Chronicle of The Cid; A Translation by Robert Southey

Robert Southey was born on the 12th of August 1774 in Bristol. A poet of the Romantic school and one of the "Lake Poets".

Although his fame has been eclipsed by that of his friends William Wordsworth and Samuel Taylor Coleridge, Southey's verse was highly influential and he wrote movingly against the horrors and injustice of the slave trade. Among his other classics are Inchcape Rock as well as a number of plays including Wat Tyler.

He was great friends with Coleridge, indeed in 1795, in a plan they soon abandoned, they thought to found a utopian commune-like society, called Pantisocracy, in the wilds of Pennsylvania.

However, that same year, the two friends married sisters Sarah and Edith Fricker. Southey's marriage was successful but Coleridge's was not. In 1810 he abandoned his wife and three children to Southey's care in the Lake District. Although his income was small and those dependent upon him growing in number he continued to write and burnish his reputation with a wider public.

In 1813 on the refusal of Walter Scott he was offered by George II the post of Poet Laureate, a post Southey accepted and kept till his death 30 years later.

Southey was also a prolific letter writer, literary scholar, essay writer, historian and biographer. His biographies included those of John Bunyan, John Wesley, William Cowper, Oliver Cromwell and Horatio Nelson.

He was a renowned scholar of Portuguese and Spanish literature and history, and translated works from those two languages into English and wrote a History of Brazil (part of his planned but un-completed History of Portugal) and a History of the Peninsular War.

Perhaps his most enduring contribution is the children's classic The Story of the Three Bears, the original Goldilocks story, first published in Southey's prose collection The Doctor.

In 1838, Edith died and Southey married Caroline Anne Bowles, also a poet, on 4 June 1839

Robert Southey died on the 21st of March, 1843 and is buried in Crosthwaite Church in Keswick,

Index of Contents

INTRODUCTION.

Robert Southey's "Chronicle of the Cid" is all translation from the Spanish, but is not translation from a single book. Its groundwork is that part of the Crónica General de España, the most ancient of the Prose Chronicles of Spain, in which adventures of the Cid are fully told. This old Chronicle was compiled in the reign of Alfonso the Wise, who was learned in the exact science of his time, and also a troubadour. Alfonso reigned between the years 1252 and 1284, and the Chronicle was written by the King himself, or under his immediate direction. It is in four parts. The first part extends from the Creation of the World to the occupation of Spain by the Visigoths, and is dull; the second part tells of the Goths in Spain and of the conquest of Spain by the Moors, and is less dull; the third part brings down the story of the nation to the reign of Ferdinand the Great, early in the eleventh century; and the fourth part continues it to the date of the accession of Alfonso himself in the year 1252. These latter parts are full of interest. Though in prose, they are based by a poet on heroic songs and national traditions of the struggle with the Moors, and the fourth part opens with an elaborate setting forth of the history of the great hero of mediaeval Spain, the Cid Campeador. The Cid is the King Arthur, or the Roland, of the Spaniards, less mythical, but not less interesting, with incidents of a real life seen through the warm haze of Southern imagination. King Alfonso, in his Chronicle, transformed ballads and fables of the Cid into a prose digest that was looked upon as history. Robert Southey translated this very distinct section of the Chronicle, not from the Crónica General itself, but from the Chronica del Cid, which, with small variation, was extracted from it, being one in substance with the history of the Cid in the fourth part of the General Chronicle, and he has enriched it. This he has done by going himself also to the Poem of the Cid and to the Ballads of the Cid, for incidents, descriptions, and turns of thought, to weave into the texture of the old prose Chronicle, brightening its tints, and adding new life to its scenes of Spanish chivalry.

"The Poem of the Cid," the earliest and best of the heroic songs of Spain, is a romance of history in more than three thousand lines, celebrating the achievements of the hero little more than fifty years after his death. Ruy Diaz, or Rodrigo Diaz de Bivar, was born at Burgos about the year 1040, and died in the year 1099. He was called the Cid, because five Moorish Kings acknowledged him in one battle as their Seid, or Lord and Conqueror, and he was Campeador or Champion of his countrymen against the Moors. Thus he was styled The Lord Champion—El Cid Campeador. The Cid died at the end of the eleventh century, and "The Poem of the Cid" was composed before the end of the twelfth. It was written after the year 1135, but before the year 1200.

The Cid is also the foremost hero of the ancient Spanish Ballads. The ballads invent or record more incidents of his life than are to be found in the Poem and the Chronicle; and of these Southey, in the translation here reprinted, has made frequent and skilful use. Thus it is from the Chronicle, the Poem, and the whole group of Ballads, as collated by an English poet with a fine relish for Spanish literature and a keen sense of the charm of old historical romance, that we get the translation from the Spanish which Southey published at the age of thirty-four, in the year 1808, as "The Chronicle of the Cid."

Robert Southey was born at Bristol on the 12th of August, 1774. He was the son of an unprosperous linen-draper, and was cared for in his childhood and youth by two of his mother's relations, a maiden aunt, with whom he lived as a child, and an uncle, the Rev. Herbert Hill, who assisted in providing for his education. Mr. Hill was Chaplain to the British Factory at Lisbon, and had a well-grounded faith in Southey's genius and character. He secured for his nephew some years of education at Westminster School, and when Southey was expelled by an unwise headmaster for a boyish jest, his uncle's faith in him held firm, and he was sent on to Balliol College, Oxford. Those were days of wild hope among the young. They felt all that was generous in the aspiration of idealists who saw the golden cities of the future in storm-clouds of revolution. Robert Southey at Oxford dreamed good dreams as a poetical Republican. He joined himself with other young students—Coleridge among them—who planned an experiment of their own in ideal life by the Susquehanna. He became engaged, therefore, at Bristol in mysterious confabulation with strange youths. This alarmed his maiden aunt. Uncle Hill, then in England, and about to return to his work at Lisbon, shrewdly proposed to set his nephew right, and draw him out of any confederacy that he might be in, by tempting him with an offer that would take strong hold of his imagination. He offered to take him for a run through Spain and Portugal. That was a chance not to be lost. Southey went to Lisbon with his uncle, but secured, before he went, the accomplishment of what he considered the best part of his design, by secretly marrying Miss Edith Fricker. During that first run over ground with which he became afterwards familiar, the young husband wrote letters to his wife, thriftily planned for future publication in aid of housekeeping. They were published in 1797, as "Letters from Spain and Portugal." It was thus that Southey was first drawn to Spanish studies. When he came back, and had to tell his aunt that he was married, he and his wife were thrown upon their own resources. He worked manfully; his uncle still abiding by him. In 1800 Southey went with his wife to visit Mr. Hill, in Lisbon.

While winning his place among the English poets, Robert Southey more than once turned to account his Spanish studies. He produced versions of the old Spanish romances of chivalry. "Amadis of Gaul" he published in 1803, and in 1807 "Palmerin of England." In 1807 he also published "Espriella's Letters," an original book of his own, professing to translate the letters of a Spaniard, who gave, as a traveller, his view of life in England. This was a pleasant book, designed, like Goldsmith's "Citizen of the World," to help us to see ourselves as others see us. In the following year, 1808, Southey—already known as the author of "Thalaba," published in 1802, and of "Madoc," published in 1805—produced this "Chronicle of the Cid." It was a time for him of energetic production and of active struggle, with a manly patience to sustain it through years rich in gentle thoughts and kindly deeds that kept his heart at rest. Sara Coleridge, to whom Southey was giving a father's care and shelter in the days when the Chronicle was being prepared, saw in him "upon the whole the best man she had ever known." All qualities that should make a good translator of such a Chronicle as this were joined in Robert Southey. As for the true Cid, let us not ask whether he was ever—as M. Dozy, in his excellent Recherches sur l'Histoire Politique et Líttéraíre de l'Espagne pendant le Moyen Age, says that he could be—treacherous and cruel. What lives of him is all that can take form as part of the life of an old and haughty nation, proud in arms. Let the rest die.

HENRY MORLEY.

PROFESSOR OF ENGLISH LITERATURE,
UNIVERSITY COLLEGE, LONDON
August, 1883.

THE CHRONICLE OF THE CID

BOOK I.

I.

King Don Ferrando succeeded to the states of Castille after the death of his father King Don Sancho el Mayor, in the era 1072, which was the year of the Incarnation 1034, and from the coming of the Patriarch Tubal to settle in Spain 3197, and from the general deluge 3339, and from the creation of the world 4995, according to the computation of the Hebrews, and from the beginning of the false sect of the Moors 413. And in the year 1037 Ferrando slew Bermudo the King of Leon in battle, who was his wife's brother, and conquered his kingdom, and succeeded to it in right of his wife Doña Sancha. So he was the first person who united the states of Castille and Leon, and the first who was called King of Castille; for till this time the lords of that country had been called Counts. He was a good king, and one who judged justly and feared God, and was bold in all his doings. Before he reigned he had by Doña Sancha his wife the Infanta Doña Urraca, his eldest daughter, who was a right excellent lady, of good customs and bounty and beauty; and after her he had the Infante Don Sancho, his eldest son and heir; and then the Infanta Doña Elvira, whom after the death of the King her father, her brother King Don Alfonso married to the Count Don Garci de Cabra. And after he became King he had the Infante Don Alfonso, and the Infante Don Garcia, who was the youngest of all. And he put his sons to read, that they might be of the better understanding, and he made them take arms, and be shown how to demean themselves in battle, and to be huntsmen. And he ordered that his daughters should be brought up in the studies beseeming dames, so that they might be of good customs, and instructed in devotion and in all things which it behoved them to know.

II.

In those days arose Rodrigo of Bivar, who was a youth strong in arms and of good customs; and the people rejoiced in him, for he bestirred himself to protect the land from the Moors. Now it behoves that ye should know whence he came, and from what men he was descended, because we have to proceed with his history. Ye are to know therefore, that after the treason which King Don Ordoño the Second committed upon the Counts of Castille, that country remained without a chief: the people therefore chose two judges, of whom the one was called Nuño Rasuera, and the other Layn Calvo, who married Nuño's daughter, Elvira Nuñez. From Nuño Rasuera King Don Ferrando descended, and from Layn Calvo, Diego Laynez, who took to wife Doña Teresa Rodríguez, the daughter of Don Rodrigo Alvarez, Count and Governor of Asturias, and had by her this Rodrigo. In the year of the Incarnation 1026 was Rodrigo born, of this noble lineage, in the city of Burgos, and in the street of St. Martin, hard by the palace of the Counts of Castille, where Diego Laynez had his dwelling. In the church of St. Martin was he baptized, a good priest of Burgos, whose name was Don Pedro de Pernegas, being his godfather: and to this church Rodrigo was always greatly affectionate, and he built the belfry tower thereof.

III.

At this time it came to pass that there was strife between Count Don Gomez the Lord of Gormaz, and Diego Laynez the father of Rodrigo; and the Count insulted Diego and gave him a blow. Now Diego was a man in years, and his strength had passed from him, so that he could not take vengeance, and he retired to his home to dwell there in solitude and lament over his dishonour. And he took no pleasure in his food, neither could he sleep by night, nor would he lift up his eyes from the ground, nor stir out of his house, nor commune with his friends, but turned from them in silence as if the breath of his shame would taint them. Rodrigo was yet but a youth, and the Count was a mighty man in arms, one who gave his voice first in the Cortes, and was held to be the best in the war, and so powerful that he had a thousand friends among the mountains. Howbeit all these things appeared as nothing to Rodrigo when he thought of the wrong done to his father, the first which had ever been offered to the blood of Layn Calvo. He asked nothing but justice of Heaven, and of man he asked only a fair field; and his father seeing of how good heart he was, gave him his sword and his blessing. The sword had been the sword of Mudarra in former times, and when Rodrigo held its cross in his hand, he thought within himself that his arm was not weaker than Mudarra's. And he went out and defied the Count and slew him, and smote off his head and carried it home to his father. The old man was sitting at table, the food lying before him untasted, when Rodrigo returned, and pointing to the head which hung from the horse's collar, dropping blood, he bade him look up, for there was the herb which should restore to him his appetite. The tongue, quoth he, which insulted you is no longer a tongue, and the hand which wronged you is no longer a hand. And the old man arose and embraced his son and placed him above him at the table, saying, that he who had brought home that head should be the head of the house of Layn Calvo.

IV.

After this Diego being full of years fell asleep and was gathered to his fathers. And the Moors entered Castille, in great power, for there came with them five Kings, and they past above Burgos, and crost the mountains of Oca, and plundered Carrion, and Vilforado, and Saint Domingo de la Calzada, and Logroño, and Najara, and all that land; and they carried away many captives both male and female, and brood mares, and flocks of all kinds. But as they were returning with all speed, Rodrigo of Bivar raised the country, and came up with them in the mountains of Oca, and fell upon them and discomfited them, and won back all their booty, and took all the five Kings prisoners. Then he went back to his mother, taking the Kings with him, and there he divided the whole spoil with the hidalgos and his other companions, both the Moorish captives and all the spoil of whatever kind, so that they departed right joyfully, being well pleased with what he had done. And he gave thanks to God for the grace which had been vouchsafed to him, and said to his mother, that he did not think it good to keep the Kings in captivity, but to let them go freely; and he set them at liberty and bade them depart. So they returned each to his own country, blessing him for their deliverance, and magnifying his great bounty; and forthwith they sent him tribute and acknowledged themselves to be his vassals.

V.

King Don Ferrando was going through Leon, putting the Kingdom in order, when tidings reached him of the good speed which Rodrigo had had against the Moors. And at the same time there came before him Ximena Gomez, the daughter of the Count, who fell on her knees before him and said, Sir, I am the daughter of Count Don Gomez of Gormaz, and Rodrigo of Bivar has slain the Count my father, and of three daughters whom he has left I am the youngest. And, Sir, I come to crave of you a boon, that you will give me Rodrigo of Bivar to be my husband, with whom I shall hold myself well married, and greatly honoured; for certain I am that his possessions will one day be greater than those of any man in your dominions. Certes, Sir, it behoves you to do this, because it is for God's service, and because I may pardon Rodrigo with a good will. The King held it good to accomplish her desire; and forthwith ordered letters to be drawn up to Rodrigo of Bivar, wherein he enjoined and commanded him that he should come incontinently to Palencia, for he had much to communicate to him, upon an affair which was greatly to God's service, and his own welfare and great honour.

VI.

When Rodrigo saw the letters of his Lord the King, he greatly rejoiced in them, and said to the messengers that he would fulfil the King's pleasure, and go incontinently at his command. And he dight himself full gallantly and well, and took with him many knights, both his own and of his kindred and of his friends, and he took also many new arms, and came to Palencia to the King with two hundred of his peers in arms, in festival guise; and the King went out to meet him, and received him right well, and did him honour; and at this were all the Counts displeased. And when the King thought it a fit season, he spake to him and said, that Doña Ximena Gomez, the daughter of the Count whom he had slain, had come to ask him for her husband, and would forgive him her father's death; wherefore he besought him to think it good to take her to be his wife, in which case he would show him great favour. When Rodrigo heard this it pleased him well, and he said to the King that he would do his bidding in this, and in all other things which he might command; and the King thanked him much. And he sent for the Bishop of Palencia, and took their vows and made them plight themselves each to the other according as the law directs. And when they were espoused the King did them great honour, and gave them many noble gifts, and added to Rodrigo's lands more than he had till then possessed: and he loved him greatly in his heart, because he saw that he was obedient to his commands, and for all that he had heard him say.

VII.

So Rodrigo departed from the King, and took his spouse with him to the house of his mother, and gave her to his mother's keeping. And forthwith he made a vow in her hands that he would never accompany with her, neither in the desert nor in the inhabited place, till he had won five battles in the field. And he besought his mother that she would love her even as she loved him himself, and that she would do good to her and show her great honour, for which he should ever serve her with the better good will, his mother promised him so to do: and then he departed from them and went out against the frontier of the Moors.

VIII.

Now the history relates that King Don Ferrando contended with King Don Ramiro of Aragon for the city of Calahorra, which each claimed as his own; in such guise that the King of Aragon placed it upon the trial by combat, confiding in the prowess of Don Martin Gonzalez, who was at that time held to be the best knight in all Spain, King Don Ferrando accepted the challenge, and said that Rodrigo of Bivar should do battle on his part, but that he was not then present. And they plighted homage on both parts to meet and bring each his knight, and the knight who conquered should win Calahorra for his Lord. Having ratified this engagement, they returned into their own lands. And immediately Ferrando sent for Rodrigo of Bivar, and told him all the matter as it then stood, and that he was to do battle. Well pleased was Rodrigo when he heard this, and he accorded to all that the King had said that he should, do battle for him upon that cause; but till the day arrived he must needs, he said, go to Compostella, because he had vowed a pilgrimage; and the King was content therewith, and gave him great gifts.

IX.

Rodrigo forthwith set out upon the road, and took with him twenty knights. And as he went he did great good, and gave alms, feeding the poor and needy. And upon the way they found a leper, struggling in a quagmire, who cried out to them with a loud voice to help him for the love of God; and when Rodrigo heard this, he alighted from his beast and helped him, and placed him upon the beast before him, and carried him with him in this manner to the inn where he took up his lodging that night. At this were his knights little pleased. And when supper was ready he bade his knights take their seats, and he took the leper by the hand, and seated him next himself, and ate with him out of the same dish. The knights were greatly offended at this foul sight, insomuch that they rose up and left the chamber. But Rodrigo ordered a bed to be made ready for himself and for the leper, and they twain slept together. When it was midnight and Rodrigo was fast asleep, the leper breathed against him between his shoulders, and that breath was so strong that it passed through him, even through his breast; and he awoke, being astounded, and felt for the leper by him, and found him not; and he began to call him, but there was no reply. Then he arose in fear, and called for light, and it was brought him; and he looked for the leper and could see nothing; so he returned into the bed, leaving the light burning. And he began to think within himself what had happened, and of that breath which had passed through him, and how the leper was not there. After a while, as he was thus musing, there appeared before him one in white garments, who said unto him, Sleepest thou or wakest thou, Rodrigo? and he answered and said, I do not sleep; but who art thou that bringest with thee such brightness and so sweet an odour? Then said he, I am Saint Lazarus, and know that I was the leper to whom thou didst so much good and so great honour for the love of God; and because thou didst this for his sake hath God now granted thee a great gift; for whensoever that breath which thou hast felt shall come upon thee, whatever thing thou desirest to do, and shalt then begin, that shalt thou accomplish to thy heart's desire, whether it be in battle or aught else, so that thy honour shall go on increasing from day to day; and thou shalt be feared both by Moors and Christians, and thy enemies shall never prevail against thee, and thou shalt die an honourable death in thine own house, and in thy renown, for God hath blessed thee;—therefore go thou on, and evermore persevere in doing good; and with that he disappeared. And Rodrigo arose and prayed to our lady and intercessor St. Mary, that she would pray to her blessed son for him to watch over both his body and soul in all his undertakings; and he continued in prayer till the day broke. Then he proceeded on his way, and performed his pilgrimage, doing much good for the love of God and of St. Mary.

X.

Now the day came which had been appointed for the combat concerning Calahorra, between Rodrigo and Don Martin Gonzalez, and Rodrigo was not arrived; therefore his cousin Alvar Fañez Minaya undertook the battle in his stead, and ordered his horse to be harnessed right well. While he was arming himself Rodrigo came up and took the horse of Alvar Fañez, and entered the lists; Don Martin Gonzalez did the same, and the judges placed them fairly, each in his place, so that neither should have the sun in his eyes. They ran their career, one against the other, and met so fiercely that their lances brake, and both were sorely wounded; but Don Martin began to address Rodrigo, thinking to dismay him: Greatly dost thou now repent, Don Rodrigo, said he, that thou hast entered into these lists with me: for I shall so handle thee that never shalt thou marry Doña Ximena thy spouse, whom thou lovest so well, nor ever return alive to Castílle. Rodrigo waxed angry at these words, and he replied, You are a good knight, Don Martin Gonzalez, but these words are not suitable to this place, for in this business we have to contend with hands and not with empty speeches; and the power is in God who will give the honour as he thinketh best. And in his anger he made at him, and smote him upon his helmet, and the sword cut through and wounded as much of the head as it could reach, so that he was sorely hurt and lost much blood. And Don Martín Gonzalez struck at Rodrigo, and the sword cut into the shield, and he plucked it towards him that with main force he made Rodrigo lose the shield; but Rodrigo did not forget himself, and wounded him again in the face. And they both became greatly enraged, and cruel against each other, striking without mercy, for both of them were men who knew how to demean themselves. But while they thus struggled Don Martin Gonzalez lost much blood, and for very weakness he could not hold himself upon his horse, but fell from his horse upon the ground; and Rodrigo alighted and went to him and slew him; and when he had slain him he asked the judges if there was any thing more to be done for the right of Calahorra: and they made answer that there was not. Then came the King Don Ferrando to him, and alighted by him, and helped to disarm him, and embraced him much; and when he was disarmed he went with him from the field, he and all the Castillians greatly rejoicing; but as great as was the pleasure of King Don Ferrando and his people, so great was the sorrow of King Don Ramiro of Aragon and of his. And he ordered them to take up Don Martin Gonzalez, and they carried the body into his own lands, and he went with it, and Calahorra remained in the power of King Don Ferrando.

XI.

But when the Counts of Castille saw how Rodrigo increased day by day in honour, they took counsel together that they should plot with the Moors, and fix a day of battle with them on the day of the Holy Cross in May, and that they should invite Rodrigo to this battle, and contrive with the Moors that they should slay him; by which means they should be revenged upon him, and remain masters of Castille, which now because of him they could not be. This counsel they sent to communicate to the Moors and to the Moorish Kings who were Rodrigo's vassals, being those whom he had made prisoners and set at liberty. But they, when they saw this counsel and the falsehood which was devised, took the letters of the Counts, and sent them to Rodrigo their Lord, and sent to tell him all the secret of the treason. And Rodrigo thanked them greatly for their good faith, and took the letters and carried to the King, and showed him all the enmity of the Counts, and especially of the Count Don Garcia, who was afterwards called of Cabra. When the King saw this as it was, he was astonished at their great falsehood, and he issued his letters in which he ordered them to leave his dominions; then he went to Santiago on a pilgrimage, and ordered Rodrigo to cast these Counts out of the land; and Rodrigo did as the King commanded him. Then Doña Elvira his kinswoman, the wife of the Count Don Garcia, came and fell on her knees before him; but Rodrigo took her by the hand and raised her up, and would not hear her till she was arisen. And when he had raised her up she said. I beseech you, cousin, since you have banished me and my husband, that you would give us a letter to some King who is one of your vassals, enjoining him to befriend us, and give us something for your sake whereon we may live. So he gave her a letter to the King of Cordova, who received her and her husband well for the love of Rodrigo, and gave Cabra to him, that he and his people might dwell therein. This Count was afterwards so ungrateful to the King of Cordova that he made war upon him from Cabra which the King had given him, till Rodrigo came and took it.

XII.

The history relateth that at this time while the King was in Galicia, the Moors entered Estremadura, and the people called upon Rodrigo of Bivar to help them. And when he heard the summons he made no delay, but gathered together his kinsmen and his friends, and went against the misbelievers. And he came up with them between Atienza and San Estevan de Gormaz, as they were carrying away a great booty in captives and in flocks, and there he had a brave battle with them in the field; and in fine Rodrigo conquered, smiting and slaying, and the pursuit lasted for seven leagues, and he recovered all the spoil, which was so great that two hundred horses were the fifth, for the whole spoil was worth a hundred times a thousand maravedís. Rodrigo divided the whole among his people without covetousness, and returned with great honour.

XIII.

Now the greater part of these Moors had been they of Merida, Badajoz, Beja and Evora, and the King was minded to requite them in their own land according to their deeds; and he entered into the heart of their country, carrying with him fire and sword, and pressed them sorely so that they yielded vassalage. Then turning through Portugal, he won the town of Sea, which was upon the western slope of the Serra da Estrella; and also another town called Gamne, the site whereof cannot now be known, for in course of years names change and are forgotten. And proceeding with his conquests he laid siege to the city of Viseu, that he might take vengeance for the death of King Don Alfonso, his wife's father, who had been slain before that city. But the people of Viseu, as they lived with this fear before their eyes, had fortified their city well, and stored it abundantly with all things needful, and moreover, they put their trust in their Alcayde, who was an African, by name Cid Alafum, a man tried in arms. He encouraged them, saying that the city could not be taken in ten years, by a greater power than the Christians; and there were many good arbalisters in the city, who shot so strong that neither shield nor armour availed against their quarrels. King Don Ferrando therefore ordered mantles to be made, and also pavaises to protect his people; and moreover he enjoined them to fasten boards upon their shields, so that the quarrels from the crossbows might not pierce through. And he continued for eighteen days to combat the city, keeping such good watch, that neither could they within receive help from without, nor themselves issue forth; and on the eighteenth day, which was the Vesper of St. Peter's, he won the city by force of arms; and few were they who escaped from the sword of the conquerors, except those who retreated with Alafum into the castle. And on the following day at the hour of tierce they also came to terms, and yielded themselves to his mercy, saving their lives. In this manner was Viseu recovered by the Christians, and never after did that city fall into the hands of the barbarians. And the Moor who had slain King Don Alfonso fell into Ferrando's power, and the King took vengeance and punished him in all the parts which had offended; he cut off the foot which had prest down the Armatost, and lopt off the hands which had held the bow and fitted the quarrel, and plucked out the eyes which had taken the mark; and the living trunk was then set up as a butt for the archers.

XIV.

In all these wars there was not a man who bore greater part, or did better feats in arms, than Rodrigo of Bivar. And the King went up against Lamego, and besieged it. Now Zadan Aben Huim, son of Huim Alboazem, the King thereof, was mightier than all the Kings who had reigned before him in Lamego, and he had peopled many places from the Douro even to the rivers Tavora and Vouga. And because he was well beloved and his city well stored and strong, all the chief Moors in that district being dismayed by the fall of Viseu, retired into it, to be under his protection. But maugre all their power. King Don Ferrando girt the city round about, and brought against it so many engines, and so many bastilles, that Zadan submitted, and opened his gates on the twenty-second of July, the day of

St. Mary Magdalene, being twenty-five days after the capture of Viseu. And Zadan became tributary to the King, and the King took with him many of the Moors, to be employed in building up the churches which had fallen to ruin since the land was lost.

XV.

All this while was Coimbra in the power of the misbelievers. And the Abbot of Lorvam took counsel with his Monks, and they said, Let us go to King Ferrando and tell him the state of the city. And they chose out two of the brethren for this errand. When the Moors therefore who came to hunt among the mountains took up their lodging in the Monastery as they were wont to do, these twain said unto them, We would go to the holy Dominicum, to say prayers there for our sins. So feigning this to be their errand they set forth, and came to the King in the town of Carrion, and spake unto him in council, saying, Sir King, we come to you through waters and over mountains and by bad ways, to tell you concerning Coimbra in what plight it is, if you desire to know, and in what guise the Moors dwell therein, what they are and how many, and with how little heed they keep the city. And he said unto them. I beseech ye, for the love of God, say on. Then told they him what they knew: and the King took counsel upon this matter with Rodrigo of Bivar, and Rodrigo said, that certes the Lord would help him to win the city; and he said that he would fain be knighted by the King's hand, and that it seemed to him now that he should receive knighthood at his hand in Coimbra. A covenant was then made with the two Monks, that they should go with the army against the city in the month of January without fail. Now this was in October. Incontinently the King sent to summon his knights and people, and when one part of them had assembled at Santa Maria, he bade them do all the damage they could against Coimbra, and ravage the country, which accordingly they did. In the meantime the King made a pilgrimage to Santiago, as Rodrigo had exhorted him to do; and he remained there three days and nights in prayer, offering great gifts, and taking upon himself great devotion, that it might please God to fulfil his desire. And with the help of Santiago he gathered together a great host, and went up against Coimbra in the month of January, even as he had covenanted, and laid siege to it. And he fought against the city all February, and March, and April, May and June, five months did he fight, and could not prevail against it. And when July came the food of the besiegers failed them, insomuch that they had only the dole for a few days left; then the baggage was made ready, and the sumpter-beasts and serving-men were ordered to depart for Leon, and proclamation was made in the camp that the army should remain yet four days, and on the fifth they might break up and depart every one to his own house. But then the Monks of Lorvam and the Abbot consulted together and said, Let us now go to the King and give him all the food which we have, both oxen and cows, and sheep and goats and swine, wheat and barley and maize, bread and wine, fish and fowl, even all that we have; for if the city, which God forbid, should not be won, by the Christians, we may no longer abide here. Then went they to the King and gave him all their stores, both of flocks and herds, and pulse, and wine beyond measure, which they had for a long time stored. Then was there abundance in the camp; but they who were within the city waxed feeble for hunger long suffering, because the Christians beset them on all sides, and warred upon them hotly, and brought their engines to bear on every part, and the walls of the city were broken down. When the Moors saw this they came to the King, and fell at his feet, and besought him of his mercy that he would let them depart, leaving to him the city and all that they had therein, for they asked for nothing but their lives. And the King had compassion upon them and granted their prayer; and the city was yielded to him on a Sunday at the hour of tierce, which was before a week had run out since the Monks of Lorvam had succoured the host.

XVI.

Now it came to pass that while the King lay before Coimbra, there came a pilgrim from the land of Greece on pilgrimage to Santiago; his name was Estiano, and he was a Bishop. And as he was praying in the church he heard certain of the townsmen and of the pilgrims saying that Santiago was wont to appear in battle like a knight, in aid of the Christians. And when he heard this it nothing pleased him, and he said unto them, "Friends, call him not a knight, but rather a fisherman." Upon this it pleased God that he should fall asleep, and in his sleep Santiago appeared to him with a good and cheerful countenance, holding in his hand a bunch of keys, and said unto him, "Thou thinkest it a fable that they should call me a knight, and sayest that I am not so: for this reason am I come unto thee that thou never more mayest doubt concerning my knighthood; for a knight of Jesus Christ I am, and a helper of the Christians against the Moors." While he was thus saying a horse was brought him the which was exceeding white, and the Apostle Santiago mounted upon it, being well clad in bright and fair armour, after the manner of a knight. And he said to Estiano, "I go to help King Don Ferrando who has lain these seven months before Coimbra, and to-morrow, with these keys which thou seest, will I open the gates of the city unto him at the hour of tierce, and deliver it into his hand." Having said this he departed. And the Bishop when he awoke in the morning called together the clergy and people of Compostella, and told them what he had seen and heard. And as he said, even so did it come to pass; for tidings came that on that day, and at the hour of tierce, the gates of the city had been opened.

XVII.

King Don Ferrando then assembled his Counts and chief captains, and told them all that the Monks of Lorvam had done, in bringing him to besiege the city, and in supplying his army in their time of need: and the Counts and chief captains made answer and said, Certes, O King, if the Monks had not given us the stores of their Monastery, thou couldest not have taken the city at this time. The King then called for the Abbot and the brethren, for they were with him in the host, and said the hours to him daily, and mass in St. Andre's, and buried there and in their Monastery as many as had died during the siege, either of arrow-wounds or by lances, or of their own infirmities. So they came before him and gave him joy of his conquest; and he said unto them, Take ye now of this city as much as ye desire, since by God's favour and your council I have won it. But they made answer, Thanks be to God and to you, and to your forefathers, we have enough and shall have, if so be that we have your favour and dwell among Christians. Only for the love of God, and for the remedy of your own soul, give us one church with its dwelling-houses within the city, and confirm unto us the gifts made to us in old times by your forefathers, and the good men to whom God give a happy rest. With that the King turned to his sons and his soldiers, and said, Of a truth, by our Creator, these who desire so little are men of God. I would have given them half the city, and they will have only a single church! Now therefore, since they require but this, on the part of God Almighty let us grant and confirm unto them what they ask, to the honour of God and St. Mamede. And the brethren brought him their charters of King Ramiro, and King Bermudo, and King Alfonso, and of Gonzalo Moniz, who was a knight and married a daughter of King Bermudo, and of other good men. And the King confirmed them, and he bade them make a writing of all which had passed between him and them at the siege of Coimbra; and when they brought him the writing, they brought him also a crown of silver and of gold, which had been King Bermudo's and which Gonzalo Moniz had given to the Monastery in honour of God and St. Mamede. The King saw the crown, how it was set with precious stones, and said to them, To what end bring ye hither this crown? And they said, That you should take it, Sire, in return for the good which you have done us. But he answered, Far be it from me that I should take from your Monastery what the good men before me have given to it! Take ye back the crown, and take also ten marks of silver, and make with the money a good cross, to remain with you for ever. And he who shall befriend you, may God befriend him; but he who shall disturb you or your Monastery, may he be cursed by the living God and by his Saints. So the King signed the writing which he had commanded to be made, and his sons and chief captains signed it also, and in the writing he enjoined his children and his children's children, as many as should come after him, to honour and protect the Monastery of Lorvam, upon his blessing he charged them so to do, because he had found the brethren better than all the other Monks in his dominions.

XVIII.

Then King Don Ferrando knighted Rodrigo of Bivar in the great mosque of Coimbra, which he dedicated to St. Mary. And the ceremony was after this manner: the King girded on his sword, and gave him the kiss, but not the blow. To do him more honour the Queen gave him his horse, and the Infanta Doña Urraca fastened on his spurs; and from that day forth he was called Ruydiez. Then the King commanded him to knight nine noble squires with his own hand; and he took his sword before the altar, and knighted them. The King then gave Coimbra to the keeping of Don Sisnando, Bishop of Iria, a man, who having more hardihood than religion, had by reason of his misdeeds gone over to the Moors, and sorely infested the Christians in Portugal. But during the siege he had come to the King's service, and bestirred himself well against the Moors; and therefore the King took him into his favour, and gave him the city to keep, which he kept, and did much evil to the Moors till the day of his death. And the King departed and went to Compostella to return thanks to Santiago.

XIX.

But then Benalfagi, who was the Lord of many lands in Estremadura, gathered together a great power of the Moors and built up the walls of Montemor, and from thence waged war against Coimbra, so that they of Coimbra called upon the King for help. And the King came up against the town, and fought against it, and took it. Great honour did Ruydiez win at that siege; for having to protect the foragers, the enemy came out upon him, and thrice in one day was he beset by them; but he, though sorely prest by them, and in great peril, nevertheless would not send to the camp for succour, but put forth his manhood and defeated them. And from that day the King gave more power into his hands, and made him head over all his household.

XX.

Now the men of Leon besought the King that he would repeople Zamora, which had lain desolate since it was destroyed by Almanzor. And he went thither and peopled the city, and gave to it good privileges. And while he was there came messengers from the five Kings who were vassals to Ruydiez of Bivar, bringing him their tribute; and they came to him, he being with the King, and called him Cid, which signifyeth Lord, and would have kissed his hands, but he would not give them his hand till they had kissed the hand of the King. And Ruydiez took the tribute and offered the fifth thereof to the King, in token of his sovereignty; and the King thanked him, but would not receive it, and from that time he ordered that Ruydiez should be called the Cid, because the Moors had so called him.

XXI.

In those days Pope Victor II. held a council at Florence, and the Emperor Henry there made his complaint against King Don Ferrando, that he did not acknowledge his sovereignty, and pay him tribute like all other Kings; and he besought the Pope to admonish him so to do. And the Pope being a German, and the friend of Henry, sent to the King to admonish him, and told him that unless he obeyed he would proclaim a crusade against him; and in like manner the Emperor, and the King of France, and the other Kings, sent to exhort him to obedience, defying him if he should refuse. When the King saw their letters he was troubled, for he knew that if this thing were done, great evil would follow to Castille and Leon. And he took counsel with his honourable men. They seeing on the one hand the great power of the Church, and on the other the great evil that it would be if Castille and Leon should be made tributary, knew not what counsel to give: howbeit at length they said to him that he should do the Pope's bidding. At this council the Cid was not present, for he had lately completed his marriage with Doña Ximena Gomez, and was then with her; but at this time he arrived, and the King showed him the letters, and told him the matter how it then stood, and what had been the advice of his good men, and besought him to speak his advice, as a good and true vassal to his Lord. When the Cid heard what had passed it grieved him to the heart, more for the counsel which had been given to the King, than because of the Pope's commands; and he turned to the King and said, In an ill day, Sir, were you born in Spain, if it be in your time to be made tributary, which it never was before; for all the honour which God hath given you, and whatever good he hath done to you, is lost if it should be so. And, Sir, whoever hath given you this counsel is not a true man, neither one who regardeth your honour nor your power. But send to defy them since they will have it so, and let us carry the war home to them. You shall take with you five thousand knights, all of whom are hidalgos, and the Moorish Kings who are your vassals will give you two thousand knights; and, Sir, you are such a one as God loves, and he will not that your honour should perish. And the King thought that he was well counselled by him, for the King was of a great heart.

XXII.

Then the King ordered letters to be written, in which he besought the Pope not to proceed farther against him without just cause, for Spain had been conquered by those who dwelt therein, by the blood of them and of their fathers, and they had never been tributary, and never would be so, but would rather all die. Moreover he sent his letters to the Emperor and to the other Kings, telling them that they well knew the wrong which the Emperor did him, having no jurisdiction over him, nor lawful claim; and he besought them to let him alone that he might continue to wage war against the enemies of the faith; but if they persisted to speak against him he then sent them back their friendship, and defied them, and where they all were there would he go seek them. While this reply was on its way he gathered together his people, as he and the Cid had advised, and set forward with eight thousand and nine hundred knights, both of his own and of the Cid, and the Cid led the advanced guard. When they had passed the passes of Aspa they found that the country was up, and the people would not sell them food; but the Cid set his hand to, to burn all the country before him, and plunder from those who would not sell, but to those who brought food he did no wrong. And after such manner did he proceed, that wherever the King and his army arrived they found all things of which they could stand in need; and the news went sounding throughout all the land, so that all men trembled.

XXIII.

Then Count Remon, Lord of Savoy, with the power of the King of France, gathered together twenty thousand knights and came beyond Tolosa, to hold the road against King Don Ferrando. And he met with his harbinger the Cid, who went before him to prepare lodgings, and they had a hard battle; and the men of the Count were discomfited, and he himself made prisoner and many with him, and many were slain. And the Count besought the Cid of his mercy to set him free, saying that he would give him a daughter he had, the which was right fair; and the Cid did as he besought him, and the daughter was given to him, and he set the Count free. And by this woman King Don Ferrando had his son the Cardinal Ferrando, who was so honourable a man.

XXIV.

After this the Cid had another battle with all the power of France, and discomfited them, and at neither of these battles did the King and his main army arrive. So the news went sounding before them to the council, of the fierceness of the Cid; and as they all knew that he was the conqueror of battles, they knew not what to advise; and they besought the Pope that he would send to them, begging them to turn back, and saying that they did not require tribute. These letters came to the King when he had past Tolosa, and he took counsel with the Cid and with his good men, and they advised that he should send two of his good men to the Pope, who should tell him to send a Cardinal with power to make a covenant, that this demand should never again be made upon Spain; and that persons from the Emperor and from the other Kings also should come to ratify this, and meanwhile he would abide where he was. But if they did not come he would go on to them. Count Don Rodrigo, and Alvar Fañez Minaya, and certain learned men, were sent with this bidding. And when they came to the Pope and gave him their letters, he was much dismayed, and he assembled the good and honourable men of the council, and asked of them what he should do. And they made answer that he must do as the King willed him, for none was so hardy as to fight against the good fortune of his vassal the Cid. Then the Pope sent Master Roberto, the Cardinal of St. Sabina, with full powers, and the representatives of the Emperor and of the other Kings came also and signed the covenant, that this demand should never again be made upon the King of Spain. And the writings which they made were confirmed by the Pope and by the Emperor and the other Kings, and sealed with their seals.

XXV.

While this was doing the King abode where he was, beyond Tolosa; six months did he abide there. And the Pope sent to ask of him the daughter of Count Remon; and she was then five months gone with child; and by the advice of his vassal the Cid the King sent her, and sent to tell the Pope the whole truth, requesting that he would see she was taken care of; and the Pope ordered that she should be taken care of till the event should be. And she was delivered of the Abbot Don Ferrando; the Pope was his godfather, and brought him up right honourably, and dispensed with his bastardry that he might hold any sacred dignity; and in process of time he was made an honourable Cardinal. So the King returned with great honour into his own land, and from that time he was called Don Ferrando the Great, the Emperor's Peer; and it was said of him in songs that he had passed the passes of Aspa in despite of the Frenchmen.

XXVI.

Many other things did King Don Ferrando, which are written in the book of the Chronicles of the Kings of Spain, enriching churches and monasteries, and honouring the saints and martyrs, and making war upon the misbelievers. And it came to pass when he was waxed old, that as he was one day saying his prayers, the confessor St. Isidro appeared unto him, and told him the day and hour when he should die, to the intent that he might make ready and confess his sins, and make atonement for them, and take thought for his soul, that so he might appear clean from offence before the face of God. From that day he, being certain that his end was at hand, began to discharge his soul. And he devised within himself how to dispose of the kingdoms which God had given him, that there might be no contention between his sons after his death; and he thought it best to divide his lands among them; but this which he thought best proved to be the worst, and great evil came thereof, for better had it been that he had left all to the eldest. Howbeit it was his pleasure to divide them: he had three sons, Don Sancho who was the eldest, and Don Alfonso who was the second born, and Don Garcia who was the youngest; and two daughters, Doña Urraca and Doña Elvira. The manner in which he divided his lands was this: he gave to Don Sancho the kingdom of Castille as far as to the river Pisuerga, on the side of Leon, with the border, which included the dioceses of Osma, and Segovia, and Avila, and on the side of Navarre as far as the Ebro, as he had won it from his nephew Don Sancho Garcia, King of Navarre. To Don Alfonso he gave the kingdom of Leon, and in Asturias as far as the river Deva, which runs by Oviedo, and part of Campos as far as Carrion and the river Pisuerga, with the border, which contained the dioceses of Zamora, Salamanca, and Ciudad Rodrigo, and the city of Astorga, and other lands in Galicia, with the town of Zebreros. To Don Garcia he gave the kingdom of Galicia, and all the lands which he had won in Portugal, with the title of King of Galicia, which country had had no King of its own since the kingdom of the Suevi had been overthrown by King Leovegildo. And to Doña Urraca he gave the city of Zamora with all its dependencies, and with half the Infantazgo: and the other half, with the city of Toro and its dependencies, to Doña Elvira.

XXVII.

When the Infante Don Sancho knew that the King his father had made this allotment it displeased him, for he was the eldest son; and he said to his father that he neither could nor ought to make this division; for the Gothic Kings had in old time made a constitution for themselves, that the kingdom and empire of Spain never should be divided, but remain one dominion under one Lord. But the King replied that he would not for this forbear to do as he had resolved, for he had won the kingdom; then the Infante made answer, Do as you will, being my father and Lord; but I do not consent unto it. So the King made this division against the right of the Infante Don Sancho, and it displeased many in the kingdom, and many it pleased; but they who were of good understanding perceived the evil which would arise.

XXVIII.

After this the King fell sick with the malady whereof he died. And he made himself be carried to Leon, and there on his knees before the bodies of the saints he besought mercy of them. And putting his crown upon his head before the holy body of St. Isidro he called upon God, saying, O Lord Jesus Christ, thine is the power over all, and thine is the kingdom, for thou art King of all kingdoms, and of all Kings, and of all nations, and all are at thy command. And now Lord I return unto thee the kingdom which thou hast given me, but I beseech thee of thy mercy that my soul may be brought to the light which hath no end. Having said thus, he stript himself of the royal robes adorned with gold in which he was arrayed, and took the crown from his head and placed it upon the altar; and he put sackcloth upon the carrion of his body, and prayed to God, confessing all the sins which he had committed against him, and took his acquittal from the Bishops, for they absolved him from his sins; and forthwith he there received extreme unction, and strewed ashes upon himself. After this, by his own order he was carried to St. Mary of Almazan in pilgrimage, and there he remained thrice nine days, beseeching St. Mary that she would have mercy upon him and intercede with her blessed Son for his soul. From thence they carried him to Cabezon, and there the Abbot Don Ferrando came to him, an honourable man, and many other honourable men of his realms, and the Cid Ruydiez, whom the King commended to the Infante Don Sancho, his son. And after he had put all his affairs in order he remained three days lamenting in pain, and on the fourth, being the day of St. John the Evangelist, he called for the Cardinal Abbot, and commended Spain and his other sons to him, and gave him his blessing, and then at the hour of sexts he rendered up his soul without stain to God, being full of years. So they carried him to Leon and buried him near his father, in the Church of St. Isidro, which he had built. Thirty and one years did King Don Ferrando the Great who was peer with the Emperor, Reign over Castille. The Queen his wife lived two years after him, leading a holy life; a good Queen had she been and of good understanding, and right loving to her husband: alway had she counselled him well, being in truth the mirror of his kingdoms, and the friend of the widows and orphans. Her end was a good end, like that of the King her husband: God give them Paradise for their reward. Amen.

BOOK II

I.

The history relates how after the death of King Don Ferrando, the three Kings his sons reigned each in his kingdom, according to the division made by their father, who had divided that which should all by right have descended to the King Don Sancho. Now the Kings of Spain were of the blood of the Goths, which was a fierce blood, for it had many times come to pass among the Gothic Kings, that brother had slain, brother upon this quarrel; from this blood was King Don Sancho descended, and he thought that it would be a reproach unto him if he did not join together the three kingdoms under his own dominion, for he was not pleased with what his father had given him, holding that the whole ought to have been his. And he went through the land setting it in order, and what thing soever his people asked at his hand that did he grant them freely, to the end that he might win their hearts.

II.

Now when King Don Sancho of Navarre saw that there was a new King in Castille, he thought to recover the lands of Bureva and of Old Castille as far as Laredo, which had been lost when the King his father was defeated and slain at Atapuerca in the mountains of Oca. And now seeing that the kingdom of Ferrando was divided, he asked help of his uncle Don Ramiro, King of Aragon; and the men of Aragon and of Navarre entered Castille together. But King Don Sancho gathered together his host, and put the Cid at their head; and such account did he give of his enemies, that he of Navarre was glad to enjoy Rioja in peace, and lay no farther claim to what his father had lost. Now the King of Castille was wroth against the King of Aragon, that he should thus have joined against him without cause; and in despite of him he marched against the Moors of Zaragoza, and laying waste their country with fire and sword, he came before their city, and gave orders to assault it, and began to set up his engines. When the King of Zaragoza saw the great will which the King had to do evil unto him, and that there was none to help him, he thought it best to come to his mercy, paying tribute, or serving him, or in any manner whatsoever. And he sent interpreters to King Don Sancho saying, that he would give him much gold and silver, and many gifts, and be his vassal, and pay him tribute yearly. The King received them right honourably, and when he had heard their bidding he answered resolutely, being of a great heart, All this which the King of Zaragoza sends to say unto me is well, but he hath another thing in his heart. He sends to bid me break up the siege and depart from his land, and as soon as I should have departed, he would make friends unto himself among Christians and among Moors, and fail me in all which he covenants. Nevertheless I will do this thing which your King requires of me; but if in the end he lie, I will come back upon him and destroy him, trusting in God that he cannot defend himself against me. And when the interpreters heard this they were greatly dismayed, and they returned and told their King all that he had said. And the Moors seeing that they could not help themselves, made such terms with him as it pleased him to grant, and gave him hostages that they might not be able to prove false. And they gave him gold and silver and precious stones in abundance, so that with great riches and full honourably did he and all his men depart from the siege.

III.

Greatly was the King of Aragon displeased at this which King Don Sancho had done, thinking that it was to his great injury and abasement, for Zaragoza he held to be within his conquest. And he came out with all his power to cut off the King's return, and took possession of the way, and said unto him that he should not pass till he had made amends for the great dishonour which he had wrought him, in coming into his conquest and against his vassals: the amends which he required was, that he should yield unto him all the spoil, and all which the King of Zaragoza had given him, else should he not pass without battle. When King Don Sancho heard this, being a man of great heart, he made answer, that he was the head of the kingdoms of Castille and Leon, and all the conquests in Spain were his, for the Kings of Aragon had no conquests appertaining unto them, being by right his tributaries, and bound to appear at his Cortes. Wherefore he counselled him to waive this demand, and let him pass in peace. But the King of Aragon drew up his host for battle, and the onset was made, and heavy blows were dealt on both sides, and many horses were left without a master. And while the battle was yet upon the chance, King Don Sancho riding light bravely through the battle, began to call out Castille! Castille! and charged the main body so fiercely that by fine force he broke them; and when they were thus broken, the Castillians began cruelly to slay them, so that King Don Sancho had pity thereof, and called out unto his people not to kill them, for they were Christians. Then King Don Ramiro being discomfited, retired to a mountain, and King Don Sancho beset the mountain round about, and made a covenant with him that he should depart, and that the King of Zaragoza should remain tributary to Castille; and but for this covenant the King of Aragon would then have been slain, or made prisoner. This was the battle whereof the Black Book of Santiago speaketh, saying, that in this year, on the day of the Conversion of St. Paul, was the great slaughter of the Christians in Porca. In all these wars did my Cid demean himself after his wonted manner; and because of the great feats which he performed the King loved him well, and made him his Alferez; so that in the whole army he was second only to the King. And because when the host was in the field it was his office to chuse the place for encampment, therefore was my Cid called the Campeador.

IV.

While King Don Sancho was busied in these wars, King Don García of Galicia took by force from Doña Urraca his sister a great part of the lands which the King their father had given her. And when she heard this she began to lament aloud, saying, Ah King Don Ferrando, in an evil hour didst thou divide thy kingdom, for thereby will all the land be brought to destruction. And now also will be accomplished that which my fosterer Arias Gonzalo said, for now that King Don García who is my younger brother, hath dispossessed me and broken the oath which he made unto my father, what will not the elder do, who made the vow by compulsion, and alway made protestation against the division! God send that as thou hast disherited me, thou mayest speedily thyself in like manner be disherited, Amen! But when King Don Sancho heard what his brother had done he was well pleased thereat, thinking that he might now bring to pass that which he so greatly desired; and he assembled together his Ricos-omes and his knights, and said unto them, The King my father divided the kingdoms which should have been mine, and therein he did unjustly; now King Don Garcia my brother hath broken the oath and disherited Doña Urraca my sister; I beseech ye therefore counsel me what I shall do, and in what manner to proceed against him, for I will take his kingdom away from him. Upon this Count Don Garcia Ordoñez arose and said, There is not a man in the world, Sir, who would counsel you to break the command of your father, and the vow which you made unto him. And the King was greatly incensed at him and said, Go from before me, for I shall never receive good counsel from thee. The King then took the Cid by the hand and led him apart, and said unto him, Thou well knowest my Cid, that when the King my father commended thee unto me, he charged me upon pain of his curse that I should take you for my adviser, and whatever I did that I should do it with your counsel, and I have done so even until this day; and thou hast alway counselled me for the best, and for this I have given thee a county in my kingdom, holding it well bestowed. Now then I beseech you advise me how best to recover these kingdoms, for if I have not counsel from you I do not expect to have it from any man in the world.

V.

Greatly troubled at this was the Cid, and he answered and said, Ill, Sir, would it behove me to counsel you that you should go against the will of your father. You well know that when I went to Cabezon unto him, after he had divided his kingdoms, how he made me swear to him that I would alway counsel his sons the best I could, and never give them ill counsel; and while I can, thus must I continue to do. But the King answered, My Cid, I do not hold that in this I am breaking the oath made to my father, for I ever said that the partition should not be, and the oath which I made was forced upon me. Now King Don García my brother hath broken the oath, and all these kingdoms by right are mine: and therefore I will that you counsel me how I may unite them, for from so doing there is nothing in this world which shall prevent me, except it be death. Then when the Cid saw that he could by no means turn him from that course, he advised him to obtain the love of his brother King Don Alfonso, that he might grant him passage through his kingdom to go against Don García: and if this should be refused he counselled him not to make the attempt. And the King saw that his counsel was good, and sent his letters to King Don Alfonso beseeching him to meet him at Sahagun. When King Don Alfonso received the letters he marvelled to what end this might be: howbeit he sent to say that he would meet him. And the two kings met in Sahagun. And King Don Sancho said, Brother, you well know that King Don Garcia our brother hath broken the oath made unto our father, and disherited our sister Doña Urraca: for this I will take his kingdom away from him, and I beseech you join with me. But Don Alfonso answered that he would not go against the will of his father, and the oath which he had sworn. Then King Don Sancho said, that if he would let him pass through his kingdom he would give him part of what he should gain: and King Don Alfonso agreed to this. And upon this matter they fixed another day to meet; and then forty knights were named, twenty for Castille and twenty for Leon, as vouchers that this which they covenanted should be faithfully fulfilled on both sides.

VI.

Then King Don Sancho gathered together a great host, Castillians and Leonese, and they of Navarre and Biscay, Asturians, and men of Aragon and of the border. And he sent Alvar Fañez, the cousin of the Cid, to King Don Garcia, to bid him yield up his kingdom, and if he refused to do this to defy him on his part. Alvar Fañez, albeit unwillingly, was bound to obey the bidding of his Lord, and he went to King Don Garcia and delivered his bidding. When King Don Garcia heard it he was greatly troubled, and he cried out in his trouble and said, Lord Jesus Christ, thou rememberest the oath which we made to our father! for my sins I have been the first to break it, and have disherited my sister. And he said to Alvar Fañez, Say to my brother that I beseech him not to break the oath which he made to our father; but if he will persist to do this thing I must defend myself as I can. And with this answer Alvar Fañez returned. Then King Don Garcia called unto him a knight of Asturias, whose name was Ruy Ximenez, and bade him go to his brother King Don Alfonso and tell him what had past, and how King Don Sancho would take away his kingdom from him; and to beseech him as a brother that he would not let him pass through his dominions. And King Don Alfonso replied, Say to my brother that I will neither help King Don Sancho, nor oppose him; and tell him that if he can defend himself I shall be well pleased. And with this answer, Ruy Ximenez returned, and bade the King look to himself for defence, for he would find no help in his brother.

VII.

Now Don Garcia was not beloved in his kingdom of Galicia, neither in Portugal, for as much as he showed little favour to the hidalgos, both Galegos and Portugueze, and vexed the people with tributes which he had newly imposed. The cause of all this was a favourite, by name Verna, to whom the King gave so much authority, that he displeased all the chief persons in his dominions, and hearkened unto him in all things; and by his advice it was that he had despoiled his sister Doña Urraca of her lands, and his sister Doña Elvira also, and had done other things, whereby Portugal and Galicia were now in danger to be lost. And the knights and hidalgos took counsel together how they might remedy these evils, and they agreed that the King should in the name of them all be advised how ill he was served, and intreated to put away his favourite. Don Rodrigo Frojaz was the one named to speak unto the King; for being a man of approved valour, and the Lord of many lands, it was thought that the King would listen more to him than to any other. But it fell out otherwise than they had devised, for Verna had such power over the mind of the King, that the remonstrance was ill received, and Don Rodrigo and the other hidalgos were contumeliously treated in public by the King. Don Rodrigo would not bear this, being a right loyal and valiant man; and he went one day into the palace, and finding Verna busied in affairs of state, he drew forth his sword and slew him; then leaving the palace, for none cared to lay hands on him, he left Portugal, and took the road toward France; many of his vassals and kinsmen and friends following him, to seek their fortunes in a country where valour would be esteemed, for they were weary of the bad Government of King Don García.

VIII.

But when King Don Garcia knew of the league which his brethren had made to divide his kingdom between them, it was a greater trouble to him than the death of Verna, and he called his chief captains together and consulted with them; and they advised him that he should send to recall Don Rodrigo Frojaz, for having him the realm would be secure, and without him it was in danger to be lost. So two hidalgos were sent after him, and they found him in Navarre, on the eve of passing into France. But when he saw the King's letters, and knew the peril in which he then stood, setting aside the remembrance of his own wrongs, like a good and true Portugueze, he turned back, and went to the King at Coimbra. In good time did he arrive, for the captains of King Don Sancho had now gained many lands in Galicia and in the province of Beira, finding none to resist them, and the Count Don Nuño de Lara, and the Count of Monzon, and Don Garcia de Cabra, were drawing nigh unto Coimbra. When Don Rodrigo heard this and knew that the Castillians were approaching, and who they were, he promised the King either to maintain his cause, or die for it; and he besought him not to go into the battle himself, having so many vassals and so good; for it was not fitting that he should expose himself when there was no King coming against him. And it came to pass that when the scouts gave notice that the Castillians were at hand, he ordered the trumpets to be sounded, and the Portugueze sallied, and a little below the city, at the place which is now called Agoa de Mayas, the two squadrons met. Then was the saying of Arias Gonzalo fulfilled, that kinsmen should kill kinsmen, and brother fall by his brother's hand. But the Portugueze fought so well, and especially Don Rodrigo, and his brothers Don Pedro and Don Vermui Frojaz, that at length they discomfited the Castillians, killing of them five hundred and forty, of whom three hundred were knights, and winning their pennons and banners. Howbeit this victory was not obtained without great loss to themselves: for two hundred and twenty of their people were left upon the field, and many were sorely wounded, among whom, even to the great peril of his life, was Don Rodrigo Frojaz, being wounded with many and grievous wounds. In this battle was slain the Count Don Fafes Sarracem de Lanhoso, with many of his vassals, he from whom the Godinhos are descended: he was a right good knight.

IX.

A sorrowful defeat was that for King Don Sancho, more for the quality of the slain than for their number; and he put himself at the head of his army, and hastened through the midst of Portugal, to go against his brother. And King Don Garcia hearing of his approach, called together his knights and hidalgos, and said unto them, Friends, we have no land whereunto to fly from the King Don Sancho my brother, let us therefore meet him in battle, and either conquer him or die; for better is it to die an honourable death than to suffer this spoiling in our country. And to the Portugueze he said, Friends, ye are right noble and haughty knights, and it is your custom to have among you few lords and good ones; now therefore make me a good one, which will be to your own great honour and profit; and if I come out of this struggle well, I shall guerdon ye well, so that ye shall understand the will I have to do good towards ye. And they made answer and said that they would stand by him to the last, and that he should not be put down by their default. Then spake he to the Galegos and said. Friends, ye are right good and true knights, and never was it yet said that lord was forsaken by you in the field. I put myself in your hands, being assured that ye will well and loyally advise me, and help me to the utmost of your power. Ye see how King Don Sancho my brother presses upon us, and we have nothing left us but to die or to conquer; but if ye know any other counsel. I beseech ye tell it now. And the Galegos answered, that they would serve and defend him loyally, and that they held it best to fight. Nevertheless they were too few in number to stand against the King Don Sancho: so they retired before him. And Don Garcia took with him three hundred horsemen, and went to the Moors, and besought them to lend him aid against his brother, saying that he would give them the kingdom of Leon. And the Moors made answer, O King, thou canst not defend thyself; how then canst thou give unto us the kingdom of Leon? Howbeit they did him honour and gave him great gifts, and he returned to his people and recovered many of the castles which he had lost.

X.

Then King Don Sancho came against his brother, to besiege him in Santarem. And the Portugueze and Galegos took counsel together what they should do; for some were of advice that it was better to defend the cities and fortresses which they held, and so lengthen out the war; others that they should harass the army of the Castillians with frequent skirmishes and assaults, and never give them battle power to power, thinking that in this manner they might baffle them till the winter came on. Don Rodrigo Frojaz was at this time recovering of the wounds which he had received at Agoa de Mayas, and he said unto the King that it behoved him above all things to put his kingdom upon the hazard of a battle; for his brother being a greater lord of lands than he, and richer in money and more powerful in vassals, could maintain the war longer than he could do, who peradventure would find it difficult another year to gather together so good an army as he had now ready. For this cause he advised him to put his trust in God first, and then in the hidalgos who were with him, and without fear give battle to the King his brother, over whom God and his good cause would give him glorious victory. And to show his own good will to the King, he besought of him the leading of the van for himself and the Counts Don Pedro and Don Vermui Frojaz his brethren, and his two nephews.

Greatly was the King Don Garcia encouraged by his gallant cheer, and he bade his host make ready to give battle to King Don Sancho, as soon as he should arrive; and he marched out from the city, and took his stand near unto it in a field where afterwards were the vineyards of the town. And when the banners of the Castillians were seen advancing, the Galegos and Portugueze drew up in battle array, Don Rodrigo and his brethren having the van, as he had requested, and a body of chosen knights with them.

Count Don Garcia came in the front of King Don Sancho's army, and in the one wing was the Count de Monzon and Count Don Nuño de Lara; and the Count Don Fruela of Asturias in the other; and the King was in the rear, with Don Diego de Osma, who carried his banner: and in this manner were they arrayed on the one side and on the other, being ready for the onset. And King Don Garcia bravely encouraged his men, saying, Vassals and friends, ye see the great wrong which the King my brother doth unto me, taking from me my kingdom; I beseech ye help me now to defend it; for ye well know that all which I had therein I divided among ye, keeping ye for a season like this. And they answered, Great benefits have we received at your hands, and we will serve you to the utmost of our power. Now when the two hosts were ready to join battle, Alvar Fañez came to King Don Sancho and said to him, Sir, I have played away my horse and arms; I beseech you give me others for this battle, and I will be a right good one for you this day; if I do not for you the service of six knights, hold me for a traitor. And the Count Don Garcia, who heard this, said to the King, Give him, Sir, what he asketh; and the King ordered that horse and arms should be given him. So the armies joined battle bravely on both sides, and it was a sharp onset; many were the heavy blows which were given on both sides, and many were the horses that were slain at that encounter, and many the men. Now my Cid had not yet come up into the field.

Now Don Rodrigo Frojaz and his brethren and the knights who were with them had resolved to make straight for the banner of the King of Castille. And they broke through the ranks of the Castillians, and made their way into the middle of the enemy's host, doing marvellous feats of arms. Then was the fight at the hottest, for they did their best to win the banner, and the others to defend it; the remembrance of what they had formerly done, and the hope of gaining more honours, heartened them; and with the Castillians there was their King, giving them brave example as well as brave words. The press of the battle was here; here died Gonzalo de Sies, a right valiant Portugueze, on the part of Don García; but on Don Sancho's part the Count Don Ñuño was sorely wounded and thrown from his horse; and Count Don García Ordoñez was made prisoner, and the banner of King Don Sancho was beaten down, and the King himself also. The first who encountered him was Don Gomes Echiguis, he from whom the old Sousas of Portugal derived their descent; he was the first who set his lance against King Don Sancho, and the other one was Don Moninho Hermigis, and Don Rodrigo made way through the press and laid hands on him and took him. But in the struggle his old wounds burst open, and having received many new ones he lost much blood, and perceiving that his strength was failing, he sent to call the King Don García with all speed. And as the King came, the Count Don Pedro Frojaz met him and said, An honourable gift, Sir, hath my brother Don Rodrigo to give you, but you lose him in gaining it. And tears fell from the eyes of the King, and he made answer and said, It may indeed be that Don Rodrigo may lose his life in serving me, but the good name which he hath gained, and the honour which be leaveth to his descendants, death cannot take away. Saying this, he came to the place where Don Rodrigo was, and Don Rodrigo gave into his hands the King Don Sancho his brother, and asked him three times if he was discharged of his prisoner; and when the King had answered Yes, Don Rodrigo said, For me, Sir, the joy which I have in your victory is enough; give the rewards to these good Portugueze, who with so good a will have put their lives upon the hazard to serve you, and in all things follow their counsel, and you will not err therein. Having said this he kissed the King's hand, and lying upon his shield, for he felt his breath fail him, with his helmet for a pillow, he kissed the cross of his sword in remembrance of that on which the incarnate Son of God had died for him, and rendered up his soul into the hands of his Creator. This was the death of one of the worthy knights of the world, Don Rodrigo Frojaz. In all the conquests which King Don Ferrando had made from the Moors of Portugal, great part had he borne, insomuch that that King was wont to say that other Princes might have more dominions than he, but two such knights as his two Rodrigos, meaning my Cid and this good knight, there was none but himself who had for vassals.

XIII.

Then King Don Garcia being desirous to be in the pursuit himself, delivered his brother into the hands of six knights that they should guard him, which he ought not to have done. And when he was gone King Don Sancho said unto the knights, Let me go and I will depart out of your country and never enter it again; and I will reward ye well as long as ye live; but they answered him, that for no reward would they commit such disloyalty, but would guard him well, not offering him any injury, till they had delivered him to his brother the King Don Garcia. While they were parleying Alvar Fañez Minaya came up, he to whom the King had given horse and arms before the battle; and he seeing the King held prisoner, cried out with a loud voice, Let loose my Lord the King: and he spurred his horse and made at them; and before his lance was broken he overthrew two of them, and so bestirred himself that he put the others to flight; and he took the horses of the two whom he had smote down, and gave one to the King, and mounted upon the other himself, for his own was hurt in the rescue; and they went together to a little rising ground where there was yet a small body of the knights of their party, and Alvar Fañez cried out to them aloud, Ye see here the King our Lord, who is free; now then remember the good name of the Castillians, and let us not lose it this day. And about four hundred knights gathered about him. And while they stood there they saw the Cid Ruydiez coming up with three hundred knights, for he had not been in the battle, and they knew his green pennon. And when King Don Sancho beheld it his heart rejoiced, and he said, Now let us descend into the plain, for he of good fortune cometh: and he said, Be of good heart, for it is the will of God that I should recover my kingdom, for I have escaped from captivity, and seen the death of Don Rodrigo Frojaz who took me, and Ruydiez the fortunate one cometh. And the King went down to him and welcomed him right joyfully, saying, In happy time are you come, my fortunate Cid; never vassal succoured his Lord in such season as you now succour me, for the King my brother had overcome me. And the Cid answered, Sir, be sure that you shall recover the day, or I will die; for wheresoever you go, either you shall be victorious or I will meet my death.

XIV.

By this time King Don García returned from the pursuit, singing as he came full joyfully, for he thought that the King his brother was a prisoner, and his great power overthrown. But there came one and told him that Don Sancho was rescued and in the field again, ready to give him battle a second time. Bravely was that second battle fought on both sides; and if it had not been for the great prowess of the Cid, the end would not have been as it was: in the end the Galegos and Portugueze were discomfited, and the King Don García taken in his turn. And in that battle the two brethren of Don Rodrigo Frojaz, Don Pedro and Don Vermui, were slain, and the two sons of Don Pedro, so that five of that family died that day. And the King Don Sancho put his brother in better ward than his brother three hours before had put him, for he put him in chains and sent him to the strong castle of Luna.

XV.

When King Don Sancho had done this he took unto himself the kingdom of Galicia and of Portugal, and without delay sent to his brother King Don Alfonso, commanding him to yield up to him the kingdom of Leon, for it was his by right. At this was the King of Leon troubled at heart; howbeit he answered that he would not yield up his kingdom, but do his utmost to defend it. Then King Don Sancho entered Leon, slaying and laying waste before him, as an army of infidels would have done; and King Don Alfonso sent to him to bid him cease from this, for it was inhuman work to kill and plunder the innocent: and he defied him to a pitched battle, saying that to whichsoever God should give the victory, to him also would he give the kingdom of Leon: and the King of Castille accepted the defiance, and a day was fixed for the battle, and the place was to be Lantada, which is near unto Carrion. The chief counsellor of King Don Alfonso was Don Pero Ansures, a notable and valiant knight, of the old and famous stock of the Ansures, Lords of Monzon, which is nigh unto Palencia; the same who in process of time was Count of Carrion and of Saldaña and Liebana, and Lord of Valladolid, a city which was by him greatly increased. This good knight commanded the army of his King Don Alfonso, and on the part of King Don Sancho came Ruydiez the Cid. Both Kings were in the field that day, and full hardily was the battle contested, and great was the mortality on either side, for the hatred which used to be between Moors and Christians was then between brethren. And that day also was the saying of Arias Gonzalo fulfilled. But in the end the skill and courage of my Cid prevailed, and King Don Alfonso was fain to avail himself of his horse's feet to save himself.

XVI.

Nevertheless the power of King Don Alfonso was not yet destroyed, and he would not yield up his kingdom: and he sent to his brother a second time to bid him battle, saying that whosoever conquered should then certainly remain King of Leon; and the place appointed was at Vulpegera, beside the river Carrion. And the two armies met and joined battle, and they of Leon had the victory, for my Cid was not in the field. And King Don Alfonso had pity upon the Castillians because they were Christians, and gave orders not to slay them; and his brother King Don Sancho fled. Now as he was flying, my Cid came up with his green pennon; and when he saw that the King his Lord had been conquered it grieved him sorely: howbeit he encouraged him saying, This is nothing, Sir! to fail or to prosper is as God pleases. But do you gather together your people who are discomfited, and bid them take heart. The Leonese and Galegos are with the King your brother, secure as they think themselves in their lodging, and taking no thought of you; for it is their custom to extol themselves when their fortune is fair, and to mock at others, and in this boastfulness will they spend the night, so that we shall find them sleeping at break of day, and will fall upon them. And it came to pass as he had said. The Leonese lodged themselves in Vulpegera, taking no thought of their enemies, and setting no watch; and Ruydiez arose betimes in the morning and fell upon them, and subdued them before they could take their arms. King Don Alfonso fled to the town of Carrion, which was three leagues distant, and would have fortified himself there in the Church of St. Mary, but he was surrounded and constrained to yield.

XVII.

Now the knights of Leon gathered together in their flight, and when they could not find their King they were greatly ashamed, and they turned back and smote the Castillians; and as it befell, they encountered King Don Sancho and took him prisoner, not having those in his company whom he should have had, for his people considered the victory as their own, and all was in confusion. And thirteen knights took him in their ward and were leading him away,—but my Cid beheld them and galloped after them: he was alone, and had no lance, having broken his in the battle. And he came up to them and said, Knights, give me my Lord and I will give unto you yours. They knew him by his arms, and they made answer, Ruydiez, return in peace and seek not to contend with us, otherwise we will carry you away prisoner with him. And he waxed wroth and said, Give me but a lance and I will, single as I am, rescue my Lord from all of ye: by God's help I will do it. And they held him as nothing because he was but one, and gave him a lance. But he attacked them therewith so bravely that he slew eleven of the thirteen, leaving two only alive, on whom he had mercy; and thus did he rescue the King. And the Castillians rejoiced greatly at the King's deliverance: and King Don Sancho went to Burgos, and took with him his brother prisoner.

XVIII.

Great was the love which the Infanta Doña Urraca bore to her brother King Don Alfonso, and when she heard that he was made prisoner, she feared least he should be put to death: and she took with her the Count Don Peransures, and went to Burgos. And they spake with the Cid, and besought him that he would join with them and intercede with the King that he should release his brother from prison, and let him become a Monk at Sahagun. Full willing was the Cid to serve in any thing the Infanta Doña Urraca, and he went with her before the King. And she knelt down before the King her brother, and besought mercy for Don Alfonso, his brother and hers. And the King took her by the hand and raised her from her knees, and made her sit beside him, and said unto her, Now then, my sister, say what you would have. And she besought him that he would let their brother Don Alfonso take the habit of St. Benedict, in the royal Monastery of Sahagun, and my Cid, and Count Peransures and the other chief persons who were there present, besought him in like manner. And the King took my Cid aside, and asked counsel of him what he should do; and the Cid said, that if Don Alfonso were willing to become a Monk, he would do well to set him free upon that condition, and he besought him so to do. Then King Don Sancho, at my Cid's request, granted to Doña Urraca what she had asked. And he released King Don Alfonso from prison, and Don Alfonso became a Monk in the Monastery at Sahagun, more by force than of free will. And being in the Monastery he spake with Don Peransures, and took counsel with him, and fled away by night from the Monks, and went among the Moors to King Alimaymon of Toledo. And the Moorish King welcomed him with a good will, and did great honour to him, and gave him great possessions and many gifts.

XIX.

When Doña Urraca knew that her brother King Don Alfonso had fled to Toledo, she sent to him three good men of the kingdom of Leon, that they should be his counsellors, for she loved him well. These were Don Pero Ansures, and Don Ferran Ansures, and Don Gonzalo Ansures, all three brethren: and they went with King Don Sancho's permission, for it was God's pleasure. Now Alimaymon rejoiced in the King Don Alfonzo, and loved him as if he had been his own son. And Don Alfonso made a covenant with him to love him and defend him and serve him alway, so long as he should remain with him, and not to depart from him without his leave; and the King covenanted on his side to love him and honour him, and defend him to the utmost of his power. And Alimaymon ordered fair palaces to be edified for him, by the wall of the Alcazar, on the outer part, that the Moors of the city might do no displeasure neither to him nor to his companions: and they were hard by a garden of the King's, that he might go out and disport himself therein whensoever it pleased him. And for these things King Don Alfonso loved to serve King Alimaymon. Nevertheless when he saw the great honour of the King of Toledo, and how powerful he was, and that he was the Lord of so great chivalry, and of the noblest city which had belonged unto the Gothic Kings, from whom he himself was descended, it grieved him in his heart to see that city in the hands of the Moors: and he said within his heart, Lord God and Father Jesus Christ, it is wholly in thy power to give and to take away, and right it is that thy will should be done, even as thou hast done it to me, to whom thou gavest a kingdom, and it was thy will to take it away from me, and thou hast made me come hither to serve the enemies who were at the service of the King my father. Lord, I put my hope in thee that thou wilt deliver me from this servitude, and give me a land and kingdom to command, and that thou wilt show unto me such favour that this land and this city shall by me be won, that thy holy body may be sacrificed in it to the honour of Christendom. This prayer he made with great devotion and with many tears; and the Lord God heard him, as hereafter you shall hear in this history. In those days King Alimaymon was at war with other Moorish Kings his enemies, and King Don Alfonso fought against them on his side, and did such good service that he quelled their power, and they durst no longer offend him. And in time of peace Don Alfonso and his companions went fowling along the banks of the Tagus, for in those days there was much game there, and venison of all kinds; and they killed venison among the mountains. And as he was thus spoiling he came to a place which is now called Brihuega, and it pleased him well, for it was a fair place to dwell in, and abounded with game, and there was a dismantled castle there, and he thought that he would ask the King for this place. And he returned to Toledo and asked it of the King, and King Alimaymon gave it him, and he placed there his huntsmen and his fowlers who were Christians, and fortified the place as his own. And the lineage of these people continued there till Don Juan, the third archbishop of Toledo, enlarged it, and peopled the parish of St. Pedro.

XX.

It came to pass after this that both the Kings one day came out of Toledo, and past over the bridge of Alcantara, and went into the royal garden to disport themselves therein and take their pleasure. And at evening Don Alfonso lay down upon a bed to sleep, and King Alimaymon fell in talk with his favourites concerning his city of Toledo, how strong it was and how well provided with all things, and that he feared neither war of Moor nor Christian against it; and he asked them if it could, by any, means be lost in war. Then one of them answered and said, Sir, if you would not hold it ill, I would tell you how it might be lost, and by no other manner in the world could it be so. And the King bade him say on. And the favourite then said, If this city were beset for seven years, and the bread and the wine and the fruits should be cut down year by year, it would be lost for lack of food. All this King Don Alfonso heard, for he was not sleeping, and he took good heed of it. Now the Moors knew not that he was lying there. And when they had thus spoken, Alimaymon arose to walk in the palace, and he saw King Don Alfonso lying there as if he were sleeping: and it troubled him, and he said to his favourites, We did not heed Alfonso who is lying there, and has heard all that we have said. And the favourites made answer, Kill him, Sir. But the King said, How shall I go against my true promise? moreover he sleepeth, and peradventure hath heard nothing. And they said to him, Would you know whether or not he sleepeth? and he answered, Yea: and they said, Go then and wake him, and if he have drivelled he hath slept, but if not he hath been awake and hath heard us. Then King Don Alfonso immediately wetted the pillow, and feigned himself hard to be awakened, so that Alimaymon thought he slept.

XXI.

And when the Easter of the Sheep was come, which the Moors celebrate, the King of Toledo went out of the city to kill the sheep at the place accustomed, as he was wont to do, and King Don Alfonso went with him. Now Don Alfonso was a goodly personage and of fair demeanour, so that the Moors liked him well. And as he was going by the side of the King, two honourable Moors followed them, and the one said unto the other, How fair a knight is this Christian, and of what good customs! well doth he deserve to be the lord of some great land. And the other made answer, I dreamed a dream last night, that this Alfonso entered the city riding upon a huge boar, and many swine after him, who rooted up all Toledo with their snouts, and even the Mosques therein: Certes, he will one day become King of Toledo. And while they were thus communing every hair upon King Don Alfonso's head stood up erect, and Alimaymon laid his hand upon them to press them down, but so soon as his hand was taken off they rose again; and the two Moors held it for a great token, and spake with each other concerning it, and one of King Alimaymon's favourites heard all which they said. And after the sheep had been sacrificed they returned into the city, and the favourite told the King what he had heard the two Moors say; and the King sent for them forthwith, and questioned them, and they repeated to him what they had said, even as ye have heard. And King Alimaymon said unto them, What then shall I do? and they made answer, that he should put Don Alfonso to death; but the King replied, that this he would not do, nor go against the true promise which he had given him, but that he would so deal that no evil should ever come towards himself from Alfonso. So he sent for Don Alfonso and bade him swear that he would never come against him, nor against his sons, and that no evil should come against them from him; and King Don Alfonso did as Alimaymon required, and did him homage to this effect. And thenceforth was the King of Toledo more secure of him, and held him even in greater favour than before. All this while did King Don Alfonso govern himself by the advice of Count Peransures, who alway advised him discreetly and well.

XXII.

But when King Don Sancho heard how his brother had fled from the Monastery, he drew out his host and went against the city of Leon. The Leonese would fain have maintained the city against him, but they could not, and he took the city of Leon, and all the towns and castles which had been under the dominion of his brother King Don Alfonso. And then he put the crown upon his head, and called himself King of the three kingdoms. He was a fair knight and of marvellous courage, so that both Moors and Christians were dismayed at what they saw him do, for they saw that nothing which he willed to take by force could stand against him. And when the Infanta Doña Urraca, and the men of Zamora, saw that he had quiet possession of both his brother's kingdoms, they feared that he would come against them and disherit his sister also. And for this reason they took Don Arias Gonzalo to be their chief captain, Doña Urraca's foster-father, that by his means they might protect themselves, if need should be. And it came to pass as they had feared, for King Don Sancho knew that his sisters greatly loved Don Alfonso, and he thought that by their counsel he had fled from the Monastery, especially by Doña Urraca's, because Don Alfonso guided himself in all things by her counsel, holding her in place of a mother, for she was a lady of great understanding. And he went forth with his army, and took from the Infanta Doña Elvira the half of the Infantazgo which she possessed, and also from Doña Urraca the other half. And he went against Toro, the city of Doña Elvira, and took it; and then he went to Zamora to Doña Urraca, bidding her yield him up the city, and saying that he would give her lands as much as she required in the plain country. But she returned for answer, that she would in no manner yield unto him that which the King her father had given her; and she besought him that he would suffer her to continue to dwell peaceably therein, saying that no disservice should ever be done against him on her part.

XXIII.

Then King Don Sancho went to Burgos, because it was not the season for besieging a town, being winter. And he sent his letters through all the land, calling upon his vassals to assemble together upon the first day of March in Sahagun, upon pain of forfeiting his favour. Now though the King was yet but a young man, whose beard was but just coming, he was of so great courage that the people feared him, and dared not do otherwise than as he commanded. And they assembled together in Sahagun on the day appointed; and when the King heard in what readiness they were, it gladdened him, and he lifted up his hands to God and said, Blessed be thy name, O Lord, because thou hast given me all the kingdoms of my father. And when he had said this he ordered proclamation to be made through the streets of Burgos, that all should go forth to protect the host and the body of the King their Lord. And the day in which they left Burgos they took up their lodging at Fromesta; and the next day they came to Canion, but the King would not lodge there, and he went on to Sahagun, where the army awaited him, and took up his lodging without the town; and on the following morning he bade the host advance, and they made such speed that in three days they arrived before Zamora, and pitched their tents upon the banks of the Douro; and he ordered proclamation to be made throughout the host that no harm should be done until he had commanded it. And he mounted on horseback with his hidalgos and rode round the town, and beheld how strongly it was situated upon a rock, with strong walls, and many and strong towers, and the river Douro running at the foot thereof; and he said unto his knights, Ye see how strong it is, neither Moor nor Christian can prevail against it; if I could have it from my sister either for money or exchange, I should be Lord of Spain.

XXIV.

Then the King returned to his tents, and incontinently he sent for the Cid, and said unto him, Cid, you well know how manifoldly you are bound unto me, both by nature, and by reason of the breeding which the King my father gave you; and when he died he commended you to me, and I have ever shown favour unto you, and you have ever served me as the loyalest vassal that ever did service to his Lord; and I have for your good deserts given unto you more than there is in a great county, and have made you the chief of all my household. Now therefore I beseech you as my friend and true vassal, that you go to Zamora to my sister Doña Urraca, and say unto her again, that I beseech her to give me the town either for a price, or in exchange, and I will give to her Medina de Rio-seco, with the whole Infantazgo, from Villalpando to Valladolid, and Tiedra also, which is a good Castle; and I will swear unto her, with twelve knights of my vassals, never to break this covenant between us; but if she refuseth to do this I will take away the town from her by force. And my Cid kissed the hand of the King and said unto him, This bidding, Sir, should be for other messenger, for it is a heavy thing for me to deliver it; for I was brought up in Zamora by your father's command, in the house of Don Arias Gonzalo, with Doña Urraca and with his sons, and it is not fitting that I should be the bearer of such bidding. And the King persisted in requiring of him that he should go, insomuch that he was constrained to obey his will. And he took with him fifteen of his knights and rode towards Zamora, and when he drew nigh he called unto those who kept guard in the towers not to shoot their arrows at him, for he was Ruydiez of Bivar, who came to Doña Urraca with the bidding of her brother King Don Sancho. With that there came down a knight who was nephew to Arias Gonzalo, and had the keeping of the gate, and he bade the Cid enter, saying that he would order him to be well lodged while he went to Doña Urraca to know if she would be pleased to see him. So the Cid went in, and the knight went to the Infanta, and told her that Ruydiez of Bivar was come with a message from King Don Sancho; and it pleased her well that he should be the messenger, and she bade him come before that she might know what was his bidding; and she sent Arias Gonzalo and the other knights of her party to meet him and accompany him. And when the Cid entered the palace Doña Urraca advanced to meet him, and greeted him full well, and they seated themselves both upon the Estrado. And Doña Urraca said unto him, Cid, you well know that you were brought up with me here in Zamora, in the house of Don Arias Gonzalo, and when my father was at the point of death he charged you that you should alway counsel his sons the best you could. Now therefore tell me I beseech you what is it which my brother goes about to do, now that he has called up all Spain in arms, and to what lands he thinks to go, whether against Moors or Christians. Then the Cid answered and said, Lady, to messenger and a letter no wrong should be done; give me safe assurance and I will tell unto you that which the King your brother hath sent me to say. And she said she would do as Don Arias Gonzalo should advise her. And Don Arias answered that it was well to hear what the King her brother had sent to say: Peradventure, said he, he goeth against the Moors, and requires aid of you, which it would be right to give; and for such service I and my sons would go with him, and I would give fifteen of my people well mounted and armed, and supply them with food for ten years, if he needed them. Doña Urraca then said to the Cid, that he might speak his bidding safely. Then said my Cid, The King your brother sends to greet you, and beseeches you to give him this town of Zamora, either for a price or in exchange; and he will give to you Medina de Rio-seco, with the whole Infantazgo, from Villalpando to Valladolid, and the good castle of Tiedra, and he will swear unto you, with twelve knights his vassals, never to do you hurt or harm; but if you will not give him the town, he will take it against your will.

XXV.

When Doña Urraca heard this she was sorely grieved, and in her great sorrow she lamented aloud, saying, Wretch that I am, many are the evil messages which I have heard since my father's death! He hath disherited my brother King Don Garcia of his kingdom, and taken him, and now holds him in irons as if he were a thief or a Moor; and he hath taken his lands from my brother King Don Alfonso, and forced him to go among the Moors, and live there exiled, as if he had been a traitor; and would let none go with him except Don Peransures and his brethren, whom I sent; and he hath taken her lands from my sister Doña Elvira against her will, and now would he take Zamora from me also! Now then let the earth open and swallow me, that I may not see so many troubles! And with that, in her strong anger against her brother King Don Sancho, she said, I am a woman, and well know that I cannot strive with him in battle; but I will have him slain either secretly or openly. Then Don Arias Gonzalo stood up and said, Lady Doña Urraca, in thus complaining and making lamentation you do inconsiderately; for in time of trouble it befits us to take thought of what best is to be done, and so must we do. Now then, Lady, give order that all the men of Zamora assemble in St. Salvador's and know of them whether they will hold with you, seeing that your father gave them to you to be your vassals. And if they will hold with you, then give not you up the town, neither for a price, nor in exchange; but if they will not, let us then go to Toledo among the Moors, where your brother King Don Alfonso abideth. And she did as her foster-father had advised, and it was proclaimed through the streets that the men of Zamora should meet in council at St. Salvador's. And when they were all assembled, Doña Urraca arose and said, Friends and vassals, ye have seen how my brother King Don Sancho hath disherited all his brethren, against the oath which he made to the King my father, and now he would disherit me also. He hath sent to bid me give him Zamora, either for a price or in exchange. Now concerning this I would know whereunto ye advise me, and if you will hold with me as good vassals and true, for he saith that he will take it from me whether I will or no; but if ye will keep my career I think to defend it by God's mercy and with your help. Then by command of the council there rose up a knight who was called Don Nuño, a man of worth, aged, and of fair speech; and he said, God reward you, Lady, this favour which you have shown us in thinking good to come to our council, for we are your vassals, and should do what you command. And we beseech you give not up Zamora, neither for price nor for exchange, for he who besieges you upon the rock would soon drive you from the plain. The council of Zamora will do your bidding, and will not desert you neither for trouble nor for danger which may befall them, even unto death. Sooner, Lady, will we expend all our possessions, and eat our mules and horses, yea sooner feed upon our children and our wives, than give up Zamora, unless by your command. And they all with one accord confirmed what Don Nuño had said. When the Infanta Doña Urraca heard this she was well pleased, and praised them greatly; and she turned to the Cid and said unto him, You were bred up with me in this town of Zamora, where Don Arias Gonzalo fostered you by command of the King my father, and through your help it was that the King my father gave it unto me to be my inheritance. I beseech you help me now against my brother, and intreat him that he will not seek to disherit me; but if he will go on with what he hath begun, say to him that I will rather die with the men of Zamora, and they with me, than give him up the town, either for price or exchange. And with this answer did the Cid return unto the King.

XXVI.

When King Don Sancho heard what the Cid said, his anger kindled against him, and he said, You have given this counsel to my sister because you were bred up with her. And my Cid answered and said, Faithfully have I discharged your bidding, and as a true vassal. Howbeit, O King, I will not bear arms against the Infanta your sister, nor against Zamora, because of the days which are passed;—and I beseech you do not persist in doing this wrong. But then King Don Sancho was more greatly incensed, and he said unto him, If it were not that my father left you commended to me, I would order you this instant to be hanged. But for this which you have said I command you to quit my kingdom within nine days. And the Cid went to his tent in anger, and called for his kinsmen and his friends, and bade them make ready on the instant to depart with him. And he set forth with all the knights and esquires of his table, and with all their retainers horse and foot, twelve hundred persons, all men of approved worth, a goodly company;—and they took the road to Toledo, meaning to join King Don Alfonso among the Moors. And that night they slept at Castro Nuño. But when the Counts and Ricos-omes, and the other good men of the host saw this, they understood the great evil and disservice which might arise to the King, and to the land, from the departure of the Cid, who went away in wrath. And they went to the King and said unto him, Sir, wherefore would you lose so good a vassal, who has done you such great service? If he should go unto your brother Don Alfonso among the Moors, he would not let you besiege this city thus in peace. And the King perceived that they spake rightly, and he called for Don Diego Ordoñez, the son of Count Don Bermudo, who was the son of the Infante Don Ordoño of Leon, and bade him follow the Cid, and beseech him in his name to return; and whatever covenant he should make it should be confirmed unto him; and of this he ordered his letters of credence to be made out. And Don Diego Ordoñez went to horse, and rode after the Cid, and overtook him between Castro Nuño and Medina del Campo. And when it was told unto the Cid that Don Diego Ordoñez was coming, he turned to meet him, and greeted him well, and asked him wherefore he was come. And he delivered the King's bidding, and showed unto him his letters of credence, and said unto him that the King besought him not to bear in mind the words which he had spoken unto him, being in anger. Then the Cid called together his kinsmen and friends, and asked them what they should do. And they counselled him that he should return to the King, for it was better to remain in his land and serve God, than to go among the Moors. And he held their counsel good, and called for Don Diego, and said unto him that he would do the will of the King: and Don Diego sent to the King to tell him how he had sped. And when the Cid drew nigh unto the host, the King went out with five hundred knights to meet him, and received him gladly, and did him great honour. And the Cid kissed his hand and asked him if he confirmed what Don Diego had said; and the King confirmed it before all the knights who were there present, promising to give him great possessions. And when they came to the army great was the joy because of the Cid's return, and great were the rejoicings which were made: but as great was the sorrow in Zamora, for they who were in the town held that the siege was broken up by his departure. Nevertheless my Cid would not bear arms against the Infanta, nor against the town of Zamora, because of the days which were past.

XXVII.

And the King ordered proclamation to be made throughout the host that the people should make ready to attack the town. And they fought against it three days and three nights so bravely that all the ditches were filled up, and the barbicans thrown down, and they who were within fought sword in hand with those without, and the waters of the Douro, as they past below the town, were all discoloured with blood. And when Count Don García de Cabra saw the great loss which they were suffering, it grieved him; and he went unto the King and told him that many men were slain, and advised him to call off the host that they should no longer fight against the town, but hold it besieged, for by famine it might soon be taken. Then the King ordered them to draw back, and he sent to each camp to know how many men had died in the attack, and the number was found to be a thousand and thirty. And when the King knew this he was greatly troubled for the great loss which he had received, and he ordered the town to be beleaguered round about, and in this manner he begirt it, that none could enter into it, neither go out therefrom; and there was a great famine within the town. And when Don Arias Gonzalo saw the misery, and the hunger, and the mortality which were there, he said to the Infanta Doña Urraca, You see, Lady, the great wretchedness which the people of Zamora have suffered, and do every day suffer to maintain their loyalty; now then call together the Council, and thank them truly for what they have done for you, and bid them give up the town within nine days to the King your brother. And we, Lady, will go to Toledo to your brother King Don Alfonso, for we cannot defend Zamora; King Don Sancho is of so great heart and so resolute, that he will never break up the siege, and I do not hold it good, that you should abide here longer. And Doña Urraca gave orders that the good men of Zamora should meet together in Council; and she said unto them, Friends, ye well see the resoluteness of King Don Sancho my brother; and already have ye suffered much evil and much wretchedness for doing right and loyally, losing kinsmen and friends in my service. Ye have done enough, and I do not hold it good that ye should perish; I command ye therefore give up the town to him within nine days, and I will go to Toledo to my brother King Don Alfonso. The men of Zamora when they heard this had great sorrow, because they had endured the siege so long, and must now give up the town at last; and they determined all to go with the Infanta, and not remain in the town.

XXVIII.

When Vellido Dolfos heard this, he went to Doña Urraca and said, Lady, I came here to Zamora to do you service with thirty knights, all well accoutred, as you know; and I have served you long time, and never have I had from you guerdon for my service, though I have demanded it: but now if you will grant my demand I will relieve Zamora, and make King Don Sancho break up the siege. Then said Doña Urraca, Vellido, I shall repeat to thee the saying of the wise man, A man bargains well with the slothful and with him who is in need; and thus you would deal with me. I do not bid thee commit any evil thing, if such thou hast in thy thought; but I say unto you, that there is not a man in the world to whom if he should relieve Zamora, and make the King my brother raise the siege, I would not grant whatsoever he might require. And when Vellido heard this he kissed her hand, and went to a porter who kept one of the gates of the town, and spake with him, saying, that he should open the gate unto him when he saw him flying toward it, and he gave him his cloak. Then went he to his lodging and armed himself, and mounted his horse, and rode to the house of Don Arias Gonzalo, and cried with a loud voice, We all know the reason, Don Arias Gonzalo, why you will not let Doña Urraca exchange Zamora with her brother; it is because you deal with her as a harlot, like an old traitor. When Arias Gonzalo heard this, it grieved him to the heart, and he said, In an evil day was I born, that so shameful a falsehood as this should be said to me in mine old age, and there should be none to revenge me! Then his sons arose and armed themselves hastily, and went after Vellido, who fled before them toward the gate of the town. The porter when he saw him coming opened the gate, and he rode out and galloped into the camp of the King Don Sancho, and the others followed him till they were nigh the camp, but farther they did not venture. And Vellido went to the King and kissed his hand, and said unto him these false words with a lying tongue: Sir, because I said to the Council of Zamora that they should yield the town unto you, the sons of Arias Gonzalo would have slain me, even as you have seen. And therefore come I to you, Sir, and will be your vassal, if I may find favour at your hands. And I will show you how in a few days you may have Zamora, if God pleases; and if I do not as I have said, then let me be slain. And the King believed all that he said, and received him for his vassal, and did him great honour. And all that night they talked together of his secrets, and he made the King believe that he knew a postern by means of which he would put Zamora into his hands.

XXIX.

On the morrow in the morning, one of the knights who were in the town went upon the wall, and cried out with a loud voice, so that the greater part of the host heard him, King Don Sancho, give ear to what I say; I am a knight and hidalgo, a native of the land of Santiago; and they from whom I spring were true men and delighted in their loyalty, and I also will live and die in my truth. Give ear, for I would undeceive you, and tell you the truth, if you will believe me, I say unto you, that from this town of Zamora there is gone forth a traitor to kill you; his name is Vellido Dolfos; he is the son of Adolfo, who slew Don Nuño like a traitor, and the grandson of Laino, another traitor, who killed his gossip and threw him into the river; and this is as great a traitor as the rest of his race; look to yourself therefore and take heed of him. I say this to you, that if peradventure evil should befall you by this traitor, it may not be said in Spain that you were not warned against him. Now the name of this knight was Bernal Diañez de Ocampo. And the men of Zamora sent also to the King to bid him beware of Vellido, and the king took their warning in good part, and sent to say unto them, that when he had the town he would deal bountifully with them, for this which they had done; nevertheless he gave no heed to the warning. And Vellido, when he heard this went to the King, and said, Sir, the old Arias Gonzalo is full crafty, and hath sent to say this unto you, because he knows that by my means you would have won the town. And he called for his horse, feigning that he would depart because of what had been said. But the King took him by the hand and said, Friend and vassal, take no thought for this; I say unto you, that if I may have Zamora, I will make you chief therein, even as Arias Gonzalo is now. Then Vellido kissed his hand and said, God grant you life, Sir, for many and happy years, and let you fulfil what you desire. But the traitor had other thoughts in his heart.

XXX.

After this Vellido took the King apart and said to him, If it please you, Sir, let us ride out together alone; we will go round Zamora, and see the trenches which you have ordered to be made; and I will show unto you the postern which is called the Queen's, by which we may enter the town, for it is never closed. When it is night you shall give me a hundred knights who are hidalgos, well armed, and we will go on foot, and the Zamorans because they are weak with famine and misery, will let us conquer them, and we will enter and open the gate, and keep it open till all your host shall have entered in; and thus shall we win the town of Zamora. The King believed what he said, and they took horse and went riding round the town, and the King looked at the trenches, and that traitor snowed him the postern whereof he had spoken. And after they had ridden round the town the King had need to alight upon the side of the Douro and go apart; now he carried in his hand a light hunting spear which was gilded over, even such as the Kings from whom he was descended were wont to bear; and he gave this to Vellido to hold it while he went aside, to cover his feet. And Vellido Dolfos, when he saw him in that guise, took the hunting spear and thrust it between his shoulders, so that it went through him and came out at his breast. And when he had stricken him he turned the reins and rode as fast as he could toward the postern; this was not the first treason which he had committed, for he had killed the Count Don Nuño treacherously. Now it chanced that the Cid saw him riding thus, and asked him wherefore he fled, and he would not answer; and then the Cid understood that he had done some treason, and his heart misgave him that he had slain the King; and he called in haste for his horse, but while they were bringing it, Vellido had ridden far away; and the Cid being eager to follow him, took only his lance and did not wait to have his spurs buckled on. And he followed him to the postern and had well nigh overtaken him, but Vellido got in; and then the Cid said in his anger, Cursed be the knight who ever gets on horseback without his spurs. Now in all the feats of the Cid never was fault found in him save only in this, that he did not enter after Vellido into the town; but he did not fail to do this for cowardice, neither for fear of death, or of imprisonment; but because he thought that peradventure this was a device between him and the King, and that he fled by the King's command; for certes, if he had known that the King was slain, there was nothing which would have prevented him from entering the town, and slaying the traitor in the streets, thereright.

XXXI.

Now the history saith, that when Vellido Dolfos had got within the postern, he was in such fear both of those who were in the town and of those who were without, that he went and placed himself under the mantle of the Infanta Doña Urraca. And when Don Arias Gonzalo knew this he went unto the Infanta and said, Lady, I beseech you that you give up this traitor to the Castillians, otherwise be sure that it will be to your own harm; for the Castillians will impeach all who are in Zamora, and that will be greater dishonour for you and for us. And Doña Urraca made answer, Counsel me then so that he may not die for this which he hath done. Don Arias Gonzalo then answered, Give him unto me, and I will keep him in custody for three days, and if the Castillians impeach us we will deliver him into their hands; and if they do not impeach us within that time, we will thrust him out of the town so that he shall not be seen among us. And Don Arias Gonzalo took him from thence, and secured him with double fetters, and guarded him well.

XXXII.

Meantime the Castillians went to seek their King, and they found him by the side of the Douro, where he lay sorely wounded, even unto death; but he had not yet lost his speech, and the hunting spear was in his body, through and through, and they did not dare to take it out least he should die immediately. And a master of Burgos came up who was well skilled in these things, and he sawed off the ends of the spear, that he might not lose his speech, and said that he should be confessed, for he had death within him. Then Count Don García de Cabra, the curley-haired one of Grañon, said unto him, Sir, think of your soul, for you have a desperate wound. And the King made answer, Blessed be you, Count, who thus counsel me, for I perceive that I am slain; the traitor Vellido has killed me, and I well know that this was for my sins, because I broke the oath which I made unto the King my father. And as the King was saying this the Cid came up and knelt before him and said, I, Sir, remain more desolate than any other of your vassals, for for your sake have I made your brethren mine enemies, and all in the world who were against you, and against whom it pleased you to go. The King your father commended me to them as well as to you, when he divided his kingdoms, and I have lost their love for your sake, having done them great evil. And now neither can I go before King Don Alfonso, your brother, nor remain among the Christians before Doña Urraca your sister, because they hold that whatsoever you have done against them was by my counsel. Now then, Sir, remember me before you depart. The King then commanded that they should raise him up in the bed, and the Counts and Ricos-omes stood round about him, and the Bishops and Archbishops who had come thither to make accord between him and his sister Doña Urraca, and they heard what the Cid said, and knew that he said truly; for whatever good speed King Don Sancho had had in his doings was all by means of my Cid. And the King said unto them, I beseech all ye who are here present, Counts and Ricos-omes, and all my other vassals, that if my brother King Don Alfonso should come from the land of the Moors, ye beseech him to show favour unto you, my Cid, and that he always be bountiful unto you, and receive you to be his vassal; and if he alway doth this and listen unto you, he will not be badly advised. Then the Cid arose and kissed his Wand, and all the chief persons who were there present did the like. And after this the King said unto them, I beseech ye intreat my brother King Don Alfonso to forgive me whatever wrong I have done him, and to pray to God to have mercy upon my soul. And when he had said this he asked for the candle, and presently his soul departed. And all who were there present made great lamentation for the King.

BOOK III.

I.

Now when the King was dead, the townsmen who were in the camp forsook their tents and fled, and much did they lose in their flight; but the noble Castillians, thinking rather of what they were bound to do as men who had always preserved their loyalty, like their ancestors before them, would not depart from Zamora, nor break up the siege thereof, but remained bravely before it, though they had lost their Lord. And they summoned all the Bishops, and took the body of the King and sent it full honourably to the Monastery of Oña, and buried him there as beseemed a King: and while one part of the chief men of the host accompanied the body, the rest remained in the camp before Zamora. And when the prelates and good men had returned to the army, they took counsel together how they should proceed against the men of Zamora for this great treason which had been committed. Then Count Don García de Cabra arose and said, Friends, ye see that we have lost our Lord the King Don Sancho; the traitor, Vellido, being his vassal, slew him, and they of Zamora have received and harboured him within their walls; and therefore as we think, and as has been said unto us, he did this treason by their counsel. Now then if there be one here who will impeach them for this thing, we will do whatever may be needful that he may come off with honour, and the impeachment be carried through. Then Don Diego Ordoñez arose, the son of Count Don Ordono, a man of royal lineage and great hardihood; and he said unto them, If ye will all assent to this which ye have heard, I will impeach the men of Zamora, for the death of the King our Lord: and they all assented, promising to fulfil what had been said. Now my Cid did not make this impeachment against the people of Zamora, because of the oath which he had sworn.

II.

Then Don Diego Ordoñez went to his lodging and armed himself well, and armed his horse also, and mounted and rode toward Zamora. And when he drew nigh unto the town, he covered himself with his shield that they might not hurt him from the walls, and began to cry aloud, asking if Don Arias Gonzalo were there, for he would speak with him. A squire who was keeping guard upon the wall went to Don Arias and told him that there was a knight well armed calling for him, without the walls, and he said that if it pleased Don Arias he would shoot at him with a cross-bow, and strike him or kill his horse; but Don Arias forbade him, saying that he should no ways harm him. And Don Arias Gonzalo went with his sons upon the wall to see who called for him, and he spake to the knight, saying, Friend, what wouldest thou? And Don Diego Ordoñez answered, The Castillians have lost their Lord; the traitor Vellido slew for him, being his vassal, and ye of Zamora have received Vellido and harboured him within your walls. Now therefore I say that he is a traitor who hath a traitor with him, if he knoweth and consenteth unto the treason. And for this I impeach the people of Zamora, the great as well as the little, the living and the dead, they who now are and they who are yet unborn; and I impeach the waters which they drink and the garments which they put on; their bread and their wine, and the very stones in their walls. If there be any one in Zamora to gainsay what I have said, I will do battle with him, and with God's pleasure conquer him, so that the infamy shall remain upon you. Don Arias Gonzalo replied, If I were what thou sayest I am, it had been better for me never to have been born; but in what thou sayest thou liest. In that which the great do the little have no fault, nor the dead for the deeds of the living, which they neither see nor hear: but setting aside these and the things which have no understanding, as to the rest I say that thou liest, and I will do battle with thee upon this quarrel, or give thee one in my stead. But know that you have been ill advised in making this impeachment, for the manner is, that whosoever impeacheth a Council must do battle with five, one after another, and if he conquer the five he shall be held a true man, but if either of the five conquer him, the Council is held acquitted and he a liar. When Don Diego heard this it troubled him; howbeit he dissembled this right well, and said unto Don Arias Gonzalo, I will bring twelve Castillians, and do you bring twelve men of Zamora, and they shall swear upon the Holy Gospel to judge justly between us, and if they find that I am bound to do battle with five, I will perform it. And Don Arias made answer that he said well, and it should be so. And truce was made for three times nine days, till this should have been determined and the combat fought.

III.

Then when the truce was made, Don Arias Gonzalo went out from the town into the host of the Castillians, and his sons with him, and many of the knights of the town; and all the Ricos-omes and knights who were in the host assembled together with them, and consulted what was to be done in this impeachment. And they chose out twelve alcades on the one part, and twelve on the other, who should decide in what manner he was bound to perform combat who impeached a Council. And the four and twenty alcades accorded concerning what was the law in this case; and two of them who were held the most learned in these things arose, the one being a Castillian and the other of Zamora, and said that they had found the law as it was written to be this: That whosoever impeacheth the Council of a town which was a bishop's seat, must do battle with five in the field, one after another; and that after every combat there should be given unto him fresh arms and horse, and three sops of bread, and a draught either of wine or of water, as he chose. And in this sentence which the twain pronounced, the other twenty and two accorded.

IV.

On the morrow before the hour of tierce, the four and twenty alcades marked out the lists upon the sand beside the river, at the place which is called Santiago, and in the middle of the lists they placed a bar, and ordained that he who won the battle should lay hand on the bar, and say that he had conquered: and then they appointed a term of nine days for the combatants to come to those lists which had been assigned. And when all was appointed as ye have heard, Don Arias returned to Zamora, and told the Infanta Doña Urraca all that had been done, and she ordered a meeting to be called, at which all the men of the town assembled. And when they were gathered together, Don Arias Gonzalo said unto them, Friends, I beseech ye, if there be any here among ye who took counsel for the death of King Don Sancho, or were privy thereunto, that ye now tell me, and deny it not; for rather would I go with my sons to the land of the Moors, than be overcome in the field, and held for a traitor. Then they all replied, that there was none there who knew of the treason, nor had consented unto it. At this was Don Arias Gonzalo well pleased, and he bade them go each to his house; and he went to his house also with his sons, and chose out four of them to do combat, and said that he would be the fifth himself; and he gave them directions how to demean themselves in the lists, and said, that he would enter first; and if, said he, what the Castillian saith be true, I would die first, not to see the infamy; but if what he saith be false, I shall conquer him, and ye shall ever be held in honour.

V.

When the day appointed was come, Don Arias Gonzalo early in the morning armed his sons, and they armed him; and it was told him that Don Diego Ordoñez was already in the lists. Then he and his sons mounted their horses, and as they rode through the gates of their house, Doña Urraca, with a company of dames met them, and said to Don Arias, weeping, Remember now how my father, King Don Ferrando, left me to your care, and you swore between his hands that you would never forsake me; and lo! now you are forsaking me. I beseech you remain with me, and go not to this battle, for there is reason enough why you should be excused, and not break the oath which you made unto my father. And she took hold on him, and would not let him go, and made him be disarmed. Then came many knights around him, to demand arms of him, and request that they might do battle in his stead; nevertheless he would give them to none. And he called for his son Pedro Arias, who was a right brave knight, though but of green years, and who had greatly intreated his father before this, that he would suffer him to fight in his stead. And Don Arias armed him compleatly with his own hands, and instructed him how to demean himself, and gave him his blessing with his right hand, and said unto him, that in such a point he went to save the people of Zamora, as when our Lord Jesus Christ came through the Virgin Mary, to save the people of this world, who were lost by our father Adam. Then went they into the field, where Don Diego Ordoñez was awaiting them, and Pedrarias entered the lists, and the judges placed them each in his place, and divided the sun between them, and went out, leaving them in the lists.

VI.

Then they turned their horses one against the other, and ran at each other full bravely, like good knights. Five times they encountered, and at the sixth encounter their spears brake, and they laid hand upon their swords, and dealt each other such heavy blows that the helmets failed; and in this manner the combat between them continued till noon. And when Don Diego Ordoñez saw that it lasted so long, and he could not yet conquer him, he called to mind that he was there fighting to revenge his Lord, who had been slain by a foul treason, and he collected together all his strength. And he lifted up his sword and smote Pedrarias upon the helmet, so that he cut through it, and through the hood of the mail also, and made a wound in the head. And Pedrarias with the agony of death, and with the blood which ran over his eyes, bowed down to the neck of the horse; yet with all this he neither lost his stirrups, nor let go his sword. And Don Diego Ordoñez seeing him thus, thought that he was dead, and would not strike him again; and he called aloud, saying, Don Arias, send me another son, for this one will never fulfil your bidding. When Pedrarias heard this, grievously wounded as he was, he wiped the blood away with the sleeve of his mail, and went fiercely against him: and he took the sword in both hands, and thought to give it him upon his head; but the blow missed, and fell upon the horse, and cut off great part of his nostrils, and the reins with it; and the horse immediately ran away because of the great wound which he had received. And Don

Diego had no reins wherewith to stop him, and perceiving that he should else be carried out of the lists, he threw himself off. And while he did this, Pedrarias fell down dead, just without the mark. And Don Diego Ordoñez laid hand on the bar, and said. Praised be the name of God, one is conquered. And incontinently the judges came and took him by the hand, and led him to a tent and disarmed him, and gave him three sops, and he drank of the wine and rested awhile. And afterwards they gave him other arms, and a horse that was a right good one, and went with him to the lists.

VII.

Then Don Arias Gonzalo called for another son, whose name was Diego Arias, and said unto him, To horse! and go fight to deliver this Council and to revenge the death of your brother; and he answered, For this am I come hither. Then his father gave him his blessing and went with, him to the lists. And the judges took the reins of the two champions and led them each to his place, and went out and left them in the lists. And they ran against each other with such force that both shields failed, and in another career they brake their lances. Then laid they hand on their good swords, and delivered such blows that their helmets were cut away, and the sleeves of the mail. And at length Diego Arias received such a blow near the heart that he fell dead. And Don Diego Ordoñez went to the bar and laid hold on it, and cried out to Don Arias Gonzalo, Send me another son, for I have conquered two, thanks be to God. Then the judges came and said that the dead knight was not yet out of the lists, and that he must alight and cast him out. And Don Diego Ordoñez did as they had directed him, and alighted from his horse and took the dead man by the leg, and dragged him to the line, and then letting the leg fall he thrust him out of the lists with his feet. And then he went and laid hand upon the bar again, saying that he had liefer fight with a living man than drag a dead one out of the field. And then the judges came to him, and led him to the tent, and disarmed him, and gave him the three sops and the wine, as they had done before, and sent to say to Don Arias Gonzalo that this son also was slain, and that he should send another.

VIII.

Then Don Arias Gonzalo, in great rage and in great trouble called for his son Rodrigo Arias, who was a good knight, right hardy and valiant, the elder of all the brethren; he had been in many a tournament, and with good fortune. And Don Arias said unto him, Son, go now and do battle with Diego Ordoñez, to save Doña Urraca your Lady, and yourself, and the Council of Zamora; and if you do this, in happy hour were you born. Then Rodrigo Arias kissed his hand and answered, Father, I thank you much for what you have said, and be sure that I will save them, or take my death. And he took his arms and mounted, and his father gave him his blessing, and went with him to the lists; and the judges took his reins and led him in. And when the judges were gone out, they twain ran at each other, and Don Diego missed his blow, but Rodrigo Arias did not miss, for he gave him so great a stroke with the lance that it pierced through the shield, and broke the saddle-bow behind, and made him lose his stirrups, and he embraced the neck of his horse. But albeit that Don Diego was sorely bested with that stroke, he took heart presently, and went bravely against him, and dealt him so great a blow that he broke the lance in him; for it went through the shield and all his other arms, and great part of the lance remained in his flesh. After this they laid hand to sword, and gave each to the other great blows, and great wounds with them. And Rodrigo Arias gave so great a wound to Diego Ordoñez, that he cut his left arm through to the bone. And Don Diego Ordoñez, when he felt himself so sorely wounded, went against Rodrigo Arias and delivered him a blow upon the head which cut through the helmet and the hood of the mail, and entered into his head. When Rodrigo Arias felt himself wounded to death, he let go the reins and took his sword in both hands, and gave so great a blow to the horse of Don Diego that he cut his head open. And the horse in his agony ran out of the lists, and carried Don Diego out also, and there died. And Rodrigo Arias fell dead as he was following him. Then Don Diego Ordoñez would have returned into the field to do battle with, the other two, but the judges would not permit this, neither did they think good to decide whether they of Zamora were overcome in this third duel or not. And in this manner the thing was left undecided. Nevertheless, though no sentence was given, there remained no infamy upon the people of Zamora. But better had it been for Don Arias Gonzalo if he had given up Vellido to the Castillians, that he might have died the death of a traitor; he would not then have lost these three sons, who died like good men, in their duty. Now what was the end of Vellido the history sayeth not, through the default of the Chroniclers; but it is to be believed, that because the impeachment was not made within three days, Don Arias Gonzalo thrust him out of the town as Doña Urraca had requested, and that he fled into other lands, peradventure among the Moors. And though it may be that he escaped punishment in this world, yet certes he could not escape it in hell where he is tormented with Dathan and Abiram, and with Judas the Traitor, for ever and ever.

IX.

In the meantime the Infanta Doña Urraca wrote letters secretly and sent messengers with them to Toledo to King Don Alfonso, telling him that King Don Sancho his brother was dead, and had left no heir, and that he should come as speedily as he could to receive the kingdoms, And she bade her messengers deliver these privately that the Moors might not discover what had taken place, lest they should seize upon King Don Alfonso, whom she dearly loved. Moreover the Castillians assembled together and found that as King Don Sancho had left no son to succeed him they were bound by right to receive King Don Alfonso as their Lord; and they also sent unto him in secret. Howbeit, certain of those spies who discover to the Moors whatever the Christians design to do, when they knew the death of King Don Sancho, went presently to acquaint the Moors therewith. Now Don Peransures, as he was a man of great understanding and understood the Arabick tongue, when he knew the death of King Don Sancho, and while he was devising how to get his Lord away from Toledo, rode out every day, as if to solace himself, on the way towards Castille, to see whom he might meet, and to learn tidings. And it fell out one day that he met a man who told him he was going with news to King Alimaymon, that King Don Sancho was dead; and Don Peransures took him aside from the road as if to speak to him, and cut off his head. And Peransures returned into the road and met another man coming with the same tidings to the King, and he slew him in like manner. Nevertheless the tidings reached King Alimaymon. Now Peransures and his brethren feared that if the Moor knew this he would not let their Lord depart, but would seize him and make hard terms for his deliverance; and on the other hand, they thought that if he should learn it from any other than themselves, it would be yet worse. And while they were in doubt what they should do, King Don Alfonso, trusting in God's mercy, said unto them, When I came hither unto this Moor, he received me with great honour, and gave to me abundantly all things of which I stood in need, even as if I had been his son; how then should I conceal from him this favour which it hath pleased God to show me? I will go and tell it unto him. But Don Peransures besought him not to tell him of his brother's death. And he went to King Alimaymon and said unto him, that he would fain go into his own country, if it pleased him, to help his vassals, who stood greatly in need of him, and he besought him that he would give him men. The death of King Don Sancho he did not make known. And King Alimaymon answered that he should not do this, because he feared that King Don Sancho his brother would take him. And King Don Alfonso said, that he knew the ways and customs of his brother, and did not fear him, if it pleased the King to give him some Moors to help him. Now Alimaymon had heard of the death of King Don Sancho, and he had sent to occupy the roads and the passes, that King Don Alfonso might be stopt if he should attempt to depart without his knowledge. Howbeit he did not fully believe the tidings, seeing that King Don Alfonso did not speak of it; and he rejoiced in his heart at what the King said, and he said unto him, I thank God, Alfonso, that thou hast told me of thy wish to go into thine own country; for in this thou hast dealt loyally by me, and saved me from that which might else have happened, to which the Moors have alway importuned me. And hadst thou departed privily thou couldest not have escaped being slain or taken. Now then go and take thy kingdom; and I will give thee whatever thou hast need of to give to thine own people and win their hearts that they may serve thee. And he then besought him to renew the oath which he had taken, never to come against him nor his sons, but alway to befriend them; and this same oath did the King of Toledo make unto him. Now Alimaymon had a grandson whom he dearly loved, who was not named in the oath, and King Don Alfonso therefore was not bound to keep it towards him. And King Don Alfonso made ready for his departure, and Alimaymon and the chief persons of the court went out from the city with him and rode with him as far as the Sierra del Dragon, which is now called Valtome; and he gave him great gifts, and there they took leave of each other with great love.

X.

As soon as King Don Alfonso arrived at Zamora, he pitched his tents in the field of Santiago, and took counsel with his sister. And the Infanta Doña Urraca, who was a right prudent lady and a wise, sent letters throughout the land, that a Cortes should assemble and receive him for their Lord. And when the Leonese and the Gallegos knew that their Lord King Don Alfonso was come, they were full joyful, and they came to Zamora and received him for their Lord and King. And afterwards the Castillians arrived, and they of Navarre, and they also received him for their Lord and King, but upon this condition, that he should swear that he had not taken counsel for the death of his brother King Don Sancho. Howbeit they did not come forward to receive the oath, and they kissed his hands in homage, all, save only Ruydiez, my Cid. And when King Don Alfonso saw that the Cid did not do homage and kiss his hand, as all the other chief persons and prelates and Councils had done, he said, Since now ye have all received me for your Lord, and given me authority over ye, I would know of the Cid Ruydiez why he will not kiss my hand and acknowledge me; for I would do something for him, as I promised unto my father King Don Ferrando, when he commended him to me and to my brethren. And the Cid arose and said, Sir, all whom you see here present, suspect that by your counsel the King Don Sancho your brother came to his death; and therefore, I say unto you that, unless you clear yourself of this, as by right you should do, I will never kiss your hand, nor receive you for my Lord. Then said the King, Cid, what you say pleases me well; and here I swear to God and to St. Mary, that I never slew him, nor took counsel for his death, neither did it please me, though he had taken my kingdom from me. And I beseech ye therefore all, as friends and true vassals, that ye tell me how I may clear myself. And the chiefs who were present said, that he and twelve of the knights who came with him from Toledo, should make this oath in the church at St. Gadea at Burgos, and that so he should be cleared.

XI.

So the King and all his company took horse and went to Burgos. And when the day appointed for the oath was come, the King went to hear mass in the church of Gadea, and his sisters the Infantas Doña Urraca and Doña Elvira with him, and all his knights. And the King came forward upon a high stage that all the people might see him, and my Cid came to him to receive the oath; and my Cid took the book of the Gospels and opened it, and laid it upon the altar, and the King laid his hands upon it, and the Cid said unto him, King Don Alfonso, you come here to swear concerning the death of King Don Sancho your brother, that you neither slew him nor took counsel for his death; say now you and these hidalgos, if ye swear this. And the King and the hidalgos answered and said, Yea, we swear it. And the Cid said, If ye knew of this thing, or gave command that it should be done, may you die even such a death as your brother the King Don Sancho, by the hand of a villain whom you trust; one who is not a hidalgo, from another land, not a Castillian; and the King and the knights who were with him said Amen. And the king's colour changed; and the Cid repeated the oath unto him a second time, and the King and the twelve knights said Amen to it in like manner, and in like manner the countenance of the King was changed again. And my Cid repeated the oath unto him a third time, and the King and the knights said Amen; but the wrath of the King was exceeding great, and he said to the Cid, Ruydiez, why dost thou thus press me, man? To-day thou swearest me, and to-morrow thou wilt kiss my hand. And from that day forward there was no love towards my Cid in the heart of the King.

XII.

After this was King Don Alfonso crowned King of Castille, and Leon, and Galicia, and Portugal; and he called himself King and Emperor of all Spain, even as his father had done before him. And in the beginning of his reign he did in all things according to the counsel of the Infanta Doña Urraca his sister; and he was a good King, and kept his kingdom so well, that rich and poor alike dwelt in peace and security, neither did one man take arms against another, nor dare to do it, if he valued the eyes in his head. And if the King was noble and high of lineage, much more was he of heart; and in his days justice abounded in the land so, that if a woman had gone alone throughout the whole of his dominions, bearing gold and silver in her hand, she would have found none to hurt her, neither in the waste, nor in the peopled country. The merchants and pilgrims also who passed through his lands were so well protected, that none durst do them wrong. Never while the kingdom was his, had they of his land to do service to any other Lord. And he was a comforter of the sorrowful, and an increaser of the faith, and a defender of the churches, and the strength of the people; a judge without fear; there was not in Spain a consoler of the poor and of those who were oppressed, till he came. Now there was a mortal enmity between my Cid and Count Garcia Ordoñez, and in this year did my Cid gather together those of his table, and all his power, and entered into the lands of Logroño, and Navarre, and Calahorra, burning and spoiling the country before him. And he laid siege to the Castle of Faro and took it. And he sent messengers to the Count his enemy, to say that he would wait for him seven days, and he waited. And the mighty men of the land came to the Count Don Garcia, but come against my Cid that they dared not do, for they feared to do battle with him.

XIII.

In the second year of the reign of King Don Alfonso, the King of Cordova made war upon Alimaymon, King of Toledo, and did great damage in his land, and held him besieged in Toledo; and King Don Alfonso drew forth a great host and went to help the King of Toledo. When Alimaymon knew that he was coming with so great a power, he was greatly dismayed, thinking that he came against him; and he sent to remind him of the love and the honour which he had shown unto him in the days of his brother King Don Sancho, and of the oath which he had taken; and to beseech him that he would continue in peace with him. And the King detained his messengers, giving them no reply, and went on advancing into the land, doing no hurt therein. And when he came to Olias, he ordered the whole army to halt. And when the King of Cordova knew that King Don Alfonso was coming, he rose up from before Toledo, and fled away, and the men of Toledo pursued him, and inflicted great loss upon him in his flight.

XIV.

And when the army had halted at Olias, the King called for the messengers of Alimaymon, and took with him five knights, and rode to Toledo. And when they came to the gate which is called Visagra, the messengers who went with him made him enter the town, and he sent one of them to tell the King that he was there, and went on in the meantime towards the Alcazar. And when King Alimaymon heard this, he would not wait till a beast should be brought him that he might ride, but set out on foot and went to meet him; and as he was going out he met King Don Alfonso, and they embraced each other. And the King of Toledo kissed King Don Alfonso's shoulder, for the joy and pleasure that he had in his heart at seeing him; and he gave thanks to God for what he had done to King Don Alfonso, and thanked him also for the truth which was in him, in coming thus to his deliverance, and for remembering the oath which they had made each to the other. And they rejoiced together all that night, and great was the joy of the people of Toledo, because of the love which King Don Alfonso bore toward their Lord. But great was the sorrow in the host of the Castillians, for they never thought to see their Lord again; and they thought that he had committed a great folly in thus putting himself into the power of the Moors.

XV.

On the morrow, King Don Alfonso besought King Alimaymon that he would go and eat with him at Olias, and see how he came to help him. And they went both together with a little company, and when they of the host saw their Lord they were all right joyful, and the two Kings went through the camp, and they sat down to eat in the tent of the King, which was a large one. And while they were at meat King Don Alfonso gave order in secret that five hundred knights should arm themselves and surround the tent. And when the King of Toledo saw these armed knights, and that the tent was surrounded, he was in great fear, and he asked of King Don Alfonso what it should be; and the King bade him eat, and said, that afterwards they would tell him. And after they had eaten, King Don Alfonso said to Alimaymon, You made me swear and promise when you had me in Toledo in your power that no evil should ever come against you on my part: now since I have you in my power I will that you release me from this oath and covenant. And the King of Toledo consented to release him, and besought him to do him no other wrong, and he acquitted him from the promise three times. And when he had done this King Don Alfonso called for the book of the Gospels, and said unto him, Now then that you are in my power, I swear and promise unto you, never to go against you, nor against your son, and to aid you against all other men in the world. And I make this oath unto you because there was reason why I should have broken that other one, seeing that it was made when I was in your hands; but against this I must not go, for I make it when you are in mine, and I could do with you even whatever pleased me; and he laid his hands upon the book, and swore even as he had said. Right joyful was the King of Toledo at this which King Don Alfonso had done, for the loyalty which he had shown towards him. And they remained that night together; and on the morrow Alimaymon returned to his city full gladly, and King Don Alfonso made his host move on towards Cordova, and Alimaymon went with him; and they overran the land, and burnt towns and villages, and destroyed castles, and plundered whatever they could find; and they returned each into his own country with great spoils. And from thenceforward the King of Cordova durst no more attack the King of Toledo.

XVI.

In the following years, nothing is found to be related, save that my Cid did battle by command of the King with a knight called Ximen García de Tiogelos, who was one of the best of Navarre: they fought for the castle of Pazluengas, and for two other castles, and my Cid conquered him, and King Don Alfonso had the castles. And after this my Cid did battle in Medina Celi, with a Moor called Faras, who was a good knight in arms, and he defeated and slew him and another also. And in the fifth year of the reign of King Don Alfonso, the King sent the Cid to the Kings of Seville and of Cordova, for the tribute which they were bound to pay him. Now there was at this time war between Almocanis, King of Seville and Almundafar, King of Granada, and with Almundafar were these men of Castille, the Count Don Garcia Ordoñez and Fortun Sanchez, the son-in-law of King Don Garcia, of Navarre, and Lope Sanchez his brother, and Diego Perez, one of the best men of Castille; and they aided him all that they could, and went against the King of Seville, and when my Cid knew this it troubled him, and he sent unto them requiring them not to go against the King of Seville, nor to destroy his country, because he was King Don Alfonso's vassal; otherwise the King must defend him. And the King of Granada and the Ricos-omes who were with him cared nothing for his letters, but entered boldly into the land of Seville, and advanced as far as Cabra, burning and laying waste before them. When the Cid saw this he gathered together what Christians he could and went against them. And the King of Granada and the Christians who were with him, sent to tell him that they would not go out of the country for him. And the wrath of the Cid was kindled, and he went against them, and fought with them in the field, and the battle lasted from the hour of tierce even until the hour of sexts; and many died upon the part of the King of Granada, and at length my Cid overcame them and made them, take to flight. And Count Garcia Ordoñez was taken prisoner, and Lope Sanchez, and Diego Perez, and many other knights, and of other men so many that they were out of number; and the dead were so many that no man could count them; and the spoils of the field were very great. And the Cid held these good men prisoners three days and then set them free, and he returned with great honour and great riches to Seville. And King Almocanis received him full honourably, and gave him great gifts for himself, and paid him the full tribute for the King; and he returned rich to Castille, and with great honour. And King Don Alfonso was well pleased with the good fortune of the Cid in all his feats; but there were many who wished ill to him, and sought to set the King against him.

XVII.

After this King Don Alfonso assembled together all his power and went against the Moors. And the Cid should have gone with him, but he fell sick and perforce therefore abode at home. And while the King was going through Andalusia, having the land at his mercy, a great power of the Moors assembled together on the other side, and entered the land, and besieged the castle of Gormaz, and did much evil. At this time the Cid was gathering strength; and when he heard that the Moors were in the country, laying waste before them, he gathered together what force he could, and went after them; and the Moors, when they heard this, dared not abide his coming, but began to fly. And the Cid followed them to Atienza, and to Ciguenza, and Fita, and Guadalajara, and through the whole land of St. Esteban, as far as Toledo, slaying and burning, and plundering and destroying, and laying hands on all whom he found, so that he brought back seven thousand prisoners, men and women; and he and all his people returned rich and with great honour. But when the King of Toledo heard of the hurt which he had received at the hands of the Cid, he sent to King Don Alfonso to complain thereof, and the King was greatly troubled. And then the Ricos-omes who wished ill to the Cid, had the way open to do him evil with the King, and they said to the King, Sir, Ruydiez hath broken your faith, and the oath and promise which you made to the King of Toledo: and he hath done this for no other reason but that the Moors of Toledo may fall upon us here, and slay both you and us. And the King believed what they said, and was wroth against the Cid, having no love towards him because of the oath which he had pressed upon him at Burgos concerning the death of King Don Sancho his brother. And he went with all speed to Burgos, and sent from thence to bid the Cid come unto him.

XVIII.

Now my Cid knew the evil disposition of the King towards him, and when he received his bidding, he made answer that he would meet him between Burgos and Bivar. And the King went out from Burgos and came nigh unto Bivar; and the Cid came up to him and would have kissed his hand, but the King withheld it, and said angrily unto him, Ruydiez, quit my land. Then the Cid clapt spurs to the mule upon which he rode, and vaulted into a piece of ground which was his own inheritance, and answered, Sir, I am not in your land, but in my own. And the King replied full wrathfully, Go out of my kingdoms without any delay. And the Cid made answer, Give me then thirty days time, as is the right of the hidalgos; and the King said he would not, but that if he were not gone in nine days time he would come and look for him. The Counts were well pleased at this; but all the people of the land were sorrowful. And then the King and the Cid parted. And the Cid sent for all his friends and his kinsmen and vassals, and told them how King Don Alfonso had banished him from the land, and asked of them who would follow him into banishment, and who would remain at home. Then Alvar Fañez, who was his cousin-german, came forward and said, Cid, we will all go with you, through desert and through peopled country, and never fail you. In your service will we spend our mules and horses, our wealth and our garments, and ever while we live be unto you loyal friends and vassals. And they all confirmed what Alvar Fañez had said; and the Cid thanked them for their love, and said that there might come a time in which he should guerdon them.

XIX.

And as he was about to depart he looked back upon his own home, and when he saw his hall deserted, the household chests unfastened, the doors open, no cloaks hanging up, no seats in the porch, no hawks upon the perches, the tears came into his eyes, and he said, My enemies have done this ... God be praised for all things. And he turned toward the East and knelt and said, Holy Mary Mother, and all Saints, pray to God for me, that he may give me strength to destroy all the Pagans, and to win enough from them to requite my friends therewith, and all those who follow and help me. Then he called for Alvar Fañez and said unto him, Cousin, the poor have no part in the wrong which the King hath done us; see now that no wrong be done unto them along our road: and he called for his horse. And then an old woman who was standing at her door said, Go in a lucky minute, and make spoil of whatever you wish. And with this proverb he rode on, saying, Friends, by God's good pleasure we shall return to Castilla with great honour and great gain. And as they went out from Bivar they had a crow on their right hand, and when they came to Burgos they had a crow on the left.

XX.

My Cid Ruydiez entered Burgos, having sixty streamers in his company. And men and women went forth to see him, and the men of Burgos and the women of Burgos were at their windows, weeping, so great was their sorrow; and they said with one accord, God, how good a vassal if he had but a good Lord! and willingly would each have bade him come in, but no one dared so to do. For King Don Alfonso in his anger had sent letters to Burgos, saying that no man should give the Cid a lodging; and that whosoever disobeyed should lose all that he had, and moreover the eyes in his head. Great sorrow had these Christian folk at this, and they hid themselves when he came near them because they did not dare speak to him; and my Cid went to his Posada, and when he came to the door he found it fastened, for fear of the King. And his people called out with a loud voice, but they within made no answer. And the Cid rode up to the door, and took his foot out of the stirrup, and gave it a kick, but the door did not open with it, for it was well secured; a little girl of nine years old then came out of one of the houses and said unto him, O Cid, the King hath forbidden us to receive you. We dare not open our doors to you, for we should lose our houses and all that we have, and the eyes in our head. Cid, our evil would not help you, but God and all his Saints be with you. And when she had said this she returned into the house. And when the Cid knew what the King had done he turned away from the door and rode up to St. Mary's, and there he alighted and knelt down, and prayed with all his heart; and then he mounted again and rode out of the town, and pitched his tent near Arlanzon, upon the Glera, that is to say, upon the sands. My Cid Ruydiez, he who in a happy hour first girt on his sword, took up his lodging upon the sands, because there was none who would receive him within their door. He had a good company round about him, and there he lodged as if he had been among the mountains.

XXI.

Moreover the King had given orders that no food should be sold them in Burgos, so that they could not buy even a pennyworth. But Martin Antolinez, who was a good Burgalese, he supplied my Cid and all his company with bread and wine abundantly. Campeador, said he to the Cid, to-night we will rest here, and to-morrow we will be gone. I shall be accused for what I have done in serving you, and shall be in the King's displeasure; but following your fortunes, sooner or later, the King will have me for his friend, and if not, I do not care a fig for what I leave behind. Now this Martin Antolinez was nephew unto the Cid, being the son of his brother, Ferrando Diaz. And the Cid said unto him, Martin Antolinez, you are a bold Lancier; if I live I will double you your pay. You see I have nothing with me, and yet must provide for my companions. I will take two chests and fill them with sand, and do you go in secret to Rachel and Vidas, and tell them to come hither privately; for I cannot take my treasures with me because of their weight, and will pledge them in their hands. Let them come for the chests at night, that no man may see them. God knows that I do this thing more of necessity than of wilfulness; but by God's good help I shall redeem all. Now Rachel and Vidas were rich Jews, from whom the Cid used to receive money for his spoils. And Martin Antolinez went in quest of them, and he passed through Burgos and entered into the Castle; and when he saw them he said, Ah Rachel and Vidas, my dear friends! now let me speak with ye in secret. And they three went apart. And he said to them, Give me your hands that you will not discover me neither to Moor nor Christian! I will make you rich men for ever. The Campeador went for the tribute and he took great wealth, and some of it he has kept for himself. He has two chests full of gold; ye know that the King is in anger against him, and he cannot carry these away with him without their being seen. He will leave them therefore in your hands, and you shall lend him money upon them, swearing with great oaths and upon your faith, that ye will not open them till a year be past. Rachel and Vidas took counsel together and answered, We well knew he got something when he entered the land of the Moors; he who has treasures does not sleep without suspicion; we will take the chests, and place them where they shall not be seen. But tell us with what will the Cid be contented, and what gain will he give us for the year? Martin Antolinez answered like a prudent man, My Cid requires what is reasonable; he will ask but little to leave his treasures in safety. Men come to him from all parts. He must have six hundred marks. And the Jews said, We will advance him so much. Well then, said Martin Antolinez, ye see that the night is advancing; the Cid is in haste, give us the marks. This is not the way of business, said they; we must take first, and then give. Ye say well, replied the Burgalese: come then to the Campeador, and we will help you to bring away the chests, so that neither Moors nor Christians may see us. So they went to horse and rode out together, and they did not cross the bridge, but rode through the water that no man might see them, and they came to the tent of the Cid.

XXII.

Meantime the Cid had taken two chests, which were covered with leather of red and gold, and the nails which fastened down the leather were well gilt; they were ribbed with bands of iron, and each fastened with three locks; they were heavy, and he filled them with sand. And when Rachel and Vidas entered his tent with Martin Antolinez, they kissed his hand; and the Cid smiled and said to them, Ye see that I am going out of the land, because of the King's displeasure; but I shall leave something with ye. And they made answer, Martin Antolinez has covenanted with us, that we shall give you six hundred marks upon these chests, and keep them a full year, swearing not to open them till that time be expired, else shall we be perjured. Take the chests, said Martin Antolinez; I will go with you, and bring back the marks, for my Cid must move before cock-crow. So they took the chests, and though they were both strong men they could not raise them from the ground; and they were full glad of the bargain which they had made. And Rachel then went to the Cid and kissed his hand and said, Now, Campeador, you are going from Castille among strange nations, and your gain will be great, even as your fortune is. I kiss your hand, Cid, and have a gift for you, a red skin: it is Moorish and honourable. And the Cid said, It pleases me; give it me if ye have brought it, if not, reckon it upon the chests. And they departed with the chests, and Martin Antolinez and his people helped them, and went with them. And when they had placed the chests in safety, they spread a carpet in the middle of the hall, and laid a sheet upon it and they threw down upon it three hundred marks of silver. Don Martin counted them, and took them without weighing. The other three hundred they paid in gold. Don Martin had five squires with him, and he loaded them all with the money. And when this was done he said to them, Now Don Rachel and Vidas, you have got the chests, and I who got them for you well deserve a pair of hose. And the Jews said to each other, Let us give him a good gift for this which he has done; and they said to him, We will give you enough for hose and for a rich doublet and a good cloak; you shall have thirty marks. Don Martin thanked them and took the marks, and bidding them both farewell, he departed right joyfully.

XXIII.

When Martin Antolinez came into the Cid's tent he said unto him, I have sped well, Campeador! you have gained six hundred marks, and I thirty. Now then strike your tent and be gone. The time draws on, and you may be with your Lady Wife at St. Pedro de Cardeña, before the cock crows. So the tent was struck, and my Cid and his company went to horse at this early hour. And the Cid turned his horse's head toward St. Mary's, and with his right hand he blest himself on the forehead, and he said, God be praised! help me, St. Mary. I go from Castille because the anger of the King is against me, and I know not whether I shall ever enter it again in all my days. Help me, glorious Virgin, in my goings, both by night and by day. If you do this and my lot be fair, I will send rich and goodly gifts to your altar, and will have a thousand masses sung there. Then with a good heart he gave his horse the reins. And Martin Antolinez said to him, Go ye on; I must back to my wife and tell her what she is to do during my absence. I shall be with you in good time. And back he went to Burgos, and my Cid and his company pricked on. The cocks were crowing amain, and the day began to break, when the good Campeador reached St. Pedro's. The Abbot Don Sisebuto was saying matins, and Doña Ximena and five of her ladies of good lineage were with him, praying to God and St. Peter to help my Cid. And when he called at the gate and they knew his voice, God, what a joyful man was the Abbot Don Sisebuto! Out into the court yard they went with torches and with tapers, and the Abbot gave thanks to God that he now beheld the face of my Cid. And the Cid told him all that had befallen him, and how he was a banished man; and he gave him fifty marks for himself, and a hundred for Doña Ximena and her children. Abbot, said he, I leave two little girls behind me, whom I commend to your care. Take you care of them and of my wife and of her ladies: when this money be gone, if it be not enough, supply them abundantly; for every mark which you expend upon them I will give the Monastery four. And the Abbot promised to do this with a right good will. Then Doña Ximena came up and her daughters with her, each of them borne in arms, and she knelt down on both her knees before her husband, weeping bitterly, and she would have kissed his hand; and she said to him, Lo now you are banished from the land by mischief-making men, and here am I with your daughters, who are little ones and of tender years, and we and you must be parted, even in your life time. For the love of St. Mary tell me now what we shall do. And the Cid took the children in his arms, and held them to his heart and wept, for he dearly loved them. Please God and St. Mary, said he, I shall yet live to give these my daughters in marriage with my own hands, and to do you service yet, my honoured wife, whom I have ever loved, even as my own soul.

XXIV.

A great feast did they make that day in the Monastery for the good Campeador, and the bells of St. Pedro's rung merrily. Meantime the tidings had gone through Castille how my Cid was banished from the land, and great was the sorrow of the people. Some left their houses to follow him, others forsook their honourable offices which they held. And that day a hundred and fifteen knights assembled at the bridge of Arlanzon, all in quest of my Cid; and there Martin Antolinez joined them, and they rode on together to St. Pedro's. And when he of Bivar knew what a goodly company were coming to join him, he rejoiced in his own strength, and rode out to meet them and greeted them full courteously; and they kissed his hand, and he said to them, I pray to God that I may one day requite ye well, because ye have forsaken your houses and your heritages for my sake, and I trust that I shall pay ye two fold. Six days of the term allotted were now gone, and three only remained: if after that time he should be found, within the King's dominions, neither for gold nor for silver could he then escape. That day they feasted together, and when it was evening the Cid distributed among them, all that he had, giving to each man according to what he was; and he told them that they must meet at mass after matins, and depart at that early hour. Before the cock crew they were ready, and the Abbot said the mass of the Holy Trinity, and when it was done they left the church and went to horse. And my Cid embraced Doña Ximena and his daughters, and blest them; and the parting between them was like separating the nail from the quick flesh: and he wept and continued to look round after them. Then Alvar Fañez came up to him and said, Where is your courage, my Cid? In a good hour were you born of woman. Think of our road now; these sorrows will yet be turned into joy. And the Cid spake again to the Abbot, commending his family to his care;—well did the Abbot know that he should one day receive good guerdon. And as he took leave of the Cid, Alvar Fañez said to him, Abbot, if you see any who come to follow us, tell them what route we take, and bid them make speed, for they may reach us either in the waste or in the peopled country. And then they loosed the reins and pricked forward.

XXV.

That night my Cid lay at Spinar de Can, and people flocked to him from all parts, and early on the morrow he set out; Santestevan lay on his left hand, which is a good city, and Ahilon on the right, which belongs to the Moors, and he passed by Alcobiella, which is the boundary of Castille. And he went by the Calzada de Quinea, and crost the Douro upon rafts. That night, being the eighth, they rested at Figeruela, and more adventurers came to join him. And when my Cid was fast asleep, the Angel Gabriel appeared to him in a vision, and said, Go on boldly and fear nothing; for everything shall go well with thee as long as thou livest, and all the things which thou beginnest, thou shalt bring to good end, and thou shalt be rich and honourable. And the Cid awoke and blest himself; and he crost his forehead and rose from his bed, and knelt down and gave thanks to God for the mercy which he had vouchsafed him, being right joyful because of the vision. Early on the morrow they set forth; now this was the last day of the nine. And they went on towards the Sierra de Miedes. Before sunset the Cid halted and took account of his company; there were three hundred lances, all with streamers, besides foot-soldiers. And he said unto them, Now take and eat, for we must pass this great and wild Sierra, that we may quit the land of King Alfonso this night. To-morrow he who seeks us may find us. So they passed the Sierra that night.

BOOK IV

I.

Now hath my Cid left the kingdom of King Don Alfonso, and entered the country of the Moors. And at day-break they were near the brow of the Sierra, and they halted there upon the top of the mountains, and gave barley to their horses, and remained there until evening. And they set forward when the evening had closed, that none might see them, and continued their way all night, and before dawn they came near to Castrejon, which is upon the Henares. And Alvar Fañez said unto the Cid, that he would take with him two hundred horsemen, and scour the country as far as Fita and Guadalajara and Alcala, and lay hands on whatever he could find, without fear either of King Alfonso or of the Moors. And he counselled him to remain in ambush where he was, and surprise the castle of Castrejon: and it seemed good unto my Cid. Away went Alvar Fañez, and Alvar Alvarez with him, and Alvar Salvadores, and Galin García, and the two hundred horsemen; and the Cid remained in ambush with the rest of his company. And as soon as it was morning, the Moors of Castrejon, knowing nothing of these who were so near them, opened the castle gates, and went out to their work as they were wont to do. And the Cid rose from ambush and fell upon them, and took all their flocks, and made straight for the gates, pursuing them. And there was a cry within the castle that the Christians were upon them, and they who were within ran to the gates to defend them, but my Cid came up sword in hand; eleven Moors did he slay with his own hand, and they forsook the gate and fled before him to hide themselves within, so that he won the castle presently, and took gold and silver, and whatever else he would.

II.

Alvar Fañez meantime scoured the country along the Henares as far as Alcala, and he returned driving flocks and herds before him, with great stores of wearing apparel, and of other plunder. He came with the banner of Minaya, and there were none who dared fall upon his rear. And when the Cid knew that he was nigh at hand he went out to meet him, and praised him greatly for what he had done, and gave thanks to God. And he gave order that all the spoils should be heaped together, both what Alvar Fañez had brought, and what had been taken in the castle; and he said to him, Brother, of all this which God hath given us, take you the fifth, for you well deserve it; but Minaya would not, saying, You have need of it for our support. And the Cid divided the spoil among the knights and foot-soldiers, to each his due portion; to every horseman a hundred marks of silver, and half as much to the foot-soldiers: and because he could find none to whom to sell his fifth, he spake to the Moors of Castrejon, and sent to those of Fita and Guadalajara, telling them that they might come safely to purchase the spoil, and the prisoners also whom he had taken, both men prisoners and women, for he would have none with him. And they came, and valued the spoil and the prisoners, and gave for them three thousand marks of silver, which they paid within three days: they bought also much of the spoil which had been divided, making great gain, so that all who were in my Cid's company were full rich. And the heart of my Cid was joyous, and he sent to King Don Alfonso, telling him that he and his companions would yet do him service upon the Moors.

Then my Cid assembled together his good men and said unto them, Friends, we cannot take up our abode in this castle, for there is no water in it, and moreover the King is at peace with these Moors, and I know that the treaty between them hath been written; so that if we should abide here he would come against us with all his power, and with all the power of the Moors, and we could not stand against him. If therefore it seem good unto you, let us leave the rest of our prisoners here, for it does not beseem us to take any with us, but to be as free from all encumbrance as may be, like men who are to live by war, and to help ourselves with our arms. And it pleased them well that it should be so. And he said to them, Ye have all had your shares, neither is there anything owing to any one among ye. Now then let us be ready to take horse betimes on the morrow, for I would not fight against my Lord the King. So on the morrow they went to horse and departed, being rich with the spoils which they had won: and they left the castle to the Moors, who remained blessing them for this bounty which they had received at their hands. Then my Cid and his company went up the Henares as fast as they could go, and they passed by the Alcarías, and by the caves of Anquita, and through the waters, and they entered the plain of Torancio, and halted between Fariza and Cetina: great were the spoils which they collected as they went along. And on the morrow they passed Alfama, and leaving the Gorge below them they passed Bobierca, and Teca which is beyond it, and came against Alcocer. There my Cid pitched his tents upon a round hill, which was a great hill and a strong; and the river Salon ran near them, so that the water could not be cut off. My Cid thought to take Alcocer: so he pitched his tents securely, having the Sierra on one side, and the river on the other, and he made all his people dig a trench, that they might not be alarmed, neither by day nor by night.

When my Cid had thus encamped, he went to look at the Alcazar, and see if he could by any means enter it. And the Moors offered tribute to him if he would leave them in peace; but this he would not do, and he lay before the town. And news went through all the land that the Cid was come among them, and they of Calatayud were in fear. And my Cid lay before Alcocer fifteen weeks; and when he saw that the town did not surrender, he ordered his people to break up their camp, as if they were flying, and they left one of their tents behind them, and took their way along the Salon, with their banners spread. And when the Moors saw this they rejoiced greatly, and there was a great stir among them, and they praised themselves for what they had done in withstanding him, and said, that the Cid's bread and barley had failed him, and he had fled away, and left one of his tents behind him. And they said among themselves, Let us pursue them and spoil them, for if they of Teruel should be before us the honour and the profit will be theirs, and we shall have nothing. And they went out after him, great and little, leaving the gates open and shouting as they went; and there was not left in the town a man who could bear arms. And when my Cid saw them coming he gave orders to quicken their speed, as if he was in fear, and would not let his people turn till the Moors were far enough from the town. But when he saw that there was a good distance between them and the gates, then he bade his banner turn, and spurred towards them, crying, Lay on, knights, by God's mercy the spoil is our own. God! what a good joy was theirs that morning! My Cid's vassals laid on without mercy;—in one hour, and in a little space, three hundred Moors were slain, and the Cid and Alvar Fañez had good horses, and got between them and the Castle, and stood in the gateway sword in hand, and there was a great mortality among the Moors; and my Cid won the place, and Pero Bermudez planted his banner upon the highest point of the Castle. And the Cid said, Blessed be God and all his Saints, we have bettered our quarters both for horses and men. And he said to Alvar Fañez and all his knights, Hear me, we shall get nothing by killing these Moors;—let us take them and they shall show us their treasures which they have hidden in their houses, and we will dwell here and they shall serve us. In this manner did my Cid win Alcocer, and take up his abode therein.

V.

Much did this trouble the Moors of Teca, and it did not please those of Teruel, nor of Calatayud. And they sent to the King of Valencia to tell him that one who was called Ruydiez the Cid, whom King Don Alfonso had banished, was come into their country, and had taken Alcocer; and if a stop were not put to him, the King might look upon Teca and Teruel and Calatayud as lost, for nothing could stand against him, and he had plundered the whole country, along the Salon on the one side, and the Siloca on the other. When the King of Valencia, whose name was Alcamin, heard this, he was greatly troubled. And incontinently he spake unto two Moorish Kings who were his vassals, bidding them take three thousand horsemen, and all the men of the border, and bring the Cid to him alive, that he might make atonement to him for having entered his land.

VI.

Fariz and Galve were the names of these two Moorish Kings, and they set out with the companies of King Alcamin from Valencia, and halted the first night in Segorve, and the second night at Celfa de Canal. And they sent their messengers through the land to all the Councils thereof, ordering all men at arms, as well horsemen as footmen, to join them, and the third night they halted at Calatayud, and great numbers joined them; and they came up against Alcocer, and pitched their tents round about the Castle. Every day their host increased, for their people were many in number, and their watchmen kept watch day and night; and my Cid had no succour to look for except the mercy of God, in which he put his trust. And the Moors beset them so close that they cut off their water, and albeit the Castillians would have sallied against them, my Cid forbade this. In this guise were my Cid and his people besieged for three weeks, and when the fourth week began, he called for Alvar Fañez, and for his company, and said unto them. Ye see that the Moors have cut off our water, and we have but little bread; they gather numbers day by day, and we become weak, and they are in their own country. If we would depart they would not let us, and we cannot go out by night because they have beset us round about on all sides, and we cannot pass on high through the air, neither through the earth which is underneath. Now then if it please you let us go out and fight with them, though they are many in number, and either defeat them or die an honourable death.

VII.

Then Minaya answered and said. We have left the gentle land of Castille, and are come hither as banished men, and if we do not beat the Moors they will not give us food. Now though we are but few, yet are we of a good stock, and of one heart and one will; by God's help let us go out and smite them to-morrow, early in the morning, and you who are not in a state of penitence, go and shrieve yourselves and repent ye of your sins. And they all held that what Alvar Fañez had said was good. And my Cid answered, Minaya, you have spoken as you should do. Then ordered he all the Moors, both men and women, to be thrust out of the town, that it might not be known what they were preparing to do; and the rest of that day and the night also they passed in making ready for the battle. And on the morrow at sunrise the Cid gave his banner to Pero Bermudez, and bade him bear it boldly like a good man as he was, but he charged him not to thrust forward with it without his bidding. And Pero Bermudez kissed his hand, being well pleased. Then leaving only two foot-soldiers to keep the gates, they issued out; and the Moorish scouts saw them and hastened to the camp.

Then was there such a noise of tambours as if the earth would have been broken, and the Moors armed themselves in great haste. Two royal banners were there, and five city ones, and they drew up their men in two great bodies, and moved on, thinking to take my Cid and all his company alive; and my Cid bade his men remain still and not move till he should bid them.

VIII.

Pero Bermudez could not bear this, but holding the banner in his hand, he cried, God help you, Cid Campeador; I shall put your banner in the middle of that main body; and you who are bound to stand by it—I shall see how you will succour it. And he began to prick forward. And the Campeador called unto him to stop as he loved him, but Pero Bermudez replied he would stop for nothing, and away he spurred and carried his banner into the middle of the great body of the Moors. And the Moors fell upon him that they might win the banner, and beset him on all sides, giving him many and great blows to beat him down; nevertheless his arms were proof, and they could not pierce them, neither could they beat him down, nor force the banner from him, for he was a right brave man and a strong, and a good horseman, and of great heart. And when the Cid saw him thus beset he called to his people to move on and help him. Then placed they their shields before their hearts, and lowered their lances with the streamers thereon, and bending forward, rode on. Three hundred lances were they, each with its pendant, and every man at the first charge slew his Moor. Smite them, knights, for the love of charity, cried the Campeador. I am Ruydiez, the Cid of Bivar! Many a shield was pierced that day, and many a false corselet was broken, and many a white streamer dyed with blood, and many a horse left without a rider. The Misbelievers called on Mahomet, and the Christians on Santiago, and the noise of the tambours and of the trumpets was so great that none could hear his neighbour. And my Cid and his company succoured Pero Bermudez, and they rode through the host of the Moors, slaying as they went, and they rode back again in like manner; thirteen hundred did they kill in this guise. If you would know who they were, who were the good men of that day, it behoves me to tell you, for though they are departed, it is not fitting that the names of those who have done well should die, nor would they who have done well themselves, or who hope so to do, think it right; for good men would not be so bound to do well if their good feats should be kept silent. There was my Cid, the good man in battle, who fought well upon his gilt saddle; and Alvar Fañez Minaya, and Martin Antolinez the Burgalesa of prowess, and Muno Gustios, and Martin Munoz who held Montemayor, and Alvar Alvarez, and Alvar Salvadores, and Galin Garcia the good one of Aragon, and Felez Munoz the nephew of the Campeador. Wherever my Cid went, the Moors made a path before him, for he smote them down without mercy. And while the battle still continued, the Moors killed the horse of Alvar Fañez, and his lance was broken, and he fought bravely with his sword afoot. And my Cid, seeing him, came up to an Alguazil who rode upon a good horse, and smote him with his sword under the right arm, so that he cut him through and through, and he gave the horse to Alvar Fañez, saying, Mount, Minaya, for you are my right hand.

IX.

When Alvar Fañez was thus remounted, they fell upon the Moors again, and by this time the Moors were greatly disheartened, having suffered so great loss, and they began to give way. And my Cid, seeing King Fariz, made towards him, smiting down all who were in his way; and he came up to him, and made three blows at him; two of them failed, but the third was a good one, and went through his cuirass, so that the blood ran down his legs. And with that blow was the army of the Moors vanquished, for King Fariz, feeling himself so sorely wounded, turned his reins and fled out of the field, even to Teruel. And Martin Antolinez the good Burgalese came up to King Galve, and gave him a stroke on the head, which scattered all the carbuncles out of his helmet, and cut through it even to the skin; and the King did not wait for another such, and he fled also. A good day was that for Christendom, for the Moors fled on all sides. King Fariz got into Teruel, and King Galve fled after him, but they would not receive him within the gates, and he went on to Calatayud. And the Christians pursued them even to Calatayud. And Alvar Fañez had a good horse; four and thirty did he slay in that pursuit with the edge of his keen sword, and his arm was all red, and the blood dropt from his elbow. And as he was returning from the spoil he said, Now am I well pleased, for good tidings will go to Castille, how my Cid has won a battle in the field. My Cid also turned back; his coif was wrinkled, and you might see his full beard; the hood of his mail hung down upon his shoulders, and the sword was still in his hand. He saw his people returning from the pursuit, and that of all his company fifteen only of the lower sort were slain, and he gave thanks to God for this victory. Then they fell to the spoil, and they found arms in abundance, and great store of wealth; and five hundred and ten horses. And he divided the spoil, giving to each man his fair portion, and the Moors whom they had put out of Alcocer before the battle, they now received again into the castle, and gave to them also a part of the booty, so that all were well content. And my Cid had great joy with his vassals.

X.

Then the Cid called unto Alvar Fañez and said, Cousin, you are my right hand, and I hold it good that you should take of my fifth as much as you will, for all would be well bestowed upon you; but Minaya thanked him, and said, that he would take nothing more than his share. And the Cid said unto him, I will send King Don Alfonso a present from my part of the spoils. You shall go into Castille, and take with you thirty horses, the best which were taken from the Moors, all bridled and saddled, and each having a sword hanging from the saddle-bow; and you shall give them to the King, and kiss his hand for me, and tell him that we know how to make our way among the Moors. And you shall take also this bag of gold and silver, and purchase for me a thousand masses in St. Mary's at Burgos, and hang up there these banners of the Moorish Kings whom we have overcome. Go then to St. Pedro's at Cardeña, and salute my wife Doña Ximena, and my daughters, and tell them how well I go on, and that if I live I will make them rich women. And salute for me the Abbot Don Sancho, and give him fifty marks of silver; and the rest of the money, whatever shall be left, give to my wife, and bid them all pray for me. Moreover the Cid said unto him, This country is all spoiled, and we have to help ourselves with sword and spear. You are going to gentle Castille; if when you return you should not find us here, you will hear where we are.

XI.

Alvar Fañez went his way to Castille, and he found the King in Valladolid, and he presented to him the thirty horses, with all their trappings, and swords mounted with silver hanging from the saddle-bows. And when the King saw them, before Alvar Fañez could deliver his bidding, he said unto him, Minaya, who sends me this goodly present; and Minaya answered, My Cid Ruydiez, the Campeador, sends it, and kisses by me your hands. For since you were wroth against him, and banished him from the land, he being a man disherited, hath helped himself with his own hands, and hath won from the Moors the Castle of Alcocer. And the King of Valencia sent two Kings to besiege him there, with all his power, and they begirt him round about, and cut off the water and bread from us so that we could not subsist. And then holding it better to die like good men in the field, than shut up like bad ones, we went out against them, and fought with them in the open field, and smote them and put them to flight; and both the Moorish Kings were sorely wounded, and many of the Moors were slain, and many were taken prisoners, and great was the spoil which we won in the field, both of captives and of horses and arms, gold and silver and pearls, so that all who are with him are rich men. And of his fifth of the horses which were taken that day, my Cid hath sent you these, as to his natural Lord, whose favour he desireth. I beseech you, as God shall help you, show favour unto him. Then King Don Alfonso answered, This is betimes in the morning for a banished man to ask favour of his Lord; nor is it befitting a King, for no Lord ought to be wroth for so short a time. Nevertheless, because the horses were won from the Moors, I will take them, and rejoice that my Cid hath sped so well. And I pardon you, Minaya, and give again unto you all the lands which you have ever held of me, and you have my favour to go when you will, and come when you will. Of the Cid Campeador, I shall say nothing now, save only that all who choose to follow him may freely go, and their bodies and goods and heritages are safe. And Minaya said, God grant you many and happy years for his service. Now I beseech you, this which you have done for me, do also to all those who are in my Cid's company, and show favour unto them also, that their possessions may be restored unto them. And the King gave order that it should be so. Then Minaya kissed the King's hand and said, Sir, you have done this now, and you will do the rest hereafter.

XII.

My Cid remained awhile in Alcocer, and the Moors of the border waited to see what he would do. And in this time King Fariz got well of his wound, and my Cid sent to him and to the Moors, saying, that if they would give him three thousand marks of silver, he would leave Alcocer and go elsewhere. And King Fariz and the Moors of Techa, and of Ternel, and of Calatayud, were right glad of this, and the covenant was put in writing, and they sent him the three thousand marks. And my Cid divided it among his company, and he made them all rich, both knights and esquires and footmen, so that they said to one another, He who serves a good Lord, happy man is his dole. But the Moors of Alcocer were full sorry to see him depart, because he had been to them a kind master and a bountiful; and they said unto him, Wherever you go, Cid, our prayers will go before you; and they wept both men and women when my Cid went his way. So the Campeador raised his banner and departed, and he went down the Salon, and crossed it; and as he crossed the river they saw good birds, and signs of good fortune. And they of Za and of Calatayud were well pleased, because he went from them. My Cid rode on till he came to the knoll above Monte-Real; it is a high hill and strong, and there he pitched his tents, being safe on all sides. And from thence he did much harm to the Moors of Medina and of the country round about; and he made Daroca pay tribute, and Molina also, which is on the other side, and Teruel also, and Celfa de Canal, and all the country along the river Martin. And the news went to the King of Zaragoza, and it neither pleased the King nor his people.

XIII.

Ever after was that knoll called the Knoll of the Cid. And when the perfect one had waited a long time for Minaya and saw that he did not come, he removed by night, and passed by Teruel and pitched his camp in the pine-forest of Tebar. And from thence he infested the Moors of Zaragoza, insomuch that they held it best to give him gold and silver and pay him tribute. And when this covenant had been made, Almudafar, the King of Zaragoza, became greatly his friend, and received him full honourably into the town. In three weeks time after this came Alvar Fañez from Castille. Two hundred men of lineage came with him, every one of whom wore sword girt to his side, and the foot-soldiers in their company were out of number. When my Cid saw Minaya he rode up to him, and embraced him without speaking, and kissed his mouth and the eyes in his head. And Minaya told him all that he had done. And the face of the Campeador brightened, and he gave thanks to God and said, It will go well with me, Minaya, as long as you live! God, how joyful was that whole host because Alvar Fañez was returned! for he brought them greetings from their kinswomen and their brethren, and the fair comrades whom they had left behind. God, how joyful was my Cid with the fleecy beard, that Minaya had purchased the thousand masses, and had brought him the biddings of his wife and daughters! God, what a joyful man was he!

XIV.

Now it came to pass that while my Cid was in Zaragoza the days of King Almudafar were fulfilled: and he left his two sons Zulema and Abenalfange, and they divided his dominions between them; and Zulema had the kingdom of Zaragoza, and Abenalfange the kingdom of Denia. And Zulema put his kingdom under my Cid's protection, and bade all his people obey him even as they would himself. Now there began to be great enmity between the two brethren, and they made war upon each other. And King Don Pedro of Aragon, and the Count Don Ramón Berenguer of Barcelona, helped Abenalfange, and they were enemies to the Cid because he defended Zulema. And my Cid chose out two hundred horsemen and went out by night, and fell upon the lands of Alcañiz; and he remained out three days in this inroad, and brought away great booty. Great was the talk thereof among the Moors: and they of Monzon and of Huesca were troubled, but they of Zaragoza rejoiced; because they paid tribute to the Cid, and were safe. And when my Cid returned to Zaragoza he divided the spoil among his companions, and said to them, Ye know, my friends, that for all who live by their arms, as we do, it is not good to remain long in one place. Let us be off again to-morrow. So on the morrow they moved to the Puerto de Alucant, and from thence they infested Huesca and Montalban. Ten days were they out upon this inroad; and the news was sent every where how the exile from Castille was handling them, and tidings went to the King of Denia and to the Count of Barcelona, how my Cid was over-running the country.

XV.

When Don Ramon Berenguer the Count of Barcelona heard this, it troubled him to the heart, and he held it for a great dishonour, because that part of the land of the Moors was in his keeping. And he spake boastfully saying, Great wrong doth that Cid of Bivar offer unto me; he smote my nephew in my own court and never would make amends for it, and now he ravages the lands which are in my keeping, and I have never defied him for this nor renounced his friendship; but since he goes on in this way I must take vengeance. So he and King Abenalfange gathered together a great power both of Moors and Christians, and went in pursuit of the Cid, and after three days and two nights they came up with him in the pine-forest of Tebar, and they came on confidently, thinking to lay hands on him. Now my Cid was returning with much spoil, and had descended from the Sierra into the valley when tidings were brought him that Count Don Ramon Berenguer and the King of Denia were at hand, with a great power, to take away his booty, and take or slay him. And when the Cid heard this he sent to Don Ramon saying, that the booty which he had won was none of his, and bidding him let him go on his way in peace: but the Count made answer, that my Cid should now learn whom he had dishonoured, and make amends once for all. Then my Cid sent the booty forward, and bade his knights make ready. They are coming upon us, said he, with a great power both of Moors and Christians, to take from us the spoils which we have so hardly won, and without doing battle we cannot be quit of them; for if we should proceed they would follow till they overtook us: therefore let the battle be here, and I trust in God that we shall win more honour, and something to boot. They come down the hill, drest in their hose, with their gay saddles, and their girths wet; we are with our hose covered and on our Galician saddles;—a hundred such as we ought to beat their whole company. Before they get upon the plain ground let us give them the points of our lances; for one whom we run through, three will jump out of their saddles; and Ramon Berenguer will then see whom he has overtaken to-day in the pine-forest of Tebar, thinking to despoil him of the booty which I have won from the enemies of God and of the faith.

While my Cid was speaking, his knights had taken their arms, and were ready on horseback for the charge. Presently they saw the pendants of the Frenchmen coming down the hill, and when they were nigh the bottom, and had not yet set foot upon the plain ground, my Cid bade his people charge, which they did with a right good will, thrusting their spears so stiffly, that by God's good pleasure not a man whom they encountered but lost his seat. So many were slain and so many wounded, that the Moors were dismayed forthwith, and began to fly. The Count's people stood firm a little longer, gathering round their Lord; but my Cid was in search of him, and when he saw where he was, he made up to him, clearing the way as he went, and gave him such a stroke with his lance that he felled him down to the ground. When the Frenchmen saw their Lord in this plight they fled away and left him; and the pursuit lasted three leagues, and would have been continued farther if the conquerors had not had tired horses. So they turned back and collected the spoils, which were more than they could carry away. Thus was Count Ramon Berenguer made prisoner, and my Cid won from him that day the good sword Colada, which was worth more than a thousand marks of silver. That night did my Cid and his men make merry, rejoicing over their gains. And the Count was taken to my Cid's tent, and a good supper was set before him; nevertheless he would not eat, though my Cid besought him so to do. And on the morrow my Cid ordered a feast to be made, that he might do pleasure to the Count, but the Count said that for all Spain he would not eat one mouthful, but would rather die, since he had been beaten in battle by such a set of ragged fellows. And Ruydiez said to him, Eat and drink, Count, of this bread and of this wine, for this is the chance of war: if you do as I say you shall be free; and if not you will never return again into your own lands. And Don Ramond answered, Eat you, Don Rodrigo, for your fortune is fair and you deserve it; take you your pleasure, but leave me to die. And in this mood he continued for three days, refusing all food. But then my Cid said to him, Take food, Count, and be sure that I will set you free, you and any two of your knights, and give you wherewith to return into your own country. And when Don Ramond heard this, he took comfort and said, If you will indeed do this thing I shall marvel at you as long as I live. Eat then, said Ruydiez, and I will do it: but mark you, of the spoil which we have taken from you I will give you nothing; for to that you have no claim neither by right nor custom, and besides we want it for ourselves, being banished men, who must live by taking from you and from others as long as it shall please God. Then was the Count full joyful, being well pleased that what should be given him was not of the spoils which he had lost; and he called for water and washed his hands, and chose two of his kinsmen to be set free with him; the one was named Don Hugo, and the other Guillen Bernalto. And my Cid sate at the table with them, and said, If you do not eat well, Count, you and I shall not part yet. Never since he was Count did he eat with better will than that day! And when they had done he said, Now, Cid, if it be your pleasure let us depart. And my Cid clothed him and his kinsmen well with goodly skins and mantles, and gave them each a goodly palfrey, with rich caparisons, and he rode out with them on their way. And when he took leave of the Count he said to him, Now go freely, and I thank you for what you have left behind; if you wish to play for it again let me know, and you shall either have something back in its stead, or leave what you bring to be added to it. The Count answered, Cid, you jest safely now, for I have paid you and all your company for this twelve months, and shall not be coming to see you again so soon. Then Count Ramond pricked on more than apace, and many times looked behind him, fearing that my Cid would repent what he had done, and send to take him back to prison, which the perfect one would not have done for the whole world, for never did he do disloyal thing.

XVII.

Then he of Bivar returned to Zaragoza, and divided the spoil, which was so great that none of his men knew how much they had. And the Moors of the town rejoiced in his good speed, liking him well, because he protected them so well that they were safe from all harm. And my Cid went out again from Zaragoza, and rode over the lands of Monzon and Huerta and Onda and Buenar. And King Pedro of Aragon came out against him, but my Cid took the Castle of Monzon in his sight; and then he went to Tamarit: and one day as he rode out hunting from thence with twelve of his knights, he fell in with a hundred and fifty of the King of Aragon's people, and he fought with them and put them to flight, and took seven knights prisoners, whom he let go freely. Then he turned towards the sea-coast, and won Xerica and Onda and Almenar, and all the lands of Borriana and Murviedro; and they in Valencia were greatly dismayed because of the great feats which he did in the land. And when he had plundered all that country he returned to Tamarit, where Zulema then was.

XVIII.

Now Zulema had sent for my Cid, and the cause was this. His brother the King of Denia had taken counsel with Count Ramon Berenguer, and with the Count of Cardona, and with the brother of the Count of Urgel, and with the chiefs of Balsadron and Remolin and Cartaxes, that they should besiege the Castle of Almenar, which my Cid had refortified by command of King Zulema. And they came up against it while my Cid was away, besieging the Castle of Estrada, which is in the rivers Tiegio and Sege, the which he took by force. And they fought against it and cut off the water. And when my Cid came to the King at Tamarit, the King asked him to go and fight with the host which besieged Almenar; but my Cid said it would be better to give something to King Abenalfange that he should break up the siege and depart; for they were too great a power to do battle with, being as many in number as the sands on the sea-shore. And the King did as he counselled him, and sent to his brother King Abenalfange, and to the chiefs who were with him, to propose this accord, and they would not. Then my Cid, seeing that they would not depart for fair means, armed his people, and fell upon them. That was a hard battle and well fought on both sides, and much blood was shed, for many good knights on either party were in the field; howbeit he of good fortune won the day at last, he who never was conquered. King Abenalfange and Count Ramon and most of the others fled, and my Cid followed, smiting and slaying for three leagues; and many good Christian knights were made prisoners. Ruydiez returned with great honour and much spoil, and gave all his prisoners to King Zulema, who kept them eight days, and then my Cid begged their liberty and set them free. And he and the King returned to Zaragoza, and the people came out to meet them, with great joy, and shouts of welcome. And the King honoured my Cid greatly, and gave him power in all his dominions.

XIX.

At this time it came to pass that Almofalez, a Moor of Andalusia, rose up with the Castle of Rueda, which was held for King Don Alfonso. And because he held prisoner there the brother of Adefir, another Moor, Adefir sent to the King of Castille, beseeching him to come to succour him, and recover the Castle. And the King sent the Infante Don Ramiro his cousin, and the Infante Don Sancho, son to the King of Navarre, and Count Don Gonzalo Salvadores, and Count Don Nuño Alvarez, and many other knights with them; and they came to the Castle, and Almofalez said he would not open the gates to them, but if the King came he would open to him. And when King Don Alfonso heard this, incontinently he came to Rueda. And Almofalez besought him to enter to a feast which he had prepared; howbeit the King would not go in, neither would his people have permitted him so to have risked his person. But the Infante Don Sancho entered, and Don Nuño, and Don

Gonzalo, and fifteen other knights; and as soon as they were within the gate, the Moors threw down great stones upon them and killed them all. This was the end of the good Count Don Gonzalo Salvadores, who was so good a knight in battle that he was called He of the Four Hands. The bodies were ransomed, seeing that there was no remedy, the Castle being so strong, and Don Gonzalo was buried in the Monastery of Oña, according as he had appointed in his will; and the Infante Don Sancho with his forefathers the Kings of Navarre, in the royal Monastery of Naxara.

XX.

Greatly was King Don Alfonso troubled at this villainy, and he sent for the Cid, who was in those parts; and the Cid came to him with a great company. And the King told him the great treason which had been committed, and took the Cid into his favour, and said unto him that he might return with him into Castille. My Cid thanked him for his bounty, but he said he never would accept his favour unless the King granted what he should request; and the King bade him make his demand. And my Cid demanded, that when any hidalgo should be banished, in time to come, he should have the thirty days, which were his right, allowed him, and not nine only, as had been his case; and that neither hidalgo nor citizen should be proceeded against till they had been fairly and lawfully heard; also, that the King should not go against the privileges and charters and good customs of any town or other place, nor impose taxes upon them against their right; and if he did, that it should be lawful for the land to rise against him, till he had amended the misdeed. And to all this the King accorded, and said to my Cid that he should go back into Castille with him: but my Cid said he would not go into Castille till he had won that castle of Rueda, and delivered the villainous Moors thereof into his hands, that he might do justice upon them. So the King thanked him greatly, and returned into Castille, and my Cid remained before the Castle of Rueda. And he lay before it so long, and beset it so close, that the food of the Moors failed, and they had no strength to defend themselves; and they would willingly have yielded the castle, so they might have been permitted to leave it and go whither they would; but he would have their bodies, to deliver them up to the King. When they saw that it must be so, great part of them came out, and yielded themselves prisoners; and then my Cid stormed the Castle, and took Almofalez and they who held with him, so that none escaped; and he sent him and his accomplices in the treason to the King. And the King was right glad when they were brought before him, and he did great justice upon them, and sent to thank my Cid for having avenged him.

XXI.

After my Cid had done this good service to King Don Alfonso, he and King Zulema of Zaragoza entered Aragon, slaying, and burning, and plundering before them, and they returned to the Castle of Monzon with great booty. Then the Cid went into King Abenalfange's country, and did much mischief there; and he got among the mountains of Moriella, and beat down every thing before him, and destroyed the Castle of Moriella. And King Zulema sent to bid him build up the ruined Castle of Alcala, which is upon Moriella; and the Cid did so. But King Abenalfange being sorely grieved hereat, sent to King Pedro of Aragon, and besought him to come and help him against the Campeador. And the King of Aragon gathered together a great host in his anger, and he and the King of Denia came against my Cid, and they halted that night upon the banks of the Ebro; and King Don Pedro sent letters to the Cid, bidding him leave the castle which he was then edifying. My Cid made answer, that if the King chose to pass that way in peace, he would let him pass, and show him any service in his power. And when the King of Aragon saw that he would not forsake the work, he marched against him, and attacked him. Then was there a brave battle, and many were slain; but my Cid won the day, and King Abenalfange fled, and King Don Pedro was taken prisoner, and many of his Counts and knights with him. My Cid returned to Zaragoza with this great honour, taking his prisoners with him; and he set them all freely at liberty, and having tarried in Zaragoza a few days, set forth for Castille, with great riches and full of honours.

XXII.

Having done all these things in his banishment, my Cid returned to Castille, and the King received him well, and gave him the Castle of Dueñas, and of Orcejon, and Ybia, and Campo, and Gaña, and Berviesca, and Berlanga, with all their districts. And he gave him privileges with leaden seals appendant, and confirmed with his own hand, that whatever castles, towns, and places, he might win from the Moors, or from any one else, should be his own, quit and free for ever, both for him and for his descendants. Thus was my Cid received into the King's favour, and he abode with him long time, doing him great services, as his Lord.

BOOK V.

I.

In these days King Yahia reigned in Toledo, the grandson of King Alimaymon, who had been the friend of King Don Alfonso; for Alimaymon was dead, and his son Hicem also. Now Yahia was a bad King, and one who walked not in the ways of his fathers. Insolent he was towards the elders, and cruel towards his people: and his yoke was so heavy that all men desired to see his death, because there was no good in him. And the people seeing that he did not protect them, and that their lands were ravaged safely, went to him and said, Stand up, Sir, for thy people and thy country, else we must look for some other Lord who will defend us. But he was of such lewd customs that he gave no heed to their words. And when they knew that there was no hope of him, the Moors sent to the King of Badajoz, inviting him to come and be their protector, saying that they would deliver the city into his hands in spite of Yahia. And the Muzarabes who dwelt in the city sent to King Don Alfonso, exhorting him to win Toledo, which he might well do, now that he was no longer bound by his oath. Then both Kings came, thinking to have the city: and the King of Badajoz came first, and the gates were opened to him in despite of Yahia. Howbeit King Don Alfonso speedily arrived, and the King of Badajoz, seeing that he could not maintain Toledo against him, retreated, and King Don Aifonso pursued him into his own dominions and gave orders that he should be attacked along the whole of his border, and did not leave him till he had plainly submitted. In this manner was Yahia delivered from the King of Badajoz; but King Don Alfonso knowing how that city was to be taken, contented himself with overrunning the country, and despoiling it, even to the walls of the city; and thus he did for four years, so that he was master of the land.

II.

In all this time did my Cid do good service to King Don Alfonso. And in these days King Don Alfonso fought at Consuegra with King Abenalfange of Denia, and in this battle the Christians were defeated, and Diego Rodriguez, the son of my Cid, was slain. Greatly was his death lamented by the Christians, for he was a youth of great hope, and one who was beginning to tread in the steps of his father. And King Don Alfonso was fain to retire into the Castle of that town. And Abenalfange gathered together the greatest power of the Moors that he could, and entered the land of the Christians, and past the mountains, and came even to Medina del Campo, and there Alvar Fañez Minaya met him. Minaya had but five and twenty hundred horse with him, and of the Moors there were fifteen thousand; nevertheless by God's blessing he prevailed against them. And by the virtue of God Alvar Fañez gave King Abenalfange a cruel wound in the face, so that he fled away. Great honour did Minaya win for this victory.

III.

Now had King Don Alfonso for many years cut down the bread and the wine and the fruits in all the country round about Toledo, and he made ready to go against the city. The tidings of this great enterprise spread far and wide, and adventurers came from all parts lo be present; not only they of Castille and Leon, Asturias and Nagera, Galicia and Portugal, but King Sancho Ramirez of Aragon came also, with the flower of Aragon and Navarre and Catalonia, and Franks and Germans and Italians, and men of other countries, to bear their part in so great and catholic a war. And the King entertained them well, being full bountiful, insomuch that he was called He of the Open Hand. Never had so goodly a force of Christians been assembled in Spain, nor so great an enterprise attempted, since the coming of the Moors. And of this army was my Cid the leader. So soon as the winter was over they began their march. And when they came to a ford of the Tagus, behold the river was swoln, and the best horsemen feared to try the passage. Now there was a holy man in the camp, by name Lesmes, who was a monk of St. Benedict's; and he being mounted upon an ass rode first into the ford, and passed safely through the flood; and all who beheld him held it for a great miracle.

IV.

Greatly to be blamed are they who lived in those days for not handing down to everlasting remembrance the worthy feats which were atchieved at this siege. For not only was Toledo a strong city, both by nature and in its walls and towers, but the flower of the chivalry of all Spain and of all Christendom was there assembled, and the Moors of Spain also, knowing that this was, as it were, the heart of their empire, did all they could to defend it: greatly to be blamed are they who neglected to transmit to us the memory of their deeds, and greatly have they wronged the worthy knights whose exploits should else have gained for them a never-dying renown. Nothing more, owing to their default, can we say of this so notable a siege, than that when Don Cabrian, the Bishop of Leon, was earnestly engaged in prayer for the success of the Christian arms, the glorious St. Isidro appeared unto him, and certified that in fifteen days the city should be surrendered; and even so it came to pass, for the gates were opened to the King on Thursday the twenty-fifth of May, in the year of the æera 1123, which is the year of Christ 1085. The first Christian banner which entered the city was the banner of my Cid, and my Cid was the first Christian Alcayde of Toledo. Of the terms granted unto the Moors, and how they were set aside for the honour of the Catholic faith, and of the cunning of the Jews who dwelt in the city, and how the Romish ritual was introduced therein, this is not the place to speak; all these things are written in the Chronicles of the Kings of Spain.

V.

Now Yahai, when he saw that he could by no means hold Toledo, because on the one hand the Moors would give it to the King of Badajoz, and on the other King Don Alfonso warred against it, he made a covenant with King Don Alfonso to yield the city to him, if he with the help of Alvar Fañez would put him in possession of Valencia, which had belonged unto Hicem and Alimaymon, his fathers, but which the Guazil Abdalla Azis held now as his own, calling himself King thereof. And he covenanted that King Don Alfonso should also put into his hand Santa Maria de Albarrazin, and the kingdom of Denia; and the King assented to the covenant, thinking that in this manner the land would be all his own. Yahia therefore sent Abenfarat, who was his cousin, to Valencia, to spy out what the Guazil would do, whether he would peaceably deliver up the kingdom unto him, or whether he would oppose his coming, which he greatly doubted, because it was rumoured that he was about to give his daughter in marriage to the King of Zaragoza. Abenfarat went his way, and took up his abode in the house of a Moor who was called Abenlupo; and while he sojourned there the marriage of the Guazil's daughter was effected, and the Guazil himself fell sick and died. Then Abenfarat tarried yet awhile to see what would be the issue, for the men of Valencia were greatly troubled because of the death of their King. He left two sons, between whom there was no brotherly love during his life, and now that he was dead there was less. And they divided between them all that he had left, even the least thing did they divide, each being covetous to possess all that he could; and they made two factions in the town, each striving to possess himself of the power therein. But the men of Valencia who were not engaged on their side, and they also who held the castles round about, were greatly troubled because of this strife which was between them; and they also were divided between two opinions, they who were of the one wishing to give the kingdom to the King of Zaragoza, and they who were of the other to yield themselves unto Yahai the grandson of Alimaymon, because of the covenant which King Don Alfonso had made with him. When Abenfarat knew these things he returned unto Yahia, and told him all even as it was; and Yahia saw that he should have the city, because of the discord which was therein.

VI.

Then Yahia gathered together all his people, knights, and cross-bow men, and foot-soldiers, and they of his board, and the officers of his household which are the eunuchs; and he set forward on the way toward Valencia, and Alvar Fañez and his body of Christians with him. And he sent to the townsmen greeting them, and saying that he was coming to dwell among them and to be their King, and that he would deal bountifully by them; and that he should wait awhile in the town which was called Sera. The chief men of the town took counsel together what they should do, and at length they agreed to receive him for their Lord; and this they did more in fear of King Don Alfonso and of Alvar Fañez than for any love towards him. This answer they sent him by Aboeza the Alcayde. Now Aboeza would fain have departed from Valencia when the Guazil Abdalla Azis died, because of the strife which was in the city, and he thought to betake himself to his own Castle of Monviedro and dwell there, away from the troubles which were to come. Upon this purpose he took counsel with his friend Mahomed Abenhayen the Scribe, for there was great love between them; and when the Scribe heard what he purposed to do he was grieved thereat, and represented unto him that it was not fitting for him to forsake the city at such a time, so that Aboeza was persuaded. And they twain covenanted one to the other, to love and defend each other against all the men in the world, and to help each other with their persons and possessions; and Aboeza sent trusty men of his kinsfolk and friends to keep the Castles of Monviedo and Castro and Santa Cruz, and other Castles which were in his possession, and he himself abode in Valencia. And now he went out to Yahia to give unto him the keys of the city, and the good men of the city went out with him, and they made obeisance to him and promised to serve him loyally. Then Yahia, the grandson of Alimaymon, set forth with all his company from Sera, and all the people of Valencia, high and low, went out to meet him with great rejoicings. And Aboeza adorned the Alcazar right nobly, that Yahia and his women and they of his company might lodge within. The most honourable of his knights took up their lodging in the town, and the cross-bow men and others of low degree lodged round about the Alcazar, and in certain dwellings which were between it and the Mosque, and Alvar Fañez and the Christians who were with him, in the village which was called Ruzaf.

VII

Yahia being now King in Valencia, made Aboeza his Guazil, and gave him authority throughout all his kingdom. Nevertheless he bore displeasure against him in his heart, because he had served Abdalla Azis; and on his part also Aboeza secretly feared the King, and knew not whether it were better to depart from him, or not; howbeit he thought it best to remain and serve him right loyally and well, that so he might win his good will; and when the King perceived this, his anger abated and was clean put out of mind. And he made Aboeza his favourite, and made a vow unto him and confirmed it by a writing, that he would never take away his favour from him, nor change him for another, nor do any thing in his dominions without him. With this was Aboeza satisfied, and the fear which he felt in his heart was removed. And they who held the castles brought great gifts to Yahia, with much humility and reverence, such as the Moors know how to put on. This they did to set his heart at rest, that he might confide in them, and send away Alvar Fañez into his own country, and not keep him and his people at so great a charge, for it cost them daily six hundred maravedis, and the King had no treasure in Valencia, neither was he so rich that he could support his own company and supply this payment; and for this reason the Moors complained of the great cost. But on the other hand, Yahia feared that if he should send away Alvar Fañez, the Moors would rise against him; and to maintain him he laid a great tax upon the city and its district, saying that it was for barley. This tax they levied upon the rich as well as the poor, and upon the great as well as the little, which they held to be a great evil and breach of their privileges, and thought that by his fault Valencia would be lost, even as Toledo had been. This tribute so sorely aggrieved the people, that it became as it were a bye word in the city, Give the barley. They say there was a great mastiff, with whom they killed beef in the shambles, who, whenever he heard, 'Give the barley,'began to bark and growl: upon which a Trobador said, Thanks be to God, we have many in the town who are like the mastiff.

When they who held the Castles sent presents to King Yahia, there was one among them, by name Abenmazot, who held Xativa, who neither sent him gifts, nor came to offer obedience. And the King sent to bid him come before him. But then Abenmazot sent a messenger with letters and full rich presents, saying that he could by no means come himself, and this not from any feigning, and that he would alway do him service with a true good will. And he besought him as his Lord to let him remain in Xativa, and he would give him the rents thereof; but if it was his pleasure to appoint some other in his stead, he besought that he would then give him something for himself and his company to subsist upon, seeing that he desired nothing but the King's favour to be well with him. Then the King took counsel with Aboeza the Guazil, and the Guazil advised him to do unto Abenmazot even as he had requested, and let him keep Xativa; and to send away Alvar Fañez because of the great charge it was to maintain him, and to live in peace, and put his kingdom in order; in all which he advised him like a good counsellor and a true. But the King would not give heed to him; instead thereof he communicated his counsel to the two sons of Abdalla Azis who had submitted unto him, and whom he had taken into his favour, and they told him that Aboeza had advised him ill, and that it behoved him to lead out his host and bring Abenmazot to obedience. And the King believed them and went out and besieged Xativa. And the first day he entered the lower part of the town, but Abenmazot retired to the Alcazar and the fortresses, and defended the upper part; and the King besieged him there for four months, attacking him every day, till food began to fail both in the army of the King and in the town. And they of Valencia could not supply what was to be paid to Alvar Fañez and his company, much less what the King wanted. Then the King understood that he had been ill advised, and for this reason he condemned one of the sons of Abdalla Azis to pay Alvar Fañez for thirty days; and he seized a Jew who was one of his Almoxarifes in Valencia, that is to say, one who collected the taxes, and took from him all that he had, because he had advised him ill, and while this lasted the people of Valencia had some respite.

IX.

When Abenmazot saw that the King was bent upon destroying him, and that every day he prest him more and more, he sent to Abenalfange who was King of Denia and Tortosa, saying, that if he would come and help him, he would make him Lord of Xativa and of all his other Castles, and would be at his mercy; and this he did to escape from the hands of Yahia. When Abenalfange heard this it pleased him well, and he sent one of his Alcaydes, who was called the Left-handed, to enter the Alcazar, and help to defend it till he could collect a company of Christians who might deal with Alvar Fañez. So that Left-handed one entered the Alcazar with his company, and the Lord of the Castle which was called Almenar, was already there to help Abenmazot, and encourage him that he should not submit. Then Abenalfange gathered together all his host and his cavalry, and brought with him Giralte the Roman, with a company of French knights, and came towards Xativa, as a hungry lion goes against a sheep, or like the coming of a flood in its hour; so that Vahia was dismayed at the tidings of his approach, and fled as fast as he could to the Isle of Xucar, and though that Isle was so near, he thought he had done a great thing; and from thence he went to Valencia, holding himself greatly dishonoured. Then Abenalfange had Xativa and all its Castles, so that it was all one kingdom as far as Denia. And he took Abenmazot with all his women and his household and all that he had, to Denia, and gave him possessions there, and did him much honour. And when it was seen that King Yahia was thus dishonoured, and that Alvar Fañez had not helped him as had been looked for, they who held the Castles lost all fear of him, so that their hearts were changed towards him, as well they of Valencia as of the other Castles, and they said that they would rather belong to Abenalfange than to him, because the town could not bear the charge of the Christians, nor the oppressions which they suffered because of them.

X.

Abenalfange abode some days in Xativa, and then moved on towards Valencia, thinking to win the city; for he knew how greatly the people were oppressed because of the Christians, and that they could not bear it, and that there was no love between them and their Lord. And he passed by a place which was an oratory of the Moors in their festivals, which they call in Arabic Axera, or Araxea; and he halted near Valencia, so that they in the town might see him, and he went round about the town, to the right and to the left, wheresoever he would. The King of Valencia with his knights was near the wall watching him, and Alvar Fañez and his company were in readiness lest the French should defy them. And after Abenalfange had staid their awhile he drew off and went his way to Tortosa. And Yahia was perplexed with Alvar Fañez, and sought for means to pay him, and he threw the two sons of Abdalla Azis into prison, and many other good men of the town also, and took from them great riches. Then he made a covenant with Alvar Fañez, that he should remain with him, and gave him great possessions. And when the Moors saw that Alvar Fañez was in such power, all the ruffians and lewd livers in the town flocked unto him, so that Valencia was in the hands of him and his followers; and the Moors being desperate of remedy deserted the town, and went whither they could, setting at nought their inheritances, for no man was safe, neither in his goods nor person. Then Alvar Fañez made an inroad into the lands of Abenalfange, and overran the lands of Buriana, and other parts; and there went with him a great company of those Moorish desperadoes who had joined him, and of other Moorish Almogavares, and they stormed towns and castles, and slew many Moors, and brought away flocks and herds both of cattle and of brood mares, and much gold and silver, and store of wearing apparel, all which they sold in Valencia.

XI.

Now when one of the sons of Abdalla Azis was loosed from prison, he placed his love upon Alvar Fañez and gave him goodly gifts, and upon Aboeza the King's Guazil, and upon a Jew who was a messenger from King Don Alfonso. And they all sent to King Don Alfonso to beseech him that he would take the son of Abdalla Azis and all that he had under his protection, so that Yahia might do no evil unto him, neither take by force from him anything that was his; and for this protection he promised to give the King thirty thousand maravedís yearly. This request King Don Alfonso granted, and incontinently he took him under his protection, and sent to the King of Valencia to request that he would do him no wrong. Therefore the son of Abdalla Azis was from that time held in more honour because of the love of King Don Alfonso; nevertheless he was still kept under a guard in his own house, that he should not issue forth. And because of this confinement not thinking himself safe, he made a hole through the wall and got out by night in woman's apparel, and lay hid all the next day in a garden, and on the following night mounted on horseback and rode to Monviedro. When the Guazil knew this he took his son and his uncle as sureties for him for the thirty thousand maravedís, which the Jew was now come to receive for King Don Alfonso. And they went to Monviedro to him, and communed with him, and accorded with him that he should pay the one-half immediately, and whenever he returned to Valencia and was safe there in possession of all his rents and inheritances, that then he should pay the remainder; so he paid the fifteen thousand forthwith in silver, and in rings of gold, and in cloth, and in strings of pearls, and the Jew returned therewith to King Don Alfonso. At this time his brother was released from prison by desire of the King of Zaragoza, and he went unto him; and many of the rich men of the city also betook themselves to Monviedro, because they were not secure neither in their possessions nor in their bodies.

XII.

In these days the Almoravides arose in Barbary. The rise of this people and all that they did in Spain are not for me to relate in this place. Suffice it to say, that King Don Alfonso being in great danger, sent for Alvar Fañez and all his company; and that he had so much to do for himself that he took no thought for Valencia. And when they who had the keeping of Yahia's Castles saw this they rose against him, so that few remained unto him, and they of his vassals in whom he put the most trust proved false, so that the heart of the King of Denia and Tortosa grew, and he thought to win Valencia. The chief persons of the town also sent unto him, saying that if he would come they would give the city into his hands. So he gathered together his host, and a company of French also, and sent them forward under the command of his uncle, saying that he would follow and join them on a certain day. But they went forward, and Yahia thinking that if he could conquer them he should be secure, went out and fought against them; and he was defeated and lost a great part of his people and of his arms, and returned into the city with great loss. When Abenalfange, who was a day's journey off, heard this, he marched all night, and came before Valencia. And King Yahia knew not what to do, and was minded to yield up the town. And he took counsel with his people, and they advised him to send for help to King Don Alfonso, and also to the King of Zaragoza, and he did accordingly. And an Arrayaz of Cuenca, whose name was Abencaño, who was a native of Valencia, went to Zaragoza, and told the King that if he would go thither he would deliver the city into his hands, for it appertained unto him rather than to Abenalfange.

XIII.

And in those days my Cid gathered together a great force, and went to the borders of Aragon, and crost the Douro, and lodged that night in Fresno. From thence he went to Calamocha, where he kept Whitsuntide. While he lay there the King of Albarrazin, being in great fear of him, sent to him requesting that they might meet. And when they saw each other they established great love between them, and the King from that day became tributary to the Cid. Then the Cid went to Zaragoza, where he tas full honourably received. And when Abencaño came to Zaragoza inviting King Almescahen to go and take Valencia, and King Yahia sent also to beg succour at his hands, the King asked the Cid to go with him, and gave him whatever he demanded. So greatly did this King desire to have Valencia, that he looked not whether his force was great or little, nor whether that of the Cid was greater than his own, but went on as fast as he could. When the King of Denia heard that he was coming and the Cid with him, he durst not abide them. And he thought that the King of Zaragoza by the Cid's help would win the city, and that he should remain with the labour he had undergone, and the cost. Then he placed his love upon King Yahia, and sent him all the food he had, and besought him to help him, saying that he would supply him with whatever he needed. King Yahia was well pleased with this, though he well understood the reason, and firm writings were made to this effect, and then Abenalfange went to Tortosa.

XIV.

And when the King of Zaragoza and the Cid drew nigh unto Valencia, Yahia went out to Welcome them, and thanked them greatly for coming to his assistance; and he lodged them in the great garden, which was called the Garden of Villa Nueva, and honoured them greatly and sent them great presents, and he invited them afterwards to come with their honourable men and be his guests in the Alcazar. But the King of Zaragoza all this while had his eye upon the town, thinking that it would be given up to him as Abencaño had promised; but he saw no sign of this, neither knew he how he could win it. Moreover Yahia had placed his love upon the Cid, and had sent him full noble gifts when he was upon the road, in secret, so that the King of Zaragoza knew not thereof. And the King of Zaragoza asked counsel of the Cid how he might get Valencia into his hands, and besought the Cid to help him. But the Cid made answer, how could that be, seeing that Yahia had received it from the hands of King Don Alfonso, who had given it unto him that he might dwell therein. If indeed King Don Alfonso should give it to the King of Zaragoza, then might the King win it, and he would help him so to do; otherwise he must be against him. When the King heard this he perceived how the Cid stood in this matter, and he left an Alcayde with a body of knights to assist King Yahia, and also to see if he could win the town; and he himself returned to Zaragoza.

XV.

Then the Cid went to besiege the Castle called Xerica, by advice of the King of Zaragoza, that he might have a frontier against Monviedro. This he did because, when the King came to relieve Valencia, Aboeza had covenanted to give up Monviedro unto him, the which he had not done; and the King thought that if he made war upon these Castles they must either yield unto him, or be at his mercy, because they did not belong to the King of Denia. But when Aboeza knew this he sent to Abenalfange the King of Denia, saying that he would give him the Castle; and the King of Denia incontinently came and took possession of it, and Aboeza became his vassal. When the Cid saw this he understood that Valencia must needs be lost, and thought in his heart that he could win the city for himself, and keep it. Then sent he letters to King Don Alfonso, in which he besought him of his mercy not to think it ill that the people who were with him should remain with him, for he would do God service, and maintain them at the cost of the Moors, and whensoever the King stood in need of their service, he and they would go unto him and serve him freely; and at other times they would make war upon the Moors, and break their power, so that the King might win the land. Well was King Don Alfonso pleased at this, and he sent to say that they who were in the Cid's company might remain with him, and that as many as would might go join him. And my Cid went to the King to commune with him, and while my Cid was with him, Don Ramon Berenguer, Lord of Barcelona, came to Zaragoza; and the King gave him great gifts, that he might not place his love upon any other for want; for the King had now put away his love from the Cid, thinking that because of him he had lost Valencia. And presently he sent a force to besiege Valencia under Don Ramon Berenguer; and he had two Bastilles built, one in Liria, which King Yahia had given him when he came to relieve him, and the other in Juballa, and he thought to build another on the side of Albuhera, so that none might enter into the city, neither go out from it. And he re-edified the Castle of Cebolla, that the Count might retire thither if it should be needful; and every day the Count attacked the city, and King Yahia defended himself, looking for the coming of the Cid to help him, according to the covenant which was between them.

XVI.

When the Cid returned from Castille and knew that Valencia was besieged by the French, he went to Tares, which is near Monviedro, and encamped there with his people, who were many in number. And when the Count knew that the Cid was so near, he feared him, holding him to be his enemy. And the Cid sent to him to bid him move from that place and raise the siege of Valencia. The Count took counsel with his knights, and they said that they would rather give battle to the Cid. Howbeit the Cid had no wish to fight with them, because the Count was related to King Don Alfonso, and moreover he had defeated him and made him prisoner heretofore: so he sent a second time, bidding him depart. And the Count seeing that he could not abide there in the Cid's despite, broke up the siege and went his way by Requena, for he would not pass through Zaragoza. Then the Cid went to Valencia, and King Yahia received him full honourably, and made a covenant with him to give him weekly four thousand maravedis of silver, and he on his part was to reduce the Castles to his obedience, so that they should pay the same rents unto him as had been paid unto the former Kings of Valencia; and that the Cid should protect him against all men, Moors or Christians, and should have his home in Valencia, and bring all his booty there to be sold, and that he should have his granaries there. This covenant was confirmed in writing, so that they were secure on one side and on the other. And my Cid sent to all those who held the Castles, commanding them to pay their rents to the King of Valencia as they had done aforetime, and they all obeyed his command, every one striving to have his love.

XVII.

When, the Cid had thus set the land in order he went against the King of Denia, and warred against Denia and against Xativa, and he abode there all the winter, doing great hurt, insomuch that there did not remain a wall standing from Orihuela to Xativa, for he laid every thing waste; and all his booty and his prisoners he sold in Valencia, Then he went towards Tortosa, destroying every thing as he went; and he pitched his camp near unto the city of Tortosa, in a place which in Arabic is called Maurelet, and he cut down every thing before him, orchards and vines and corn. When King Abenalfange saw that the land was thus destroyed, and that neither bread, nor wine, nor flocks would be left him, he sent to Count Ramon Berenguer, beseeching him to gather together a great force, and drive the Cid out of the land, for which service he would give him whatever he might stand in need of. And the Count, thinking now to be revenged of the Cid for his former defeat, and because he had taken from him the rents which he used to receive from the land of Valencia, took what the King gave him, and assembled a great host of the Christians. This was so great a power when the Moors had joined, that they surely thought the Cid would fly before them; for the Moors held that these Frenchmen were the best knights in the world, and the best appointed, and they who could bear the most in battle. When the Cid knew that they came resolved to fight him, he doubted that he could not give them battle because of their great numbers, and sought how he might wisely disperse them. And he got among the mountain values, whereunto the entrance was by a narrow strait, and there he planted his barriers, and guarded them well that the Frenchmen might not enter. The King of Zaragoza sent to tell him to be upon his guard, for Count Ramon Berenguer would without doubt attack him: and the Cid returned for answer, Let him come. On the morrow the Count came nearer, and encamped a league off, in sight of him, and when it was night he sent his spies to view the camp of Ruydiez the Cid. The next day he sent to bid him come out and fight, and the Cid answered, That he did not want to fight nor to have any strife with him, but to pass on with his people. And they drew nearer and invited him to come out, and defied him, saying that he feared to meet them in the field; but he set nothing by all this. They thought he did it because of his weakness, and that he was afraid of them: but what he did was to wear out their patience.

XVIII.

Then the Count sent a letter to the Cid after this fashion: I Count Don Ramón Berenguer of Barcelona, and all my vassals with me, say unto thee, Ruydiez, that we have seen thy letter to King Almescahen of Zaragoza, which thou toldest him to show unto us, that we might have the more cause of quarrel against thee. Before this thou hast done great displeasure unto us, so that we ought at all times to bear ill will against thee. And now while thou hast our goods in thy possession as booty, thou sendest thy letter to King Almescahen, saying that we are like our wives. God give us means to show thee that we are not such. And thou saidst unto him, that before we could be with thee thou wouldst come to us; now we will not alight from our horses till we have taken vengeance on thee, and seen what sort of Gods these mountain crows and daws are, in whom thou puttest thy trust to fight with us; whereas we believe in one God alone, who will give us vengeance against thee. Of a truth, to-morrow morning we will be with thee, and if thou wilt leave the mountain and come out to us in the plain, then wilt thou be, as they call thee, Rodrigo the Campeador. But if thou wilt not do this, thou wilt then be what according to the custom of Castille is called alevoso, and bauzador according to the custom of France; that is to say, a false traitor. And if thou wilt not come down from the mountain it shall not avail thee, for we will not depart from hence till we have thee in our hands, either dead or alive, and we will deal with thee as thou hast done by us, and God in his mercy now take vengeance upon thee for his churches which thou hast destroyed.

XIX.

When the Cid had read this letter he wrote another in reply after this manner: I Ruydiez and my vassals: God save you Count! I have seen your letter in which you tell me that I sent one to King Almescahen of Zaragoza speaking contumeliously of you and of all your vassals; and true it is that I did so speak, and I will tell you for what reason. When you were with him you spake contumeliously of me before him, saying of me the worst you could, and affirming that I did not dare enter the lands of Abenalfange for fear of you. Moreover Ramon de Bajaran, and other of your knights who were with him, spake ill of me and of my vassals before King Don Alfonso of Castille, and you also after this went to King Don Alfonso, and said that you would have fought with me, and driven me out of the lands of Abenalfange, but that I was dismayed, and did not dare do battle with you; and you said unto him, that if it had not been for the love of him, you would not have suffered me to be one day in the land. Now then I say that I thank you because you no longer let me alone for the love of him. Come! here I am; this is the plainest ground among these mountains, and I am ready to receive you.

But I know you dare not come, for Moors and Christians know that I conquered you once, and took you and your vassals, and took from ye all that ye had with ye: and if ye come now ye shall receive the same payment at my hands as heretofore. As for what thou sayest that I am a false traitor, thou lyest, and art a false traitor thyself.

XX.

Greatly was the Count enraged when he read this letter, and he took counsel with his vassals, and in the night time took possession of the mountain above the camp of the Cid, thinking that by this means he might conquer him. On the morrow the Cid sent away certain of his company as if they were flying, and bade them go by such ways that the French might see them, and instructed them what to say when they should be taken. When the French saw them, they pursued and took them, and carried them before the Count, and he asked of them what the Cid would do. Then made they answer that he meant to fly, and had only remained that day to put his things in order for flight, and as soon as night came he would make his escape by way of the mountain. Moreover they said that the Cid did not think Count Ramon had it so much at heart to give him battle, or he would not have awaited till his coming; and they counselled the Count to send and take possession of the passes by which he meant to escape, for so he might easily take him. Then the Frenchmen divided their host into four parts, and sent them to guard the passes, and the Count himself remained with one part at the entrance of the straits. The Cid was ready with all his company, and he had sent the Moors who were with him forward to the passes whither his men had directed the Frenchmen, and they lay in ambush there; and when the Frenchmen were in the strong places, and had begun to ascend, little by little, as they could, they rose upon them from the ambush and slew many, and took others of the best, and among the prisoners was Guirabent, the brother of Giralte the Roman, who was wounded in the face. And the Cid went out and attacked the Count, and the battle was a hard one; the Count was beaten from his horse, nevertheless his men remounted him, and he bade them stand to it bravely; and the battle lasted long time; but at the end, he who was never conquered won the day. And the Cid took a good thousand prisoners; among them was Don Bernalte de Tamaris, and Giralte the Roman, and Ricarte Guillen. And he put them all in irons, and reproached them saying, that he well knew what his chivalry was, and his hardihood, and that he should thus beat them all down; and he said to them that he was in God's service, taking vengeance for the ills which the Moors had done unto the Christians, and had done them no wrong; but they being envious of him, had come to help the Moors, therefore God had helped him, because he was in his service. And he took their tents, and their horses, and their arms, which were many and good; and much gold and silver, and fine linen, and all that they had, so that he and all his company were rich men with the spoils. And when Count Ramon heard in his flight, that the Cid had taken all his chief captains, and that well nigh all his power was either slain or taken, he thought it best to come unto the Cid and trust unto his mercy, and he came full humbly and put himself into his hands. And the Cid received him full well and honoured him greatly, and let him go into his own country. And the Count offered a price for the prisoners which was a full great ransom, and moreover the swords precious above all others, which were made in other times. Bountiful was the Cid when he received this ransom, and great part of it he returned unto them again, and showed them great courtesy, and they did homage to him never to come against him with any man in the world.

XXI.

When Abenalfange the King of Denia and Tortosa heard this, he was so sorely grieved that he fell sick and died. He left one son who was a little one, and the sons of Buxar were his guardians. One of these held Tortosa for the child, and the other held Xativa, and one who was their cousin held Denia.

And they knowing that they could neither live in peace, nor yet have strength for war, unless they could have the love of the Cid, sent humbly to say unto him that if he would do no hurt to their lands they would do whatever he pleased, and pay him yearly what he should think good. And the Cid demanded of them fifty thousand maravedis of silver, every year: and the covenant was made between them, and the whole country from Tortosa to Orihuela was under his protection and at his command. And he fixed the tribute which each Castle was to pay, that it should be certain; and it was as you shall be told. The Lord of Albarrazin was to pay ten thousand, according to covenant as you heard heretofore, and the Lord of Alfuente ten thousand, and Monviedro eight thousand, and Segorbe six thousand, and Xerica four thousand, and Almenara three thousand. Liria at that time paid nothing, for it was in the Lordship of Zaragoza; but the Cid had it in his heart to fight with that King. For every thousand maravedis a hundred more were paid for a Bishop, whom the Moors called Alat Almarian. And you are to know that whatever my Cid commanded in Valencia was done, and whatever he forbad was forbidden. And because the King was sick of a malady which continued upon him long time, so that he could not mount on horseback, and was seen by none, Valencia remained under the command of his Guazil Abenalfarax, whom the Cid had appointed. And then the Cid appointed trusty men in the city who should know to how much the rents amounted, as well those of the land as of the sea; and in every village he placed a knight to protect it, so that none dared do wrong to another, nor take any thing from him. Each of these knights had three maravedis daily. And the people complained greatly of what they gave these knights, and of that also which they paid to King Yahia. Yet were they withal abundantly supplied with bread, and with flocks which the Christians brought in, and with captives both male and female, and with Moorish men and women, who gave great sums for their ransom.

XXII.

Then the Cid sent to the King of Zaragoza, bidding him yield up the Bastilles which he had built against Valencia; and the King returned for answer that he would not until King Yahia had paid him the whole cost which he had been at, when he came to his succour against King Abenalfange. Then the Cid besieged Liria, and the people submitted unto him, that they should pay him yearly two thousand maravedis. And he overran the whole of the King of Zaragoza's country, and brought great spoils to Valencia. Now at this time a Moor called Ali Abenaxa, the Adelantado of the Almoravides, that is to say, of the Moors from beyond sea, came with a great power of the Moors of Andalusia to besiege the Castle of Aledo. This he did because he knew that King Don Alfonso would come to its relief, and he thought that peradventure the King would bring with him so small a force that he might slay or take him. But when the King heard of it he assembled a great host, and sent to the Cid, bidding him come and aid him. And the Cid went to Requena, believing that he should meet the King there; but the King went another way, and the Cid not knowing this tarried some days in Requena expecting him, because that was the road. And when the Moors knew that King Don Alfonso was coming with so great a host to relieve the Castle, they departed, flying. And King Don Alfonso came to the Castle, and when he came there he found that he was short of victuals, and returned in great distress for want of food, and lost many men and many beasts who could not pass the Sierra. Nevertheless he supplied the Castle well with arms, and with such food as he could.

XXIII.

Now they who hated the Cid spake leasing of him to King Don Alfonso, saying that he had tarried in Requena, knowing that the King was gone another way, that so he might give the Moors opportunity to fall upon him. And the King believed them, and was wroth against the Cid, and ordered all that he had in Castille to be taken from him, and sent to take his wife, and his daughters. When the Cid heard this he sent presently a knight to the King to defend himself, saying, that if there were Count or Rico-ome or knight who would maintain that he had a better and truer will to do the King service than he had, he would do battle with him body to body, but the King being greatly incensed would not hear him. And when they who hated the Cid saw this, and knew that the Cid was gone against a Castle near Zaragoza, they besought the King to give them force to go against him; howbeit this the King would not. At this time Ali Abenaxa, the Adelantado of the Almoravides, besieged Murcia, and there was a dearth in the city, and Alvar Fañez who should have relieved them did not, and they were so closely beset that they were compelled to yield up the town. As soon as he had taken Murcia he went against the Castle of Aledo, of which you have heard, and assaulted it vigorously, and took it by force and by famine. And when he had won Murcia and Aledo, he wished to have Valencia also, and they of Valencia, because of the yoke of the Cid, longed to be his vassals, even as the sick man longeth after health. When King Don Alfonso heard what Ali Abenaxa had done, he made ready to go against him. And the Queen his wife, and certain knights who were friends to the Cid, wrote to him that he should now come and serve the King in such a season, that the King might thank him greatly and lay aside his wrath. Having seen these letters the Cid set out from Zaragoza where he was, and went his way with a great host, and advanced as far as Martos, where he found the King. And the King received him honourably, and they continued together till the King passed the Sierra de Elvira, and the Cid went in the plain below before him. And they who wished ill to him said to the King, The Cid came after you like one who was wearied, and now he goes before you. And after this manner they set the King again against him, so that his displeasure was greatly moved. And the Moors did not venture to give him battle, but left the Castle of Aledo and retreated to Murcia, and the King returned to Ubeda. And when the Cid saw that the heart of the King was changed, he returned to Valencia, and the King went back to Toledo.

XXIV.

After this King Don Alfonso drew forth a great host and went towards Valencia, and sent to all the Castles in that land, saying that for five years they should pay him the tribute which they were wont to pay unto the Cid. When the Cid knew this he sent to the King, saying, he marvelled why the King should thus seek to dishonour him, and that he trusted in God soon to make him know how ill he was advised by those about him. And presently the Cid gathered together a full great host both of Moors and of Christians, and entered the land of King Don Alfonso, burning and destroying whatever he found, and he took Logroño, and Alfaro also, and sacked it. While he was at Alfaro, Count Garci Ordoñez and certain other Ricos-omes of Castille sent to say to him, that if he would tarry for them seven days, they would come and give him battle. He tarried for them twelve days, and they did not dare to come; and when the Cid saw this he returned to Zaragoza. Now when King Don Alfonso knew what the Cid had done in his land, and that the Ricos-omes had not dared fight against him, he saw that he had taken an evil counsel when he set his heart against him. And he sent his letters to the Cid saying, that he forgave him all that he had done, seeing that he himself had given the occasion; and he besought him to come to Castille, where he should find all things free which appertained unto him. Much was the Cid rejoiced at these tidings, and he wrote to the King thanking him for his grace, and beseeching him not to give ear to bad counsellors, for he would alway be at his service.

XXV.

Now it came to pass, that by reason of certain affairs the Cid tarried a long time in Zaragoza. And they of Valencia being no longer kept in awe by his presence, complained one to another of the oppressions and wrongs which they endured from him and from his servants, and from Abenalfarax, the Guazil whom he had appointed; and they conspired with an Alcayde who was called Abeniaf. And when Abenalfarax the Guazil understood how Abeniaf cast about to disturb the peace of the city, he would have taken him and cast him in prison; but this he dared not do till the Cid should come, and moreover he weened that upon his coming the disturbance would cease. Now Abeniaf knew that the Guazil was minded to seize him if he could have dared so to do, and he sent his messengers to Ali Abenaxa the Adelantado of the Almoravides, who was now Lord of Murcia, telling him to come to Valencia, and he would deliver the city into his hands. Moreover he took counsel with the Alcayde of Algezira de Xucar, that the Alcayde also should send to Ali Abenaxa, exhorting him to make good speed himself, or to send an Alcayde with a fitting power, and to come to Algezira, which was near, and then presently proceed to Valencia. So soon as Ali Abenaxa had received this message he made speed to come, and as many Castles as were upon his road submitted unto him. When the Alcayde of Denia heard of his coming, and that all these Castles had submitted, he durst not abide there, but fled to Xativa; and Ali Abenaxa took possession of Denia, and he sent his Alcayde to Algezira de Xucar, and took possession of that also. When these tidings came to Valencia, the Bishop who was there, and the forty knights who were with the messenger of the King of Aragon because of the friendship between their King and the Cid, and all the other Christians who were in the city, would no longer abide there, but took of their goods each as much as he could, and went away in fear. And the Guazil was greatly dismayed, neither knew he what course to take, and Yahia, the King, though he was now healed of his malady, neither mounted on horseback, nor appeared abroad. Abenalfarax went unto him and told him the peril in which they stood. And their counsel was, that they should remove all that they had from Valencia and go to the Castle of Segorbe. Then they sent away many beasts laden with goods and with riches, under the care of a nephew of the Guazil and many others, to the Castle of Benaecab, that is to say, the Castle of the Eagle, to be in charge of the Alcayde thereof. And the King and the Guazil bestirred themselves and gathered together foot-soldiers and cross-bow men to defend the Alcazar, and sent speedily to Zaragoza, telling the Cid to come; but he could not set forth so speedily as need was; and the stir which was in the city endured for full twenty days. Then that Alcayde of Ali Abenaxa who was in Algezira de Xucar set forward in the first of the night with twenty horsemen of the Almoravides, and as many more of Algezira, all clad alike in green, that they might all be taken for Almoravides; and they came by day-break to Valencia, to the gate of Tudela, and sounded their drums, and the rumour in the town was that there were full five hundred knights of the Almoravides, and the Guazil was in great fear. And he went to the Alcazar to take counsel with the King, and they gave order that the gates of the town should be barred, and that the walls should be manned.

XXVI.

Then the King's soldiers went to the house of Abeniaf the Alcayde who had sent for the Almoravides, and called unto him to come forth that they might take him before the King; but he was trembling in great fear, and would not come out. And the men of the town came to his help, and when he saw the company that were on his side, he came forth and went with them to the Alcazar, and entered it and took the Guazil of the Cid. And the townsmen ran to the gates and drove away those of the King's party who guarded them; and they strove to beat the gates down, but they could not, and they set fire to them and burnt them. And others let down ropes from the walls, and drew up the Almoravides. King Yahia put on woman's apparel, and fled with his women, and hid himself in a dwelling near unto a bath. And the Almoravides took possession of the Alcazar, and plundered it. One Christian they slew who guarded the gates, and another who was of St. Maria de Albarrazin, who guarded one of the towers of the wall. In this manner was Valencia lost.

XXVII.

Now when Abeniaf saw that all the people were on his side, and obeyed him, his heart grew and he was puffed up, insomuch that he despised those who were as good as himself or better. Albeit he was of good parentage, for his fathers before him had all been Alcaydes ever since Valencia was in the hands of the Moors. And because he knew that the King had not fled out of the town, he made search for him, and found him in the house where he had hidden himself with his women. Now the King when he fled from the Alcazar had taken with him the best of his treasures, pearls, among which was one the most precious and noble that could be, so that nowhere was there a better one to be found, nor so good; and precious stones, sapphires and rubies and emeralds; he had with him a casket of pure gold full of these things; and in his girdle he had hidden a string of precious stones and of pearls, such that no King had so rich and precious a thing as that carkanet. They say that in former times it had belonged to Queen Seleyda, who was wife to Abanarrexit King of Belcab, which is beyond sea; and afterwards it had come to the Kings called Benivoyas, who were Lords of Andalusia; after that King Alimaymon of Toledo possessed it, and gave it to his wife, and she gave it to the wife of her son, who was the mother of this Yahia. Greatly did Abeniaf covet these treasures and this carkanet, and incontinently he thought in his heart that he might take them and none know thereof, which could no ways be done unless he slew King Yahia. When therefore it was night he gave order to cut off his head, and to throw it into a pond near the house in which he had been taken. This was done accordingly, and Abeniaf took the treasures, and they who were set over King Yahia to guard him and murder him, took also each what he could, and concealed it. And the body lay where it had been slain till the following day; but then a good man who grieved for the death of his Lord took it up, and laid it upon the cords of a bed, and covered it with an old horsecloth, and carried it out of the town, and made a grave for it in a place where camels were wont to lie, and buried it there, without gravecloaths and without any honours whatsoever, as if the corpse had been the corpse of a villain.

BOOK VI.

I.

When Abeniaf had slain his Lord, as you have heard, he became haughty like a King, and gave no thought to anything save to building his own houses, and setting guards round about them by day and by night; and he appointed secretaries who should write his secret letters, and chose out a body from among the good men of the city to be his guard. And when he rode out he took with him many knights and huntsmen, all armed, who guarded him like a King; and when he went through the streets the women came out to gaze at him, and shouted and rejoiced in him; and he being elated and puffed up with these vanities, demeaned himself in all things after the manner of a King. This he did for the sake of abasing a certain kinsman of his, who was chief Alcayde, and who was better and wiser than he. Moreover he made no account of the Alcayde of the Almoravides who held the Alcazar, neither took counsel with him concerning anything, and he gave no heed to him except to supply him and his company with their charges, which he did right sparingly.

II.

But when King Yahia was slain, his servants and eunuchs and they of his household fled to Juballa, a Castle which was held by a kinsman of the Guazil Abenalfarax, who lay in prison; other some fled to Zaragoza, and told the Cid all that had befallen. The Cid was greatly grieved when he heard it, and without delay he set forth with all his people, and went as fast as he could go to Juballa, and there they who had escaped from Valencia met him, and besought him to help them to revenge the death of their Lord, saying that they would follow him for life or for death, and do whatsoever he commanded them. Then the Cid sent letters to Abeniaf, saying disdainfully unto him, that by God's help he had kept his Lent well, and accomplished his fast with a worthy sacrifice by murdering the King his master! and he reproached him for the shame he had done the King in casting his head into the pond and letting the body be buried in a dunghill; and at the end of the letter he bade Abeniaf give him his corn which he had left in his granaries at Valencia. Abeniaf returned for answer that his granaries had all been plundered, and that the city now "belonged to the King of the Almoravides;" and he said that if the Cid would serve that King he would do his best to help him that he might win his love. When the Cid read this letter he saw that Abeniaf was a fool, for he had sent to reproach him for the death of his Lord, and the answer which he had returned was concerning another matter; and he then knew that Abeniaf was not a man to keep the power which he coveted. So he sent other letters to him, calling him and all who were with him traitors, and saying that he would never leave from making war against them till he had taken vengeance for the death of King Yahia.

III.

And the Cid sent letters to all the Castles round about, bidding them supply his host with victuals, and do it speedily, or he would do all he could to destroy them. And there was none to gainsay him; and all obeyed his commands in this matter, saving Aboeza Abenlupo, for he was a discreet man, and perceived what was to come, and in what this was to end; moreover he feared that if he should not do as the Cid commanded, the Cid would put him out of the world, and no one would be able to protect him; and if he should do it, then he feared least he should be banished. So he sent to the Cid to say he would do his pleasure, and he sent also to Abenrazin, the Lord of Albarrazin, saying that he would give him Monviedro and the other Castles in his possession, and bidding him make his terms with the Cid, for as touching himself, he desired to have no dispute, but to come off with his company and his own person in peace. When Abenrazin heard this he was well pleased; and he went to Monviedro with all speed, and took possession of the Castle. From the time that King Yahia was slain till this time, was twenty and six days. And when Abenrazin had got possession of the Castle of Monviedro he came to the Cid, and established love with him, and made a covenant that there should be buying and selling between his Castles and the host, and that he would provide food, and that the Cid should not make war upon him. And upon this they made their writings, which were full fast; and Abenrazin returned to his own land, and left one to keep Monviedro for him; and Abenlupo went with him, taking with him his wives and his children and his people and all that he had, and he thought himself well off that he had escaped with his body, for he desired to have nothing to do with the Cid. And the Cid lay before Juballa, and sent out his foragers towards Valencia twice a day; one party went in the morning, and another towards night; and they slew many Moors, and made many prisoners, and made prey of all the flocks which they found without the walls; nevertheless the Cid commanded that no hurt should be done to those of the land of Moya, nor to the husbandmen, but that they who laboured to produce bread and wine should be protected and encouraged; and this he did thinking that what they raised would be for him when he should lay siege unto the town; and he said this to his knights and Adalides and Almocadenes, and took homage of them that they should obey him therein. All this time the Cid held that Castle besieged, so that none could enter in nor come out thereof; and it is said that terms had secretly been made with him to yield it up, but that it was so to be done that the other Moors might believe they had yielded from great necessity, for it was not stored so as to be able to hold out long. And while the Cid lay before Juballa, all the spoil which his Almogavares took they brought to the host, and from the host it was taken and sold at Monviedro. Many laden beasts came every day, and there was plenty in the host.

IV.

Abeniaf gathered together the knights who were natives of the city and vassals to the King whom he had slain, and sent for others who were in Denia, so that in all they were three hundred knights, and maintained them with the bread which was in the granaries of the Cid Ruydiez, and with the rents and possessions of those who had been the King's officers, and who were gone from Valencia, and with the customs; from all these did he give these knights whatsoever they stood in need of. And he took no counsel with the Alcayde of the Almoravides concerning any thing which he did, neither with any one, nor did he care a jot for them. And when the Alcayde and the Almoravides saw that he made himself master in the city, and how every thing that he did was by his own will, they were offended therewith. The sons of Aboegib were offended also: and they and the Almoravides placed their love upon each other, and took counsel together against him, and became of one party, and they bare great hatred against him, and he against them. All this while the Cid lay before Juballa, and every day he scoured the country to the gates of Valencia, early in the morning, and at noon day, and at night, so that he never let them rest. And the three hundred knights whom Abeniaf had collected went out against his foragers, with the men of the town, and the Christians slew many of them, so that there were lamentations daily within the walls, and wailings over the dead that were brought in. And in one of these skirmishes, a rich Moor was taken who was Alcayde of Acala, which is near Torralva, and they gave him grievous torments till he ransomed himself for ten thousand marks of silver; and moreover he gave the houses which he had in Valencia, which were called the houses of Añaya, to be theirs if peradventure the town should be yielded up.

V.

When the Cid knew that there was great hatred between Abeniaf and the Almoravides and the sons of Aboegib, he devised means how to set farther strife between them, and sent privily to proffer his love to Abeniaf on condition that they should expel the Almoravides out of the town; saying, that if he did this, he would remain Lord thereof, and the Cid would help him in this, and would be good to him, as he knew he had been to the King of Valencia, and would defend him. When Abeniaf heard this he was well pleased, thinking that he should be King of Valencia. And he took counsel with Abenalfarax the Guazii of the Cid, whom he held prisoner, and Abenalfarax, with the hope of getting out of prison, counselled him to do thus, and to accept the love of the Cid. Then sent he to the Cid, saying that he would do all which he commanded to gain his love, and he began to stop the allowance of the Almoravides, saying that he could give them nothing, for he had nothing whereof to give: this did he to the end that they might go their way, for he lacked not means.

VI.

At this time Ali Abenaxa, the Alcayde who was in Denia, sent to Abeniaf, saying unto him that he should send of that treasure, and of those jewels which he had taken from King Yahia, to the Miramamolin beyond sea; with the which he would gather together a great power, and cross the sea, and come against the Cid, to help the people of Valencia, and protect them against the Cid, who did so much evil to them all. And Abeniaf took counsel with the men of Valencia concerning this matter, whether he should send this to the Miramamolin beyond sea or not. And the old men advised him that he should, and the others that he should not. And Abeniaf took the treasures, and hid the best part thereof for himself, for none knew what it was; and the rest he sent by his messengers, Abenalfarax the Guazil of the Cid being one; and they took their departure from Valencia with great secrecy, least the Cid should know it and overtake them upon the road. But Abenalfarax devised means to let the Cid know, and sent him a messenger. And the Cid sent horsemen to follow their track, who caught them, and took the treasure, and brought it to the Cid. Greatly did he thank Abenalfarax for having served him so well at that season, and putting the treasure into his hands, and he promised him goodly guerdon; and he made him chief over all the Moors who were his subjects. At this time the Alcayde of Juballa yielded up the Castle to the Cid, and the Cid placed another therein, and went up with his host against Valencia, and encamped in a village which is called Deroncada. And as the seed time was now over, he burnt all the villages round about, and wasted all that belonged to Abeniaf and his lineage, and he burnt the mills, and the barks which were in the river. And he ordered the corn to be cut, for it was now the season, and he beset the city on all sides, and pulled down the houses and towers which were round about, and the stone and wood thereof he sent to Juballa, to make a town there beside the Castle.

VII.

At this time there came the Guazil of the King of Zaragoza to the host of the Cid, bringing with him great treasures which the King had sent for the redemption of the captives, for ruth which he had of them, and also that he might have his reward from God in the other world. He came also to talk with Abeniaf and counsel him that he should give up the city to the King of Zaragoza, and they would send away the Almoravides, and the King would protect him; but Abeniaf would give no ear to this, and the Guazil said unto him that he would repent not having taken this advice. On the second day after this Guazil had arrived, the Cid attacked the suburb which is called Villa Nueva, and entered it by force, and slew many Moors, both men of Andalusia and Almoravides, and plundered all that they found, and pulled down the houses, and the wood and stone the Cid sent to Juballa, and he set a guard there that the Moors might not recover the place. On the morrow the Cid attacked another suburb, which is called Alcudia, and there were a great body of the Moors gathered together there. And he sent a part of his host against the gate of Alcantara, bidding them attack the gate, while he fought against them in Alcadia; and he thought that by God's mercy peradventure he should enter the town. And the Cid with his company rode among that great multitude of the Moors, smiting and slaying without mercy, and the Cid's horse trampled over the dead, and stumbled among them and fell, and the Cid remained afoot. Howbeit they brought him to horse again, and he continued smiting and laying on strenuously, so that the Moors were amazed at the great mortality which he made among them, and maugre all they could do, were fain to fly into the town. And they whom he had sent against the gate of Alcantara, attacked it so bravely that they would have entered the city, if it had not been for the boys and the women, who were upon the wall and in the towers, and threw down stones upon them. And this while the cry went forth in the city, and many horsemen sallied forth and fought with the Christians before the bridge, and the battle lasted from morning until midday, and when they separated, the Cid returned to his camp. And when the Cid had taken food, he returned after the siesta to attack the suburb of Alcudia; and this attack was so vigorous that they who dwelt therein thought the place would be forced, and they began to cry out, Peace! Peace! being in great fear. Then, the Cid bade his men give over the attack, and the good men of the suburb came out to him, and whatsoever terms of security they asked, he granted them; and he took possession of the suburb that night, and set his guards therein; and he commanded his people that they should do no wrong to them of Alcudia, and if any one offended he said that his head should be smitten off; so he returned that night to the camp. And on the morrow he came there, and assembled together the Moors of that place, and comforted them much with his speeches, and promised that he would favour them greatly and not oppress them, and bade them till their fields and tend their flocks securely, saying that he would take only a tenth of the fruit thereof, as their law directed. And he placed a Moor there named Yucef to be his Almoxarife, that is to say, his Receiver. And he gave orders that all Moors who would come and dwell therein might come securely, and they also who would bring food thither for sale, and other merchandize. So much food and much merchandize were brought there from all parts, and that suburb became like a city, and there was plenty therein.

VIII.

Now when the Cid Ruydiez had gotten possession of the suburbs, he cut off from Valencia both the ingress and the egress, and they of the town were greatly straightened, and knew not what they should do, and they repented them that they had not listened to what the King of Zaragoza sent to counsel them, for they had none to help them; and the Almoravides were in the like straight, for they had none to look to, and the pay which they were wont to receive failed, both to them and to the other knights. All this time Abeniaf secretly continued his love with the Cid, for he had not departed from the promise which he had made him to send away the Almoravides, and put himself under his protection. And they took counsel together in this distress, both the Almoravides and the men of the town, how they might obtain the love of the Cid, in whatever manner they could, so that they might remain in peace in the city till they had sent to the Miramamolin beyond sea, and received his commands; and they sent to the Cid to say this. But he made answer that he would make no treaty with them till they had sent away the Almoravides. And they of the town told the Almoravides what the Cid had said, and these Africans were well pleased, being full weary of that place, and said that they would go their way, and that it would be the happiest day of their lives, that, wherein they should depart. So they made their covenant that the Almoravides should be placed in safety, and that they should pay the Cid for all the corn which was in his granaries at the time when King Yahia was slain. And moreover the thousand maravedis per week, which they were wont to pay him should be paid for the whole time which they had been in arms, and also from that time forth. And that the suburb which he had won should be his; and that his host should remain in Juballa so long as they continued in that land. And upon this they made their writings, and confirmed them. And the Almoravides departed from Valencia, and horsemen were sent with them, who conducted them in safety, and the Moors of Valencia were left in peace.

IX.

Then the Cid went with all his host to Juballa, leaving none but such as were to collect his rents with his Almoxarife. And Abeniaf cast about how he might pay the Cid for the corn, and also what else was to be given him. And he made terms with those who held the Castles round about Valencia, that they should pay him the tenth of all their fruits and of all their other rents. Now this was the season for gathering in the fruit, and he appointed men in every place who should look to it, and see it valued, and receive the tenth; a Moor and a Christian did he appoint in every place, who were to receive this, and to gather the corn also into the granaries: and this was done after such manner that the Cid had his tribute well paid. At this time came tidings to Valencia, that the Almoravides were coming again with a great power, and the Cid devised how he might prevent their coming, or if they came how he might fight against them. And he sent to tell Abeniaf to forbid them from coming, for if they should enter the town he could not be Lord thereof, which it was better he should be, and the Cid would protect him against all his enemies. Well was Abeniaf pleased at this; and he held a talk with the Alcayde of Xativa, and with him who held the Castle of Carchayra; and they agreed to be of one voice. And they came to Valencia, and the Cid came to his suburb; and they confirmed love with him in great secrecy. But he who had the Castle of Algezira would not be in this covenant with them and the Cid sent parties into his lands, and did him much evil; and the Alcayde of Juballa went against him, and cut down all his corn and brought it to Juballa, which the Cid had made a great town with a church and with towers, and it was a goodly place; and there he had his corn and his other things, and his rents were all brought thither, and it abounded with all things; and men held it for a great marvel that in so short time he had made so great a town, which was so rich and so plentiful. And the Cid thought to have Valencia if the Almoravides did not come, and for this reason did all that he could to prevent their coming.

X.

At this time Abenrazin the Lord of Albarrazin covenanted with the King of Aragon that the King should help him to win Valencia, and he would give him great treasures; and he gave him in pledge a Castle which is called Toalba. And in this which he did he gained nothing, but he lost the Castle. Now this Abenrazin had made covenant with the Cid, so that they were friends, and the Cid had never done hurt in his lands. And when he knew this that he had done with the King of Aragon, he held himself to have been deceived and dealt falsely with; howbeit he dissembled this, and let none of his company wit, till they had gathered in all the corn from about Algezira de Xucar, and carried it to Juballa. When this was done, he bade his men make ready, and he told them not whither they were to go, and he set forward at night toward Albarrazin, and came to the Fountain. Now that land was in peace, and the dwellers thereof kept neither watch nor ward; and his foragers slew many, and made many prisoners, and drove great flocks and herds, sheep and kine, and brood mares, and prisoners all together, and they carried away all the corn; and they sent all the spoil to Juballa, and it was so great that Valencia and Juballa and all their dependencies were rich with cattle and with other things. While the Cid lay before Albarrazin, as he one day rode forth with five of his knights to disport himself, there came twelve knights out of the town, thinking to slay him or take him. And he pricked forward against them, and encountered them so bravely that he slew twain, and other twain he overthrew, so that they were taken, and the rest were put to flight: but he remained with a wound in his throat from the push of a spear, and they thought he would have died of that wound; and it was three weeks before it was healed.

XI.

Now came true tidings to Valencia that the host of the Almoravides were coming, and that they were now at Lorca, and the son in law of the Miramamolin at their head, for he himself could not come, by reason that he ailed. They of Valencia took courage at these tidings, and waxed insolent, and began to devise how they should take vengeance upon Abeniaf, and upon all those who had oppressed them. And Abeniaf was in great trouble at this which was said openly concerning him, and he sent privily to the Cid, telling him to come as soon as might be. The Cid was then before Albarrazin, doing all the evil that he could, and he brake up his camp and came with his host to Juballa; and Abeniaf and the Alcaydes of Xativa and Carchayra came unto him, and they renewed their covenant to stand by each other, and be of one voice. And they took counsel and made a letter for the leader of the army of the Almoravides, wherein they told him that the Cid had made a treaty with the King of Aragon, whereby the King bound himself to help him against them; and they bade him beware how he came towards Valencia, unless he chose to do battle with eight thousand Christian horsemen, covered with iron, and the best warriors in the world. This did they thinking that he would be dismayed and turn back: but the Moor did not cease to advance, notwithstanding this letter.

XII.

There was a garden nigh unto Valencia which had belonged to Abenalhazis, and the Cid asked Abeniaf to give it him, that he might take his pleasure there when he was disposed to solace himself.

This he did cunningly, that when the Almoravides heard how this garden had been given him which was so nigh unto the city, they should ween that the men of Valencia had given it, and that they were better pleased with his company than with theirs, Abeniaf granted it. And the Cid was wary, and would not enter it till a gateway had been opened into the garden, for the entrance was through narrow streets, and the Cid would not trust himself in those strait places: so Abeniaf ordered the gate to be made, and told the Cid that he would be his host on a day appointed. And Abeniaf bedecked the gate of this garden full richly, and spread costly carpets, and ordered the way to be strewn with rushes, and made a great feast, and expected him all the day, but he did not come. And when it was night he sent to say that he was sick and could not come: and he prayed him to hold him excused. This he did to see whether they of Valencia would murmur against him. And the sons of Aboegib and all the people murmured greatly, and would fain in their hearts have risen against Abeniaf, but they durst not because of the Cid, with whom they would not fall out least he should lay waste all that was without the walls. And they looked daily for the Almoravides, and one day they said, Lo! now they are coming: and on the morrow they said, They are coming not. And in this manner some days past on. And the murmur which there had been concerning the garden died away; and then the Cid entered it, and took possession of the whole suburb of Alcudia round about it: and this he did peaceably, for the Moors and Christians dwelt there together.

XIII.

Now came true tidings that the host of the Almoravides, which was at Lorca, was coming on through Murcia, and that the tarriance which they had made had been by reason of their Captain, who had fallen sick, but he was now healed, and they were advancing fast. And the sons of Aboegib and great part of the people rejoiced in these tidings, and took heart: and Abeniaf was in great fear, and he began to excuse himself to the men of the town, and said unto them to pacify them, that they did him wrong to complain of him for the garden which the Cid had asked of him, inasmuch as he had only given it him to disport himself therein for some days and take his pleasure, and that he would make him leave it again whenever it should please them. Moreover he said, that seeing they were displeased with what he had done, he would take no farther trouble upon him; but would send to break off his covenant with the Cid, and send to bid him look out for others to collect his payments, for he would have the charge no longer. This he said in his cunning, thinking that he should pacify them; but they understood his heart, and they cried aloud against him that they would not stand to his covenant, nor by his counsel, but that the sons of Aboegib should counsel them, and whatsoever they should think good, that would they do. And they gave order to fasten the gates of the town, and to keep watch upon the towers and walls. When Abeniaf saw this he ceased to do as he had been wont for fear of the people and of the sons of Aboegib, and took unto himself a greater company to be his guard. And the war was renewed between the Cid and the people of Valencia.

XIV.

Now came true tidings that the host of the Almoravides was nigh unto Xativa; and the people of Valencia were glad and rejoiced, for they thought that they were now delivered from their great misery, and from the oppression of the Cid. And when he heard these tidings he left the garden and went to the place where his host was encamped, which was called Xarosa, and remained there in his tents, and he was at a stand what he should do, whether to abide the coming of the Almoravides, or to depart; howbeit he resolved to abide and see what would befall. And he gave order to break down the bridges and opea the sluices, that the plain might be flooded, so that they could only come by one way, which was a narrow pass. Tidings now came that the host of the Almoravides was at Algezira de Xucar, and the joy of the people of Valencia increased, and they went upon the walls and upon the towers to see them come. And when night came they remained still upon the walls, for it was dark, and they saw the great fires of the camp of the Almoravides, which they had pitched near unto a place called Bacer; and they began to pray unto God, beseeching him to give them good speed against the Christians, and they resolved as soon as the Almoravides were engaged in battle with the Cid, that they would issue forth and plunder his tents. But our Lord Jesus Christ was not pleased that it should be so, and he ordered it after another guise; for he sent such a rain that night, with such a wind and flood as no man living remembered, and when it was day the people of Valencia looked from the wall to see the banners of the Almoravides and the place where they had encamped, and behold they could see nothing: and they were full sorrowful, and knew not what they should do, and they remained in such a state as a woman in her time of childing, till the hour of tierce, and then came tidings that the Almoravides had turned back, and would not come unto Valencia. For the rains and floods had dismayed them, and they thought the waters would have swept them away, and that the hand of God was against them, and therefore they turned back. And when the people of Valencia heard this they held themselves for dead men, and they wandered about the streets like drunkards, so that a man knew not his neighbour, and they smeared their faces with black like unto pitch, and they lost all thought like one who falls into the waves of the sea. And then the Christians drew nigh unto the walls, crying out unto the Moors with a loud voice like thunder, calling them false traitors and renegados, and saying, Give up the town to the Cid Ruydiez, for ye cannot escape from him. And the Moors were silent, and made no reply because of their great misery.

XV.

Then Abenalfarax, a Moor of Valencia, he who wrote this history in Arabic, took account of the food which was in the city, to see how long it could hold out. And he says that the cafiz of wheat was valued at eleven maravedís, and the cafiz of barley at seven maravedís, and that of pulse or other grain at six; and the arroba of honey at fifteen dineros; and the arroba of carobs the third of a maravedí, and the arroba of onions two thirds of a maravedí, and the arroba of cheese two maravedís and a half, and the measure of oil frhich the Moors call maron, a maravedí, and the quintal of figs five maravedís, and the pound of mutton six dineros of silver, and the pound of beef four. These maravedis were silver ones, for no other money was current among them. The Moors who dwelt in the suburbs carried all the best of their goods into the city, and the rest they buried. And when the Cid was certain that the Almoravides were not coming, he returned again to lodge in the garden, and gave order to spoil the suburbs, save that of Alcudia, because the inhabitants of that had received him without resistance; and the Moors fled into the city with their wives and children. And when the Christians began to plunder the suburbs they of the town came out and plundered also those houses which were nearest unto the walls, so that every thing was carried away and nothing but the timbers left; and then the Christians took that to build them lodgments in the camp; and when the Moors saw this they came out, and carried away what timber they could into the city. And the Christians pulled down all the houses, save only such as could be defended with arrows, and these which they dared not pull down they set fire to by night. And when all the houses had been levelled they began to dig in the foundations, and they found great wealth there, and store of garments, and hoards of wheat; and when the Cid saw this he ordered them to dig every where, so that nothing might be lost. And when all had been dug up the Cid drew nearer to the city, and girt it round about, and there was fighting every day at the barriers, for the Moors came out and fought hand to hand, and many a sword-stroke was given and many a push with the spear. While the Moors were thus beleaguered came letters from the Captain of the Almoravides, saying that he had not turned back to Algezira de Xucar for fear, nor for cowardice, neither as one who fled, but for lack of food, and also by reason of the waters; and that it was his set purpose at all events to succour them and deliver them from the oppression which they endured, and he was preparing to do this with all diligence. And he bade them take courage, and maintain the city. And when the Moors of Valencia heard, these letters they took heart, and joined with the sons of Aboegib, and their resolve was that they would be firm and maintain the city. And they said that Abeniaf had made the Almoravides retreat, because he had told them that there was discord in the town. And Abeniaf kept great watch, having a great guard to secure him, least the people should attempt aught against him. And the price of all things in Valencia was doubled.

XVI.

Then the Cid drew nearer to the walls, so that no man could either enter in or issue out, but whosoever attempted it was either slain or taken. And he gave orders to till all the lands which lay round about Alcudia, for this was now become a great place, even like a city, and the Moors who dwelt there were safe; and tents and shops were made there for all kinds of merchandize, and merchants came there safely from all parts to buy and to sell, so that they who dwelt there were greatly enriched. And justice was administered to all full righteously, so that there was none who could complain of the Cid nor of his Almoxarife, nor of any of his people; and the Moors were judged by their own law, and were not vexed, and he took from them only a tenth. Now came true tidings from Denia that the Almoravides had returned into their own country, and that there was no hope of succour at their hands. And when they of Valencia heard this they were greatly troubled. And they who held the Castles round about came humbly to the Cid, to place their love upon him, and besought him that he would accept tribute from them, and have them under his protection; and he gave orders that they might travel the roads in peace: and in this manner his rents increased, so that he had plenty to give. And he sent to them who held the Castles, bidding them provide him with cross-bow men, and foot-soldiers, to fight against the city; and there was none who dared disobey his bidding, and they sent him cross-bow men and foot-men in great numbers, with their arms and provisions. Thus was Valencia left desolate, and forsaken by all the Moorish people; and it was attacked every day, and none could enter in, neither could any come out; and they were sore distressed, and the waves of death compassed them round about.

XVII.

Then was there a Moor in the city who was a learned man and a wise, and he went upon the highest tower, and made a lamentation, and the words with which he lamented he put in writing, and it was rendered afterwards from the Arabic into the Castillian tongue, and the lamentation which he made was this:

Valencia! Valencia! trouble is come upon thee, and thou art in the hour of death; and if peradventure thou shouldst escape, it will be a wonder to all that shall behold thee.

But if ever God hath shown mercy to any place, let him be pleased to show mercy unto thee; for thy name was joy, and all Moors delighted in thee and took their pleasure in thee.

And if it should please God utterly to destroy thee now, it will be for thy great sins, and for the great presumption which thou hadst in thy pride.

The four corner stones whereon thou art founded would meet together and lament for thee, if they could!

Thy strong wall which is founded upon these four stones trembles, and is about to fall, and hath lost all its strength.

Thy lofty and fair towers which were seen from far, and rejoiced the hearts of the people,...little by little they are falling.

Thy white battlements which glittered afar off, have lost their truth with which they shone like the sunbeams.

Thy noble river Guadalaver, with all the other waters with which thou hast been served so well, have left their channel, and now they run where they should not.

Thy water courses, which were so clear and of such great profit to so many, for lack of cleansing are choked with mud.

Thy pleasant gardens which were round about thee;...the ravenous wolf hath gnawn at the roots, and the trees can yield thee no fruit.

Thy goodly fields, with so many and such fair flowers, wherein thy people were wont to take their pastime, are all dried up.

Thy noble harbour, which was so great honour to thee, is deprived of all the nobleness which was wont to come into it for thy sake.

The fire hath laid waste the lands of which thou wert called Mistress, and the great smoke thereof reacheth thee.

There is no medicine for thy sore infirmity, and the physicians despair of healing thee.

Valencia! Valencia! from a broken heart have I uttered all these things which I have said of thee.

And this grief would I keep unto myself that none should know it, if it were not needful that it should be known to all.

XVIII.

Now all the trouble and distress which the men of Valencia endured, pleased Abeniaf well, because they had forsaken him and followed the sons of Aboegib; and he said that it did not behove a man to give advice unto those who would not listen to it, and that if the people had hearkened to him they would not have been brought to this misery; and what evil they endured was because of the sons of Aboegib, who lacked wit to be well with any one, or to do any thing. These things Abeniaf said daily to all who came to visit him: so that the people great as well as little began to talk thereof, saying that Abeniaf spake truly. And the Christians fought against them every day, and prest them close, and the price of food increased daily: and they withdrew themselves from the love of the sons of Aboegib, and thought that they had been ill advised to follow their counsel, and that because of them all this evil was come upon them, and they held them for fools. And the people cried out upon Abeniaf that he should forgive them for having forsaken him, and that he should protect them, and devise means for their deliverance from this great trouble. And Abeniaf said that he would have nothing to do with them more than as one of them; for if they were in trouble, so was he: and what they stood in fear of, that did he fear also; and that he could not give counsel to men who were divided among themselves; and he said unto them that they must agree among themselves, and be all of one mind to do one of these two things;...either to forsake the sons of Aboegib and their counsel; or to stand by it. And when he should see that they no longer opposed him with their evil counsels and the bad way in which they were going on, that he would then take counsel for them in such guise that they should be at peace; for they knew how they had sped so long as they let him direct them, and he trusted in God so to speed as that they should have no war with the Cid, neither with any other. And they made answer with one accord that they would trust in him and obey him, and do all which he should command, for it had alway been well with them when they followed his advice.

XIX.

Then the men of Valencia made Abeniaf their Adelantado, and promised to abide by his counsel; howbeit this could not lightly be done, for many of the people held with the others. And when Abeniaf saw that they would have him for their chief, he said that they should make a writing, and the chief persons of the town confirm it with their names; and the people accorded that it should be so, and it was done accordingly. Then he made offers to the Cid that they should pay him tribute, and took counsel with him how to put the sons of Aboegib, and those who held with them, out of the town; and their counsel was, that the Cid should draw nigh to the walls, and speak unto the men of the town, saying, that so long as they followed after the ways of the sons of Aboegib, he would never grant them his love; and that all the evil which he did unto them was because of them, and because they were guided by them and by their evil counsel. And if they desired to speed well they should send away the sons of Aboegib, and take Abeniaf to be their chief, and give ear unto him. And the Cid came nigh unto the walls and said these things, and moreover that he had great ruth for them, for he loved them well; and if they would do according to his words he would help them and protect them, as he had been wont to do in the days of King Yahia; and he bade them look well to what they were doing, and not suffer themselves to be brought to destruction. And Abeniaf also said these things to those of his household and to all those who talked with him, and asked of them why they would let themselves be brought to destruction by the counsel of foolish men and unwise. And this he said so often that they thought it was truth, and they besought him that as he was their Adelantado now, he would devise means for their deliverance, and how they might live in peace; and he made answer that they were not to think he had forgotten this, for he had laboured greatly with the Cid to obtain his love for them, but the Cid had sworn that they should never have his love till they had put the sons of Aboegib out of the town; when they had done that, he would do whatsoever they should think good, but till they had done it there should be no covenant between him and them. But when the men of the town heard this they murmured greatly, and said that he demanded a hard thing, and that it were better they should all die than do this; and they talked concerning this matter three days, being in doubt what they should do. And when Abeniaf saw that the people were thus at a stand, he took counsel privily with the Cid, and with the knights, and the good men who were on his side, how he might take them. And one of the chief persons of Abeniaf's household went out with a great company of horse and foot to seize the sons of Aboegib; and they when they knew this, took shelter in the house of an Alfaqui, that is to say, one learned in the law, who was held in much honour by the Moors; and in this house, which was surrounded with an embattled wall, they thought with the little company that they had with them, to defend themselves, till the cry could go forth through the city, and their friends come to their succour. And they who went to take them set fire to the outer gates, and many of the baser sort gathered together to see what the stir was. And they ascended the roof and threw down tiles upon the assailants till they made them take shelter under the eaves, and then the house was forced, and they plundered all that they could find, and laid hands on the sons of Aboegib and carried them to prison. All this was done before the cry could go forth through the town; and all the kinsmen of the sons of Aboegib were taken also: they were kept that day in prison, and when it was night they were taken to the Cid, to his lodging in Alcudia, and delivered into his hands.

XX.

On the morrow there was a great stir among the men of the town, and they were greatly troubled at this foul thing which Abeniaf had done. But Abeniaf thinking that he should now have his desire, and that all was done, took horse and rode forth with all his company to the Bridge-end, to see Ruydiez the Cid. And the Bishop, as he was called, of Albarrazin, came to meet him with a great company of knights, being the chiefs of the company of the Cid, and they did great honour unto him, thinking that he would give them something. And they brought him to the lodging of the Cid, which was in the Garden of the New Town; and the Cid came out to meet him at the garden gate, and embraced him, and made much of him. And the first thing which he said, was, to ask him why he had not put on kingly garments, for King he was: and he bade him take off the coif which he wore, for it was not what beseemed him now, and made semblance as if he would have held his stirrups. And they stood talking awhile. Now the Cid thought that Abeniaf would not come to him with empty hands, and looked that he should give him of the treasures and jewels that he had taken from King Yahia whom he had slain; but when he saw that he brought nothing, then began the Cid to talk of terms, and said unto him that if he desired to have his love, and that there should be peace between them, he must divide with him the rents of the town, as well what was collected within as without, and that he would have his own Almoxarife to see to this and collect his share. And Abeniaf made answer that it should be so. And the Cid demanded of him his son as hostage, that he might keep him in Juballa, for otherwise he said he could not be secure. And Abeniaf agreed to this also; so they parted for that day, having appointed that they should meet on the morrow, and confirm this covenant by writings so that it should be good. Then Abeniaf returned into the city, full sorrowful and taking great thought; and then he saw the foolishness that he had done in sending away the Almoravides out of the land, and in putting his trust in men of another law. And on the morrow the Cid sent for him that he should come out and confirm the covenant; but Abeniaf sent him word that he would not give him his son, even though he knew he should lose his head for refusing. And the Cid sent him a letter with great threats, saying, that since he had thus deceived him, there should never more be love between them, nor would he ever believe aught which he should say. And then the hatred between them waxed very great. And the Cid sent unto that Moor who had taken the sons of Aboegib and bade him leave the town, and go unto the Castle which was called Alcala; and he obeyed and went thither, for he dared not do otherwise than as the Cid commanded. And he did great honours to the sons of Aboegib and to their kinsmen, and gave orders that they should be provided with all things which they needed, and gave them garments, and promised that he would be their great friend. At this time three good men of Valencia died, who were the most honourable of the town and of the most discretion, and Abeniaf was left as Chief, for there was none to gainsay him.

XXI.

And the Cid made war afresh upon the city as cruelly as he could, and the price of bread was now three times as great as it had been at the beginning; the load of wheat was worth an hundred maravedís of silver, and the pound of flesh was a maravedí. And the Cid drew nigh unto the walls, so as to fight hand to hand with the townsmen. And Abeniaf waxed proud and despised the people, and when any went to make complaint before him, and ask justice at his hands, he dishonoured them, and they were evil entreated by him. And he was like a King, retired apart, and trobadors and gleemen and masters disported before him which could do the best, and he took his pleasure. And they of the town were in great misery, from the Christians who warred upon them from without, and the famine whereof they died within. Moreover Abeniaf oppressed them greatly, and he took unto himself all the goods of those who died, and he made all persons equal, the good and the bad, and took from all all that he could; and those who gave him nothing he ordered to be tormented with stripes, and cast into rigorous prisons, till he could get something from them. And he had no respect neither for kinsman nor friend. There was but one measure for all, and men cared nothing now for their possessions, so that the sellers were many and the buyers none. And with all these miseries the price of food became exceeding great, for the cafiz of wheat was priced at ninety maravedis, and that of barley at eighty, and that of painick eighty and five, and that of all pulse sixty, and the arroba of figs seven, and of honey twenty, and of cheese eighteen, and of carobs sixteen, and of onions twelve, and the measure of oil twenty: flesh there was none, neither of beast nor of anything else; but if a beast died, the pound was worth three maravedis. And they were so weak with hunger that the Christians came to the walls and threw stones in with the hand, and there was none who had strength to drive them back.

XXII.

And the Cid having it at heart to take the town, let make an engine, and placed it at one of the gates, and it did great hurt both to the walls and within the town; and the Moors made other engines, with the which they brake that of the Cid. And the Cid in his anger let make three engines, and placed them at the three gates of the town, and they did marvellous great hurt. And food waxed dearer every day, till at last dear nor cheap it was not to be had, and there was a great mortality for famine; and they eat dogs and cats and mice. And they opened the vaults and privies and sewers of the town, and took out the stones of the grapes which they had eaten, and washed them, and ate them. And they who had horses fed upon them. And many men, and many women, and many children watched when the gates were open, and went out and gave themselves into the hands of the Christians, who slew some, and took others, and sold them to the Moors in Alcudia; and the price of a Moor was a loaf and a pitcher of wine: and when they gave them food, and they took their fill, they died. Them that were stronger they sold to merchants who came there by sea from all parts. And the Moors of Alcudia, and of the town which the Cid had made there, had plenty of all things, and as great as was their abundance, even so great was the misery of those in the town: and they spake the verse which sayeth, If I go to the right the water will destroy me, and if I go to the left the lion will kill me, and if I turn back there is the fire.

XXIII.

Now the Moors of Valencia being in this great misery because of the siege which the Cid laid unto the town, Abeniaf bethought him that he would send a messenger to the King of Zaragoza, and beseech him to come to his succour, even as he had succoured the grandson of Alimaymon, when the Lord of Denia and Tortosa came against him. And the good men of the town took counsel whether they should say in these letters, To you the King, or whether they should humble themselves before him and call him Lord; and they debated upon this for three days, and agreed that they would call him Lord, that he might have the more compassion upon them. And though Abeniaf was troubled at heart at this determination, nevertheless he said in the letter as they had appointed. And he called a Moor who spake the mixed language, and instructed him how to get out of the city by night, so that the Christians might not see him, and told him that when he had given that letter to the King of Zaragoza, the King would give him garments, and a horse, and a mule to ride on, and that he himself would show favour unto him as long as he lived. So the messenger departed with the letter. And the famine in the town waxed greater, and food was not now bought by the cafiz, neither by the fanega, but by ounces, or at most by the pound. And the pound of wheat cost a maravedí and a half, and that of barley a maravedi, and that of painick a maravedi and a quarter, and of pulse a maravedi, and of flax-seed three parts of a maravedi, and of cheese three dineros, and of honey three, and of figs one; and the panilla of oil was eight dineros, and the pound of colewort five, and the ounce of carobs three parts of a dinero, and the ounce of onions the same, and the head of garlick the same; and a pound of beast's flesh was six maravedis, and grape-stones were half a dinero the pound, and the skins of kine and of beasts five dineros; the dinero was silver, for there was no money current save silver and gold.

XXIV.

When the King of Zaragoza saw the letter which Abeniaf and the men of Valencia had sent him, he gave no heed to it, neither cared he for the messenger, neither did he give him even a draught of water for his reward. And the messenger waited for his answer from day to day for three weeks, and he dared not depart without it for fear least Abeniaf should slay him; and he thought also that some of the King's people would come out after him and slay him upon the way; and he was urgent for his answer, and began at last to cry aloud at the gate of the King's house, so that the King asked of what that messenger was making his complaint. Then they told the King that he wanted his answer that he might be gone. And the King wrote an answer and said, that this aid which they besought of him he could not give till he had sent to ask help of King Don Alfonso of Castille, for he could not else venture to do battle with the Cid. And he exhorted them to defend themselves the best they could while he procured horsemen from King Don Alfonso to help them, and that they should from time to time send him word how they went on. So the messenger returned in great sorrow that he had sped no better, and that nothing had been given him as Abeniaf had promised: and all this which the King of Zaragoza said was only delay, and meant nothing. And the famine now waxed so great, that there was no food to sell, and many died of hunger. And many for great misery went out to the Christians, recking not whether they should be made captive, or slain, for they thought it better to be slain than to perish for lack of food. And Abeniaf searched all the houses in the town for food, and where he found any store, he left only what would suffice for a fortnight, and took the rest, saying that in that time the King of Zaragoza would come and relieve them, for that he only tarried to collect great store of food, that he might bring it with him. This he said to keep the people quiet, and to encourage them. And of the food which he carried away he took the most part for himself and for his guards, and the rest he ordered to be sold in such manner that none should buy more than would suffice him for the day. And what he took he did not pay for, and when the people demanded payment he put them off till another day; and he bade them not complain, for they would be relieved from this misery, and then he would pay them well. And they who had any food left buried it for fear, and for this reason there was none to be bought, neither dear nor cheap. And they who had nothing else, ate herbs, and leather, and electuaries from the apothecaries which they bought at a great price, and the poor ate the dead bodies.

XXV.

Now Abeniaf had no hope of succour save only from the King of Zaragoza, who had sent to bid him hold out; and he sent to him every night to tell him of the great misery which there was in Valencia, and the King of Zaragoza returned for answer that King Don Alfonso had sent him a great body of horsemen with Garcia Ordoñez, and would come himself after them; and he sent in this letter another letter written with his own hand, and which was to be shown to the good men of the town, privily; and he said therein, with great oaths to confirm it, that he would without fail come and deliver them, for it was a great grief to him to think what they endured, and that this was as great sorrow to him, as theirs could be. And certain of the King's favourites wrote to Abeniaf also after the same manner, telling him that he would surely come; howbeit one of his favourites who had compassion upon the men of Valencia sent a covert message to warn them, saying, That the King of Zaragoza would build a tower in Alcudia de Tudela; the meaning of this was, that all the King said, was only to put them off. Abeniaf did not understand it, and sent to ask him what it was that he had said; but the other made him no reply. Then the King of Zaragoza sent two messengers to the Cid with jewels and rich presents, and besought him that he would not distress the men of Valencia so greatly, and also that he would let his messengers enter the town that they might speak with Abeniaf. This the Cid would not permit; howbeit they found means to send in a letter, saying, Wit ye that I send to entreat the Cid that he will not do so great evil unto you, and I give him jewels and rich presents that he may do my will in this, and I believe that he will do it. But if he should not, I will gather together a great host, and drive him out of the land. Howbeit these were but dissembling words, for the King of Zaragoza and the Cid were friends and were of one accord, that the Cid should take Valencia and give it the King, who should give him great treasures in return.

XXVI.

Then the Cid began to treat with a great Moor of the town, named Abenmoxiz that he should rise up against Abeniaf, and kill him or deliver him into his hands, and that he would make him Lord over Valencia, and the country as far as Denia. And Abenmoxiz took counsel with his friends, and they advised him that he should do this: but Abeniaf knew of their counsel, and took them, and put them in prison, and gave them in charge to two of his household in whom he had great trust. And Abenmoxiz talked with his keepers, and told them all that he proposed to do, and promised them, if they would release him, to reward them greatly when he had succeeded, saying, that he undertook this with the consent and advice of the King of Zaragoza: so they were persuaded and promised to join with him. And when it was night Abenmoxiz and his friends and the two keepers agreed to seize the Alcazar, which was the place wherein they were imprisoned, and to beat the alarm, and raise a cry for the King of Zaragoza; and they thought the men of the town would join with them, and then they would go to the house of Abeniaf and lay hands on him. And they did accordingly, and beat a drum, and sent a cryer upon the tower of the Mosque to bid all the people assemble at the Alcazar. And when the people heard that drum and that cryer they were in great fear, and knew not what to think: and they assembled some to guard their own houses, other some to guard the tower, till they knew what it was. And when Abeniaf heard it, he was greatly dismayed, and he asked of all whom he found at his gates, what the uproar was, and what this thing might be. In short time all they who were on his side, both horse and foot, assembled together, and then they knew what it was; and he bade them go to the Alcazar and take Abenmoxiz, and all that held with him. Abenmoxiz this while was at the gate of the Alcazar with his little company, thinking that the whole town would join him; and behold Abeniaf's company came up and charged him; and he thought to defend himself with the few that were with him, but the most part fled, and he with four others were taken; and they led them with great shame to the house of Abeniaf, who sent him to prison, and gave orders to smite off the heads of the others. And Abeniaf sent to lay hands on all whom he suspected, and took from them all that they had. And he sent messengers to the King of Zaragoza, to tell him what had chanced, and they took with them Abenmoxiz prisoner, and they were charged to remain at Zaragoza, and send him true tidings from thence.

XXVII.

Now there was no food to be bought in the city, and the people were in the waves of death: and men were seen to drop and die in the streets, and the Place of the Alcazar round about the walls thereof was full of graves, and there was no grave which had fewer than ten bodies in it. As many as could fled out of the town, and delivered themselves up to the Christians to be made prisoners. The Cid thought that they who were the Chiefs within the walls, thrust out the poor and feeble, that they might be able to hold out longer; and it troubled him, for he thought to take the town by starving it, and he feared the coming of the Almoravides. Sometimes it troubled him, and at other times he seemed pleased that the Moors should come out and give themselves prisoners to his people. Now it befel that once, at such time as it seemed to please him, some of the chief men of the town came out in this manner, and counselled him that he should attack it, for they said the men at arms were few, and weak for hunger, and that he might presently win it: and the Cid took thought upon this matter, and resolved to do as they said; and he gathered together his host and advanced against the gate which is called Belfanhanes, that is to say, the Gate of the Snake, and they drew nigh unto the wall. And all the people of the town assembled, even all the force which was therein, and threw down stones from the gate and from the wall, and shot their arrows, so that neither stone nor arrow fell in vain; and the Cid and they who had advanced with him went into a bath which was near the wall, to be under cover from the arrows. And Abeniaf's company opened the gate and sallied out, seeing that the stones and arrows from the wall had hurt many, and made the Christians draw back; and the Cid and they who were with him remained in the bath, being shut up there, for they could not go out by the door where at they had entered, and they broke through the wall on the other side, and the Cid escaped that way, being thus put to rout. Then he thought himself ill advised in having attacked the town, and in putting himself into a place from whence he had escaped with such great danger; and he held that the worst war which he could make upon the men of Valencia was to let them die of hunger. So he ordered proclamation to be made so loud that all the Moors upon the walls could hear, bidding all who had come out from the town to return into it, or he would burn as many as he should find; and saying also that he would slay all who came out from that time forth. Nevertheless they continued to let themselves down from the walls, and the Christians took them without his knowledge. But as many as he found he burnt alive before the walls, so that the Moors could see them; in one day he burnt eighteen, and cast others alive to the dogs, who tore them in pieces. They who could hide any sent them away by sea and by land to be sold; the most whom they sent were young men and girls, for others they would not take; and many virgins they kept for themselves. And if they knew that any who came out, had left kinsmen or friends in the town who would give any thing for them, they tortured them before the walls, or hung them from the towers of the Mosques which were without the city, and stoned them; and when they in the town saw this they gave ransom for them, that they might be permitted to dwell in Alcudia with the Moors who were in peace with the Cid. This continued for two months, till there were only four beasts left in the town, and one was a mule of Abeniaf's, and another was a horse of his son's; and the people were so wasted that there were but few who had strength to mount the wall.

XXVIII.

The company of Abeniaf and of his kinsmen despaired now of holding out, and of the help of the King of Zaragoza, or of the Almoravides, and they desired rather to die than endure this misery. And the good men of the city, as many as were left, went to an Alfaqui, who was a good man, and one who was held in great esteem, and besought him to give them counsel, for he saw their great distress, and how they were out of all hope of succour; and they besought him that he would go to Abeniaf, and know of him what he thought to do, or what hope he had, that he let them all perish thus. The Alfaqui gave ear to them, and said that if they would all hold together, and be of one heart, and show great anger at having been brought to this misery, he would do all he could to relieve them; and they promised to do whatever he should advise. Now Abeniaf knew of the talk which the good men of the town had had with the Alfaqui, and understood that it was because of the great misery which they endured; and he thought in his heart that he would humble himself, and do whatever his people should think good. And the Alfaqui thought that happy man was his dole now that the people had committed themselves to his guidage, and he went to Abeniaf and communed with him, and their accord was to give up all hope of succour. And Abeniaf put himself in the hands of the Alfaqui, that he should go between him and the Cid and the people of Valencia, and make the best terms for them that he could, seeing that they could no longer hold out, and maintain the town.

XXIX.

Here the history relates that at this time Martin Pelaez the Asturian came with a convoy of laden beasts, carrying provisions to the host of the Cid; and as he passed near the town the Moors sallied out in great numbers against him; but he, though he had few with him, defended the convoy right well, and did great hurt to the Moors, slaying many of them, and drove them into the town. This Martin Pelaez who is here spoken of, did the Cid make a right good knight, of a coward, as ye shall hear. When the Cid first began to lay siege to the city of Valencia, this Martin Pelaez came unto him; he was a knight, a native of Santillana in Asturias, a hidalgo, great of body and strong of limb, a well made man and of goodly semblance, but withal a right coward at heart, which he had shown in many places when he was among feats of arms. And the Cid was sorry when he came unto him, though he would not let him perceive this; for he knew he was not fit to be of his company. Howbeit he thought that since he was come he would make him brave whether he would or not. And when the Cid began to war upon the town, and sent parties against it twice and thrice a day, as ye have heard, for the Cid was alway upon the alert, there was fighting and tourneying every day. One day it fell out that the Cid and his kinsmen and friends and vassals were engaged in a great encounter, and this Martin Pelaez was well armed; and when he saw that the Moors and Christians were at it, he fled and betook himself to his lodging, and there hid himself till the Cid returned to dinner. And the Cid saw what Martin Pelaez did, and when he had conquered the Moors he returned to his lodging to dinner. Now it was the custom of the Cid to eat at a high table, seated on his bench, at the head. And Don Alvar Fañez, and Pero Bermudez, and other precious knights, ate in another part, at high tables, full honourably, and none other knights whatsoever dared take their seats with them, unless they were such as deserved to be there; and the others who were not so approved in arms ate upon estrados, at tables with cushions. This was the order in the house of the Cid, and every one knew the place where he was to sit at meat, and every one strove all he could to gain the honour of sitting to eat at the table of Don Alvar Fañez and his companions, by strenuously behaving himself in all feats of arms; and thus the honour of the Cid was advanced. This Martin Pelaez, thinking that none had seen his badness, washed his hands in turn with the other knights, and would have taken his place among them. And the Cid went unto him, and took him by the hand and said, You are not such a one as deserves to sit with these, for they are worth more than you or than me; but I will have you with me: and he seated him with himself at table. And he, for lack of understanding, thought that the Cid did this to honour him above all the others. On the morrow the Cid and his company rode towards Valencia, and the Moors came out to the tourney; and Martin Pelaez went out well armed, and was among the foremost who charged the Moors, and when he was in among them he turned the reins, and went back to his lodging; and the Cid took heed to all that he did, and saw that though he had done badly he had done better than the first day. And when the Cid had driven the Moors into the town he returned to his lodging, and as he sate down to meat he took this Martin Pelaez by the hand, and seated him with himself, and bade him eat with him in the same dish, for he had deserved more that day than he had the first. And the knight gave heed to that saying, and was abashed; howbeit he did as the Cid commanded him: and after he had dined he went to his lodging and began to think upon what the Cid had said unto him, and perceived that he had seen all the baseness which he had done; and then he understood that for this cause he would not let him sit at board with the other knights who were precious in arms, but had seated him with himself, more to affront him than to do him honour, for there were other knights there better than he, and he did not show them that honour. Then resolved he in his heart to do better than he had done heretofore. Another day the Cid and his company and Martin Pelaez rode toward Valencia, and the Moors came out to the tourney full resolutely, and Martin Pelaez was among the first, and charged them right boldly; and he smote down and slew presently a good knight, and he lost there all the bad fear which he had had, and was that day one of the best knights there; and as long as the tourney lasted there he remained, smiting and slaying and overthrowing the Moors, till they were driven within the gates, in such manner that the Moors marvelled at him, and asked where that Devil came from, for they had never seen him before. And the Cid was in a place where he could see all that was going on, and he gave good heed to him, and had great pleasure in beholding him, to see how well he had forgotten the great fear which he was wont to have. And when the Moors were shut up within the town, the Cid and all his people returned to their lodging, and Martin Pelaez full leisurely and quietly went to his lodging also, like a good knight. And when it was the hour of eating the Cid waited for Martin Pelaez, and when he came, and they had washed, the Cid took him by the hand and said, My friend, you are not such a one as deserves to sit with me from henceforth, but sit you here with Don Alvar Fañez, and with these other good knights, for the good feats which you have done this day have made you a companion for them; and from that day forward he was placed in the company of the good. And the history saith that from that day forward this knight Martin Pelaez was a right good one, and a right valiant, and a right precious, in all places where he chanced among feats of arms, and he lived alway with the Cid, and served him right well and truly. And the history saith, that after the Cid had won the city of Valencia, on the day when they conquered and discomfited the King of Seville, this Martin Pelaez was so good a one, that setting aside the body of the Cid himself, there was no such good knight there, nor one who bore such part, as well in the battle as in the pursuit. And so great was the mortality which he made among the Moors that day, that when he returned from the business the sleeves of his mail were clotted with blood, up to the elbow; insomuch that for what he did that day his name is written in this history, that it may never die. And when the Cid saw him come in that guise, he did him great honour, such as he never had done to any knight before that day, and from thenceforward gave him a place in all his actions and in all his secrets, and he was his great friend. In this knight Martin Pelaez was fulfilled the example which saith, that he who betaketh himself to a good tree, hath good shade, and he who serves a good Lord winneth good guerdon; for by reason of the good service which he did the Cid, he came to such good state that he was spoken of as ye have heard: for the Cid knew how to make a good knight, as a good groom knows how to make a good horse. The history now leaves to speak of him, and returns to the accord of the Alfaqui and Abeniaf, which they propounded unto the Cid.

XXX.

This Alfaqui sent his messengers to an Almoxarife of the Cid whose name was Abdalla Adiz; who was a good man and one whom the Cid loved, and who never left him after he had obtained his favour. And when Abdalla Adiz heard that they wished to propose terms, he spake with the Cid upon this matter, and the Cid bade him enter the town, and speak with them, and know of them what they would have. And he went into the town, and spake with them as the Cid had commanded, and came out again, and reported unto him what they had said, till he had made terms between them, Abeniaf sent three good men with him to confirm the terms which were made, and the covenant was after this manner, that they of Valencia should send messengers to the King of Zaragoza, and to Ali Abenaxa who was Adelantado of the Almoravides and Lord of Murcia, beseeching them to succour them within fifteen days; and if within that time they were not succoured they should then give up the city to the Cid, with such conditions, that Abeniaf should remain mighty in the town, as he had been before, his person being secure and all that he had, and his wives, and his children, and that he should remain Veedor, that is to say. Overseer, of all the rents of the town, he and the Almoxarife of the Cid, and a Moor who was called Musa should be Guazil of the town; this Musa had looked after the affairs of the Cid in the time of King Yabia, and never forsook him after the death of the King his

Lord; and the Cid made him Alcayde of a Castle, and alway found him loyal, and at his service, and for this reason trusted he in him so as to make him Guazil, who should keep the keys of the town, with a guard of Almocadenes, and of Christian foot-men of Almogavares who had been born in the land of the Moors. And it was appointed that the Cid should dwell in Juballa, in the town which he had made, and that he should alter none of their privileges, nor of their customs, nor the rents which they paid, nor their money.

XXXI

Presently on the morrow they sent five good men as messengers to the King of Zaragoza, and as many more to Murcia; and it had been covenanted that neither of these messengers should take with him more than fifty maravedís for his journey, and that they should go by sea as far as Denia, in a ship of the Christians, and from thence by land. These messengers embarked with their company on board that ship, and the Cid sent orders to the master thereof not to sail till he came; and the Cid came himself in his own body and bade them search the messengers to see if they took with them more than had been agreed; and he found upon them great riches in gold and in silver and in pearls and in precious stones; part was their own, and part belonged to other merchants in the city, who thought to send it to Murcia, not being minded to abide in Valencia: and he took it all, leaving them no more than fifty maravedís each, according to the covenant. This was the price of food on the day when these messengers departed: the pound of wheat was three maravedís, and the pound of barley one and a half, and the pound of painick three, saving a quarter; the ounce of cheese three dineros, and the ounce of hemp seed four, and the pound of colewort one maravedí and two dineros of silver, and the pound of neat-skin one maravedí. In the whole town there was only one mule of Abeniaf's, and one horse: another horse which belonged to a Moor he sold to a butcher for three hundred and eighty doblas of gold, bargaining that he should have ten pounds of the flesh. And the butcher sold the flesh of that horse at ten maravedís the short pound, and afterwards at twelve, and the head for twenty doblas of gold.

The Moors of Valencia were now something comforted, for they weened that they should receive help, and the Christians did not now war upon them; nevertheless they kept guard, and went the rounds, as before, and waited for the day appointed, as one who looked to be released from prison. And for this reason men began to bring out the food which they had hidden, and to sell of it, and thus they went on til the time expired, and the messengers were not returned. And Abeniaf besought them that they would wait yet three days more, but they made answer that they would not, for they could bear it no longer. And the Cid sent unto them bidding them yield up the town, as they had covenanted to do; and he swore with great oaths, that if they delayed a single hour after the time was expired, he would not keep the terms which he had made, and moreover that he would slay the hostages; nevertheless they let a day pass over and above the term. And then they who made the covenant with the Cid went out unto him and besought him to come and receive the town, but the Cid said wrathfully to them that he was not bound to keep the terms, seeing they had let the time appointed pass; and they yielded themselves into his hands that he should do with them according to his pleasure; then he was moved to compassion, and had pity upon them. And Abeniaf and other good men came out, and the writings were made and were confirmed on both sides, by the Chiefs of the Christians and of the Moors, and the gates were opened at the hour of noon, upon Thursday the last day of June, after the feast of St. John, which the Moors call Alhazaro. And when the gate was opened Abeniaf was there within, with a great company round about him, both of his own people and of those of the town; and the Christians as they entered ascended the walls and towers. And Abeniaf asked why so many went up, for it was not in the terms; but they would not cease for that, and they took possession of all, little to his liking.

BOOK VII.

I.

And all the people of the town gathered together, like men risen from their graves,...yea, like the dead when the trumpet shall sound for the day of judgment, and men shall come out of their graves and be gathered together before the Majesty of God. And hucksters came from Alcudia and brought bread and pulse to sell, and others of the town went out to Alcudia to buy food; and they who were poor, and had not wherewith to buy, plucked of the herbs of the field and ate them, and they held themselves rich because they could go out when they would, and enter in again without fear. And such as were wise among them abstained from taking much food, fearing what would happen, and they took it little by little till they had gotten strength; all they who took their fill died, and the mortality among them was so great that all the fields were full of graves.

II.

On the following day after the Christians had taken possession of the town, the Cid entered it with a great company, and he ascended the highest tower of the wall, and beheld all the city; and the Moors came unto him, and kissed his hand, saying he was welcome. And the Cid did great honour unto them. And then he gave order that all the windows of the towers which looked in upon the town should be closed up, that the Christians might not see what the Moors did in their houses; and the Moors thanked him for this greatly. And he commanded and requested the Christians that they should show great honour to the Moors, and respect them, and greet them when they met: and the Moors thanked the Cid greatly for the honour which the Christians did them, saying that they had never seen so good a man, nor one so honourable, nor one who had his people under such obedience.

III.

Now Abeniaf thought to have the love of the Cid; and calling to mind the wrath with which he had formerly been received, because he had not taken a gift with him, he took now great riches which he had taken from those who sold bread for so great a price during the siege of Valencia, and this he carried to the Cid as a present. Among those who had sold it were some men from the Islands of Majorca, and he took from them all that they had. This the Cid knew, and he would not accept his gifts. And the Cid caused proclamation to be made in the town and throughout the whole district thereof, that the honourable men and knights and castellans should assemble together in the garden of Villa Nueva, where the Cid at that time sojourned. And when they were all assembled, he went out unto them, to a place which was made ready with carpets and with mats, and he made them take their seats before him full honourably, and began to speak unto them, saying, I am a man who have never possessed a kingdom, neither I nor any man of my lineage. But the day when I first beheld this city I was well pleased therewith, and coveted it that I might be its Lord; and I besought the Lord our God that he would give it me. See now what his power is, for the day when I sate down before Juballa I had no more than four loaves of bread, and now by God's mercy I have won Valencia. And if I administer right and justice here God will let me enjoy it, but if I do evil, and demean myself proudly and wrongfully, I know that he will take it away. Now then let every one go to his own lands, and possess them even as he was wont to have and to hold them. He who shall find his field, or his vineyard, or his garden, desert, let him incontinently enter thereon; and he who shall find his husbanded, let him pay him that hath cultivated it the cost of his labour, and of the seed which he hath sown therein, and remain with his heritage, according to the law of the Moors. Moreover I have given order that they who collect my dues take from you no more than the tenth, because so it is appointed by the custom of the Moors, and it is what ye have been wont to pay. And I have resolved in my heart to hear your complaints two days in the week, on the Monday and the Thursday; but if causes should arise which require haste, come to me when ye will and I will give judgment, for I do not retire with women to sing and to drink, as your Lords have done, so that ye could obtain no justice, but will myself see to these things, and watch over ye as friend over his friend, and kinsman over his kinsman. And I will be Cadi and Guazil, and when dispute happens among ye I will decide it. When he had said these things they all replied that they prayed God to preserve him through long and happy years, and four of the most honourable among them rose and kissed his hands, and the Cid bade them take their seats again.

IV.

Then the Cid spake unto them and said, It is told me that Abeniaf hath done much evil, and committed great wrong toward some of ye, in that he hath taken great riches from ye to present them to me, saying, that this he did because ye sold food for a great price during the siege. But I will accept of no such gift; for if I were minded to have your riches, I could take them, and need not ask them neither from him, nor from any other; but thing so unseemly as to take that which is his from any one, without just cause, I will not do. They who have gotten wealth thus, God hath given it them; let them go to Abeniaf, and take back what he hath forced from them, for I will order him to restore the whole. Then he said, Ye see the riches which I took from the messengers who went to Murcia; it is mine by right, for I took it in war because they brake the covenant which they had made, and would have deceived me: nevertheless I will restore it to the uttermost farthing, that nothing thereof shall be lost. And ye shall do homage to me that ye will not withdraw yourselves, but will abide here, and do my bidding in all things, and never depart from the covenant which ye make with me; for I love ye, and am grieved to think of the great evil and misery which ye endured from the great famine, and of the mortality which there was. And if ye had done that before which ye have done now, ye would not have been brought to these sufferings and have bought the cafiz of wheat at a thousand maravedís; but I trust in God to bring it to one maravedí. Be ye now secure in your lands, and till your fields, and rear cattle; for I have given order to my men that they offer ye no wrong, neither enter into the town to buy nor to sell; but that they carry on all their dealings in Alcudia, and this I do that ye may receive no displeasure. Moreover I command them not to take any captive into the town, but if this should be done, lay ye hands on the captive and set him free, without fear, and if any one should resist, kill him and fear not. I myself will not enter your city nor dwell therein, but I will build me a place beside the Bridge of Alcantara, where I may go and disport myself at times, and repair when it is needful. When he had said these things he bade them go their way.

V.

Well pleased were the Moors when they departed from him, and they marvelled at the greatness of his promises, and they set their hearts at rest, and put away the fear which they had had, thinking all their troubles were over; for in all the promises which the Cid had made unto them, they believed that he spake truth; but he said these things only to quiet them, and to make them come to what he wished, even as came to pass. And when he had done, he sent his Almoxarife, Abdalla Adiz, to the Custom House, and made him appoint men to collect the rents of the town for him, which vas done accordingly. And when the Cid had given order concerning his own affairs at his pleasure, the Moors would fain have entered again into possession of their heritages as he told them; but they found it all otherwise, for of all the fields which the Christians had husbanded; they would not yield up one; albeit they let them enter upon such as were left waste; some said that the Cid had given them the lands that year, instead of their pay, and other some that they rented them and had paid rent for the year. So the Moors seeing this, waited till Thursday, when the Cid was to hear complaints, as he had said unto them. When Thursday came all the honourable men went to the Garden, but the Cid sent to say unto them that he could not come out that day, because of other causes which he had to determine; and he desired that they would go their way for that time, and come again on the Monday: this was to show his mastery. And when it was Monday they assembled again in the Garden, and the Cid came out to them, and took his seat upon the estrado, and the Moors made their complaint. And when he had heard them, he began to make similitudes, and offer reasons which were not like those which he had spoken the first day, for he said to them, I ask of ye, whether it is weil that I should be left without men? for if I were without them, I should be like unto one who hath lost his right arm, or to a bird that hath no wings, or to one who should do battle and hath neither spear nor sword. The first thing which I have to look to is to the well-being of my people, that they may live in wealth and honour, so that they may be able to serve me, and defend my honour; for since it has pleased God to give me the city of Valencia, I will not that there be any other Lord here than me. Therefore I say unto you and command you, if you would be well with me, and would that I should show favour unto you, that ye see how to deliver that traitor Abeniaf into my hands. Ye all know the great treason which he committed upon King Yahia, his Lord and yours, how he slew him, and the misery which he brought upon you in the siege; and since it is not fitting that a traitor who hath slain his Lord should live among you, and that his treason should be confounded with your loyalty, see to the obeyment of my command.

VI.

When the honourable Moors heard this they were dismayed; verily they knew that he spake truth touching the death of the King, but it troubled them that he departed from the promise which he had made; and they made answer that they would take counsel concerning what he had said, and then reply. Then five of the best and most honourable among them withdrew, and went to Abdalla Adiz, and said unto him, Areed us thy reed now the best and truest that thou canst, for thou art of our law, and oughtest to do this; and the reason why we ask counsel of thee is this. The Cid promised us many things, and now behold he says nothing to us of what he said before, but moveth other new reasons, at which great dismay hath seized us. And because thou better knowest his ways, tell us now what is his pleasure, for albeit we might wish to do otherwise, this is not a time wherein anything but what he shall command can be done. When the Almoxarife heard this he made answer, Good men, it is easy to understand what he would have, and to do what should be done. We all know the great treason which Abeniaf committed against we all in killing your Lord the King: for albeit, at that time ye felt the burden of the Christians, yet it was nothing so great as after he had killed him, neither did ye suffer such misery. And since God hath brought him who was the cause to this state, see now by all means how ye may deliver him into the hands of the Cid. And fear not, neither take thought for the rest; for though the Cid may do his pleasure in some things, better is it to have him for Lord, than this traitor who hath brought so much evil upon ye. Moreover the things of this world soon pass away, and my heart tells me that we shall ere long come out of the bondage of the Cid, and of the Christians, for the Cid is well nigh at the full of his days, and we who remain alive after his death, shall then be masters of our city. When the good men heard what he said, they thanked him much, and held themselves to be well advised, and said that they would do willingly what he bade them: and they returned forthwith to the Cid, and said unto him that they would fulfil his commandment. Incontinently did the good men dispeed themselves of the Cid, and they went into the city, and gathered together a great posse of armed men, and went to the place where Abeniaf dwelt; and they assaulted the house and brake the doors, and entered in and laid hands on him, and his son, and all his company, and carried them before the Cid. And the Cid ordered Abeniaf to be cast into prison, and all those who had taken counsel with him for the death of King Yahia.

VII.

When this was done, the Cid said unto the good men, Now that ye have fulfilled my bidding, I hold it good to show favour unto you in that which ye yourselves shall understand to be fitting for me to grant. Say therefore what ye would have, and I will do that which I think behoveth me: but in this manner, that my dwelling place be within the city of Valencia, in the Alcazar, and that my Christian men have all the fortresses in the city. And when the good men heard this, they were greatly troubled; howbeit they dissembled the sorrow which they resented, and said unto him, Sir Cid, order it as you think good, and we consent thereto. Then said he unto them that he would observe towards them all the uses and customs of their law, and that he would have the power, and be Lord of all; and they should till their fields and feed their flocks and herds, and give him his tenth, and he would take no more. When the Moors heard this they were well pleased, and since they were to remain in the town, and in their houses and their inheritances, and with their uses and customs, and that their Mosques were to be left them, they held themselves not to be badly off. Then they asked the Cid to let their Guazil be the same as he had first appointed, and that he would give them for their Cadi the Alfaqui Alhagi, and let him appoint whom he would to assist him in distributing justice to the Moors; and thus he himself would be relieved of the wearisomeness of hearing them, save only when any great occasion might befall. This Alhagi was he who made the lamentation for Valencia, as ye have heard; and when the Cid was peaceably established in Valencia, he was converted, and the Cid made him a Christian. And the Cid granted this which they required, and they kissed his hand, and returned into the town. Nine months did the Cid hold Valencia besieged, and at the end of that time it fell into his power, and he obtained possession of the walls, as ye have heard. And one month he was practising with the Moors that he might keep them quiet, till Abeniaf was delivered into his hands; and thus ten months were fulfilled, and they were fulfilled on Thursday the last day of June, in the year of the æra one thousand one hundred and thirty and one, which was in the year one thousand ninety and three of the Incarnation of our Lord Jesus Christ. And when the Cid had finished all his dealings with the Moors, on this day he took horse with all his company in good array, his banner being carried before him, and his arms behind: and in this guise, with great rejoicings he entered the city of Valencia. And he alighted at the Alcazar, and gave order to lodge all his men round about it, and he bade them his banner upon the highest tower of the Alcazar.

Glad was the Campeador, and all they who were with him when they saw his banner planted in that place. And from that day forth was the Cid possessed of all the Castles and fortresses which were in the kingdom of Valencia, and established in what God had given him, and lie and ail Ins people rejoiced.

VIII.

On the morrow the Cid sent Abeniaf to Juballa, and they gave him great tortures till he was at the point of death; and they kept him there two days, and then brought him to Valencia to the Garden of the Cid, and the Cid gave order that he should write with his own hand an account of all that he had. And he did this, and wrote down the carkanets, and rings, and costly garments, and rich apparel which he had, and also many other precious household things, and the debts which were due unto him. This the Cid did that he might see if all was there which Abeniaf had taken when he slew the King his Master; and the writing was read before the Cid. And the Cid sent for certain Moors who were good and honourable men, and made Abeniaf be brought before him, and demanded of him if he had nothing more than what was there written down; and he answered that he had not; and he bade him swear this before the Moors, and Abeniaf swore accordingly. Then the Cid sent privily to make search in all the houses of the friends of Abeniaf, swearing unto them, that if they had anything of his and denied it, and it should afterwards be discovered, he would put them to death, and moreover take from them all that they had. And they when they heard this, partly in the fear of the Cid, and partly that they might find favour with him, brought each of them great riches, saying, Sir, Abeniaf gave us this in keeping, that if it might be saved, he might share it with us. And he gave order to search and dig in the houses of Abeniaf, and they found great treasure there in gold and in silver, and in pearls, and in precious stones, all which a servant discovered unto them. And when the Cid saw it all before him it pleased him much, and he called for the Moors before whom Abeniaf had taken the oath, and he took his seat upon the estrado full nobly, and there in the presence of Christians and Moors he ordered Abeniaf and all the other prisoners to be brought forth. And he bade that Alfaqui whom he had made Cadi, and the other good men, judge by what death he who had slain his Lord deserved to die, according to their law, and who moreover was perjured, for he had sworn that he possessed nothing more than what he had set down in writing: and the Cadi and the other Moors said that according to their law, he and his accomplices should be stoned: This, they said, we find in our law, but you will do as you think good. Nevertheless we ask mercy of you for his son, who is but a child; may it please you to set him free, for he hath no fault in what his father hath done. And the Cid answered, that for the love of them he pardoned the child, but that he should depart from the city, for he would not have the son of a traitor dwell therein. And he commanded them that they should stone Abeniaf and all them who had taken counsel with him for the death of the King, according as they had given sentence. Then the honourable Moors rose and kissed his feet and his hands for the mercy which he had shown to the son of Abeniaf; and they took out Abeniaf to stone him, and other twenty and two with him. And the Cid bade them come again to him on the morrow, and he would appoint what should be the manner of his dwelling among them.

IX.

That night the Cid spake with Alvar Fañez and with Pero Bermudez, and all them who were of his council, and they resolved in what manner they would live among the Moors. And on the morrow the honourable Moors of Valencia assembled together in the Alcazar as they had been commanded to do, and the Cid took his seat upon the estrado, and all the honourable men round about him, and he spake unto them after this manner: Good men of the Aljama of Valencia, ye know how I served and defended King Yahia your Lord, and ye also, until his death. And I had great sorrow for him, and strove to revenge him, as ye know, and endured great hardships in winning Valencia.

And since God hath thought it good that I should be Lord thereof, I will have it for myself, and for those who have helpen me to win it, saving the sovereignty of King Don Alfonso of Castille, my Lord, whom God preserve for his service long and happy years. Ye are all now in my power, to do with ye whatever I will, both with your persons and your riches, and your wives and your children; but I will not do thus. And I hold it good that the honourable men among ye who have alway been loyal, remain in the city in their dwellings and with all their family; and that none among ye keep more than one beast, which shall be a mule, and that ye do not use arms, neither have them in your possession, except when it is needful and I shall give command. And all the rest of the people shall go out of the town and dwell in the suburb of Alcudia, where I was wont to be. Ye shall have two

Mosques, one in the city and one in the suburb; and ye shall have your Alfaquis and follow your own law; and ye shall have your Cadis, and your Guazil, as I have appointed; and ye shall have your inheritances, and pay me the tenth of the fruits thereof as your service; and the power of justice shall be mine, and I will order such money to be coined as I shall think good. Do ye therefore who are minded to abide with me in the land, abide: and let those who are not, go, in God's name, and good luck with them, but they shall take only their own persons, and I will give command to see them escorted in safety. When the Moors of Valencia heard this they were full sorrowful; howbeit it was now a time when they could do no otherwise than as he commanded. And incontinently they began to go out of the city with their wives and children, all except those whom the Cid had commanded to abide there; and as the Moors went out the Christians who dwelt in Alcudia entered in. And the history saith, that so great was the multitude which departed, that they were two whole days in going out. Great was the joy of the Cid and his people that day, and from thenceforward he was called My Cid the Campeador, Lord of Valencia.

X.

Now was it bruited abroad throughout all lands, how the Cid Ruydiez had won the noble city of Valencia. And when Ali Abenaxa the Adelantado of the Almoravides knew it, he sent his son-in-law the King of Seville to besiege him in Valencia, and gave him thirty thousand men at arms. And this King came in great haste to Valencia, and besieged the Cid therein. And the Cid made ready with all his people, and went out to fight him. And the battle was nigh unto Valencia, beside the garden which is called the Garden of Villa Nueva; and it was a good battle, and at length he of the good fortune conquered; and the pursuit continued as far as Xativa; even so far did the Christians pursue them, smiting and slaying. And at the passage of the Xucar there might you have seen confusion, and there the Moors without liking it drank plenty of water. They say that fifteen thousand Moors died in the river; and the King of Seville fled with three great blows. This day did Martin Pelaez the Asturian approve himself a right good one: there was no knight so good that day in arms as he, nor who bore away such honour. And when the pursuit was ended the Cid returned to the field of battle, and ordered the spoils of the field and of the tents to be collected. Be it known that this was a profitable day's work. Every foot soldier shared a hundred marks of silver that day. And the Cid returned full honourably to Valencia. Great was the joy of the Christians in the Cid Ruydiez, he who was born in a good hour. His beard was grown, and continued to grow a great length. My Cid said of his chin, For the love of King Don Alfonso, who hath banished me from his land, no scissars shall come upon it, nor shall a hair be cut away, and Moors and Christians shall talk of it.

XI.

That night the Cid took counsel with Alvar Fañez, who departed not from his side, and with the other honourable men who were of his council, concerning what should be done: for now that his people were all rich, he feared least they should return into their own country, for my Cid saw that if they might go they would. And Minaya advised him that he should cause proclamation to be made through the city, that no man should depart without permission of the Cid, and if any one went who had not dispeeded himself and kist his hand, if he were overtaken he should lose all that he had, and moreover be fixed upon a stake. And that they might be the more certain, he said unto Minaya that he would take account of all the people who were with him, both horsemen and foot, and Pero Bermudez and Martin Antolinez made the roll; and there were found a thousand knights of lineage, and five hundred and fifty other horsemen, and of foot soldiers four thousand, besides boys and others; thus many were the people of my Cid, he of Bivar. And his heart rejoiced, and he smiled and said, Thanks be to God, Minaya, and to Holy Mary Mother!...we had a smaller company when we left the house of Bivar!

XII.

At this time there came a crowned one from the parts of the East, that is to say, one who was shaven and shorn; his name was the Bishop Don Hieronymo, a full learned man and a wise, and one who was mighty both on horseback and a-foot: and he came enquiring for the Cid, wishing that he might see himself with the Moors in the field, for if he could once have his fill of smiting and slaying them, Christians should never lament him. And when the Cid knew this it pleased him in his heart, and he took horse and went to visit him, and rejoiced greatly that he was come; and he resolved to make Valencia a bishopric and give it to this good Christian. And they took counsel, and it was that on the morrow the Bishop and his clergy should turn the Mosques into Churches, wherein they might sing masses, and sacrifice the body of Jesus Christ. And rents were appointed for the table of the Bishop and for his Canons, and for all the clergy in the city of Valencia. And nine parish Churches were made. And the greatest was called St. Pedro's, and another was called St. Mary of the Virtues. This was near the Alcazar, and there the Cid went oftenest to hear service. After this manner the Cid ordered his city that it should be a Bishopric, for the honour of the Catholic faith. God! how joyful was all Christendom that there was a Lord Bishop in the land of Valencia!

XIII.

Now the Cid bethought him of Doña Ximena his wife, and of his daughters Doña Elvira and Doña Sol, whom he had left in the Monastery of St. Pedro de Cardeña; and he called for Alvar Fañez and Martin Antolinez of Burgos, and spake with them, and besought them that they would go to Castille, to King Don Alfonso his Lord, and take him a present from the riches which God had given them; and the present should be a hundred horses, saddled and bridled; and that they would kiss the King's hand for him, and beseech him to send him his wife Doña Ximena, and his daughters, and that they would tell the King all the mercy which God had shown him, and how he was at his service with Valencia and with all that he had. Moreover he bade them take a thousand marks of silver to the Monastery of St. Pedro de Cardeña, and give them to the Abbot, and thirty marks, of gold for his wife and daughters, that they might prepare themselves and come in honourable guise. And he ordered three hundred marks of gold to be given them, and three hundred marks of silver, to redeem the chests full of sand which he had pledged in Burgos to the Jews; and he bade them ask Rachel and Vidas to forgive him the deceit of the sand, for he had done it because of his great need: and he said, You, Martin Antolinez, were aiding and abetting herein, but praised be the name of the Lord for ever, he hath let me quit myself truly; tell them that they shall have more profit than they asked. And he bade them each take with him his whole company, that they might be better advised and accompanied, and that Doña Ximena might come with the greater honour: and the company was this: two hundred knights who were of Don Alvar Fañez, and fifty of Martin Antolinez: and he ordered money to be given them for their disbursement, and for all things needful, in abundance.

XIV.

Alvar Fañez and Martin Antolinez went their way, and they found the King in the city of Palencia. When they arrived he was coming from mass, and seeing this goodly company of horsemen he stopped in the church porch, and asked who they were. And it was told him that they were people of the Cid, who came to him with a full great present. And Alvar Fañez and Martin Antolinez alighted, and came to the King, and kissed his hand; and he received them right well, and said, What tidings bring ye me of the Cid, my true vassal, the most honourable knight that ever was knighted in Castille? Well was Minaya pleased when he heard this, and he said, A boon, Sir King Don Alfonso, for the love of your Maker: My Cid sendeth to kiss your hands and your feet, as his natural Lord, at whose service he is, and from whom he expecteth much bounty and good. You banished him from the land; but though in another's country, he hath only done you service. Five pitched battles hath he won since that time, some with Moors and some with bad Christians; and he hath taken Xerica, and Ondra, and Almenar, and Monviedro which is a bigger place, and Cebola also, and Castrejon, and Peña Cadiella which is a strong eminence, and with all the right noble city of Valencia, for the honour of the faith of Jesus Christ, and of you our Lord and King; and he hath made it a Bishopric, and made the Honourable Don Hieronymo Bishop thereof with his own hand. And behold here are a hundred horses of the spoils which he hath won; they are great and swift, and are all bridled and saddled, and he kisseth your hand and beseecheth you as his natural Lord to receive them. When the King heard this he was greatly astonished, and he lifted up his right hand and blessed himself, and said, As St. Isidro shall keep me, I rejoice in the good fortune of the Cid, and receive his gift full willingly. But though this pleased the King it did not please Garci Ordoñez, and he said, It seemeth there is not a man left in the land of the Moors, that the Cid can thus do his pleasure! And the King said unto him, Hold thy peace, for in all things he serves me better than thou.

Then Alvar Fañez kissed the King's hand again, and said, Sir, the Cid beseecheth you of your bounty that he may have his wife Doña Ximena and his two daughters, that they may go to Valencia unto him, from the Monastery where he left them, for it is many days since he saw them, and if it please you this would rejoice him. And the King made answer, It pleases me well, and I will give them a guard throughout my dominions, that they may be conducted honourably to the border: when they have past it, the Campeador himself will look to them. And he said, Hear me! all those whom I have disseized of their inheritances for following the Campeador, I restore again to the possession thereof, and all those who desire to serve him I freely licence: let them go in the grace of God. Moreover the King said, I grant him Valencia and all that he hath won and shall win hereafter, that he be called Lord thereof, and that he hold it of no other Lordship save of me, who am his liege Lord. Alvar Fañez and Martin Antolinez kissed his hand for this in the Cid's name. And the King called a porter, who should go with them, bearing a writing from the King, that all things needful should be given unto them so long as they were in his lands. Then Alvar Fañez and Martin Antolinez dispeeded themselves of the King, and took their way towards Burgos.

XV.

When they reached Burgos they sent for Rachel and for Vidas, and demanded from them the chests, and paid unto them the three hundred marks of gold and the three hundred of silver as the Cid had commanded, and they besought them to forgive the Cid the deceit of the chests, for it was done because of his great necessity. And they said they heartily forgave him, and held themselves well paid; and they prayed God to grant him long life and good health, and to give him power to advance Christendom, and put down Pagandom. And when it was known through the city of Burgos the goodness and the gentleness which the Cid had shown to these merchants in redeeming from them the chests full of sand and earth and stones, the people held it for a great wonder, and there was not a place in all Burgos where they did not talk of the gentleness and loyalty of the Cid; and they besought blessings upon him, and prayed that he and his people might be advanced in honour. When they had done this, they went to the Monastery of St. Pedro de Cardeña, and the porter of the King went with them, and gave order every where that every thing which they wanted should be given them. If they were well received, and if there was great joy in St. Pedro de Cardeña over them, it is not a thing to ask, for Doña Ximena and her daughters were like people beside themselves with the great joy which they had, and they came running out on foot to meet them, weeping plenteously for great joy. And Alvar Fañez and Martin Antolinez, when they saw them coming, leapt off their horses and went to them, and Minaya embraced Doña Ximena and both his cousins, Doña Elvira and Doña Sol, and so great was the rejoicing which they made together that no man can tell it you. And when this great joy was somewhat abated, Doña Ximena asked how the Cid fared, for since he had parted from her she had heard no news of him. And Alvar Fañez said he had left him safe and sound in Valencia; and he bade her and her daughters thank God for the great favour that he had shown him, for he had won sundry castles from the Moors, and the noble city of Valencia, whither he was now come to carry her and her daughters, for the Cid had sent for them, and when he should see them his heart's desire would be accomplished. When Doña Ximena and her daughters heard this, they set their knees to the ground, and lifted up their hands and thanked God for the favour he had shown to the Cid, and to them with him, in giving him the Lordship of Valencia. While they were preparing for the journey, Alvar Fañez sent three knights to the Cid to tell him how they had sped with the King, and of the great favour which they had found at his hands, and how he only tarried now to equip Doña Ximena, that she might come full honourably. That good one Minaya then began to deck them out for the journey with the best trappings which could be found in Burgos: right noble garments did he provide for them, and a great company of damsels, and good palfreys, and great mules, which were not bad ones. And he gave the Abbot the thousand marks of silver which the Cid had sent for the Monastery, with which to discharge all the debt that Doña Ximena and his daughters had contracted. Great was the stir throughout all that land of the honour of the Cid, and of the licence which the King gave to as many as should chuse to join him; and for this reason full sixty knights came to St. Pedro de Cárdena, and a great number of squires on foot. Don Alvar Fañez was well pleased to see them, and he promised them that he would obtain the Cid's grace for them, and would befriend them all he could. Great dole did the Abbot make when they departed; and he said, As God shall help you, Minaya, kiss the hand of the Campeador for me. This Monastery will never forget him, to pray for him every day in the year. The Cid will alway prosper more and more. Minaya promised to do this, and dispeeded himself, and they went their way. Five days they travelled, and then they came to Medina Celi; and alway the porter of the King was with them, and made all that they wanted be given unto them, even as the King had commanded.

XVI.

Now the three knights whom Alvar Fañez had sent, came to the Cid and delivered their message. When my Cid heard it his heart rejoiced and he was glad, and he spake with his mouth and said, He who sends good messengers looks for good tidings. Blessed be the name of God, since King Don Alfonso rejoices in my good fortune. And he called for Muño Gustios, and Pero Bermudez, and the Bishop Don Hieronymo, and bade them take a hundred knights least there should be need to fight, and go to Molina, to Abencaño, who was his friend and vassal, and bid him take another hundred knights, and go with them to Medina Celi as fast as they could go. There, said he, ye will find Alvar Fañez and my wife and daughters; bring them to me with great honour: I will remain here in Valencia which has cost me so much; great folly would it be if I were to leave it: I will remain in it, for I hold it for my heritage. And they did as he commanded them. And when they came to Molina, Abencaño received them right well, and did them great honour; and though the Cid had bidden him take only one hundred horse, he took two. On the morrow they went to horse: they crossed the mountains which are great and wild, and they passed Mata de Toranz without fear, and they thought to come through the valley of Arbuxedo. There was good look out kept in Medina, and Alvar Fañez sent two knights to know who they were. They made no tarriance in doing this, for they had it at heart; one tarried with them, and the other returned, and said it was the host of the Campeador with Pero Bermudez, and Muño Gustios, and the Bishop Hieronymo, and the Alcayaz Abencaño. This instant, said Minaya, let us to horse; incontinently this was done, for they would make no delay. And they rode upon goodly horses with bells at their poitrals and trappings of sandall silk, and they had their shields round their necks, and lances with streamers in their hands. Oh, how Alvar Fañez went out from Castille with these ladies! They who pricked forward, couched their spears and then raised them, and great joy was there by Salon where they met. The others humbled themselves to Minaya: when Abencaño carne up he kissed him on the shoulder, for such was his custom. In a good day, Minaya, said he, do you bring these ladies, the wife and daughters of the Cid, whom we all honour. Whatever ill we may wish him we can do him none; in peace or in war he will have our wealth, and he must be a fool who does not acknowledge this truth. Alvar Fañez smiled and told him he should lose nothing by this service which he had done the Cid: and now, said he, let us go rest, for the supper is ready. Abencaño said he was well pleased to partake it, and that within three days he would return him the entertainment two-fold. Then they entered Medina, and Minaya served them; all were full glad of the service which they had undertaken, and the King's porter paid for all. The night is gone, morning is come, mass is said, and they go to horse. They left Medina and past the river Salon, and pricked up Arbuxuelo, and they crost the plain of Torancio. That good Christian the Bishop Don Hieronymo, night and day he guarded the ladies; on a goodly horse he rode, and they went between him and Alvar Fañez. They came to Molina and there were lodged in a good and rich house, and Abencaño the Moor waited on them. Nothing did they want which they could wish to have; he even had all their beasts new shod, and for Minaya and the ladies, Lord! how he honoured them! On the morrow they left Molina, and the Moor went with them. When they were within three leagues of Valencia, news of their coming was brought to the Cid. Glad was the Cid, never was he more joyful, never had he such joy, for tidings were come to him of what he loved best. Two hundred knights did he order out to meet them, others he bade to keep the Alcazar, and the other high towers, and all the gates and entrances. And he commanded that they should bring him Bavieca. It was but a short time since he had won this horse; my Cid, he who girt on sword in a happy hour, did not yet know if he was a good goer, and if he stopt well. The Bishop Don Hieronymo, he pricked forward and entered the city. He left his horse and went to the Church, and collected all the clergy; they put on their surplices, and with crosses of silver went out to meet the ladies, and that good one Minaya. He who was born in happy hour made no tarriance; they saddled him Bavieca and threw his trappings on. My Cid wore light armour, and his surcoat over it: long was his beard. He went out upon this horse, and ran a career with him; Bavieca was the name of the horse, and when he was running all marvelled at him: from that day Bavieca was famous all over Spain. At the end of the course my Cid alighted and went toward his wife and his daughters. Who can tell the joy that was made at their meeting? They fell at his feet, and their joy was such that they could not speak. And he raised them up and embraced them, and kissed them many times, weeping for joy that he saw them alive. Hear what he said who was born in happy hour! You dear and honoured wife, and ye my daughters, my heart and my soul; enter with me into Valencia;...this is the inheritance which I have won for you. While they were thus rejoicing the Bishop Don Hieronymo came with the procession. Doña Ximena brought good relicks and other sacred things, which she gave to ennoble the new Church of Valencia. In this guise they entered the city. Who can tell the rejoicings that were made that day, throwing at the board, and killing bulls! My Cid led them to the Alcazar, and took them up upon the highest tower thereof, and there they looked around and beheld Valencia, how it lay before them, and the great Garden with its thick shade, and the sea on the other side; and they lifted up their hands to thank God. Great honour did the Cid do to Abencaño the Lord of Molina, for all the service which he had done to Doña Ximena. Then said Abencaño, This, Sir, I was bound to do, for since I have been your vassal I have alway been respected, and defended from all my enemies, and maintained in good estate; how then should I do otherwise than serve you? If I did not, I should lack understanding. And the Cid thanked him for what he had done, and what he had said, and promised also to show favour unto him. And Abencaño took his leave and returned to Molina.

XVII.

The winter is past, and March is coming in. Three months Doña Ximena had been in Valencia, when tidings came to the Cid from beyond sea, that King Yucef, the son of the Miramamolin, who dwelt in Morocco, was coming to lay siege unto Valencia with fifty thousand men. When the Cid heard this he gave command to store all his Castles, and had them well repaired. And he had the walls of the city prepared, and stored it well with food and with all things needful for war, and gathered together a great power of Christians and of the Moors of his seignory. Hardly had he done this before he heard that Yucef was near at hand, and coming as fast as he could come. Then the Cid assembled together the Christians in the Alcazar, and when they were assembled, he rose upon his feet and said, Friends and kinsmen and vassals, praised be God and holy Mary Mother, all the good which I have in the world I have here in Valencia; with hard labour I won the city, and hold it for my heritage, and for nothing less than death will I leave it. My daughters and my wife shall see me fight, they shall see with their own eyes our manner of living in this land, and how we get our bread. We will go out against the Moors and give them battle, and God who hath thus far shown favour unto us will still continue to be our helper. When they heard this they cried out with one accord that they would do his bidding, and go out with him and fight under his banner, for certain they were that by his good fortune the Moors would be overthrown.

XVIII.

On the morrow the Cid took Doña Ximena by the hand, and her daughters with her, and made them go up upon the highest tower of the Alcazar, and they looked toward the sea and saw the great power of the Moors, how they came on and drew nigh, and began to pitch their tents round about Valencia, beating their tambours and with great uproar. And Ximena's heart failed her, and she asked the Cid if peradventure God would deliver him from these enemies. Fear not, honoured woman, said he; you are but lately arrived, and they come to bring you a present, which shall help marry your daughters. Fear not, for you shall see me fight by the help of God and holy Mary Mother; my heart kindles because you are here! The more Moors the more gain! The tambours sounded now with a great alarum, and the sun was shining. Cheer up, said my Cid; this is a glorious day. But Ximena was seized with such fear as if her heart would have broken; she and her daughters had never been in such fear since the day that they were born. Then the good Cid Campeador stroked his beard and said, Fear not, all this is for your good. Before fifteen days are over, if it please God, those tambours shall be laid before you, and shall be sounded for your pleasure, and then they shall be given to the Bishop Don Hieronymo, that he may hang them up in the Church of St. Mary, Mother of God. This vow the Cid Campeador made. Now the Moors began to enter the gardens which were round about the town, and the watchman saw them and struck the bell. My Cid looked back and saw Alvar Salvadores beside him, and he said, go now, take two hundred horse, and sally upon yonder Moors who are entering the gardens; let Doña Xiraena and her daughters see the good will you have to serve them. Down went Alvar Salvadores in great haste, and ordered a bell to be rung which was a signal for two hundred knights to make ready; for the history saith, that the Cid, by reason that he was alway in war, had appointed, such signals for his people, that they knew when one hundred were called for, and when two, and so forth. Presently they were ready at the place of meeting, and the gate was opened which was nearest the gardens where the Moors had entered, without order; and they fell fiercely upon them, smiting and slaying. Great was the pleasure of the Cid at seeing how well they behaved themselves. And Doña Ximena and her daughters stood trembling, like women who had never seen such things before: and when the Cid saw it he made them seat themselves, so as no longer to behold it. Great liking had the Bishop Don Hieronymo to see how bravely they fought. Alvar Salvadores and his companions bestirred themselves so well that they drove the enemy to their tents, making great mortality among them, and then they turned back, whereat my Cid was well pleased; but Alvar Salvadores went on, hacking and hewing all before him, for he thought the ladies were looking on, and he pressed forward so far, that being without succour he was taken. The others returned to the city, falling back in brave order till they were out of reach of the enemy: and they had done no little in that exploit, for they slew above two hundred and fifty Moors. When my Cid saw that they who eat his bread were returned, he went down from the tower, and received them right well, and praised them for what they had done like good knights: howbeit he was full sorrowful for Alvar Salvadores that he should be in the hands of the Moors, but he trusted in God that he should deliver him on the morrow.

XIX.

And the Cid assembled his chief captains and knights and people, and said unto them, Kinsmen and friends and vassals, hear me: to-day has been a good day, and to-morrow shall be a better. Be you all armed and ready in the dark of the morning; mass shall be said, and the Bishop Don Hieronymo will give us absolution, and then we will to horse, and out and smite them in the name of the Creator and of the Apostle Santiago. It is fitter that we should live than that they should gather in the fruits of this land. But let us take counsel in what manner we may go forth, so as to receive least hurt, for they are a mighty power, and we can only defeat them by great mastery in war. When Alvar Fañez Minaya heard this, he answered and said, Praised be God and your good fortune, you have achieved greater things than this, and I trust in God's mercy that you will achieve this also. Give me three hundred horse, and we will go out when the first cock crows, and put ourselves in ambush in the valley of Albuhera; and when you have joined battle we will issue out and fall upon them on the other side, and on one side or the other God will help us. Well was the Cid pleased with this counsel, and he said that it should be so; and he bade them feed their horses in time and sup early, and as soon as it was cock-crow come to the Church of St. Pedro, and hear mass, and shrive themselves, and communicate, and then take horse in the name of the Trinity, that the soul of him who should die in the business might go without let to God.

XX.

Day is gone, and night is come. At cock-crow they all assembled together in the Church of St. Pedro, and the Bishop Don Hieronymo sung mass, and they were shriven and assoyled, and howselled. Great was the absolution which the Bishop gave them: He who shall die, said he, fighting face forward, I will take his sins, and God shall have his soul. Then said he, A boon, Cid Don Rodrigo; I have sung mass to you this morning: let me have the giving the first wounds in this battle! and the Cid granted him this boon in the name of God. Then being all ready they went out through the gate which is called the Gate of the Snake, for the greatest power of the Moors was on that side, leaving good men to guard the gates. Alvar Fañez and his company were already gone forth, and had laid their ambush. Four thousand, lacking thirty, were they who went out with my Cid, with a good will, to attack fifty thousand. They went through all the narrow places, and bad passes, and leaving the ambush on the left, struck to the right hand, so as to get the Moors between them and the town. And the Cid put his battles in good array, and bade Pero Bermudez bear his banner. When the Moors saw this they were greatly amazed; and they harnessed themselves in great haste, and came out of their tents. Then the Cid bade his banner move on, and the Bishop Don Hieronymo pricked forward with his company, and laid on with such guise, that the hosts were soon mingled together. Then might you have seen many a horse running about the field with the saddle under his belly, and many a horseman in evil plight upon the ground. Great was the smiting and slaying in short time; but by reason that the Moors were so great a number, they bore hard upon the Christians, and were in the hour of overcoming them. And the Cid began, to encourage them with a loud voice, shouting God and Santiago! And Alvar Fañez at this time issued out from ambush, and fell upon them, on the side which was nearest the sea; and the Moors thought that a great power had arrived to the Cid's succour, and they were dismayed, and began to fly. And the Cid and his people pursued, punishing them in a bad way. If we should wish to tell you how every one behaved himself in this battle, it is a thing which could not be done, for all did so well that no man can relate their feats. And the Cid Ruydiez did go well, and made such mortality among the Moors, that the blood ran from his wrist to his elbow! great pleasure had he in his horse Bavieca that day, to find himself so well mounted. And in the pursuit he came up to King Yucef, and smote him three times: but the King escaped from under the sword, for the horse of the Cid passed on in his course, and when he turned, the King being on a fleet horse, was far off, so that he might not be overtaken; and he got into a Castle called Guyera, for so far did the Christians pursue them, smiting and slaying, and giving them no respite, so that hardly fifteen thousand escaped of fifty that they were. They who were in the ships, when they saw this great overthrow, fled to Denia.

XXI.

Then the Cid and his people returned to the field and began to plunder the tents. And the spoil was so great that there was no end to the riches, in gold and in silver, and in horses and arms, so that men knew not what to leave and what to take. And they found one tent which had been King Yucef's; never man saw so noble a thing as that tent was; and there were great riches therein, and there also did they find Alvar Salvadores, who had been made prisoner the yesterday, as ye have heard. Greatly did the Cid rejoice when he saw him alive and sound, and he ordered his chains to be taken off; and then he left Alvar Fañez to look to the spoil, and went into Valencia with a hundred knights. His wrinkled brow was seen, for he had taken off his helmet, and in this manner he entered, upon Bavieca, sword in hand. Great joy had Doña Ximena and her daughters, who were awaiting him, when they saw him come riding in; and he stopt when he came to them, and said, Great honour have I won for you, while you kept Valencia this day! God and the Saints have sent us goodly gain, upon your coming. Look, with a bloody sword, and a horse all sweat, this is the way that we conquer the Moors! Pray God that I may live yet awhile for your sakes, and you shall enter into great honour, and they shall kiss your hands. Then my Cid alighted when he had said this, and the ladies knelt down before him, and kissed his hand, and wished him long life. Then they entered the Palace with him, and took their seats upon the precious benches. Wife Doña Ximena, said he, these damsels who have served you so well, I will give in marriage to these my vassals, and to every one of them two hundred marks of silver, that it may be known in Castille what they have got by their services. Your daughters'marriage will come in time. And they all rose and kissed his hand: and great was the joy in the Palace, and it was done according as the Cid had said.

XXII.

Alvar Fañez this while was in the field writing and taking account of the spoil: but the tents and arms and precious garments were so many that they cannot be told, and the horses were beyond all reckoning; they ran about the field, and there was no body to take them, and the Moors of the land got something by that great overthrow. Nevertheless so many horses were taken that the Campeador had to his share of the good ones a thousand and five hundred. Well might the others have good store when he had so many. And my Cid won in this battle from King Yucef, his good sword Tizona, which is to say, the firebrand. The tent of the King of Morocco, which was supported by two pillars wrought with gold, he gave order not to be touched, for he would send it to Alfonso the Castillian. The Bishop Don Hieronymo, that perfect one with the shaven crown, he had his fill in that battle, fighting with both hands; no one could tell how many he slew. Great booty came to him, and moreover the Cid sent him the tithe of his fifth. Glad were the Christian folk in Valencia for the great booty which they had gotten, and glad was Doña Ximena and her daughters, and glad were all those ladies who were married.

XXIII.

King Yucef, after the pursuit was given over, and he saw that he might come forth from the Castle, fled to Denia, and embarked in his ships, and returned to Morocco. And thinking every day how badly he had sped, and how he had been conquered by so few, and how many of his people he had lost, he fell sick and died. But before he died he besought his brother, who was called Bucar, that for the tie there was between them, he would take vengeance for the dishonour which he had received from the Cid Campeador before Valencia; and Bucar promised to do this, and swore also upon the Koran, which is the book of their law. And accordingly he came afterwards across the sea, with nine and twenty Kings, as shall be related when the time comes.

XXIV.

Then the Cid sent Alvar Fañez and Pero Bermudez with a present to King Alfonso his Lord. And the present which he sent was two hundred horses saddled and bridled, with each a sword hanging from the saddle-bow: and also the noble tent which he had won from King Yucef of Morocco. This present he gave, because the King had sent him his wife and daughters when he asked for them, and because of the honour which he had done them, and that the King might not speak ill of him who commanded in Valencia. Alvar Fañez and Pero Bermudez went their way towards Castille, over sierras and mountains and waters; and they asked where the King was, and it was told them that he was at Valladolid, and thither they went. And when they drew nigh unto the city, they sent to let him know of their coming, and to ask of him whether he thought it good for them to come into the city unto him, or if he would come out to them, for they were a great company, and the present a full great one, which he would see better without, than in the town. And the King thought this best, and he went to horse, and bade all the hidalgos who were with him do the like. Now the Infantes of Carrion were there, Diego Gonzalez and Ferrando Gonzalez, the sons of Count Don Gonzalo. And they found the company of the Cid about half a league from the town, and when the King saw how many they were, he blest himself, for they seemed like a host. And Minaya and Pero Bermudez pricked on when they saw him, and came before him, and alighted, and knelt down, and kissed the ground and kissed both his feet; and he bade them rise and mount their horses, and would not hear them till they had mounted, and taken their places one at his right hand, and the other at his left. And they said, Sir, the Cid commends himself to your grace as his liege Lord, and thanks you greatly for having sent him with such honour his wife and daughters. And know. Sir, that since they arrived, he hath achieved a great victory over the Moors, and their King Yucef of Morocco, the Miramamolin, who besieged him in Valencia with fifty thousand men. And he went out against them, and smote them, and hath sent you these two hundred horses from his fifth. Then Alvar Fañez gave order that the horses should be led forward. And this was the manner in which they came. The two hundred horses came first, and every one was led by a child, and every one had a sword hanging from the saddle, on the left side; and after them came the pages of all the knights in company, carrying their spears, and then the company, and after them, an hundred couple with spears in rest. And when they had all past by, the King blest himself again, and he laughed and said that never had so goodly a present been sent before to King of Spain by his vassal. And Alvar Fañez said moreover, Sir, he hath sent you a tent, the noblest that ever man saw, which he won in this battle: and the King gave order that the tent should be spread, and he alighted and went into it, he and all his people, and he was greatly pleased; and they all said that they had never seen so noble a tent as this; and the King said he had won many from the Moors, but never such as this. But albeit that all the others were well pleased, Count Don Garcia was not so; and he and ten of his lineage talked apart, and said that this which the Cid had done was to their shame, for they hated the Cid in their hearts. And King Don Alfonso said, Thanks be to God and to Sir Saint Isidro of León, these horses may do me good service; and he gave three of them to Minaya, and Pero Bermudez, and bade them chuse, and he ordered food and cloathing to be given them while they remained, and said that he would give them compleat armour when they returned, such as was fit for them to appear in before my Cid. And they were lodged, and all things that were needful provided for them and their people.

XXV.

When the Infantes of Carrion, Diego Gonzalez and Ferrando Gonzalez, saw the noble present which the Cid had sent unto the King, and heard how his riches and power daily increased, and thought what his wealth must needs be when he had given those horses out of the fifth of one battle, and moreover that he was Lord of Valencia: they spake one with the other, and agreed, that if the Cid would give them his daughters to wife, they should be well married, and become rich and honourable. And they agreed together that they would talk with the King in private upon this matter. And they went presently to him, and said, Sir, we beseech you of your bounty to help us in a thing which will be to your honour; for we are your vassals, and the richer we are the better able shall we be to serve you. And the King asked of them what it was they would have, and they then told him their desire. And the King thought upon it awhile, and then came to them, and said, Infantes, this thing which you ask lies not in me, but in the Cid; for it is in his power to marry his daughters, and peradventure he will not do it as yet. Nevertheless that he ye may not fail for want of my help, I will send to tell him what ye wish. Then they kissed his hand for this favour. And the King sent for Alvar Fañez and Pero Bermudez, and went apart with them, and praised the Cid, and thanked him for the good will which he had to do him service, and said that he had great desire to see him. Say to him, he said, that I beseech him to come and meet me, for I would speak with him concerning something which is to his good and honour. Diego and Ferrando, the Infantes of Carrion, have said unto me that they would fain wed with his daughters, if it seemeth good to him; and methinks this would be a good marriage. When Alvar Fañez and Pero Bermudez heard this, they answered the King, and said, Certain we are, Sir, that neither in this, nor in anything else will the Cid do aught but what you, Sir, shall command or advise. When ye have your meeting ye will agree concerning it as is best. Then they kissed his hand, and took their leave.

XXVI.

On the morrow the messengers of the Cid departed from Valladolid, and took their way towards Valencia; and when the Cid knew that they were nigh at hand he went out to meet them, and when he saw them he waxed joyful, and he embraced them, and asked what tidings of his Lord Alfonso. And they told him how they had sped, and how greatly the King loved him; and when we departed, said they, he bade us beseech you to come and meet him anywhere where you will appoint, for he desireth to speak with you, concerning the marriage of your daughters with the Infantes of Carrion, if it should please you so to bestow them: now by what the King said it seemeth unto us that this marriage pleaseth him. And when the Cid heard this he became thoughtful, and he said to them after awhile, What think ye of this marriage? And they answered him, Even as it shall please you. And he said to them, I was banished from my own country, and was dishonoured, and with hard labour gained I what I have got; and now I stand in the King's favour, and he asketh of me my daughters for the Infantes of Carrion. They are of high blood and full orgullous, and I have no liking to this match; but if our Lord the King adviseth it we can do no otherwise; we will talk of this, and God send it for the best. So they entered Valencia, and the Cid spake with Doña Ximena touching this matter, and when she heard it it did not please her; nevertheless she said, if the King thought it good they could do no otherwise. Then the Cid gave order to write letters to the King, saying, that he would meet the King as he commanded, and whatever the King wished that he would do. And he sealed the letters well, and sent two knights with them. And when the King saw the letters he was well pleased, and sent others to say that the time of their meeting should be three weeks after he received these letters, and the place appointed was upon the Tagus, which is a great river.

XXVII.

Now began they to prepare on both sides for this meeting. He who should relate to you the great preparations, and the great nobleness which were made for the nonce, would have much to recount. Who ever saw in Castille so many a precious mule, and so many a good-going palfrey, and so many great horses, and so many goodly streamers set upon goodly spears, and shields adorned with gold and with silver, and mantles, and skins, and rich sendals of Adria? The King sent great store of food to the banks of the Tagus, where the place of meeting was appointed. Glad were the Infantes of Carrion, and richly did they bedight themselves; some things they paid for, and some they went in debt for: great was their company, and with the King there were many Leonese and Galegos, and Castillians out of number. My Cid the Campeador made no tarriance in Valencia; he made ready for the meeting: there was many a great mule, and many a palfrey, and many a good horse, and many a goodly suit of arms, cloaks, and mantles both of cloth and of peltry; ... great and little are all clad in colours. Alvar Fañez Minaya, and Pero Bermudez, and Martin Munoz, and Martin Antolinez that worthy Burgalese, and the Bishop Don Hieronymo that good one with the shaven crown, and Alvar Alvarez, and Alvar Salvadores, and Muño Gustios that knight of prowess, and Galind Garcia of Aragon; all these and all the others made ready to go with the Cid. But he bade Alvar Salvadores and Galind Garcia and all those who were under them, remain and look with heart and soul to the safety of Valencia, and not open the gates of the Alcazar neither by day nor by night, for his wife and daughters were there, in whom he had his heart and soul, and the other ladies with them; he like a good husband gave order that not one of them should stir out of the Alcazar till he returned. Then they left Valencia and pricked on more than apace; more than a thousand knights, all ready for war, were in this company. All those great horses that paced so well and were so soft of foot, my Cid won; they were not given to him.

XXVIII.

King Don Alfonso arrived first by one day at the place of meeting, and when he heard that the Cid was at hand, he went out with all his honourable men, more than a long league to meet him. When he who was born in a good hour had his eye upon the King, he bade his company halt, and with fifteen of the knights whom he loved best he alighted, and put his hands and his knees to the ground, and took the herbs of the field between his teeth, as if he would have eaten them, weeping for great joy; ... thus did he know how to humble himself before Alfonso his Lord; and in this manner he approached his feet and would have kissed them. And the King drew back and said, The hand, Cid Campeador, not the foot! And the Cid drew nigh upon his knees and besought grace, saying, In this guise grant me your love, so that all present may hear. And the King said that he forgave him, and granted him his love with his heart and soul. And the Cid kissed both his hands, being still upon his knees; and the King embraced him, and gave him the kiss of peace. Well pleased were all they who beheld this, save only Alvar Diez and García Ordoñez, for they did not love the Cid. Then went they all toward the town, the King and the Cid talking together by the way. And the Cid asked the King to eat with him, and the King answered, Not so, for ye are not prepared; we arrived yesterday, and ye but now. Eat you and your company therefore with me, for we have made ready. To-day, Cid

Campeador, you are my guest, and to-morrow we will do as pleases you. Now came the Infantes of Carrion up and humbled themselves before the Cid, and he received them well, and they promised to do him service. And the company of the Cid came up, and kissed the King's hand. So they alighted and went to meat; and the King said unto the Cid that he should eat with him at his table; howbeit he would not. And when the King saw that he would not take his seat with him, he ordered a high table to be placed for the Cid and for Count Don Gonzalo, the father of the Infantes of Carrion. All the while that they ate the King could never look enough at the Cid, and he marvelled greatly at his beard, that it had grown to such length. And when they had eaten they were merry, and took their pleasure. And on the morrow the King and all they who went with him to this meeting, ate with the Cid, and so well did he prepare for them that all were full joyful, and agreed in one thing, that they had not eaten better for three years. There was not a man there who did not eat upon silver, and the King and the chief persons ate upon dishes and trenchers of gold. And when the Infantes saw this they had the marriage more at heart than before.

XXIX.

On the morrow as soon as it was day, the Bishop Don Hieronymo sung mass before the King, in the oratory of the Cid; and when it was over, the King said before all who were there assembled, Counts and Infanzones and knights, hear what I shall say unto the Cid. Cid Ruydiez, the reason wherefore I sent for you to this meeting was two-fold: first, that I might see you, which I greatly desired, for I love you much because of the many and great services which you have done me, albeit that at one time I was wroth against you and banished you from the land. But you so demeaned yourself that you never did me disservice, but contrariwise, great service both to God and to me, and have won Valencia, and enlarged Christendom, wherefore I am bound to show favour unto you and to love you alway. The second reason was, that I might ask you for your two daughters Doña Elvira and Doña Sol, that you would give them in marriage to the Infantes of Carrion, for this methinks would be a fit marriage, and to your honour and good. When the Cid heard this, he was in a manner bound to consent, having them thus demanded from him; and he answered and said, Sir, my daughters are of tender years and if it might please you, they are yet too young for marriage. I do not say this as if the Infantes of Carrion were not worthy to match with them, and with better than they. And the King bade him make no excuse, saying, that he should esteem himself well served if he gave his consent. Then the Cid said, Sir, I begat them, and you give them in marriage; both I and they are yours, ... give them to whom you please, and I am pleased therewith. When the King heard this he was well pleased, and he bade the Infantes kiss the hand of the Cid Campeador, and incontinently they changed swords before the King, and they did homage to him, as sons-in-law to their father-in-law. Then the King turned to the Cid, and said, I thank thee, Ruydiez, that thou hast given me thy daughters for the Infantes of Carrion: and here I give them to the Infantes to be their brides; I give them and not you, and I pray God that it may please him, and that you also may have great joy herein. The Infantes I put into your hands; they will go with you, and I shall return from hence, and I order that three hundred marks of silver be given to them for their marriage, and they and your daughters will all be your children.

XXX.

Eight days this meeting lasted; the one day they dined with the King, and the other with the Cid. Then was it appointed that on the morrow at sunrise every one should depart to his own home. My Cid then began to give to every one who would take his gifts, many a great mule, and many a good palfrey, and many a rich garment, ... every one had what he asked, ... he said no to none. Threescore horses did my Cid give away in gifts; well pleased were all they who went to that meeting. And now they were about to separate, for it was night. The King took the Infantes by the hand, and delivered them into the power of my Cid the Campeador, ... See here your sons: from this day, Campeador, you will know what to make of them. And the Cid answered, Sir, may it please you, seeing it is you who have made this marriage for my daughters, to appoint some one to whom I may deliver them, and who may give them, as from your hand, to the Infantes. And the King called for Alvar Fañez Minaya, and said. You are sib to the damsels; I command you, when you come to Valencia, to take them with your own hands, and give them to the Infantes, as I should do if that I were there present: and be you the bride's father. Then said the Cid, Sir, you must accept something from me at this meeting. I bring for you twenty palfreys, these that are gaily trapped, and thirty horses fleet of foot, these that are well caparisoned, ... take them, and I kiss your hand. Greatly have you bound me, said King Don Alfonso; I receive this gift, and God and all Saints grant that it may well be requited; if I live you shall have something from me; Then my Cid sprung up upon his horse Bavieca, and he said, Here I say before my Lord the King, that if any will go with me to the wedding, I think they will get something by it! and he besought the King that he would let as many go with him as were so minded; and the king licensed them accordingly. And when they were about to part, the company that went with the Cid was greater than that which returned with the King. And the Cid kissed the King's hand and dispeeded himself with his favour, and the King returned to Castille.

XXXI.

My Cid went his way toward Valencia, and he appointed Pero Bermudez and Muño Gustios, than whom there were no better two in all his household, to keep company with the Infantes of Carrion and be their guard, and he bade them spy out what their conditions were; and this they soon found out. The Count Don Suero González went with the Infantes; he was their father's brother, and had been their Ayo and bred them up, and badly had he trained them, for he was a man of great words, good of tongue, and of nothing else good; and full scornful and orgullous had he made them, so that the Cid was little pleased with them, and would willingly have broken off the marriage; but he could not, seeing that the King had made it. And when they reached Valencia, the Cid lodged the Infantes in the suburb of Alcudia, where he had formerly lodged himself; and all the company who were come to the marriage were quartered with them. And he went to the Alcazar.

XXXII.

On the morrow the Cid mounted his horse and rode ínto Alcudia, and brought the Infantes his sons-in-law from thence with him into the city to the Alcazar, that they might see their brides Doña Elvira and Doña Sol. Doña Ximena had her daughters ready to receive them in full noble garments, for since midnight they had done nothing but prink and prank themselves. Full richly was the Alcazar set out that day, with hangings both above and below, purple and samite, and rich cloth. The Cid entered, between the Infantes, and all that noble company went in after them; and they went into the chief hall of the Alcazar, where Doña Ximena was with her daughters: and when they saw the Cid and the Infantes, they rose up and welcomed them right well. And the Cid took his seat upon his bench with one of the Infantes on one side of him, and one on the other, and the other honourable men seated themselves on the estrados, each in the place where he ought to be, and which belonged to him; and they remained awhile silent. Then the Cid rose and called for Alvar Fañez and said, Thou knowest what my Lord the King commanded; fulfil now his bidding, ... take thy cousins, and deliver them to the Infantes, for it is the King who gives them in marriage, and not I. And Alvar Fañez arose and took the damsels one in each hand, and delivered them to the Infantes, saying. Diego Gonzalez, and Ferrando Gonzalez, I deliver unto you these damsels, the daughters of the Cid Campeador, by command of King Don Alfonso my Lord, even as he commanded. Receive you them as your equal helpmates, as the law of Christ enjoineth. And the Infantes took each his bride by the hand, and went to the Cid and kissed his hand, and the same did they to their mother Doña Ximena Gomez: and the Bishop Don Hieronymo espoused them, and they exchanged rings. When this was done, the Cid went and seated himself on the estrado with the ladies, he and Doña Ximena in the middle, and beside him he placed Doña Elvira his eldest daughter, and by her, her spouse the Infante Diego Gonzalez; and Doña Sol was seated on the other side, by her mother, and the Infante Ferrando by her. And when they had solaced themselves awhile, the Cid said that now they would go eat, and that the marriage should be performed on the morrow, and he besought and commanded the Bishop Don Hieronymo to perform it in such a manner that no cost should be spared, but that every thing should be done so compleatly, that they who came from Castille to this wedding might alway have something to tell of.

XXXIII.

On the morrow they went to the Church of St. Mary, and there the Bishop Don Hieronymo sate awaiting them, and he blest them all four at the altar. Who can tell the great nobleness which the Cid displayed at that wedding, the feasts and the bull-fights, and the throwing at the target, and the throwing canes, and how many joculars were there, and all the sports which are proper at such weddings? As soon as they came out of Church they took horse and rode to the Glera; three times did the Cid change his horse that day; seven targets were set up on the morrow, and before they went to dinner all seven were broken. Fifteen days did the feasts at this wedding continue; then all they who had come there to do honour to the Cid took leave of him and of the Infantes. Who can tell the great and noble gifts which the Cid gave to them, both to great and little, each according to his quality, vessels of gold and silver, rich cloth, cloaks, furs, horses, and money beyond all reckoning, so that all were well pleased. And when it was told in Castille with what gifts they who had been to the wedding were returned, many were they who repented that they had not gone there.

BOOK VIII.

I.

Now the history relateth that Gilbert, a sage who wrote the history of the Moorish Kings who reigned in Africa, saith, that Bucar remembering the oath which he had made to his brother King Yucef, how he would take vengeance for him for the dishonour which he had received from the Cid Ruydiez before Valencia, ordered proclamation to be made throughout all the dominions of his father, and gathered together so great a power of Moors, that among the Captains of his host there were twenty and nine Kings; this he could well do, for his father was Miramamolin, which is as much as to say Emperor. And when he had gathered together this mighty host, he entered into his ships and crost the sea, and came unto the port of Valencia, and what there befell him with the Cid the history shall relate in due time.

II.

Two years after their marriage did the Infantes of Carrion sojourn in Valencia in peace and pleasure, to their own great contentment, and their uncle Suero Gonzalez with them; and at the end of those two years, there came to pass a great misadventure, by reason of which they fell out with the Cid, in whom there was no fault. There was a lion in the house of the Cid, who had grown a large one, and a strong, and was full nimble: three men had the keeping of this lion, and they kept him in a den which was in a court yard, high up in the palace; and when they cleansed the court they were wont to shut him up in his den, and afterward to open the door that he might come out and eat: the Cid kept him for his pastime, that he might take pleasure with him when he was minded so to do. Now it was the custom of the Cid to dine every day with his company, and after he had dined, he was wont to sleep awhile upon his seat. And one day when he had dined there came a man and told him that a great fleet was arrived in the port of Valencia, wherein there was a great power of the Moors, whom King Bucar had brought over, the son of the Miramamolin of Morocco. And when the Cid heard this, his heart rejoiced and he was glad, for it was nigh three years since he had had a battle with the Moors. Incontinently he ordered a signal to be made that all the honourable men who were in the city should assemble together. And when they were all assembled in the Alcazar and his sons-in-law with them, the Cid told them the news, and took counsel with them in what manner they should go out against this great power of the Moors. And when they had taken counsel the Cid went to sleep upon his seat, and the Infantes and the others sate playing at tables and chess. Now at this time the men who were keepers of the lion were cleaning the court, and when they heard the cry that the Moors were coming, they opened the den, and came down into the palace where the Cid was, and left the door of the court open. And when the lion had ate his meat and saw that the door was open he went out of the court and came down into the palace, even into the hall where they all were; and when they who were there saw him, there was a great stir among them; but the Infantes of Carrion showed greater cowardice than all the rest. Ferrando González having no shame, neither for the Cid nor for the others who were present, crept under the seat whereon the Cid was sleeping, and in his haste he burst his mantle and his doublet also at the shoulders. And Diego González, the other, ran to a postern door, crying, I shall never see Carrion again! this door opened upon a court yard where there was a wine press, and he jumped out, and by reason of the great height could not keep on his feet, but fell among the lees and defiled himself therewith. And all the others who were in the hall wrapt their cloaks around their arms, and stood round about the seat whereon the Cid was sleeping, that they might defend him. The noise which they made awakened the Cid, and he saw the lion coming towards him, and he lifted up his hand and said, What is this?... and the lion hearing his voice stood still; and he rose up and took him by the mane, as if he had been a gentle mastiff, and led him back to the court where he was before, and ordered his keepers to look better to him for the time to come. And when he had done this he returned to the hall and took his seat again; and all they who beheld it were greatly astonished.

III.

After some time Ferrando Gonzalez crept from under the seat where he had hidden himself, and he came out with a pale face, not having yet lost his fear, and his brother Diego got from among the lees: and when they who were present saw them in this plight you never saw such sport as they made; but my Cid forbade their laughter. And Diego went out to wash himself and change his garments, and he sent to call his brother forth, and they took counsel together in secret, and said to each other, Lo now, what great dishonour this Ruydiez our father-in-law hath done us, for he let this lion loose for the nonce, to put us to shame. But in an evil day were we born if we do not revenge this upon his daughters. Badly were we matched with them, and now for the after-feast he hath made this mockery of us! But we must keep secret this which we bear in mind, and not let him wit that we are wroth against him, for otherwise he would not let us depart from hence, neither give us our wives to take with us, and he would take from us the swords Colada and Tizona which he gave us.... We will therefore turn this thing into merriment before him and his people, to the end that they may not suspect what we have at heart. While they were thus devising their uncle Suero Gonzalez came in, and they told him of their intent. And he counselled them to keep their wrath secret, as they said, till this stir of the Moors from beyond sea was over, and then they should demand their wives of the Cid that they might take them to their own country; This, said he, the Cid can have no reason to deny, neither for detaining ye longer with him, and when ye are got away far out of his land, then may ye do what ye will with his daughters, and ill will ye do if ye know not how to revenge yourselves; so shall ye remove the dishonour from yourselves, and cast it upon him and his children. This wicked counsel did Suero González give unto his nephews, which he might have well excused giving, and then both he and they would not have come off so badly as the history will in due season relate.

IV.

After Suero González and his nephews had taken this evil counsel together, they went to their lodging, and on the morrow they went to the Alcazar and came to the Cid where he was preparing for business. And when they drew nigh, the Cid rose and welcomed them right well, and they carried a good countenance towards him, and made sport of what had happened about the lion. And the Cid began to give order in what array they should go out to battle. While they were in this discourse, a great cry was heard in the town and a great tumult, and this was because King Bucar was come with his great power into the place which is called the Campo del Quarto, which is a league from Valencia, and there he was pitching his tents and when this was done the camp made a mighty show, for the history saith that there were full five thousand pavilions, besides common tents. And when the Cid heard this, he took both his sons-in-law and Suero González with him, and went upon the highest tower of the Alcazar, and showed them the great power which King Bucar of Morocco had brought; and when he beheld this great power he began to laugh and was exceeding glad: but Suero González and his nephews were in great fear: howbeit they would not let it be seen. And when they came down from the tower the Cid went foremost, and they tarried behind, and said, If we go into this battle we shall never return to Carrion. Now it so chanced that Muño Gustios heard them, and he told it to the Cid, and it grieved the Cid at heart; but he presently made sport of it, and turned to his sons-in-law, and said, You my sons shall remain in Valencia and guard the town, and we who are used to this business will go out to battle; and they when they heard this were ashamed, for they weened that some one had overheard what they said; and they made answer, God forefend, Cid, that we should abide in Valencia! we will go with you to the work, and protect your body as if we were your sons, and you were the Count Don Gonzalo Gomez our father. And the Cid was well pleased hearing them say this.

V.

While they were thus saying, word was brought to the Cid that there was a messenger from King Bucar at the gate of the town, who would fain speak with him. The name of this Moor was Ximen de Algezira, and the Cid gave order that he should be admitted. Now the history saith, God had given such grace to my Cid that never Moor beheld his face without having great fear of him; and this Ximen began to gaze upon his countenance, and said nothing, for he could not speak. And so great was the fear which came upon him that the Cid perceived it, and bade him take courage and deliver the bidding of his Lord, without fear or shame, for he was a messenger. And when the Moor heard this he laid aside his fear, and recovered heart, and delivered his bidding fully, after this wise. Sir Cid Campeador, King Bucar my Lord hath sent me to thee saying, great wrong hast thou done him in holding Valencia against him, which belonged to his forefathers; and moreover thou hast discomfited his brother King Yucef. And now he is come against thee with twenty and nine Kings, to take vengeance for his brother, and to win Valencia from thee in spite of thee and of all who are with thee. Nevertheless, King Bucar saith, that inasmuch as he hath heard that thou art a wise man and of good understanding, he will show favour unto thee, and let thee leave Valencia with all the lands thereof, and go into Castille, and take with thee all that is thine. And if thou wilt not do this he sends to say that he will fight against Valencia, and take thee and thy wife and thy daughters, and torment thee grievously, in such manner that all Christians who shall hear tell of it shall talk thereof for evermore. This is the bidding of my Lord King Bucar.

VI.

When the Cid heard this, notwithstanding he was wroth at heart, he would not manifest it, but made answer in few words and said, Go tell thy Lord King Bucar I will not give him up Valencia: great labour did I endure in winning it, and to no man am I beholding for it in the world, save only to my Lord Jesus Christ, and to my kinsmen and friends and vassals who aided me to win it. Tell him that I am not a man to be besieged, and when he does not expect it I will give him battle in the field; and would that even as he has brought with him twenty and nine Kings, so he had brought all the Moors of all Pagandom, for with the mercy of God in which I trust, I should think to conquer them all. Bear this answer to your Lord, and come here no more with messages, neither on this account nor on any other. When Ximen de Algezira, the Moorish messenger, heard this, he left Valencia, and went unto his Lord and told him before the twenty and nine Kings all that the Cid had said. And they were astonished at the brave words of the Cid, for they did not think that he would have resisted, so great was their power, neither did they ween that he would so soon come out to battle. And they began to give order to set their siege round about Valencia, as the history, and as Gilbert also relateth. This King Bucar and his brother King Yucef were kinsmen of Alimaymon, who had been King of Toledo and Valencia, and this was the reason why Bucar said that Valencia had belonged to his forefathers.

VII.

No sooner had Ximen, the messenger of King Bucar, left the city, than the Cid ordered the bell to be struck, at the sound of which all the men at arms in Valencia were to gather together. Incontinently they all assembled before the Cid, and he told them all to be ready full early on the morrow to go out and give battle to the Moors. And they made answer with one accord that they were well pleased to do this, for they trusted in God and in his good fortune that they should overcome them. On the morrow therefore at the first cock-crow, they confessed and communicated, as was their custom, and before the morning brake they went forth from Valencia. And when they had got through the narrow passes among the gardens, the Cid set his army in array. The van he gave to Alvar Fañez Minaya, and to Pero Bermudez who bore his banner; and he gave them five hundred horsemen, and a thousand and five hundred men a-foot. In the right wing was that honourable one with the shaven crown, Don Hieronymo the Bishop, with the like number both of horse and foot; and in the left Martin Antolinez of Burgos and Alvar Salvadores, with as many more. The Cid came in the rear with a thousand horsemen all in coats of mail, and two thousand five hundred men a-foot. And in this array they proceeded till they came in sight of the Moors. As soon as the Cid saw their tents he ordered his men to slacken their pace, and got upon his horse Bavieca, and put himself in the front before all his army, and his sons-in-law the Infantes of Carrion advanced themselves with him. Then the Bishop Don Hieronymo came to the Cid and said, This day have I said the mass of the Holy Trinity before you, I left my own country and came to seek you, for the desire I had to kill some Moors, and to do honour to my order and to my own hands. Now would I be the foremost in this business; I have my pennon and my armorial bearing, and will employ them by God's help, that my heart may rejoice. And my Cid, if you do not for the love of me grant this I will go my ways from you. But the Cid bade him do his pleasure, saying that it would please him also. And then the great multitude of the Moors began to come out of their tents, and they formed their battle in haste, and came against the Christians, with the sound of trumpets and tambours, and with a great uproar; and as they came out upon the alarm, not expecting that the Cid would come against them so soon, they did not advance in order, as King Bucar had commanded. And when the Cid saw this, he ordered his banner to be advanced, and bade his people lay on manfully. The Bishop Don Hieronynio he pricked forward; two Moors he slew with the two first thrusts of the lance; the haft broke, and he laid hand on his sword, God,... how well the Bishop fought! two he slew with the lance and five with the sword; the Moors came round about him and laid on load of blows, but they could not pierce his arms. He who was born in happy hour had his eyes upon him, and he took his shield and placed it before him, and lowered his lance, and gave Bavieca the spur, that good horse. With heart and soul he went at them, and made his way into their first battle; seven the Campeador smote down, and four he slew. In short time they joined battle in such sort that many were slain and many overthrown, on one side and on the other, and so great was the din of strokes and of tambours that none could hear what another said; and they smote away cruelly, without rest or respite.

VIII.

Now it came to pass in this battle that the Infante Diego Gonzalez encountered a Moor of Africa who was of great stature and full valiant withal, and this Moor came fiercely against him; and when the Infante saw how fiercely he was coming, he turned his back and fled. No one beheld this but Felez Muñoz the nephew of the Cid, who was a squire; he set himself against the Moor with his lance under his arm, and gave him such a thrust in the breast, that the streamer of the lance came out all red with blood between his shoulders, and he down'd with the dead man and took his horse by the bridle, and began to call the Infante Diego Gonzalez. When the Infante heard himself called by his name he turned his head to see who called him, and when he saw that it was his cousin Felez Muñoz, he turned and awaited him. And Felez Muñoz said, Take this horse, cousin Diego Gonzalez, and say that you killed the Moor; nobody shall ever know otherwise from me, unless you give just cause. While they were talking the Cid came up, after another Moorish knight, whom he reached just as he came up to them, and smote him with his sword upon the head, so that he split it down to the teeth. When Felez Muñoz saw the Cid, he said, Sir, your son-in-law Don Diego Gonzalez hath great desire to serve and help you in this day's work, and he hath just slain a Moor from whom he hath won this horse: and this pleased the Cid much, for he weened that it was true. And then they all three advanced themselves toward the midst of the battle, giving great strokes, and smiting and slaying. Who can tell how marvellously the Bishop Don Hieronymo behaved himself in this battle, and how well all the rest behaved, each in his way, and above all, the Cid Campeador, as the greatest and best of all! nevertheless the power of the Moors was so great that they could not drive them to flight, and the business was upon the balance even till the hour of nones. Many were the Christians who died that day among the foot-soldiers; and the dead, Moors and Christians together, were so many, that the horses could scant move among their bodies. But after the hour of nones the Cid and his people smote the Moors so sorely that they could no longer stand against them, and it pleased God and the good fortune of the Cid that they turned their backs; and the Christians followed, hewing them down, and smiting and slaying; ana they tarried not to lay hands on those whom they felled, but went on in the pursuit as fast as they could. Then might you have seen cords broken, and stakes plucked up as the Christians came to the tents; my Cid's people drove King Bucar's through their camp, and many an arm with its sleeve-mail was lopt off, and many a head with its helmet fell to the ground; and horses ran about on all sides without riders. Seven full miles did the pursuit continue. And while they were thus following their flight the Cid set eyes upon King Bucar, and made at him to strike him with the sword; and the Moorish King knew him when he saw him coming; Turn this way Bucar, cried the Campeador, you who came from beyond sea, to see the Cid with the long beard. We must greet each other and cut out a friendship! God confound such friendship, cried King Bucar, and turned his bridle, and began to fly towards the sea, and the Cid after him, having great desire to reach him. But King Bucar had a good horse and a fresh, and the Cid went spurring Bavieca who had had hard work that day, and he came near his back; and when they were nigh unto the ships, and the Cid saw that he could not reach him, he darted his sword at him, and struck him between the shoulders; and King Bucar being badly wounded rode into the sea, and got to a boat, and the Cid alighted and picked up his sword. And his people came up, hewing down the Moors before them, and the Moors in their fear of death ran into the sea, so that twice as many died in the water as in the battle; nevertheless so many were they who were slain in the field, that they were thought to be seventeen thousand persons and upward: but a greater number died in the sea. And so many were they who were taken prisoner, that it was a wonder; and of the twenty and nine Kings who came with King Bucar, seventeen were slain. And when the Cid saw that of the Moors some had gotten to the ships and the others were slain or taken, he returned toward their tents.

IX.

My Cid Ruydiez the Campeador returned from the slaughter; the hood of his mail was thrown back, and the coif upon his head bore the marks of it. And when he saw his sons-in-law the Infantes of Carrion, he rejoiced over them, and said to them to do them honour, Come here, my sons, for by your help we have conquered in this battle. Presently Alvar Fañez came up: the shield which hung from his neck was all battered: more than twenty Moors had he slain, and the blood was running from his wrist to his elbow. Thanks be to God, said he, and to the Father who is on high, and to you, Cid, we have won the day. All these spoils are yours and your vassals. Then they spoiled the field, where they found great riches in gold, and in silver, and in pearls, and in precious stones, and in sumptuous tents, and in horses, and in oxen, which were so many that it was a wonder. The poorest man among the Christians was made full rich that day. So great was the spoil that six hundred horses fell to the Cid as his fifth, beside sumpter beasts and camels, and twelve hundred prisoners; and of the other things which were taken no man can give account, nor of the treasure which the Cid won that day in the Campo del Quarto. God be praised! said the Campeador...once I was poor, but now am I rich in lands and in possessions, and in gold and in honour. And Moors and Christians both fear me. Even in Morocco, among their Mosques, do they fear least I should set upon them some night. Let them fear it! I shall not go to seek them, but here will I be in Valencia, and by God's help they shall pay me tribute. Great joy was made in Valencia for this victory, and great was the joy of the Infantes of Carrion; five thousand marks came to them for their portion of the spoil. And when they saw themselves so rich, they and their uncle Suero Gonzalez took counsel together, and confirmed the wicked resolution which they had taken.

X.

One day the companions of the Cid were talking before him of this victory, and they were saying who were the young knights that had demeaned themselves well in the battle and in the pursuit, and who had not; but no mention was made of the Infantes; for though some there were who whispered to each other concerning them, none would speak ill of them before the Cid. And the Infantes saw this, and took counsel with their uncle, who ought not to have given them the evil counsel that he did, and they determined forthwith to put their wicked design in execution. So they went before the Cid, and Ferrando Gonzalez, having enjoined silence, began to say thus. Cid, thou knowest well the good tie which there is between thee and us, for we hold thee in the place of a father, and thou didst receive us as thy sons on the day when thou gavest us thy daughters to be our wives; and from that day we have alway abode with thee, and have alway endeavoured to do that which was to thy service; and if we have at any time failed therein it hath not been wilfully, but for lack of better understanding. Now inasmuch as it is long time since we departed from Castille, from our father and from our mother, and because neither we know how it fares with them, nor they how it fares with us, we would now, if you and Doña Ximena should so think good, return unto them, and take our wives with us: so shall our father and our mother and our kinsmen see how honourably we are mated, and how greatly to our profit, and our wives shall be put in possession of the towns which we have given them for their dower, and shall see what is to be the inheritance of the children whom they may have. And whensoever you shall call upon us, we will be ready to come and do you service. Then the Cid made answer, weening that this was spoken without deceit, My sons, I am troubled at what ye say, for when ye take away my daughters ye take my very heart-strings: nevertheless, it is fitting that ye do as ye have said. Go when ye will, and I will give unto you such gifts that it shall be known in Gallicia and in Castille and in Leon, with what riches I have sent my sons-in-law home.

XI.

When the Cid had made this reply, he rose from his seat and went to Doña Ximena his wife, and spake with her and with Alvar Fañez, and told them what had passed with his sons-in-law, and what answer he had given. Greatly was Doña Ximena troubled at this, and Alvar Fañez also, that he had consented to what they asked; and she said, I do not think it is wisely done to let them take our daughters from us, and carry them into another country; for these our sons-in-law are traitorous and false at heart, and if I areed them right they will do some dishonour to our daughters, when there will be none there to call them to account. And Alvar Fañez was of the same mind; but the Cid was displeased at this, and marvelled greatly at what they said; and he bade them speak no more thereof, for God would not let it be so, ... neither were the Infantes of such a race as that they should do this; neither, quoth he, would it come into their minds to do it, if only because our Lord King Don Alfonso was he who made the marriage; but if the Devil should tempt them, and they should commit this wickedness, dearly would it cost them!

XII.

So the Infantes of Carrion made ready for their departure, and there was a great stir in Valencia. And the two sisters Doña Elvira and Doña Sol, came and knelt before the Cid and before Doña Ximena their mother, and said, You send us to the lands of Carrion, and we must fulfil your command: now then give us your blessing, and let us have some of your people with us in Carrion, we beseech you. And the Cid embraced them and kissed them, and the mother kissed them and embraced them twice as much, and they gave them their blessing, and their daughters kissed their hands. And the Cid gave unto his sons-in-law great store of cloth of gold, and of serge, and of wool, and an hundred horses bridled and saddled, and an hundred mules with all their trappings, and ten cups of gold, and an hundred vessels of silver, and six hundred marks of silver in dishes and trenchers and other things. When all this was done they took their departure and went out of Valencia, and the Cid rode out a long league with them. He looked at the birds, and the augury was bad, and he thought that these marriages would not be without some evil. And his heart smote him, and he began to think on what Doña Ximena had said, and to fear lest evil should befall him from these sons-in-law, for the manner of their speech was not as it was wont to be. Where art thou my nephew, where art thou Felez Muñoz? thou art the cousin of my daughters, said he, both in heart and in soul. Go with them even unto Carrion, and see the possessions which are given them, and come back with tidings thereof And Felez Muñoz said that he would do this. And the Cid bade him salute the Moor Abengalvon in his name, with whom they should tarry a night at Molina, and bid him do service unto his daughters, and his sons-in-law, and accompany them as far as Medina; and for all that he shall do; said the Cid, I will give him good guerdon. And when the ladies came to take their leave of their father the Cid, and of their mother Doña Ximena, great were the lamentations on both sides, as if their hearts had divined the evil which was to come; and the Cid strove to comfort them, saying, that he should alway think of them, and would maintain them in good estate: and he gave them his blessing and turned back toward Valencia, and they went their way with their husbands, and that parting was like plucking the nail from the flesh.

XIII.

So the Infantes of Carrion went their way, by the Campo del Quarto to Chiva, and to Bonilla, and to Requena, and to Campo-Robres, and they took up their lodging at Villa Taxo. And on the morrow they took the road to Amaja, and leaving it on the right came to Adamuz, and passed by Colcha, and rested at Quintana. And when Abengalvon knew that the daughters of the Cid were coming, he went out joyfully from Molina to meet them, and pitched tents for them in the field, and had food brought there in abundance. God, how well he served them! and on the morrow the Moor gave full rich and noble gifts to the daughters of his Lord the Cid, and to each of the Infantes he gave a goodly horse. And he took horse himself and rode on with them, having two hundred knights in his company. They crossed the mountains of Luzon and passed Arbuxuelo, and came to Salon, and the Moor lodged them in the place which is called Ansarera; all this he did for the love of the Cid Campeador. Now the Infantes seeing the riches which this Moor had with him, took counsel together for treason, and said, Lo now if we could slay this Moor Abengalvon, we should possess all these riches as safely as if we were in Carrion, and the Cid could never take vengeance. And a Moor who understood the Latin of the country, heard them and knew what they said, and he went to Abengalvon, and said unto him, Acaiaz, that is to say, Sire, take heed, for I heard the Infantes of Carrion plotting to kill thee. Abengalvon the Moor was a bold Baron, and when this was told him, he went with his two hundred men before the Infantes, and what he said to them did not please them. Infantes of Carrion, he said, tell me, what have I done? I have served ye without guile, and ye have taken counsel for my death. If it were not for the sake of my Cid, never should you reach Carrion! I would carry back his daughters to the loyal Campeador, and so deal with you that it should be talked of over the whole world. But I leave ye for traitors as ye are. Doña Elvira and Doña Sol, I go with your favour. God grant that this marriage may please your father! Having said this the good Moor returned to Molina.

XIV.

They went on by Valdespino, and by Parra, and Berrocal, and Val de Endrinas, and they left Madina Celi on the right, and crost the plain of Barahona, and past near Berlanga; and they crost the Douro by a ford below the town, and rode on and came into the Oak-wood of Corpes. The mountains were high, and the trees thick and lofty, and there were wild beasts in that place. And they came to a green lawn in the midst of that oak forest, where there was a fountain of clear water, and there the Infantes gave order that their tents should be pitched; and they passed the night there, making show of love to their wives, which they badly fulfilled when the sun was risen, for this was the place where they thought to put them to shame. Early in the morning they ordered the sumpter beasts to be laden, and the tent struck, and they sent all their company on, so that none remained with them, neither man nor woman, but they and their wives were left alone that they might disport with them at pleasure. And Doña Elvira said to her husband, Why wouldst thou that we should remain alone in this place? And he said, Hold thy peace, and thou shall see! And the Infantes tore away the mantles from off their wives, and the garments which they wore, save only their inner garment, and they held them by the hair of their head with one hand, and with the other took the girths of their horses. And the women said, Don Diego and Don Ferrando, ye have strong swords and of sharp edge; the one is called Colado and the other Tizona; cut off our heads and we shall become martyrs! But set not this evil example upon us, for whatever shame ye do unto us shall be to your own dishonour. But the Infantes heeded not what they said, and beat them cruelly with the saddle-girths, and kicked them with their spurs, so that their garments were torn, and stained with blood. Oh, if the Cid Campeador had come upon them at that hour! And the women cried out, and called upon God and Holy Mary to have mercy upon them; but the more they cried, the more cruelly did those Infantes beat and kick them, till they were covered with blood, and swooned away. Then the Infantes took their mantles and their cloaks, and their furs of ermine and other garments, and left them for dead, saying, Lie there, daughters of the Cid of Bivar, for it is not fitting that ye should be our wives, nor that ye should have your dower in the lands of Carrion! We shall see how your father will avenge you, and we have now avenged ourselves for the shame he did us with the Lion. And they rode away as they said this, leaving them to the mountain birds and to the beasts of the forest. Oh if the Cid Campeador had come upon them at that hour! And the Infantes rode on glorying in what they had done, for they said that the daughters of the Cid were worthy to be their harlots, but not their wives.

XV.

When the Infantes, before they committed this great cruelty, ordered their company to ride forward, Felez Muñoz the nephew of the Cid, rode on with the rest: but this order nothing pleased him, and he was troubled at heart, insomuch that he went aside from his companions, and struck into the forest, and there waited privily till he should see his cousins come, or learn what the Infantes had done to them. Presently he saw the Infantes, and heard what they said to each other. Certes if they had espied him he could not have escaped death. But they pricked on not seeing him, and he rode back to the fountain, and there he found the women lying senseless, and in such plight as ye have heard. And he made great lamentation over them, saying, Never can it please God that ye my cousins should receive such dishonour! God and St. Mary give them who have done this an evil guerdon! for ye never deserved this, neither are ye of a race to deserve that this or any other evil should betide ye! By this time the women began to come to themselves, but they could not speak, for their hearts were breaking. And Felez Muñoz called out to them, Cousins! Cousins! Doña Elvira! Doña Sol! for the love of God rouse yourselves that we may get away before night comes, or the wild beasts will devour us! and they came to themselves and began to open their eyes, and saw that he who spake to them was Felez Muñoz; and he said to them, For the love of God take heart and let us be gone; for the Infantes will soon seek for me, and if God do not befriend us we shall all be slain. And Doña Sol said to him in her great pain, Cousin, for all that our father hath deserved at your hands, give us water. Felez Muñoz took his hat and filled it with water and gave it to them. And he comforted them and bade them take courage, and besought them to bear up. And he placed them upon his horse, and covered them both with his cloak, and led them through the oak forest, into the thickest part thereof, and there he made a bed of leaves and of grass, and laid them on it, and covered them with his cloak, and he sate down by them and began to weep, for he knew not what he should do: for he had no food, and if he went to seek it, great danger was there because they were wounded and bloody, that the wild beasts and the birds of the mountain would attack them; and on the other hand, unless he went to his uncle the Cid, to tell him of this wickedness, none other knew what had been done, and thus there would be no vengeance taken.

XVI.

While Felez Muñoz was in this great trouble the Infantes joined their company, and their spurs were bloody and their hands also from the wounds which they had given their wives. And when their people saw them in this plight, and that their wives were not with them, they weened that some wickedness had been done; and all they who were of good heart and understanding among them went apart, to the number of an hundred, with one who was named Pero Sanchez; and he spake unto them, saying, Friends, these Infantes have done a foul deed upon their wives, the daughters of our Lord the Cid; and they are our liege Ladies, for we did homage to them before their father, and accepted them as such; and the Cid made us knights that we should discharge the duty which we owe to them. Now then, it behoveth us that we arm ourselves, and demand of the Infantes what they have done with our ladies, and require them at their hands. And if they will not deliver them to us, then will we fight against them even to death; for thus shall we do right, and otherwise we shall be ill spoken of, and not worthy to live in the world. This was the counsel which Pero Sanchez gave, and they all held it good and did accordingly. And the Infantes, when they saw them coming and heard their demand, were greatly afraid, and they said, Go to the fountain in the Oak-forest of Corpes, and there ye may find them; we left them safe and sound, and no harm have we done unto them; but we would not take them with us. Ill have ye done, replied those knights, to forsake such wives, and the daughters of such a father, and ill will ye fare for it! And from henceforward, we renounce all friendship with ye, and defy ye for the Cid, and for ourselves, and for all his people. And the Infantes could not reply. And when they saw that the Infantes did not answer, they said, Get ye gone for traitors and false caitiffs: there is no way in the world by which ye can escape from the enemies whom ye have now made! But for all this the Infantes made no reply, and went their way.

XVII.

Pero Sanchez and those other knights rode back to the green lawn in the Oak-forest, where they had left the dames; and when they came to the fountain they saw that there was blood round about, but the dames were not there; and they were greatly troubled, and knew not where to seek them. And they went about the forest seeking them, calling them aloud, and making great lamentation for the ill that had befallen, and also, because they could not find them. Now Felez Muñoz and the women heard their voices, and were in great fear, for they weened that it was the Infantes and their company, who were returned with intent to kill them; and in their great fear they remained still, and would fain have been far from that place. So Pero Sanchez and they who were with him went about seeking them in vain. Then spake up a knight called Martin Ferrandez, who was a native of Burgos, saying, Friends, it boots us to turn back from hence and follow after the Infantes, and do battle with them, even unto death, because of this wickedness which they have committed, rather than return to the Cid; for if we do not strive to take vengeance, we are not worthy to appear before him. And if, peradventure, we cannot come up with them upon the road, let its go before the King Don Alfonso, and discover unto him this foul deed, and tell him the truth thereof, to the intent that he may order justice to be done for such a thing; for certes, greatly will he be troubled when he knoweth it, and greatly will he be incensed against them, inasmuch as he it was who besought the Cid to give them his daughters to wife. And we will not depart from the King's house, nor take unto ourselves any other Lord till the Cid shall have obtained justice in this matter. And all those knights held this counsel to be good, and agreed to do so. And they took their way and followed after the Infantes as fast as they could, taking no rest; but the Infantes had ridden away full speed, and they could not overtake them. And when they saw this they went their way to King Don Alfonso who was at Palencia, and they came before him and kissed his hands, and then with sorrowful hearts told him of the evil which had befallen the Cid, in this dishonour done unto his daughters by the Infantes of Carrion. And when the King heard it he was grievously offended, as one who had great part therein; and he said unto him, It must needs be, that before many days we shall receive tidings of this from the Cid Campeador, and then upon his complaint we will enter into the business in such wise, that every one shall have justice. Then Pero Sanchez and the other knights kissed the King's hands for what he had said; and they abode in his court, waiting tidings from the Cid.

When Felez Muñoz saw that the voices which they heard had ceased, he went after awhile to a village which was at hand, to seek food for the dames and for himself; and in this manner he kept them for seven days. And in that village he found a good man, who was a husbandman, and who lived a godly life with his wife and with his daughters; and this good man knew the Cid Ruydiez, for the Cid had lodged in his house, and he had heard tell of his great feats. And when Felez Muñoz knew this he took the man aside, seeing how good a man he was, and how well he spake of the Cid, and told him what had befallen those dames, and how he had hidden them in the wood. And when the good man heard it he had great ruth for them, but he held himself a happy man in that he could do them service; and he took two asses and went with Felez Muñoz to the place where they were hidden, and took with him his two sons, who were young men. And when the dames saw them they marvelled who they might be, and were ashamed and would have hidden themselves; but they could not. And the good man bent his knees before them, weeping, and said, Ladies, I am at the service of the Cid your father, who hath many times lodged in my house, and I served him the best I could, and he alway was bountiful toward me. And now, this young man, who saith his name is Felez Muñoz, hath told me the great wrong and dishonour which your husbands, the Infantes of Carrion, have done unto you. And when I heard it I was moved to great sorrow, and for the great desire I have to do service to the Cid and to you, I am come hither, to carry you, if you will be so pleased, upon these beasts, to my house; for you must not remain in this wild forest, where the beasts would devour you. And when you are there, I and my wife and my daughters will serve you the best we can; and you may then send this squire to your father, and we will keep you secretly and well till your father shall send for you; this place is not fit for you, for you would die of cold and hunger. When the good man had said this, Doña Sol turned to Doña Elvira and said, Sister, the good man saith well, and it is better that we should go with him than remain and die here, for so shall we see the vengeance which I trust in God our father will give us. So they gave thanks to God, and to that man. And he set them upon his beasts, and led them to the village, when it was now night; and they entered his house secretly, so that none knew of their coming save the good man and his family, whom he charged that they should tell no man thereof. And there his wife and his daughters ministered uoto them with pure good will.

Then these dames wrote a letter to their father the Cid, which was a letter of credence, that he should believe the tidings which Felez Muñoz would deliver, and they wrote it with the blood from their wounds. And Felez Muñoz went his way toward Valencia; and when he came to Santesteban he spake with Diego Tellez, who had been of the company of Alvar Fañez, and told him of what had befallen. He, so soon as he heard this great villainy, took beasts and seemly raiment, and went for those dames, and brought them from the house of that good man to Santesteban, and did them all honour that he could. They of Santesteban were always gentlemen; and they comforted the daughters of the Cid, and there they were healed of their hurts. In the mean time Felez Muñoz proceeded on his journey; and it came to pass that he met Alvar Fañez Minaya, and Pero Bermudez on the way, going to the King with a present which the Cid had sent him; and the present was this, ... two hundred horses, from those which he had won in the battle of Quarto from King Bucar, and an hundred Moorish prisoners, and many good swords, and many rich saddles. And as Alvar Fañez and Pero Bermudez rode on in talk, they thought that it was he, and marvelled greatly; and he when he drew nigh began to tear his hair, and make great lamentation, so that they were greatly amazed. And they alighted, asking him what it was. And he related unto them all that had befallen. But when they heard this, who can tell the lamentation which they made? And they took counsel together what they should do, and their counsel was this, ... that they should proceed to the King, and demand justice at his hands in the name of the Cid, and that Felez Muñoz should proceed to Valencia. So he told them the name of the good man with whom he had left the dames, and the place where he dwelt, and also how he had spoken with Diego Tellez at Santesteban, and then they parted.

Alvar Fañez and Pero Bermudez held on their way, and came to the King, whom they found in Valladolid. And he received them right well, and asked them for the Cid, and they kissed his hand and said, Sir, the Cid commends himself to your grace; he hath had a good affair with King Bucar of Morocco, and hath defeated him, and nine and twenty Kings who came with him, in the field of Quarto, and great booty did he gain there in gold and in silver, and in horses and tents and cattle; and he hath slain many and taken many prisoners. And in acknowledgment of you as his natural Lord, he sends you two hundred horses, and an hundred black Moors, and many rich saddles and precious swords, beseeching you to accept them at his hand, in token of the desire he hath to do service to God and to you, maintaining the faith of Jesus Christ. And King Don Alfonso made answer and said, that he took the present of the Cid with a right good will, as of the truest and most honourable vassal that ever Lord had: and he gave order to his people to receive it, and bade Alvar Fañez and Pero Bermudez seat themselves at his feet. After a while Alvar Fañez rose and said, Sir, when we departed from the Cid we left him in great honour and prosperity; but on our way we met a squire who is his nephew, by name Felez Muñoz, and he hath told us the evil and the dishonour which both we and the Cid endure in the villainy which the Infantes of Carrion have committed upon his daughters. You, Sir, know how great this villainy hath been, and how nearly it toucheth you, for the marriage was of your appointment, and I gave them by your command to the Infantes. Pero Sánchez hath told you that the dames were dead, as he believed them to be; but we, Sir, know that they are yet alive, having been grievously hurt and wounded with bridles and spurs, and stript of their garments, ... in which plight Felez Muñoz found them. Certes such a thing as this cannot please God in heaven, and ought to offend you who are Lord here in your own realm. Now therefore we beseech you that you take justice for yourself, and give us and the Cid ours. And let not the Cid be dishonoured in your time, for blessed be God, he hath never been dishonoured yet, but hath gone on alway advancing in honour since King Don Ferrando your father knighted him in Coimbra. To this the King made answer and said, God knoweth the trouble which I resent for this dishonour which hath been done to the Cid, and the more I hear of it the more doth it trouble me, and many reasons are there why it should; for my own sake, and for the sake of the Cid, and for the sake of his daughters; but since they are yet alive the evil is not so great, for as they have been wrongfully put to shame, nothing meriting such treatment, they may be rightfully avenged, as my Cortes shall determine. Moreover it is a grief to me that my vassals the Infantes of Carrion should have erred so badly and with such cruelty; but since it hath been so I cannot but do justice. I hold it good therefore to summon them to my Cortes, which I will assemble for this matter in Toledo, and the time assigned them shall be three months from this day; and do ye tell the Cid to come there with such of his people as he shall think good. Glad were Alvar Fañez and Pero Bermudez of this reply, and they kissed his hand, and dispeeded themselves. And the King ordered mules to be given them for the dames, with right noble saddles and trappings of gold and cloth of gold and of wool, with menever and gris.

XXI

Then Alvar Fañez and Pero Bermudez went their way, and Pero Sanchez and his company departed with them. They went up Val de Esgueva to Peñafiel, and by Roa and Arrueco, and they entered the

Oak-forest of Corpes, and Pero Sanchez showed the place beside the fountain where the villainy had been committed; and they made such lamentation there as if they had seen the dames lie dead before them. Then rode they to the village where the good man dwelt, and went to his dwelling, and good guerdon did they give unto him for the service which he had done, so that he was full well requited. And they took with them the two sons and the two daughters of the good man, that they might recompense them for the good deeds of their father; and the dames gave them in marriage, and made them full rich, and held them even as brothers and as sisters, because of the service which they had received from them. When it was known at Santesteban that Minaya was coming for his kinswomen, the men of that town welcomed him and his company, and they brought him in payment the efurcion, that is to say, the supper-money, and it was full great. But Minaya would not accept it at their hands, and he thanked them, and said, Thanks, men of Santesteban, for what ye have done, and my Cid the Campeador will thank ye, as I do, and God will give ye your guerdon. Then went they to visit their kinswomen, and when they saw the dames, who can tell the great lamentation which was made on both sides? albeit that they rejoiced to see each other. And Minaya said unto them, By God, cousins, he knoweth the truth, and your father and mother know it also, ... I misdoubted this when you went away with those false ones; and it grieved me when your father said that he had given his consent that ye should go, and your mother gainsaid it also; but we could not prevail, for he said he had consented. Howbeit, since ye are alive, of evils let us be thankful for the least: you have lost one marriage, and may gain a better, and the day will come when we shall avenge ye. That night they rested at Santesteban, and on the morrow they set forward and took the road towards Atienza, and the men of Santesteban escorted them as far as the river Damor, to do them pleasure. And they past Alcoceba, and went on to the King's Ford, and there took up there lodging at the Casa de Berlanga. On the morrow they lodged at Medina Celi, and from thence they went to Molina, and Abengalvon came out with a right good will to welcome them, for love of the Cid, and he did them all the honour that he could. And it was accorded between them that the dames should rest there some days, because of their weakness, and that they should send and let the Cid know what had been done.

XXII.

Then Pero Bermudez went on to Valencia, and Alvar Fañez and the rest of his company abode with the dames in Molina. And when Pero Bermudez arrived he found the Cid Ruydiez just risen with his chivalry from dinner, and when the Cid saw him he welcomed him right well; howbeit he could not refrain from weeping; for before this Felez Muñoz had told him all. And he stroked his beard and said, Thanks be to Christ, the Lord of this world, by this beard which no one hath ever cut, the Infantes of Carrion shall not triumph in this! And he began to take comfort, hearing how King Don Alfonso had appointed the Cortes. And he took Pero Bermudez by the hand and led him to Doña Ximena, who wept greatly at seeing him, and said, Ah, Pero Bermudez, what tidings bringest thou of my daughters? And he comforted her and said, Weep not, Lady, for I left them alive and well at Molina, and Alvar Fañez with them; by God's blessing you shall have good vengeance for them! Then the Cid seated himself near his wife, and Pero Bermudez took his seat before them, and told them all that he had done, and how the King had summoned them to the Cortes at Toledo. And he said unto the Cid, My uncle and Lord, I know not what to say, but ill is my luck that I could not take vengeance before I returned here; and certes, if I could have found them I would have died, or have compleated it: but they when they had done this villainy dared not appear before the King, neither in his Court, and therefore he hath issued this summons to them that they should come. Manifestly may it be seen that the King well inclineth to give you justice, if you fail not to demand it. Now then I beseech you tarry not, but let us to horse and confront them and accuse them, for this is not a thing to be done leisurely. And the Cid answered and said, Chafe not thyself, Pero Bermudez, for the man who thinketh by chafing to expedite his business, leaveth off worse than he began. Be you certain, that if

I die not I shall take vengeance upon those traitors, and I trust in God not to die till I have taken it. Now therefore, give me no more anger than I feel in my own heart, for Felez Muñoz hath given me enough. I thank my Lord King Don Alfonso for the answer which he gave you, and for appointing the Cortes, and in such guise will I appear there as shall gall them who wish ill to me. God willing, we will take our departure in good time! Do you now return to Molina, and bring on my daughters, for I would fain see them; and I will talk with them that they may tell me the whole truth of this thing, that I may know the whole when I go to the court of the King to demand vengeance.

XXIII.

Pero Bermudez returned the next day to Molina, where Abengalvon had done great honour to the dames, and to Alvar Fañez, and all that were with him. And they departed from Molina, and Abengalvon with them, for he would not leave them till he had brought them to Valencia to his Lord the Cid. And when the Cid knew that they were drawing nigh he rode out two leagues to meet them, and when they saw him they made great lamentation, they and all his company, not only the Christians but the Moors also who were in his service. But my Cid embraced his daughters, and kissed them both, and smiled and said, Ye are come, my children, and God will heal you! I accepted this marriage for you, but I could do no other; by God's pleasure ye shall be better mated hereafter. And when they reached Valencia and went into the Alcazar to their mother Doña Ximena, who can tell the lamentation which was made by the mother over her daughters, and the daughters with their mother, and by the women of their household. Three days did this great lamentation last. And the Cid thanked Abengalvon, his vassal, for the honour which he had shown to his children and their company, and promised to protect him from all who should come against him. And Abengalvon returned to Molina well pleased.

BOOK IX.

I.

My Cid the Campeador made ready to appear at the Cortes in Toledo, and he left the Bishop Don Hieronymo, and Martin Pelaez the Asturian, to command in Valencia, and five hundred knights with them, all hidalgos. And he spake with his daughters, and commanded and besought them to tell him the whole truth, how this matter had been, and not say the thing which was false; and they did accordingly, and related unto him all, even as it had befallen them. And the Cid departed from Valencia, and with him went Alvar Fañez Minaya with two hundred knights, and Pero Bermudez with one hundred; and Martin Antolinez with fifty, and Martin Ferrandez with other fifty, and Felez Ferruz and Benito Sanchez with fifty each; ... these were five hundred knights. And there went fifty with Martin Garcia and Martin Salvadorez, and fifty with Pero Gonzalvez and Martin Muñoz, and Diego Sanchez of Arlanza went with fifty, and Don Nuño, he who colonized Cubiella, and Alvar Bermudez he who colonized Osma, went with forty, and Gonzalo Muñoz of Orbaneja, and Muño Ravia, and Yvañez Cornejo with sixty, and Muño Fernandez the Lord of Monteforte, and Gomez Fernandez he who colonized Pampliego with sixty; and Don Garcia de Roa and Serrazin his brother, Lord of Aza, with ninety; and Antolin Sanchez of Soria took with him forty knights who were his children or his kin: ... nine hundred knights were they in all. And there went with them five hundred esquires on foot, all hidalgos, beside those who were bred in his household, and beside other foot-men, who were many in number. All these went well clad in right good garments, and with good horses, to serve the Cid both in Cortes and in the war.

II.

King Don Alfonso made no delay, but sent out his letters through Leon and Santiago, to the Portugueze and the Calicians, and they of Carrion, and the Castillians, that he would hold a Cortes in Toledo at the end of seven weeks, and that they who did not appear should no longer be accounted his vassals. At this greatly were the Infantes of Carrion troubled, for they feared the coming of my Cid the Campeador. And they took counsel with their kin and prayed the King that he would hold them excused from that Cortes; and the King made answer, that nothing but God should excuse them from it, for the Campeador was coming to demand justice against them, and he, quoth the King, who will not appear, shall quit my kingdoms. So when they saw that they must needs appear, they took counsel with the Count Don Garcia, the enemy of my Cid, who alway wished him ill, and they went with the greatest company that they could assemble, thinking to dismay my Cid the Campeador. And they arrived before him.

III.

When my Cid drew nigh unto Toledo, he sent Alvar Fañez forward to kiss the King's hand, and let him wit that he should be there that night. When the King heard this it rejoiced his heart, and he took horse and went out with a great company to meet him who was born in happy hour; and there went with him his sons-in-law, the Count Don Anrrich, and the Count Don Remond; this one was the father of the good Emperor. When they came in sight, the Cid dismounted and fell to the ground, and would have abased himself to honour his Lord, but the King cried out to him and said, By St. Isidro this must not be to-day! Mount, Cid, or I shall not be well pleased! I welcome you with heart and soul; ... and my heart is grieved for your grief. God send that the court be honoured by you! Amen, said my Cid the Campeador, and he kissed his hand, and afterwards saluted him. And the Cid said, I thank God that I see you, Sir; and he humbled himself to Count Don Anrrich, and Count Don Remond, and the others, and said, God save all our friends, and chiefly you, Sir! my wife Doña Ximena kisses your hand, and my daughters also, that this thing which hath befallen us, may be found displeasing unto you. And the King said, That will it be, unless God prevent. So they rode toward Toledo. And the King said unto him, I have ordered you to be lodged in my Palaces of Galiana, that you may be near me. And the Cid answered, Gramercy, Sir! God grant you long life and happy, but in your Palaces there is none who should be lodged save you. When you hold your Cortes let it be in those Palaces of Galiana, for there is better room there than in the Alcazar. I will not cross the Tagus to-night, but will pass the night in St. Servans on this side, and hold a vigil there. To-morrow I will enter the city, and be in the court before dinner. The King said that it pleased him well, and he returned into Toledo. And the Cid went into the Church of St. Servans, and ordered candles to be placed upon the altar, for he would keep a vigil there; and there he remained with Minaya and the other good ones, praying to the Lord, and talking in private. The tents of his company were pitched upon the hills round about. Any one who beheld them might well have said, that it looked like a great host.

IV.

When the King entered the city, he bade his seneschal, Benito Perez, make ready the Palaces of Galiana for the next day, when the Cortes should begin; and he fitted the great Palace after this manner. He placed estrados with carpets upon the ground, and hung the walls with cloth of gold. And in the highest place he placed the royal chair in which the King should sit; it was a right noble chair and a rich, which he had won in Toledo, and which had belonged to the Kings thereof; and round about it right noble estrados were placed for the Counts and honourable men who were come to the Cortes. Now the Cid knew how they were fitting up the Palaces of Galiana, and he called for a squire, who was a young man, one whom he had brought up and in whom he had great trust; he was an hidalgo, and hight Ferran Alfonso; and the Cid bade him take his ivory seat which he had won in Valencia, and which had belonged to the Kings thereof, and place it in the Palace, in the best place, near the seat of the King; and that none might hurt or do dishonour unto it, he gave him a hundred squires, all hidalgos, to go with him, and ordered them not to leave it till he should come there the next day. So when they had dined, they made the seat be taken up, and went with it to the Palaces of Galiana, and placed it near the seat of the King, as the Cid had commanded; and all that day and night they remained there guarding the ivory seat, till the Cid should come and take his place thereon; every one having his sword hung from his neck. This was a right noble seat, and of subtle work, so that whoso beheld it would say it was the seat of a good man, and that it became such a one as the Cid. It was covered with cloth of gold, underneath which was a cushion.

V.

On the morrow, after the King had heard mass, he went into the Palace of Galiana, where the Cortes was to assemble, and the Infantes of Carrion and the other Counts and Ricos-omes with him, save the Cid who was not yet come; and when they who did not love the Cid beheld his ivory seat, they began to make mock of it. And Count Garcia said to the King, I beseech your Grace, tell me, for whom that couch is spread beside your seat: for what dame is it made ready; will she come drest in the almexia ... or with white alquinales on her head, or after what fashion will she be apparelled? Sir, a seat like that is fit for none but your Grace: give order to take it for yourself, or that it be removed. When Ferran Alfonso, who was there to guard the ivory seat heard this, he answered and said, Count, you talk full foolishly, and speak ill of one against whom it behoves you not to talk. He who is to sit upon this seat is better than you, or than all your lineage; and he hath ever appeared a man to all his enemies, not like a woman as you say. If you deny this I will lay hands upon you, and make you acknowledge it before my Lord the King Don Alfonso, who is here present. And I am of such a race that you cannot acquit yourself by saying I am not your peer, and the vantage of half your arms I give you! At these words was the King greatly troubled, and the Counts also, and all the honourable men who were there present. And Count García who was an angry man, wrapt his mantle under his arm, and would have struck Ferran Alfonso, saying, Let me get at the boy who dares me! And Ferran Alfonso laid hand upon his sword and came forward to meet him, saying, that if it were not for the King, he would punish him thereright for the folly which he had uttered. But the King seeing that these words went on from bad to worse, put them asunder that farther evil might not happen, and he said, None of ye have reason to speak thus of the seat of the Cid; he won it like a good knight and a valiant, as he is. There is not a King in the world who deserves this seat better than my vassal the Cid, and the better and more honourable he is, the more am I honoured through him. This seat he won in Valencia, where it had belonged to the Kings thereof; and much gold and silver, and many precious stones hath he won; and many a battle hath he won both against Christians and Moors: and of all the spoil which he hath won, he hath alway sent me part, and great presents and full rich, such as never other vassal sent to his Lord; and this he hath done in acknowledgment that I am his Lord. Ye who are talking here against him, which of ye hath ever sent me such gifts as he? If any one be envious, let him atchieve such feats as he hath done, and I will seat him with myself to do him honour.

VI.

Now the Cid had performed his vigil in the Church of St. Servan, matins and primes were said, and mass performed; and then he made ready to go to the Cortes, and with him went Alvar Fañez Minaya, whom he called his right arm, and Pero Bermudez, and Muño Gustios, and Martin Antolinez that doughty Burgalese, and Alvar Alvarez, and Alvar Salvadorez, and Martin Muñoz, and Felez Muñoz the Cid's nephew, and Malanda who was a learned man, and Galin Garciez the good one of Aragon: these and others made ready to go with him, being an hundred of the best of his company. They wore velmezes under their harness, that they might be able to bear it, and then their mail, which was as bright as the sun: over this they had ermine or other skins, laced tight that the armour might not be seen, and under their cloaks, their swords which were sweet and sharp. He who was born in happy hour made no tarriance; he drew on his legs hose of fine cloth, and put on over them shoes which were richly worked. A shirt of ranzal he wore, which was as white as the sun; all the fastenings were wrought with gold and silver: over this a brial of gold tissue; and over this a red skin with points of gold. My Cid the Campeador alway wore it. On his head he had a coif of scarlet wrought with gold, which was made that none might clip the hair of the good Cid. His was a long beard, and he bound it with a cord. And he bade Alvar Fañez and Pero Bermudez assemble their companions, and when he saw them he said, If the Infantes of Carrion should seek a quarrel, where I have a hundred such as these I may be well without fear! And he said, Let us mount now and go to the Cortes. We go to make one defiance, and peradventure it may be two or three, through the folly of those who may stir against us. Ye will be ready to aid me, saying and doing as I shall call upon ye, always saving the honour and authority of King Don Alfonso our Lord; see now that none of ye say or do ought amiss, for it would be unseemly. Then called he for his horse, and bestrode it, and rode to the Cortes.

VII.

My Cid and his company alighted at the gate of the Palaces of Galiana, and he and his people went in gravely, he in the midst and his hundred knights round about him. When he who was born in happy hour entered, the good King Don Alfonso rose up, and the Counts Don Anrrich and Don Remond did the like, and so did all the others, save the curly-headed one of Granon, and they who were on the side of the Infantes of Carrion. All the others received him with great honour. And he said unto the King, Sir, where do you bid me sit with these my kinsmen and friends who are come with me? And the King made answer, Cid, you are such a one, and have past your time so well to this day, that if you would listen to me and be commanded by me, I should hold it good that you took your seat with me; for he who hath conquered Kings, ought to be seated with Kings. But the Cid answered, That, Sir, would not please God, but I will be at your feet for by the favour of the King your father Don Ferrando was I made, his creature and the creature of your brother King Don Sancho am I, and it behoveth not that he who receiveth bounty should sit with him who dispenseth it. And the King answered, Since you will not sit with me, sit on your ivory seat, for you won it like a good man; and from this day I order that none except King or Prelate sit with you, for you have conquered so many high-born men, and so many Kings, both Christians and Moors, that for this reason there is none who is your peer, or ought to be seated with you. Sit therefore like a King and Lord upon your ivory seat. Then the Cid kissed the King's hand, and thanked him for what he had said, and for the honour which he had done him; and he took his seat, and his hundred knights seated themselves round about him. All who were in the Cortes sate looking at my Cid and at his long beard which he had bound with a cord; but the Infantes of Carrion could not look upon him for shame.

VIII.

When they were all seated the King gave command that they should be silent; and when the Cid saw that they were all still, he rose and spake after this manner. Sir King Don Alfonso, I beseech you of your mercy that you would hear me, and give command that I should be heard, and that you would suffer none to interrupt me, for I am not a man of speech, neither know I how to set forth my words, and if they interrupt me I shall be worse. Moreover, Sir, give command that none be bold enough to utter unseemly words, nor be insolent towards me, least we should come to strife in your presence. Then King Don Alfonso rose and said, Hear me, as God shall help you! Since I have been King I have held only two Cortes, one in Burgos, and one in Carrion. This third I have assembled here in Toledo for the love of the Cid, that he may demand justice against the Infantes of Carrion for the wrongs which we all know. The Counts Don Anrrich and Don Remoud shall be Alcaldes in this cause; and these other Counts who are not on either side, give ye all good heed, for ye are to take cognizance that the right may be decreed. And I give order, and forbid any one, to speak without my command, or to utter aught insolent against the Cid; and I swear by St. Isidro, that whosoever shall disturb the Cortes shall lose my love and be banished from the kingdom. I am on the side of him who shall be found to have the right. Then those Counts who were appointed Alcaldes were sworn upon the Holy Gospels, that they would judge between the Cid and the Infantes of Carrion, rightly and truly, according to the law of Castille and Leon.

IX.

When this was done the King bade the Cid make his demand; and the Cid rose and said, Sir, there is no reason for making long speeches here, which would detain the Cortes. I demand of the Infantes of Carrion, before you, two swords which I gave into their keeping; the one is Colada and the other Tizona. I won them like a man, and gave them to the keeping of the Infantes that they might honour my daughters with them, and serve you. When they left my daughters in the Oak-forest of Corpes they chose to have nothing to do with me, and renounced my love; let them therefore give me back the swords, seeing that they are no longer my sons-in-law. Then the King commanded the Alcaldes to judge upon this demand according as they should find the right; and they took counsel and judged, that the swords should be restored unto the Cid. And Count Don Garcia said they would talk concerning it; and the Infantes of Carrion talked apart with those who were on their side, and they thought that they were well off; for that the Cid would demand nothing more of them, but would leave the Cortes when he had recovered the swords. So they brought the swords Colada and Tizona, and delivered them to the King. The King drew the swords, and the whole Court shone with their brightness: their hilts were of solid gold; all the good men of the Cortes marvelled at them. And the Cid rose and received them, and kissed the King's hand, and went back to his ivory seat; and he took the swords in his hand and looked at them; they could not change them, for the Cid knew them well, and his whole frame rejoiced, and he smiled from his heart. And he laid them upon his lap and said, Ah, my swords, Colada and Tizona, truly may I say of you, that you are the best swords in Spain; and I won you, for I did not get you either by buying or by barter. I gave ye in keeping to the Infantes of Carrion that they might do honour to my daughters with ye. But ye were not for them! they kept ye hungry, and did not feed ye with flesh as ye were wont to be fed. Well is it for you that ye have escaped that thraldom and are come again to my hands, and happy man am I to recover you. Then Alvar Fañez rose and kissed the hand of the Cid, and said, I beseech you give Colada into my keeping while this Cortes shall last, that I may defend you therewith: and the Cid gave it him and said. Take it, it hath changed its master for the better. And Pero Bermudez rose and made the same demand for the sword Tizona, and the Cid gave it him in like manner. Then the Cid laid hand upon his beard as he was wont to do, and the Infantes of Carrion and they who were of their side thought that he meant to disturb the Cortes, and they were greatly afraid; but he sate still like a man of good understanding, for he was not one who did things lightly.

X.

Then the Cid rose and said, Thanks be to God and to you, Sir King, I have recovered my swords Colada and Tizona, I have now another demand against the Infantes of Carrion, King Don Alfonso, you well know that it was your pleasure to bid me meet you at Requeña, and I went there in obedience to your command. And you asked of me my daughters in marriage for the Infantes, and I did not refuse, in that I would not disobey your command; and you bade me deliver them to my kinsman here Don Alvar Fañez, and he gave them to the Infantes to be their wives, and the blessing was given them in the church of St. Mary, according to the law of Rome. You, Sir, gave them in marriage, not I; and you did it for good, not for evil; but what they did was after another wise. And though they are of great blood and honourable, yet would I not have given my daughters to them, unless in obedience to your command; and this, Sir, you well know, for so I said unto you. I gave them, when they took my daughters from Valencia, horses and mules, and cups and vessels of fine gold, and much wrought silver, and many noble garments, and other gifts, three thousand marks of silver in all, thinking that I gave it to my daughters whom I loved. Now, Sir, since they have cast my daughters off, and hold themselves to have been dishonoured in marrying them, give command that they restore unto me this which is my own, or that they show cause why they should not. Then might you have seen the Infantes of Carrion in great chafing. And Count Don Remond called upon them to speak; and they said, We gave his swords to the Cid Campeador, that he might ask nothing more of us, if it please the King. But the King said that they must answer to the demand. And they asked together to consult concerning it; and the King bade them take counsel and make answer incontinently. So they went apart, and with them eleven Counts and Ricos-omes who were on their side, but no right or reason could they find for opposing this demand which the Cid had made. Howbeit Count Don Garcia spake for them and said, Sir, this which the Cid demands back from them, it is true that he gave it, but they have expended it in your service; we hold therefore that they are not bound to make restitution of it, seeing how it hath been expended. Nevertheless if you hold it to be lawful that they should restore this money, give order that time be given them to make the payment, and they will go to Carrion, their inheritance, and there discharge the demand as you shall decree. When the Count had thus said he sate down. And the Cid arose and said, Sir, if the Infantes of Carrion have expended aught in your service, it toucheth not me. You and the Alcaldes whom you have appointed have heard them admit that I gave them this treasure, and this excuse which they set up; I pray you let judgment be given whether they are bound to pay it or not. Then King Don Alfonso answered and said, If the Infantes of Carrion have expended aught in my service, I am bound to repay it, for the Cid must not lose what is his own; and he bade the Alcaldes consult together and judge according to what they should find right. And the Alcaldes having taken counsel gave judgment, that seeing the Infantes acknowledged the Cid had given them this treasure with his daughters, and they had abandoned them, they must needs make restitution in the Cortes of the King there right: and the King confirmed this sentence, and the Cid rose and kissed the King's hand. Greatly were the Infantes of Carrion troubled at this sentence, and they besought the King that he would obtain time for them from the Cid, in which to make their payment; and the King besought him to grant them fifteen days, after this manner, that they should not depart from the Court till they had made the payment, and that they should plight homage for the observance of this. And the Cid granted what the King desired, and they plighted homage accordingly in the hands of the King, Then made they their account with the King, and it was found that what they had expended for his service was two hundred marks of silver, and the King said that he would repay this, so that there remained for them two thousand and eight hundred to pay. Who can tell the trouble in which the Infantes were, to pay this treasure to the Cid, they and all their kindred and friends, for it was full hard for them to accomplish, And they took up upon trust horses and mules and wrought silver, and other precious things, and as they could get them, delivered them over to the Cid. Then might you have seen many a good-going horse brought there, and many a good mule, and many a good palfrey, and many a good sword with its mountings. And they sent to Carrion to their father and mother to help them, for they were in great trouble; and they raised for them all they could, so that they made up the sum within the time appointed. And then they thought that the matter was at an end, and that nothing more would be demanded from them.

XI.

After this payment had been made the Cortes assembled again, and the King and all the honourable men being each in his place, the Cid rose from his ivory seat, and said, Sir, praise be to God and your favour, I have recovered my swords, and my treasure; now then I pray you let this other demand be heard which I have to make against the Infantes. Full hard it is for me to make it, though I have it rooted in my heart! I say then, let them make answer before you, and tell why it was that they besought you to marry them with my daughters, and why they took them away from me from Valencia, when they had it in heart to dishonour me, and to strike them, and leave them as they were left, in the Oak-forest of Corpes? Look, Sir, what dishonour they did them! they stript them of the garments which they had not given them, as if they had been bad women, and the children of a bad father. With less than mortal defiance I shall not let them go!... How had I deserved this, Infantes, at your hands? I gave you my daughters to take with you from Valencia; with great honour and great treasures gave I them unto you;... Dogs and Traitors,... ye took them from Valencia when ye did not love them, and with your bridles ye smote and with your spurs ye spurned and wounded them, and ye left them alone in the Oak-forest, to the wild beasts, and to the birds of the mountain! King Don Alfonso, they neither remembered God, nor you, nor me, nor their own good fortune! And here was fulfilled the saying of the wise man, that harder it is for those who have no understanding to bear with good than with evil. Praise be to God and to your grace, such a one am I, and such favour hath God shown me, from the day when I first had horse and arms, until now, that not only the Infantes of Carrion, but saving yourself, Sir, there is not a King in Christendom who might not think himself honoured in marrying with either of my daughters,... how much more then these traitors!... I beseech you give me justice upon them for the evil and dishonour which they have done me! And if you and your Cortes will not right me, through the mercy of God and my own good cause, I will take it myself, for the offence which they have committed against God and the faith, and the truth which they promised and vowed to their wives. I will pull them down from the honour in which they now are; better men than they have I conquered and made prisoners ere now! and with your license, Sir, to Carrion will I follow them, even to their inheritance, and there will I besiege them, and take them by the throat, and carry them prisoners to Valencia to my daughters, and there make them do penance for the crime which they have committed, and feed them with the food which they deserve. If I do not perform this, call me a flat traitor. When the King heard this he rose up and said, that it might be seen how he was offended in this thing. Certes, Cid Ruydiez Campeador, I asked your daughters of you for the Infantes of Carrion, because, as they well know, they besought me to do so, I never having thought thereof. It well seemeth now that they were not pleased with this marriage which I made at their request, and great part of the dishonour which they have done you, toucheth me. But seeing ye are here in my presence, it is not fitting that you make your demand in any other manner than through my Cortes; do you therefore accuse them, and let them acquit themselves if they can before my Alcaldes, who will pass sentence according to what is right. And the Cid kissed the King's hand, and returned to his place upon the ivory seat.

XII.

Then the Cid arose and said, God prosper you, Sir, in life, and honour, and estate, since you have compassion for me and for the dishonour which my daughters have received. And he turned towards the Infantes of Carrion, and said, Ferrando Gonzalez and Diego Gonzalez, I say that ye are false traitors for leaving your wives as ye left them in the Oak-forest; and here before the King I attaint you as false traitors, and defy you, and will produce your peers who shall prove it upon you, and slay you or thrust you out of the lists, or make you confess it in your throats. And they were silent. And the King said, that seeing they were there present, they should make answer to what the Cid had said. Then Ferrando Gonzalez the elder arose and said, Sir, we are your subjects, of your kingdom of Castille, and of the best hidalgos therein, sons of the Count Don Gonzalo Gonzalez; and we hold that men of such station as ourselves were not well married with the daughters of Ruydiez of Bivar. And for this reason we forsook them, because they come not of blood fit for our wives, for one lineage is above another. Touching what he says, that we forsook them, he saith truly; and we hold that in so doing we did nothing wrong, for they were not worthy to be our wives, and we are more to be esteemed for having left them, than we were while they were wedded with us. Now then, Sir, there is no reason why we should do battle upon this matter with any one. And Diego Gonzalez his brother arose and said, You know, Sir, what perfect men we are in our lineage, and it did not befit us to be married with the daughters of such a one as Ruydiez; and when he had said this he held his peace and sate down. Then Count Don García rose and said, Come away, Infantes, and let us leave the Cid sitting like a bridegroom in his ivory chair:... he lets his beard grow and thinks to frighten us with it!... The Campeador put up his hand to his beard, and said, What hast thou to do with my beard, Count? Thanks be to God, it is long because it hath been kept for my pleasure; never son of woman hath taken me by it; never son of Moor or of Christian hath plucked it, as I did yours in your castle of Cabra, Count, when I took your castle of Cabra, and took you by the beard; there was not a boy of the host but had his pull at it. What I plucked then is not yet methinks grown even!... And the Count cried out again, Come away, Infantes, and leave him! Let him go back to Rio de Ovierna, to his own country, and set up his mills, and take toll as he used to do!... he is not your peer that you should strive with him. At this the knights of the Cid looked at each other with fierce eyes and wrathful countenances; but none of them dared speak till, the Cid bade them, because of the command which he had given.

XIII.

When the Cid saw that none of his people made answer he turned to Pero Bermudez and said, Speak, Pero Mudo, what art thou silent for? He called him Mudo, which is to say, Dumb-ee, because he snaffled and stuttered when he began to speak; and Pero Bermudez was wroth that he should be so called before all that assembly. And he said, I tell you what, Cid, you always call me Dumb-ee in Court, and you know I cannot help my words; but when anything is to be done, it shall not fail for me. And in his anger he forgot what the Cid had said to him and to the others that they should make no broil before the King. And he gathered up his cloak under his arm and went up to the eleven Counts who were against the Cid, to Count Garcia, and when he was nigh him he clenched his fist, and gave him a blow which brought him to the ground. Then was the whole Cortes in an uproar by reason of that blow, and many swords were drawn, and on one side the cry was Cabra and Grañon, and on the other side it was Valencia and Bivar; but the strife was in such sort that the Counts in short time voided the Palace, King Don Alfonso meantime cried out aloud, forbidding them to fight before him, and charging them to look to his honour; and the Cid then strove what he could to quiet his people, saying to the King. Sir, you saw that I could bear it no longer, being thus maltreated in your presence; if it had not been before you, well would I have had him punished. Then the King sent to call those Counts who had been driven out; and they came again to the Palace, though they fain would not, complaining of the dishonour which they had received. And the King said unto them that they should defend themselves with courtesy and reason, and not revile the Cid, who was not a man to be reviled; and he said that he would defend as far as he could the rights of both parties. Then they took their seats on the estrados as before.

XIV

And Pero Bermudez rose and said to Count Garcia, Foul mouth, in which God hath put no truth, thou hast dared let thy tongue loose to speak of the Cid's beard. His is a praiseworthy beard, and an honourable one, and one that is greatly feared, and that never hath been dishonoured, nor overcome! and if you please you may remember when he fought against you in Cabra, hundred to hundred, he threw you from your horse, and took thee by the beard, and made thee and thy knights prisoners, and carried thee prisoner away across a pack-saddle; and his knights pulled thy beard for thee, and I who stand here had a good hand-full of it: how then shall a beard that hath been pulled speak against one that hath alway been honourable! If you deny this, I will fight you upon this quarrel before the King our Lord. Then Count Suero González rose in great haste and said, Nephews, go you away and leave these rascally companions: if they are for fighting, we will give them their fill of that, if our Lord the King should think good so to command; that shall not fail for us, though they are not our peers. Then Don Alvar Fañez Minaya arose and said, Hold thy peace, Count Suero Gonzalez! you have been to breakfast before you said your prayers, and your words are more like a drunkard's than one who is in his senses. Your kinsmen like those of the Cid!... if it were not out of reverence to my Lord and King, I would teach you never to talk again in this way. And then the King saw that these words were going on to worse, and moreover that they were nothing to the business; and he commanded them to be silent, and said, I will determine this business of the defiance with the Alcaldes, as shall be found right; and I will not have these disputes carried on before me, least you should raise another uproar in my presence.

XV

Then the King rose and called to the Alcaldes, and went apart with them into a chamber, and the Cid and all the others remained in the Hall. And when the King and the Alcaldes had taken counsel together concerning what was right in this matter, they came out from the chamber, and the King went and seated himself in his chair, and the Alcaldes each in his place, and they commanded all persons to be silent and hear the sentence which the King should give. Then the King spake thus: I have taken counsel with these Counts whom I appointed to be Alcaldes in this cause between the Cid and the Infantes of Carrion, and with other honourable and learned men: and this is the sentence which I give; that both the Infantes and Count Suero Gonzalez their fosterer and uncle, forasmuch as it is given me to understand that he was the adviser and abettor in the dishonour which they did unto the daughters of the Cid, shall do battle with such three of the Cid's people as it may please him to appoint, and thereby acquit themselves if they can. When the King had given this sentence, the Cid rose and kissed, his hand and said, May God have you, Sir, in his holy keeping long and happy years, seeing you have judged justly, as a righteous King and our natural Lord. I receive your sentence; and now do I perceive that it is your pleasure to show favour unto me, and to advance mine honour, and for this reason I shall ever be at your service. Then Pero Bermudez rose up and went to the Cid and said, A boon, Sir! I beseech you let me be one of those who shall do battle on your part, for such a one do I hold myself to be, and this which they have done is so foul a thing, that I trust in God to take vengeance for it. And the Cid made answer that he was well pleased it should be so, and that he should do battle with Ferrando Gonzalez the eldest; and upon that Pero Bermudez kissed his hand. Then Martin Antolinez of Burgos rose and besought the Cid that he might be another, and the Cid granted his desire, and said that he should do battle with Diego Gonzalez the younger brother. And then Muño Gustioz of Linquella rose and besought the Cid that he might be the third, and the Cid granted it, and appointed him to do battle with Count Suero Gonzalez. And when the Cid had appointed his three champions, the King gave command that the combat should be performed on the morrow; but the Infantes were not prepared to fight so soon, and they besought him of his favour that he would let them go to Carrion, and that they would come prepared for the battle. And the King would not allow this time which they requested; howbeit the Counts Don Anrrich and Don Remond his sons-in-law, and Count Don Nuño, spake with him, and besought him of his grace that he would allow them three weeks; and the King at their intreaty granted it with the pleasure of the Cid.

XVI.

Now when all this had been appointed, as ye have heard, and while they were all in the court, there came into the Palace messengers from the Kings of Aragon and of Navarre, who brought letters to King Don Alfonso, and to the Cid Campeador, wherein those Kings sent to ask the daughters of the Cid in marriage, the one for the Infante Don Sancho of Aragon, the other for the Infante Garcia Ramirez of Navarre. And when they came before the King, they bent their knees and gave him the letters, and delivered their message; the like did they to the Cid. Much were the King and the Cid also pleased at this news, and the King said unto him, What say you to this? And the Cid answered, I and my daughters are at your disposal, do you with us as you shall think good. And the King said, I hold it good that they wed with these Infantes, and that from henceforward they be Queens and Ladies; and that for the dishonour which they have received, they now receive this honour. And the Cid rose and kissed the hands of the King, and all his knights did the like. These messengers hight, he of Aragon Yñigo Ximenez, and he of Navarre Ochoa Perez. And the King gave order that his letters of consent to these marriages should be given, and the Cid did the like. And those knights did homage before the King, that in three months from that day the Infantes of Aragon and of Navarre should come to Valencia, to the Cid, to be wedded to his daughters. Great joy had the companions of the Cid that these marriages were appointed, seeing how their honour was increased; and contrariwise, great was the sorrow of the Infantes of Carrion and their friends, because it was to their confusion and great shame. And King Don Alfonso said aloud unto the Cid before them all, Praised be the name of God, because it hath pleased him that the dishonour which was done to me and to you and your daughters, should thus be turned into honour: for they were the wives of the sons of Counts, and now shall they be the wives of the sons of Kings, and Queens hereafter. Great was the pleasure of the Cid and his company at these words of the King, for before they had sorrow, and now it was turned into joy. And the Infantes went away from the Palace full sadly, and went to their lodging, and prepared to go to Carrion that they might make ready for the combat, which was to be in three weeks from that time.

XVII.

hen the Cid said unto the King, Sir, I have appointed those who are to do battle with the Infantes and their uncle for the enmity and treason which they committed against me and my daughters; and now, Sir, as there is nothing more for me to do here, I will leave them in your hand, knowing that you will not suffer them to receive any displeasure or wrong soever, and that you will defend their right. And if it please you I would fain return to Valencia, where I have left my wife and daughters, and my other companions; for I would not that the Moors should rise up against me during my absence, thinking peradventure that I have not sped so well in this matter as I have done, praised be God and you. And moreover I have to make ready for these marriages which you have now appointed. And the King bade him go when he pleased, and good fortune with him, and said that he would protect his knights and maintain his right in all things. Then the Cid kissed the King's hand for this which he had said, and commended the knights to his keeping. And the King called for Count

Don Remond his son-in-law, and gave the knights of the Cid to his charge, and bade them not depart from him; and then the King rose and returned to the Alcazar.

XVIII.

Then the Cid took off his coif of ranzal, which was as white as the sun, and he loosed his beard, and took it out of the cord with which it was bound. All they who were there could not be satisfied with looking at him. And the Counts Don Anrrich and Don Remond came up to him, and he embraced them, and thanked them and the other good men who had been Alcaldes in this business, for maintaining his right; and he promised to do for them in requital whatever they might require; and he besought them to accept part of his treasures. And they thanked him for his offer, but said that it was not seemly. Howbeit he sent great presents to each of them, and some accepted them and some did not. Who can tell how nobly the Cid distributed his treasure before he departed? And he forgave the King the two hundred marks which should have been paid on account of the Infantes. And to the knights who had come from Aragon and Navarre concerning the marriages, he gave many horses, and money in gold, and sent them with great honour into their own country.

XIX.

On the morrow the Cid went to take leave of the King, and the King went some way out of the town with him, and all the good men who were in the court also, to do him honour as he deserved. And when he was about to dispeed himself of the King they brought him his precious horse Bavieca, and he turned to the King and said, Sir, I should depart ill from hence if I took with me so good a horse as my Bavieca, and did not leave him for you, for such a horse as this is fit for you and for no other master: and that you may see what he is, I will do before you what it is long since I have done except in the battles which I have had with my enemies. Then he mounted his horse, with his ermine housings, and gave him the spur. Who can tell the goodness of the horse Bavieca, and of the Cid who rode him? And as the Cid was doing this the horse brake one of his reins, yet he came and stopt before the King as easily as if both the reins had been whole. Greatly did the King and all they who were with him marvel at this, saying that they had never seen or heard of so good a horse as that. And the Cid besought the King that he would be pleased to take the horse, but the King answered, God forbid that I should take him!... rather would I give you a better if I had one, for he is better bestowed on you than on me or any other, for upon that horse you have done honour to yourself, and to us, and to all Christendom, by the good feats which you have atchieved. Let him go as mine, and I will take him when I please. Then the Cid kissed the King's hand and dispeeded himself, and the King embraced him and returned to Toledo.

XX.

Now when the Cid had taken leave of the King, and of the other honourable men and Counts, and Ricos-omes who were with him, Pero Bermudez and Martin Antolinez and Muño Gustioz went on yet awhile with him: and he counselled them how to demean themselves so as to clear him of the shame which had been done him, and to be held for good knights themselves, and to take vengeance for King Don Alfonso, and for him, and for themselves, that he might receive good tidings from them in Valencia. And they took his counsel well, as they afterwards manifested when there was occasion. But Martin Antolinez made answer, Why do you say this, Sir? we have undertaken the business and we shall go through it; and they said unto him, God have you in his guidance. Sir, and be you sure and certain, that by the mercy and help of God we shall so demean ourselves as to come to you without shame. But if for our sins it should betide otherwise, never more shall we appear before you dead or living,... for slain we may be, but never vanquished. Then he bade them return to the King, praying to God to have them in his keeping, and assist them in fulfilling their demand, as he knew that their cause was right.

BOOK X.

I.

Now King Alfonso misdoubted the Infantes of Carrion that they would not appear at the time appointed, and therefore he said that he would go to Carrion, and the battle should be fought there. And he took with him the Counts whom he had appointed Alcaldes, and Pero Bermudez and Martin Antolinez and Muño Gustioz went with the Count Don Remond, to whose charge the King had given them. And on the third day after the Cid departed from Toledo the King set forth for Carrion; but it so chanced that he fell sick upon the road, and could not arrive within the three weeks, so that the term was enlarged to five. And when the King's health was restored he proceeded and reached Carrion, and gave order that the combat should be performed, and appointed the day, and named the plain of Carrion for the place thereof. And the Infantes came there with a great company of all their friends and kindred, for their kinsmen were many and powerful; and they all came with one accord, that if before the battle they could find any cause they would kill the knights of the Cid: nevertheless, though they had determined upon this they dared not put it in effect, because they stood in fear of the King.

II.

And when the night came of which the morrow was appointed for the combat, they on one side and on the other kept vigil in the Churches, each in that Church to which he had the most devotion. Night is past away, and the dawn is now breaking; and at day-break a great multitude was assembled in the field, and many Ricos-omes came there for the pleasure which they would have in seeing this battle, and the King sent and commanded the champions to make ready. Moreover he made the two Counts his sons-in-law, Don Anrrich and Don Remond, and the other Counts and their people, arm themselves and keep the field, that the kinsmen of the Infantes might not make a tumult there. Who can tell the great dole and sorrow of Count Gonzalo Gonzalez for his sons the Infantes of Carrion, because they had to do battle this day! and in the fullness of his heart he curst the day and the hour in which he was born, for his heart divined the sorrow which he was to have for his children. Great was the multitude which was assembled from all Spain to behold this battle. And there in the field near the lists the champions of the Cid armed themselves on one side, and the Infantes on the other. And Count Don Remond armed the knights of the Cid, and instructed them how to do their devoir, and Count Garci Ordoñez helped arm the Infantes of Carrion and their uncle Suero Gonzalez, and they sent to ask the King of his favour that he would give command that the swords Colada and Tizona should not be used in that combat. But the King would not, and he answered that each must take the best sword and the best arms that he could, save only that the one should not have more than the other. Greatly were they troubled at this reply, and greatly did they fear those good swords, and repent that they had taken them to the Cortes of Toledo. And from that hour the Infantes and Suero Gonzalez bewrayed in their countenances that they thought ill of what they had done, and happy men would they have thought themselves if they had not committed that great villainy, and he if he had not counselled it; and gladly would they have given all that they had in Carrion so it could now have been undone.

III.

And the King went to the place where the Infantes were arming, and said unto them, If ye feared these swords ye should have said so in the Cortes of Toledo, for that was the place, and not this; ... there is now nothing to be done but to defend yourselves stoutly, as ye have need against those with whom ye have to do. Then went he to the knights of the Cid, whom he found armed; and they kissed his hand and said unto him, Sir, the Cid hath left us in your hand, and we beseech you see that no wrong be done us in this place, where the Infantes of Carrion have their party; and by God's mercy we will do ourselves right upon them. And the King bade them have no fear for that. Then their horses were brought, and they crost the saddles, and mounted, with their shields hanging from the neck; and they took their spears, each of which had its streamer, and with many good men round about they went to the lists; and on the other side the Infantes and Count Suero Gonzalez came up with a great company of their friends and kinsmen and vassals. And the King said with a loud voice, Hear what I say, Infantes of Carrion!... this combat I would have had waged in Toledo, but ye said that ye were not ready to perform it there, and therefore I am come to this which is your native place, and have brought the knights of the Cid with me. They are come here under my safeguard. Let not therefore you nor your kinsmen deceive yourselves, thinking to overpower them by tumult, or in any other way than by fair combat; for whosoever shall begin a tumult, I have given my people orders to cut him in pieces upon the spot, and no enquiry shall be made touching the death of him who shall so have offended. Full sorrowful were the Infantes of Carrion for this command which the King had given. And the King appointed twelve knights who were hidalgos to be true-men and place the combatants in the lists, and show them the bounds at what point they were to win or to be vanquished, and to divide the sun between them. And he went with a wand in his hand, and saw them placed on both sides; then he went out of the lists, and gave command that the people should fall back, and not approach within seven spears-length of the lines of the lists.

IV.

Now were the six combatants left alone in the lists, and each of them knew now with whom he had to do battle. And they laced their helmets, and put shield upon the arm, and laid lance in rest. And the knights of my Cid advanced against the Infantes of Carrion, and they on their part against the champions of the Campeador. Each bent down with his face to the saddle-bow, and gave his horse the spur. And they met all six with such a shock, that they who looked on expected to see them all fall dead. Pero Bermudez and Ferrando Gonzalez encountered, and the shield of Pero Bermudez was pierced, but the spear past through on one side, and hurt him not, and brake in two places; and he sat firm in his seat. One blow he received, but he gave another; he drove his lance through Ferrando's shield, at his breast, so that nothing availed him. Ferrando's breast-plate was threefold: two plates the spear went clean through, and drove the third in before it, with the velmes and the shirt, into the breast, near his heart; ... and the girth and the poitral of his horse burst, and he and the saddle went together over the horse's heels, and the spear in him, and all thought him dead. Howbeit Ferrando Gonzalez rose, and the blood began to run out of his mouth, and Pero Bermudez drew his sword and went against him; but when he saw the sword Tizona over him, before he received a blow from it, he cried out that he confessed himself conquered, and that what Pero Bermudez had said against him was true. And when Pero Bermudez heard this he stood still, and the twelve true-men came up and heard his confession, and pronounced him vanquished. This Ferrando did thinking to save his life; but the wound which he had got was mortal.

V

Martin Antolinez and Diego Gonzalez brake their lances on each other, and laid hand upon their swords. Martin Antolinez drew forth Colada, the brightness of which flashed over the whole field, for it was a marvellous sword; and in their strife he dealt him a back-handed blow which sheared off the crown of his helmet, and cut away hood and coif, and the hair of his head and the skin also: this stroke he dealt him with the precious Colada. And Diego Gonzalez was sorely dismayed therewith, and though he had his own sword in his hand he could not for very fear make use of it, but he turned his horse and fled; and Martin Antolinez went after him, and dealt him another with the flat part of the sword, for he mist him with the edge, and the Infante began to cry out aloud, Great God, help me and save me from that sword! And he rode away as fast as he could, and Martin Antolinez called out after him, Get out, Don Traitor! and drove him out of the lists, and remained conqueror.

VI

Muño Gustioz and Suero Gonzalez dealt each other such strokes with their spears as it was marvellous to behold. And Suero Gonzalez being a right hardy knight and a strong, and of great courage, struck the shield of Muño Gustioz and pierced it through and through; but the stroke was given aslant, so that it passed on and touched him not. Muño Gustioz lost his stirrups with that stroke, but he presently recovered them, and dealt him such a stroke in return that it went clean through the midst of the shield, and through all his armour, and came out between his ribs, missing the heart; then laying hand on him he wrenched him out of the saddle, and threw him down as he drew the spear out of his body; and the point of the spear and the haft and the streamer all came out red. Then all the beholders thought that he was stricken to death. And Muño Gustioz turned to smite again. But when Gonzalo Ansures his father saw this, he cried out aloud for great ruth which he had for his son, and said, For God's sake do not strike him again, for he is vanquished. And Muño Gustioz, like a man of good understanding, asked the true-men whether he were to be held as conquered for what his father said, and they said not, unless he confirmed it with his own mouth. And Muño Gustioz turned again to Suero Gonzalez where he lay wounded, and lifted his spear against him, and Suero Gonzalez cried out, Strike me not, for I am vanquished. And the judges said it was enough, and that the combat was at an end.

Then the King entered the lists, and many good knights and hidalgos with him, and he called the twelve true-men, and asked them if the knights of the Cid had aught more to do to prove their accusation; and they made answer that the knights of the Cid had won the field and done their devoir, and all the hidalgos who were there present made answer, that they said true. And King Don Alfonso lifted up his voice and said, Hear me, all ye who are here present: inasmuch as the knights of the Cid have conquered, they have won the cause; and the twelve true-men made answer, that what the King said was the truth, and all the people said the same. And the King gave command to break up the lists, and gave sentence that the Infantes of Carrion and their uncle Suero Gonzalez were notorious traitors, and ordered his seneschal to take their arms and horses. And from that day forth their lineage never held up its head, nor was of any worth in Castille; and they and their uncle fled away, having been thus vanquished and put to shame. And thus it was that Carrion fell to the King after the days of Gonzalo Gonzalez, the father of the Infantes. Great was their shame, and the like or worse betide him who abuseth fair lady, and then leaveth her.

Then the King went to meat, and he took the knights of the Cid with him; and great was the multilude which followed after them, praising the good feat which they had atchieved. And the King gave them great gifts, and sent them away by night, and with a good guard to protect them till they should be in safety; and they took their leave of the King, and travelled by night and day, and came to Valencia. When the Cid knew that they drew nigh, he went out to meet them, and did them great honour. Who can tell the great joy which he made over them? And they told him all even as it had come to pass, and how the King had declared the Infantes of Carrion and their uncle to be notorious traitors. Great was the joy of the Cid at these tidings, and he lifted up his hands to heaven, and blest the name of God because of the vengeance which he had given him for the great dishonour which he had received. And he took with him Martin Antolinez and Pero Bermudez and Muño Gustioz, and went to Doña Ximena and her daughters, and said to them, Blessed be the name of God, now are you and your daughters avenged! and he made the knights recount the whole unto them, even as it had come to pass. Great was the joy of Doña Ximena and her daughters, and they bent their knees to the ground, and praised the name of Jesus Christ, because he had given them this vengeance for the dishonour which they had received; and Doña Elvira and Doña Sol embraced those knights many times, and would fain have kissed their hands and their feet. And the Cid said unto Doña Ximena, Now may you without let marry your daughters with the Infantes of Aragon and Navarre, and I trust in God that they will be well and honourably married, better than they were at first. Eight days did the great rejoicings endure which the Cid made in Valencia, for the vengeance which God had given him upon the Infantes of Carrion, and their uncle Suero Gonzalez, the aider and abettor in the villainy which they had committed.

Now it came to pass after this, that the Great Soldan of Persia, having heard of the great goodness of the Cid, and of his great feats in arms, and how he had never been vanquished by mortal man, and how he had conquered many Kings, Moor and Christian, and had won the noble city of Valencia, and had defeated King Bucar Lord of Africa and Morocco, and twenty nine Kings with him, all these things made him greatly desirous of his love. And holding him to be one of the noble men of the world, he sent messengers to him with great gifts, which will be recounted hereafter, and with them he sent one of his kinsmen, a full honourable man, with letters of great love. When this kinsman reached the port of Valencia, he sent word to the Cid that he was arrived there with a message from the Great Soldan of Persia, who had sent a present by him; and when the Cid knew this he was well pleased. And in the morning the Cid took horse, and went out with all his company, all nobly attired, and his knights rode before him with their lances erect. And when they had gone about a league they met the messenger of the Soldan coming to Valencia: and when he beheld them in what order they came, he understood what a noble man the Cid Campeador was. And when he drew nigh, the Cid stopt his horse Bavieca, and waited to receive him. And when the messenger came before the Cid and beheld him, all his flesh began to tremble, and he marvelled greatly that his flesh should tremble thus; and his voice failed him, so that he could not bring forth a word. And the Cid said that he was welcome, and went towards him to embrace him; but the Moor made him, no reply, being amazed. And when he had somewhat recovered and could speak, he would have kissed the Cid's hand; but the Cid would not give it him: and he thought this was done for haughtiness, but they made him understand that it was to do him honour; then was he greatly rejoiced, and he said, I humble myself before thee, O Cid, who art the fortunate, the best Christian, and the most honourable that hath girded on sword or bestrode horse these thousand years. The Great Soldan of Persia, my Lord, hearing of thy great fame and renown, and of the great virtue which is in thee, hath sent me to salute thee and receive thee as his friend, even as his best friend, the one whom he loveth and prizeth best. And he hath sent a present by me who am of his lineage, and beseecheth thee to receive it as from a friend. And the Cid made answer that he thanked him greatly.

X.

Then the Cid bade his people make way that the sumpter beasts which carried the present might pass, and also the strange animals which the Soldan had sent, the like whereof were not in that land. And when they were passed he and his company returned towards the town, and the messenger with him. And whensoever the messenger spake to the Cid, it came into his mind how his voice had failed and his flesh trembled when he beheld him; and he marvelled thereat, and would fain have asked the Cid why it should be. And when they entered Valencia, great was the crowd which assembled to see the sumpter beasts, and the strange animals, for they had never seen such before, and they marvelled at them. And the Cid gave order that the beasts should be taken care of, and he went to the Alcazar and took the Moor with him; and when they came to Doña Ximena the Moor humbled himself before her and her daughters, and would have kissed her hand, but she would not give it him. Then he commanded that the camels and other beasts of burthen should be unloaded in their presence, and he began to open the packages and display the noble things which were contained therein. And he laid before them great store of gold and of money, which came in leathern bags, each having its lock; and wrought silver in dishes and trenchers and basons, and pots for preparing food; all these of fine silver and full cunningly wrought, the weight whereof was ten thousand marks. Then he brought out five cups of gold, in each of which were ten marks of gold, with many precious stones set therein, and three silver barrels, which were full of pearls and of precious stones. Moreover he presented unto him many pieces of cloth of gold, and of silk, of those which are made in Tartary, and in the land of Calabria. And moreover, a pound of myrrh and of balsam, in little caskets of gold; this was a precious thing, for with this ointment they were wont to anoint the bodies of the Kings when they departed, to the end that they might not corrupt, neither the earth consume them: and with this was the body of the Cid embalmed after his death. Moreover he presented unto him a chess board, which was one of the noble ones in the world; it was of ivory riveted with gold, and with many precious stones round about it; and the men were of gold and silver, and the squares also were richly wrought with stones of many virtues. This was a full rich, and great and noble present, so that no man could tell the price thereof.

XI.

When the Moor had produced all these things before the Cid, he said unto him, All this, Sir, with the animals which thou hast seen, my Lord the Soldan of Persia hath sent unto thee, because of the great fame which he hath heard of thy goodness and loyalty; and, Sir, he beseecheth thee to accept it for the love of him. And the Cid thanked him, taking great pleasure therein, and said that he would fain do him greater honour than he had ever yet done to any one. And then he embraced him in the name of the Soldan, and said, that if he were a Christian he would give him the kiss of peace; and he asked whether among those things there was aught which had belonged to the person of the Soldan, that if so he might kiss it in his honour, and in token that if he were there present, he would kiss him on the shoulder, according to the custom of the Moors, for he knew that his Lord was one of the noblest men in all Pagandom. When the kinsman of the Soldan heard this he was greatly rejoiced, because of the great courtesy with which the Cid had spoken, and he perceived how noble a man he was. And he said unto him, Sir Cid, if you were present before my Lord the Soldan, he would do you full great honour, and would give you the head of his horse to eat, according to the custom of our country; but seeing that this is not the custom of this country, I give you my living horse, which is one of the best horses of Syria; and do you give order that he be taken in honour of my Lord the Soldan, and he will be better than his head would be boiled. And I kiss your hand, Sir Ruydiez, and hold myself more honoured and a happier man than ever I have been heretofore. And the Cid accepted the horse, and gave consent to the Moor that he should kiss his hand. And then he called for his Almoxarife, and bade him take with him this kinsman of the Soldan, and lodge him in the Garden of Villa Nueva, and do him even such honour and service as he would to himself.

XII.

Great was the honour which the Almoxarife of the Cid Ruydiez did unto the kinsman of the Soldan, and he served him even as he would have served his Lord the Cid. And when they had disported and taken solace together, the kinsman of the Soldan asked him concerning the Cid, what manner of man he was. And the Almoxarife answered that he was the man in the world who had the bravest heart, and the best knight at arms, and the man who best maintained his law; and in the word which he hath promised he never fails; and he is the man in the world who is the best friend to his friend, and to his enemy he is the mortallest foe among all Christians; and to the vanquished he is full of mercy and compassion; and full thoughtful and wise in whatsoever thing he doeth; and his countenance is such that no man seeth him for the first time without conceiving great fear. And this, said the Almoxarife, I have many times witnessed, for when any messengers of the Moors come before him, they are so abashed that they know not where they are. When the messenger of the Soldan heard this he called to mind how it had been with him, and he said unto the Almoxarife, that as they were both of one law he besought him to keep secret what he should say, and he would tell him what had befallen him himself. And the Almoxarife said that he would do as he desired. And with that he began to say, that he marvelled greatly at what he had heard, for even as he had now told him that it happened unto other messengers, even so had he himself found it the first time that he had seen the Cid; for so great was the fear which he conceived at the sight of his countenance, that for long time he had no power of speech; and according to his thinking, this could only proceed from the grace of God towards the Cid, that none of his enemies might ever behold his face without fear. When the kinsman of the Soldan had said this, the Almoxarife perceived that he was a wary man, and one of good understanding; and he began to talk with him, and asked him whether he would tell him what he should ask, and the messenger replied that he would. Then the Almoxarife asked of him if he knew what was the reason which had moved his Lord the Soldan to send so great a present to the Cid Campeador, and why he desired to have his love when he was so far away, beyond sea. Now the messenger of the Soldan conceived that the Almoxarife sought to know the state of the lands beyond sea, and he feared that this had been asked of him by command of the Cid; and he made answer, that so great was the renown of the Cid, and the report which they had heard in the lands beyond sea of his great feats in arms, that it had moved the Soldan to send him that present and desire his love. But when the Almoxarife heard this, he said that he could not believe that this had been the reason, but that some other intention had moved him. And when the messenger perceived that the Almoxarife understood him, and that he desired to know the whole of the matter, he said that he would tell him, but he besought him to keep it secret. And the Almoxarife promised to do this. Then he told him that the land beyond sea was in such state that they weened it would be lost, and that the Christians would win it, so great a Crusade had gone forth against it from Germany, and from France, and from Lombardy, and Sicily, and Calabria, and Ireland, and England, which had won the city of Antioch, and now lay before Jerusalem. And my Lord the Great Soldan of Persia, hearing of the great nobleness of the Cid, and thinking that he would pass over also, was moved to send him this present to gain his love, that if peradventure he should pass there he might be his friend. And when the Almoxarife of the Cid heard this, he said that of a truth he believed it.

XIII.

While yet that messenger of the Soldan of Persia abode in Valencia, tidings carne to the Cid that the Infantes of Aragon and Navarre were coming to celebrate their marriage with his daughters, according as it had been appointed at the Cortes of Toledo. He of Navarre hight Don Ramiro, and he was the son of King Don Sancho, him who was slain at Rueda; and he married with Doña Elvira, the elder: and the Infante of Aragon who married Doña Sol, the younger, hight Don Sancho, and was the son of King Don Pedro. This King Don Pedro was he whom the Cid Ruydiez conquered and made prisoner, as the history hath related; but calling to mind the great courtesy which the Cid had shown in releasing him from prison, and how he had ordered all his own to be restored unto him, and moreover the great worth and the great goodness of the Cid, and the great feats which he had performed, he held it good that his son should match with his daughter, to the end that the race of so good a man might be preserved in Aragon. Howbeit it was not his fortune to have a son by Doña Sol, for he died before he came to the throne, and left no issue. When the Cid knew that the Infantes were coming, he and all his people went out six leagues to meet them, all gallantly attired both for court and for war; and he ordered his tents to be pitched in a fair meadow, and there he awaited till they came up. And the first day the Infante Don Sancho of Aragon carne up, and they waited for the Infante Don Ramiro; and when they were all met they proceeded to Valencia. And the Bishop Don Hieronymo came out to meet them with a procession, full honourably. Great were the rejoicings which were made in Valencia because of the coming of the Infantes, for eight days before the marriage began. And the Cid gave order that they should be lodged in the Garden of Villa Nueva, and supplied with all things in abundance.

XIV.

When eight days were overpast the Bishop Don Hieronymo married the Infantes of Aragon and Navarre to the daughters of the Cid in this manner: the Infante Don Ramiro of Navarre to Doña Elvira; and the Infante Don Sancho of Aragon to Doña Sol. And on the day after they had been espoused they received the blessing in the great Church of St. Peter, as is commanded by the law of Jesus Christ, and the Bishop said mass. Who can tell the great rejoicings which were made at those marriages, and the great nobleness thereof? Certes there would be much to tell; for during eight days that they lasted, there was feasting every day, full honourably and plentifully, where all persons did eat out of silver; and many bulls were killed every day, and many of those wild beasts which the Soldán sent; and many sports were devised, and many garments and saddles and noble trappings were given to the joculars. And the Moors also exhibited their sports and rejoicings, after such divers manners, that men knew not which to go to first. So great was the multitude which was there assembled, that they were counted at eight thousand hidalgos. And when the marriage was concluded, the Cid took his sons-in-law and led them by the hand to Doña Ximena, and showed them all the noble things which the Soldan had sent him; and they when they beheld such great treasures and such noble things were greatly astonished, and said that they did not think there had been a man in Spain so rich as the Cid, nor who possessed such things. And as they were marvelling from whence such riches could have come, both of gold and silver, and of precious stones and pearls, the Cid embraced them and said, My sons, this and all that I have is for you and for your wives, and I will give unto you the noblest and most precious things that ever were given with women for their dowry: for I will give you the half of all that you see here, and the other half I and Doña Ximena will keep so long as we live, and after our death all shall be yours; and my days are now well nigh full. Then the Infantes made answer, that they prayed God to grant him life for many and happy years yet, and that they thanked him greatly, and held him as their father; and that they would ever have respect to his honour and be at his service, holding themselves honoured by the tie that there was between them. Three months these Infantes abode with the Cid in Valencia, in great pleasure. And then they dispeeded themselves of the Cid and of their mother-in-law Doña Ximena, and took each his wife and returned into their own lands with great riches and honour. And the Cid gave them great treasures, even as he had promised, and gave them certain of those strange beasts which the Soldan had sent. And he rode out with them twelve leagues. And when they took leave of each other there was not a knight of all those who came with the Infantes to whom the Cid did not give something, horse, or mule, or garments, or money, so that all were well pleased; and he gave his daughters his blessing, and commended them to God, and then he returned to Valencia, and they went to their own country.

XV.

After the Cid had seen his sons-in-law depart, he sent for the messenger of the Soldan, and gave him many of the rare things of his country to carry unto his Lord. And he gave him a sword which had the device of the Soldan wrought in gold, and a coat of mail and sleeve armour, and a noble gipion which was wrought of knots; and his letters of reply, which were full of great assurances of friendship. Much was the messenger of the Soldan pleased with the Cid for the great honour which he had shown him, and much was he pleased also at seeing how honourably the marriage of his daughters had been celebrated. So he departed and went to the port, and embarked on board his ship, and went to his Lord the Soldan.

XVI.

After this the Cid abode in Valencia, and he laboured a full year in settling all the Castles of the Moors who were subject unto him in peace, and in settling the Moors of Valencia well with the Christians; and this he did so that their tribute was well paid from this time till his death. And all the land from Tortoso to Origuela was under his command. And from this time he abode in peace in Valencia; and laboured alway to serve God and to increase the Catholic faith, and to make amends for the faults he had committed towards God, for he weened that his days now would be but few. And it came to pass one day, the Cid having risen from sleep and being in his Alcazar, there came before him an Alfaqui whom he had made Alcalde of the Moors; his name was Alfaraxi, and he it was who made the lamentation for Valencia, as is recorded in this history. This Alfaqui had served the Cid well in his office of Alcalde over the Moors of Valencia: for he kept them in peace, and made them pay their tribute well, being a discreet man and of great prudence, so that for this and for his speech he might have been taken for a Christian; and for this reason the Cid loved him and put great trust in him. And when the Cid saw him he asked him what he would have: and he like a prudent man bent his knees before him, and began to kiss his hand, and said, Sir Cid Ruydiez, blessed be the name of Jesus Christ who hath brought you to this state that you are Lord of Valencia, one of the best and noblest cities in Spain. What I would have is this. Sir, my forefathers were of this city, and I am a native hereof; and when I was a little lad the Christians took me captive, and I learnt their tongue among them, and then my will was to be a Christian, and to abide there in the land of the Christians; but my father and mother, being rich persons, released me. And God showed me such favour, and gave me such understanding and so subtle, that I learnt all the learning of the Moors, and was one of the most honourable and best Alfaquis that ever was in Valencia till this time, and of the richest, as you know, Sir; and you in your bounty made me Alcalde, and gave me your authority over the Moors, of which peradventure I was not worthy. And now, Sir, thinking in my heart concerning the law in which I have lived, I find that I have led a life of great error, and that all which Mahommed the great deceiver gave to the Moors for their law, is deceit: and therefore, Sir, I turn me to the faith of Jesus Christ, and will be a Christian and believe in the Catholic faith. And I beseech you of your bounty give order that I may be baptized in the name of the Holy Trinity, and give me what name you will. And from this time forward I will live the life of a Christian, and fulfil what is written in the

Gospel, and forsake wife and children and kin, and all that there is in the world, and serve God, and believe in his faith and holy law, as far as the weakness of my body can bear. When the Cid Ruydiez heard this he began to smile for very pleasure; and he rose up and took Alfaraxi with him to Doña Ximena, and said, Here is our Alcalde, who will be a Christian, and our brother in the faith of Jesus Christ: I beseech you therefore give order to provide all things that may be needful. When Doña Ximena heard this she rejoiced greatly, and gave order that all things should be full nobly prepared. And on the morrow the Bishop Don Hieronymo baptized him, and they gave him the name of Gil Diaz: and his godfathers were Don Alvar Fañez, and Pero Bermudez, and Martin Antolinez of Burgos; and Doña Ximena, with other honourable dames, were his godmothers. And from that time forward Gil Diaz was in such favour with the Cid, that he trusted all his affairs to his hands, and he knew so well how to demean himself, both towards him and all those of his company, that they all heartily loved him.

BOOK XI.

I.

It is written in the history which Abenalfarax, the nephew of Gil Diaz, composed in Valencia, that for five years the Cid Ruydiez remained Lord thereof in peace, and in all that time he sought to do nothing but to serve God, and to keep the Moors quiet who were under his dominion; so that Moors and Christians dwelt together in such accord, that it seemed as if they had alway been united; and they all loved and served the Cid with such goodwill that it was marvellous. And when these five years were over tidings were spread far and near, which reached Valencia, that King Bucar the Miramamolin of Morocco, holding himself disgraced because the Cid Campeador had conquered him in the field of Quarto near unto Valencia, where he had slain or made prisoners all his people, and driven him into the sea, and made spoil of all the treasures which he had brought with him; ... King Bucar calling these things to mind, had gone himself and stirred up the whole Paganism of Barbary, even as far as Montes Claros, to cross the sea again, and avenge himself if he could; and he had assembled so great a power that no man could devise their numbers. When the Cid heard these tidings he was troubled at heart; how beit he dissembled this, so that no person knew what he was minded to do; and thus the matter remained for some days. And when he saw that the news came thicker and faster, and that it was altogether certain that King Bucar was coming over sea against him, he sent and bade all the Moors of Valencia assemble together in his presence, and when they were all assembled he said unto them, Good men of the Aljama, ye well know that from the day wherein I became Lord of Valencia, ye have alway been protected and defended, and have past your time well and peaceably in your houses and heritages, none troubling you nor doing you wrong; neither have I who am your Lord ever done aught unto you that was against right. And now true tidings are come to me that King Bucar of Morocco is arrived from beyond sea, with a mighty power of Moors, and that he is coming against me to take from me this city which I won with so great labour. Now therefore, seeing it is so, I hold it good and command that ye quit the town, both ye and your sons and your women, and go into the suburb of Alcudia and the other suburbs, to dwell there with the other Moors, till we shall see the end of this business between me and King Bucar. Then the Moors, albeit they were loth, obeyed his command; and when they were all gone out of the city, so that none remained, he held himself safer than he had done before.

II.

Now after the Moors were all gone out of the city, it came to pass in the middle of the night that the Cid was lying in his bed, devising how he might withstand this coming of King Bucar, for Abenalfarax saith that when he was alone in his palace his thoughts were of nothing else. And when it was midnight there came a great light into the palace, and a great odour, marvellous sweet. And as he was marvelling what it might be, there appeared before him a man as white as snow; he was in the likeness of an old man, with grey hair and crisp, and he carried certain keys in his hand; and before the Cid could speak to him he said, Sleepest thou, Rodrigo, or what are thou doing? And the Cid made answer, What man art thou who askest me? And he said, I am St. Peter, the Prince of the Apostles, who come unto thee with more urgent tidings than those for which thou art taking thought concerning King Bucar, and it is, that thou art to leave this world, and go to that which hath no end; and this will be in thirty days. But God will show favour unto thee, so that thy people shall discomfit King Bucar, and thou, being dead, shalt win this battle for the honour of thy body: this will be with the help of Santiago, whom God will send to the business: but do thou strive to make atonement for thy sins, and so thou shall be saved. All this Jesus Christ vouchsafest thee for the love of me, and for the reverence which thou hast alway shown to my Church in the Monastery of Cárdena. When the Cid Campeador heard this he had great pleasure at heart, and he let himself fall out of bed upon the earth, that he might kiss the feet of the Apostle St. Peter; but the Apostle said, Strive not to do this, for thou canst not touch me; but be sure that all this which I have told thee will come to pass.

And when the blessed Apostle had said this he disappeared, and the palace remained full of a sweeter and more delightful odour than heart of man can conceive. And the Cid Ruydiez remained greatly comforted by what St. Peter had said to him, and as certain that all this would come to pass, as if it were already over.

III.

Early on the morrow he sent to call all his honourable men to the Alcazar; and when they were all assembled before him, he began to say unto them, weeping the while, Friends and kinsmen and true vassals and honourable men, many of ye must well remember when King Don Alfonso our Lord twice banished me from his land, and most of ye for the love which ye bore me followed me into banishment, and have guarded me ever since. And God hath shown such mercy to you and to me, that we have won many battles against Moors and Christians; those which were against Christians, God knows, were more through their fault than my will, for they strove to set themselves against the good fortune which God had given me, and to oppose his service, helping the enemies of the faith. Moreover we won this city in which we dwell, which is not under the dominion of any man in the world, save only of my Lord the King Don Alfonso, and that rather by reason of our natural allegiance than of anything else. And now I would have ye know the state in which this body of mine now is; for be ye certain that I am in the latter days of my life, and that thirty days hence will be my last. Of this I am well assured; for for these seven nights past I have seen visions. I have seen my father Diego Laynez, and Diego Rodríguez my son; and every time they say to me, You have tarried long here, let us go now among the people who endure for ever. Now notwithstanding man ought not to put his trust in these things, nor in such visions, I know this by other means to be certain, for Sir St. Peter hath appeared to me this night, when I was awake and not sleeping, and he told me that when these thirty days were over, I should pass away from this world. Now ye know for certain that King Bucar is coming against us, and they say that thirty and six Moorish Kings are coming with him; and since he bringeth so great a power of Moors, and I have to depart so soon, how can ye defend Valencia! But be ye certain, that by the mercy of God I shall counsel ye so, that ye shall conquer King Bucar in the field, and win great praise and honour from him, and Doña Ximena, and ye and all that ye have, go hence in safety; how ye are to do all this I will tell ye hereafter, before I depart.

IV

After the Cid had said this he sickened of the malady of which he died. And the day before his weakness waxed great, he ordered the gates of the town to be shut, and went to the Church of St. Peter; and there the Bishop Don Hieronymo being present, and all the clergy who were in Valencia, and the knights and honourable men and honourable dames, as many as the Church could hold, the Cid Ruydiez stood up, and made a full noble preaching, showing that no man whatsoever, however honourable or fortunate they may be in this world, can escape death; to which, said he, I am now full near; and since ye know that this body of mine hath never yet been conquered, nor put to shame, I beseech ye let not this befall it at the end, for the good fortune of man is only accomplished at his end. How this is to be done, and what ye all have to do, I will leave in the hands of the Bishop Don Hieronymo, and Alvar Fañez, and Pero Bermudez. And when he had said this he placed himself at the feet of the Bishop, and there before all the people made a general confession of all his sins, and all the faults which he had committed against our Lord Jesus Christ. And the Bishop appointed him his penance, and assoyled him of his sins. Then he arose and took leave of the people, weeping plenteously, and returned to the Alcazar, and betook himself to his bed, and never rose from it again; and every day he waxed weaker and weaker, till seven days only remained of the time appointed. Then he called for the caskets of gold in which was the balsam and the myrrh which the Soldan of Persia had sent him; and when these were put before him he bade them bring him the golden cup, of which he was wont to drink; and he took of that balsam and of that myrrh as much as a little spoon-full, and mingled it in the cup with rose-water, and drank of it; and for the seven days which he lived he neither ate nor drank aught else than a little of that myrrh and balsam mingled with water. And every day after he did this, his body and his countenance appeared fairer and fresher than before, and his voice clearer, though he waxed weaker and weaker daily, so that he could not move in his bed.

V.

On the twenty-ninth day, being the day before he departed, he called for Doña Ximena, and for the Bishop Don Hieronymo, and Don Alvar Fañez Minaya, and Pero Bermudez, and his trusty Gil Diaz; and when they were all five before him, he began to direct them what they should do after his death; and he said to them. Ye know that King Bucar will presently be here to besiege this city, with seven and thirty Kings whom he bringeth with him, and with a mighty power of Moors. Now therefore the first thing which ye do after I have departed, wash my body with rose-water many times and well, as blessed be the name of God it is washed within and made pure of all uncleanness to receive his holy body to-morrow, which will be my last day. And when it has been well washed and made clean, ye shall dry it well, and anoint it with this myrrh and balsam, from these golden caskets, from head to foot, so that every part shall be anointed, till none be left. And you my Sister Doña Ximena, and your women, see that ye utter no cries, neither make any lamentation for me, that the Moors may not know of my death. And when the day shall come in which King Bucar arrives, order all the people of Valencia to go upon the walls, and sound your trumpets and tambours, and make the greatest rejoicings that ye can. And when ye would set out for Castille, let all the people know in secret, that they make themselves ready, and take with them all that they have, so that none of the Moors in the suburb may know thereof; for certes ye cannot keep the city, neither abide therein after my death. And see ye that sumpter beasts be laden with all that there is in Valencia, so that nothing which can profit may be left. And this I leave especially to your charge, Gil Diaz. Then saddle ye my horse Bavieca, and arm him well; and ye shall apparel my body full seemlily, and place me upon the horse, and fasten and tie me thereon so that it cannot fall: and fasten my sword Tizona in my hand. And let the Bishop Don Hieronymo go on one side of me, and my trusty Gil Diaz on the other, and he shall lead my horse. You, Pero Bermudez, shall bear my banner, as you were wont to bear it; and you, Alvar Fañez, my cousin, gather your company together, and put the host in order as you are wont to do. And go ye forth and fight with King Bucar: for be ye certain and doubt not that ye shall win this battle; God hath granted me this. And when ye have won the fight, and the Moors are discomfited, ye may spoil the field at pleasure. Ye will find great riches. What ye are afterwards to do I will tell ye to-morrow, when I make my testament.

VI.

Early on the morrow the Bishop Don Hieronymo, and Alvar Fañez, and Pero Bermudez, and Martin Antolinez, came to the Cid. Gil Diaz and Doña Ximena were alway with him; and the Cid began to make his testament. And the first thing which he directed, after commending his soul to God, was, that his body should be buried in the Church of St. Pedro de Cardeña, where it now lies; and he bequeathed unto that Monastery many good inheritances, so that that place is at this day the richer and more honourable. Then he left to all his company and household according to the desert of every one. To all the knights who had served him since he went out of his own country, he gave great wealth in abundance. And to the other knights who had not served him so long, to some a thousand marks of silver, to others two, and some there were to whom he bequeathed three, according who they were. Moreover, to the squires who were hidalgos, to some five hundred, and others there were who had a thousand and five hundred. And he bade them, when they arrived at St. Pedro de Cardena, give clothing to four thousand poor, to each a skirt of escanforte and a mantle. And he bequeathed to Doña Ximeña all that he had in the world, that she might live honourably for the remainder of her days in the Monastery of St. Pedro de Cardena; and he commanded Cil Diaz to remain with her and serve her well all the days of her life. And he left it in charge to the Bishop Don Hieronymo, and Doña Ximena his wife, and Don Alvar Fañez, and Pero Bermudez, and Felez Muñoz, his nephews, that they should see all this fulfilled. And he commanded Alvar Fañez and Pero Bermudez, when they had conquered King Bucar, to proceed forthwith into Castille and fulfil all that he had enjoined. This was at the hour of sexts. Then the Cid Ruydiez, the Campeador of Bivar, bade the Bishop Don Hieronymo give him the body of our Lord and Saviour Jesus Christ, and he received it with great devotion, on his knees, and weeping before them all. Then he sate up in his bed and called upon God and St. Peter, and began to pray, saying, Lord Jesus Christ, thine is the power and the kingdom, and thou art above all Kings and all nations, and all Kings are at thy command, I beseech thee therefore pardon me my sins, and let my soul enter into the light which hath no end. And when the Cid Ruydiez had said this, this noble Baron yielded up his soul, which was pure and without spot, to God, on that Sunday which is called Quinquagesima, being the twenty and ninth of May, in the year of our Lord one thousand and ninety and nine, and in the seventy and third year of his life. After he had thus made his end they washed his body twice with warm water, and a third time with rose water, and then they anointed and embalmed it as he had commanded. And then all the honourable men, and all the clergy who were in Valencia, assembled and carried it to the Church of St. Mary of the Virtues, which is near the Alcazar, and there they kept their vigil, and said prayer and performed masses, as was meet for so honourable a man.

VII.

Three days after the Cid had departed King Bucar came into the port of Valencia, and landed with all his power, which was so great that there is not a man in the world who could give account of the Moors whom he brought. And there came with him thirty and six Kings, and one Moorish Queen, who was a negress, and she brought with her two hundred horsewomen, all negresses like herself, all having their hair shorn save a tuft on the top, and this was in token that they came as if upon a pilgrimage, and to obtain the remission of their sins; and they were all armed in coats of mail and with Turkish bows. King Bucar ordered his tents to be pitched round about Valencia, and Abenalfarax who wrote this history in Arabic, saith, that there were full fifteen thousand tents; and he bade that Moorish negress with her archers to take their station near the city. And on the morrow they began to attack the city, and they fought against it three days strenuously; and the Moors received great loss, for they came blindly up to the walls and were slain there. And the Christians defended themselves right well, and every time that they went upon the walls, they sounded trumpets and tambours, and made great rejoicings, as the Cid had commanded. This continued for eight days or nine, till the companions of the Cid had made ready every thing for their departure, as he had commanded. And King Bucar and his people thought that the Cid dared not come out against them, and they were the more encouraged, and began to think of making bastilles and engines wherewith to combat the city, for certes they weened that the Cid Ruydiez dared not come out against them, seeing that he tarried so long.

VIII.

All this while the company of the Cid were preparing all things to go into Castille, as he had commanded before his death; and his trusty Gil Diaz did nothing else but labour at this. And the body of the Cid was prepared after this manner: first it was embalmed and anointed as the history hath already recounted, and the virtue of the balsam and myrrh was such that the flesh remained firm and fair, having its natural colour, and his countenance as it was wont to be, and the eyes open, and his long beard in order, so that there was not a man who would have thought him dead if he had seen him and not known it. And on the second day after he had departed, Gil Díaz placed the body upon a right noble saddle, and this saddle with the body upon it he put upon a frame; and he dressed the body in a gambax of fine sendal, next the skin. And he took two boards and fitted them to the body, one to the breast and the other to the shoulders; these were so hollowed out and fitted that they met at the sides and under the arms, and the hind one came up to the pole, and the other up to the beard; and these boards were fastened into the saddle, so that the body could not move. All this was done by the morning of the twelfth day; and all that day the people of the Cid were busied in making ready their arms, and in loading beasts with all that they had, so that they left nothing of any price in the whole city of Valencia, save only the empty houses. When it was midnight they took the body of the Cid, fastened to the saddle as it was, and placed it upon his horse Bavieca, and fastened the saddle well: and the body sate so upright and well that it seemed as if he was alive. And it had on painted hose of black and white, so cunningly painted that no man who saw them would have thought but that they were grieves and cuishes, unless he had laid his hand upon them; and they put on it a surcoat of green sendal, having his arms blazoned, thereon, and a helmet of parchment, which was cunningly painted that every one might have believed it to be iron: and his shield was hung round his neck, and they placed the sword Tizona in his hand; and they raised his arm, and fastened it up so subtilly that it was a marvel to see how upright he held the sword. And the Bishop Don Hieronymo went on one side of him, and the trusty Gil Diaz on the other, and he led the horse Bavieca, as the Cid had commanded him. And when all this had been made ready, they went out from Valencia at midnight, through the gate of Roseros, which is towards Castille. Pero Bermudez went first with the banner of the Cid, and with him five hundred knights who guarded it, all well appointed. And after these came all the baggage. Then came the body of the Cid with an hundred knights, all chosen men, and behind them Doña Ximena with all her company, and six hundred knights in the rear. All these went out so silently, and with such a measured pace, that it seemed as if there were only a score. And by the time that they had all gone out it was broad day.

Now Alvar Fañez Minaya had set the host in order, and while the Bishop Don Hieronymo and Gil Diaz led away the body of the Cid, and Doña Ximena, and the baggage, he fell upon the Moors. First he attacked the tents of that Moorish Queen the Negress, who lay nearest to the city; and this onset was so sudden, that they killed full a hundred and fifty Moors before they had time to take arms or go to horse. But that Moorish Negress was so skilful in drawing the Turkish bow, that it was held for a marvel, and it is said that they called her in Arabic Nugueymat Turya, which is to say, the Star of the Archers. And she was the first that got on horseback, and with some fifty that were with her, did some hurt to the company of the Cid; but in fine they slew her, and her people fled to the camp. And so great was the uproar and confusion, that few there were who took arms, but instead thereof they turned their backs and fled toward the sea. And when King Bucar and his Kings saw this they were astonished. And it seemed to them that there came against them on the part of the Christians full seventy thousand knights, all as white as snow: and before them a knight of great stature upon a white horse with a bloody cross, who bore in one hand a white banner, and in the other a sword which seemed to be of fire, and he made a great mortality among the Moors who were flying. And King Bucar and the other Kings were so greatly dismayed that they never checked the reins till they had ridden into the sea; and the company of the Cid rode after them, smiting and slaying and giving them no respite; and they smote down so many that it was marvellous, for the Moors did not turn their heads to defend themselves. And when they came to the sea, so great was the press among them to get to the ships, that more than ten thousand died in the water. And of the six and thirty Kings, twenty and two were slain. And King Bucar and they who escaped with him hoisted sails and went their way, and never more turned their heads. Then Alvar Fañez and his people, when they had discomfited the Moors, spoiled the field, and the spoil thereof was so great that they could not carry it away. And they loaded camels and horses with the noblest things which they found, and went after the Bishop Don Hieronymo and Gil Diaz, who, with the body of the Cid, and Doña Ximena, and the baggage, had gone on till they were clear of the host, and then waited for those who were gone against the Moors. And so great was the spoil of that day, that there was no end to it: and they took up gold, and silver, and other precious things as they rode through the camp, so that the poorest man among the Christians, horseman or on foot, became rich with what he won that day. And when they were all met together, they took the road toward Castille; and they halted that night in a village which is called Siete Aguas, that is to say, the Seven Waters, which is nine leagues from Valencia.

Abenalfarax, he who wrote this history in Arabic, saith, that the day when the company of the Cid went out from Valencia, and discomfited King Bucar and the six and thirty Kings who were with him, the Moors of Alcudia and of the suburbs thought that he went out alive, because they saw him on horseback, sword in hand; but when they saw that he went towards Castille, and that none of his company returned into the town, they were astonished. And all that day they remained in such amaze, that they neither dared go into the tents which King Bucar's host had left, nor enter into the town, thinking that the Cid did this for some device; and all night they remained in the same doubt, so that they dared not go out from the suburbs. When it was morning they looked towards the town, and heard no noise there; and Abenaltarax then took horse, and taking a man with him, went toward the town, and found all the gates thereof shut, till he came to that through which the company of the Cid had gone forth; and he went into the city and traversed the greater part thereof, and found no man therein, and he was greatly amazed. Then he went out and called aloud to the Moors of the suburbs, and told them that the city was deserted by the Christians; and they were more amazed than before: nevertheless they did not yet dare either to go out to the camp or to enter into the town, and in this doubt they remained till it was mid-day. And when they saw that no person appeared on any side, Abenalfarax returned again into the town, and there went with him a great company of the best Moors; and they went into the Alcazar, and looked through all the halls and chambers, and they found neither man nor living thing; but they saw written upon a wall in Arabic characters by Gil Diaz, how the Cid Ruydiez was dead, and that they had carried him away in that manner to conquer King Bucar, and also to the end that none might oppose their going. And when the Moors saw this they rejoiced and were exceeding glad, and they opened the gates of the town, and sent to tell these tidings to those in the suburbs. And they came with their wives and children into the town, each to the house which had been his before the Cid won it. And from that day Valencia remained in the power of the Moors till it was won by King Don Jayme of Aragon, he who is called the Conqueror, which was an hundred and seventy years. But though King Don Jayme won it, it is alway called Valencia del Cid. On the morrow they went into the tents of King Bucar, and found there many arms; but the tents were deserted, save only that they found certain women who had hid themselves, and who told them of the defeat of King Bucar. And the dead were so many that they could scarcely make way among them. And they went on through this great mortality to the port, and there they saw no ships, but so many Moors lying dead that tongue of man cannot tell their numbers; and they began to gather up the spoils of the field, which were tents, and horses, and camels, and buffaloes, and flocks, and gold and silver, and garments, and store of provisions, out of all number, so that they had wherewith to suffice the city of Valencia for two years, and to sell to their neighbours also; and they were full rich from that time.

XI.

When the company of the Cid departed from the Siete Aguas, they held their way by short journies to Salvacañete. And the Cid went alway upon his horse Bavieca, as they had brought him out from Valencia, save only that he wore no arms, but was clad in right noble garments; and all who saw him upon the way would have thought that he was alive, if they had not heard the truth. And whenever they halted they took the body off, fastened to the saddle as it was, and set it upon that frame which Gil Diaz had made, and when they went forward again, they placed it in like manner upon the horse Bavieca. And when they reached Salvacañete, the Bishop Don Hieronymo, and Doña Ximena, and Alvar Fañez, and the other honourable men, sent their letters to all the kinsmen and friends of the Cid Ruydiez, bidding them come and do honour to his funeral; and they sent letters also to his sons-in-law, the Infantes of Aragon and Navarre, and to King Don Alfonso. And they moved on from Salvacañete and came to Osma, and then Alvar Fañez asked of Doña Ximena if they should not put the body of the Cid into a coffin covered with purple and with nails of gold; but she would not, for she said that while his countenance remained so fresh and comely, and his eyes so fair, his body should never be placed in a coffin, and that her children should see the face of their father; and they thought that she said well, so the body was left as it was. And at the end of fifteen days the Infante of Aragon arrived, with Doña Sol his wife, and they brought with them an hundred armed knights, all having their shields reversed hanging from the saddle bow, and all in grey cloaks, with the hoods rent. And Doña Sol came clad in linsey-woolsey, she and all her women, for they thought that mourning was to be made for the Cid. But when they came within half a league of Osma, they saw the banner of the Cid coming on, and all his company full featly apparelled. And when they drew nigh they perceived that they were weeping, but they made no wailing; and when they saw him upon his horse Bavieca, according as ye have heard, they were greatly amazed. But so great was the sorrow of the Infante that he and all his company began to lament aloud. And Doña Sol, when she beheld her father, took off her tire, and threw it upon the ground and began to tear her hair, which was like threads of gold. But Doña Ximena held her hand and said, Daughter, you do ill, in that you break the command of your father, who laid his curse upon all who should make lamentation for him. Then Doña Sol kissed the hand of the Cid and of her mother, and put on her tire again, saying, Lady mother, I have committed no fault in this, forasmuch as I knew not the command of my father.

And then they turned back to Osma, and great was the multitude whom they found there assembled from all parts to see the Cid, having heard in what manner he was brought, for they held it to be a strange thing: and in truth it was, for in ne history do we find that with the body of a dead man hath there been done a thing so noble and strange as this. Then they moved on from Osma, and came to Santesteban de Gormaz. And there after few days the King of Navarre came with the Queen Doña Elvira his wife; and they brought with them two hundred knights; howbeit their shields were not reversed, for they had heard that no mourning was to be made for the Cid. And when they were within half a league of Santesteban, the company of the Cid went out to meet them, as they had the Infante of Aragon; and they made no other lamentation, save that they wept with Doña Elvira; and when she came up to the body of her father she kissed his hand, and the hand of Doña Ximena her mother. And greatly did they marvel when they saw the body of the Cid Ruydiez how fair it was, for he seemed rather alive than dead. And they moved on from Santesteban, towards San Pedro de Cardeña. Great was the concourse of people to see the Cid Ruydiez coming in that guise. They came from Rioja, and from all Castille, and from all the country round about, and when they saw him their wonder was the greater, and hardly could they be persuaded that he was dead.

XII.

At this time King Don Alfonso abode in Toledo, and when the letters came unto him saying how the Cid Campeador was departed, and after what manner he had discomfited King Bucar, and how they brought him in this goodly manner upon his horse Bavieca, he set out from Toledo, taking long journies till he came to San Pedro de Cardeña to do honour to the Cid at his funeral. The day when he drew nigh the Infante of Aragon and the King of Navarre went out to meet him, and they took the body of the Cid with them on horseback, as far as the Monastery of San Christoval de Ybeas, which is a league from Cardeña; and they went, the King of Navarre on one side of the body, and the Infante of Aragon on the other. And when King Don Alfonso saw so great a company and in such goodly array, and the Cid Ruydiez so nobly clad and upon his horse Bavieca, he was greatly astonished. Then Alvar Fañez and the other good men kissed his hand in the name of the Cid. And the King beheld his countenance, and seeing it so fresh and comely, and his eyes so bright and fair, and so even and open that he seemed alive, he marvelled greatly. But when they told him that for seven days he had drank of the myrrh and balsam, and had neither ate nor drank of aught else, and how he had afterwards been anointed and embalmed, he did not then hold it for so great a wonder, for he had heard that in the land of Egypt they were wont to do thus with their Kings. When they had all returned to the Monastery they took the Cid from off his horse, and set the body upon the frame, as they were wont to do, and placed it before the altar. Many were the honours which King Don Alfonso did to the Cid in masses and vigils, and other holy services, such as are fitting for the body and soul of one who is departed. Moreover he did great honour to the King of Navarre, and to the Infante of Aragon, ordering that all things which were needful should be given to them and their companies.

XIII.

On the third day after the coming of King Don Alfonso, they would have interred the body of the Cid, but when the King heard what Doña Ximena had said, that while it was so fair and comely it should not be laid in a coffin, he held that what she said was good. And he sent for the ivory chair which had been carried to the Cortes of Toledo, and gave order that it should be placed on the right of the altar of St. Peter; and he laid a cloth of gold upon it, and upon that placed a cushion covered with a right noble tartarí, and he ordered a graven tabernacle to be made over the chair, richly wrought with azure and gold, having thereon the blazonry of the Kings of Castille and Leon, and the King of

Navarre, and the Infante of Aragon, and of the Cid Ruydiez the Campeador. And he himself, and the King of Navarre and the Infante of Aragon, and the Bishop Don Hieronymo, to do honour to the Cid, helped to take his body from between the two boards, in which it had been fastened at Valencia. And when they had taken it out, the body was so firm that it bent not on either side, and the flesh so firm and comely, that it seemed as if he were yet alive. And the King thought that what they purported to do and had thus begun, might full well be effected. And they clad the body in a full noble tartari, and in cloth of purple, which the Soldan of Persia had sent him, and put him on hose of the same, and set him in his ivory chair; and in his left hand they placed his sword Tizona in its scabbard, and the strings of his mantle in his right. And in this fashion the body of the Cid remained there ten years and more, till it was taken thence, as the history will relate anon. And when his garments waxed old, other good ones were put on.

XIV.

King Don Alfonso, and the sons-in-law of the Cid, King Don Ramiro of Navarre, and the Infante Don Sancho of Aragon, with all their companies, and all the other honourable men, abode three weeks in St. Pedro de Cardeña, doing honour to the Cid. And the Bishop Don Hieronymo, and the other Bishops who came with King Don Alfonso, said every day their masses, and accompanied the body of the Cid there where it was placed, and sprinkled holy water upon it, and incensed it, as is the custom to do over a grave. And after three weeks they who were there assembled began to break up, and depart to their own houses. And of the company of the Cid, some went with the King of Navarre, and other some with the Infante of Aragon; but the greater number, and the most honourable among them, betook themselves to King Don Alfonso, whose natural subjects they were. And Doña Ximena and her companions abode in San Pedro de Cardeña, and Gil Diaz with her, as the Cid had commanded in his testament. And the Bishop Don Hieronymo, and Alvar Fañez Minaya, and Pero Bermudez, remained there also till they had fulfilled all that the Cid Ruydiez had commanded in his testament to be done.

XV.

Gil Díaz did his best endeavour to fulfil all that his Lord the Cid Ruydiez had commanded him, and to serve Doña Ximena and her companions truly and faithfully; and this he did so well, that she was well pleased with his faithfulness. And Doña Ximena fulfilled all that the Cid had commanded her; and every day she had masses performed for his soul, and appointed many vigils, and gave great alms for the soul of the Cid and of his family. And this was the life which she led, doing good wherever it was needful for the love of God; and she was alway by the body of the Cid, save only at meal times and at night, for then they would not permit her to tarry there, save only when vigils were kept in honour of him. Moreover Gil Diaz took great delight in tending the horse Bavieca, so that there were few days in which he did not lead him to water, and bring him back with his own hand. And from the day in which the dead body of the Cid was taken off his back, never man was suffered to bestride that horse, but he was alway led when they took him to water, and when they brought him back. And Gil Diaz thought it fitting that the race of that good horse should be continued, and he bought two mares for him, the goodliest that could be found, and when they were with foal, he saw that they were well taken care of, and they brought forth the one a male colt and the other a female; and from these the race of this good horse was kept up in Castille, so that there were afterwards many good and precious horses of his race, and peradventure are at this day. And this good horse lived two years and a half after the death of his master the Cid, and then he died also, having lived, according to the history, full forty years. And Gil Diaz buried him before the gate of the Monastery, in the public place, on the right hand; and he planted two elms upon the grave, the one at his head and the other at his feet, and these elms grew and became great trees, and are yet to be seen before the gate of the Monastery. And Gil Diaz gave order that when he died they should bury him by that good horse Bavieca, whom he had loved so well.

XVI.

Four years after the Cid had departed that noble lady Doña Ximena departed also, she who had been the wife of that noble baron the Cid Ruydiez, the Campeador. At that time Don García Tellez was Abbot of the Monastery, a right noble monk, and a great hidalgo. And the Abbot and Gil Díaz sent for the daughters of the Cid and Doña Ximena to come and honour their mother at her funeral, and to inherit what she had left. Doña Sol, who was the younger, came first, because Aragón is nearer than Navarre, and also because she was a widow; for the Infante Don Sancho, her husband, had departed three years after the death of the Cid, and had left no child. King Don Ramiro soon arrived with the other dame, Queen Doña Elvira his wife, and he brought with him a great company in honour of his wife's mother, and also the Bishop of Pamplona, to do honour to her funeral; and the Infante Don Garcia Ramírez, their son, came with them, being a child of four years old. Moreover there came friends and kinsmen from all parts. And when they were all assembled they buried the body of Doña Ximena at the feet of the ivory chair on which the Cid was seated; and the Bishop of Pamplona said mass, and the Abbot Don García Tellez officiated. And they tarried there seven days, singing many masses, and doing much good for her soul's sake. And in that time the Bishop Don Hieronymo arrived, who abode with King Don Alfonso, and he came to do honour to the body of Doña Ximena; for so soon as he heard that she was departed, he set off taking long journies every day. And when the seven days were over, King Don Ramiro and Queen Doña Elvira his wife, and her sister, Doña Sol, set apart rents for the soul of Doña Ximena, and they appointed that Gil Díaz should have them for his life, and that then they should go to the Monastery for ever: and they ordained certain anniversaries for the souls of the Cid and of Doña Ximena. After this was done they divided between them what Doña Ximena had left, which was a great treasure in gold and in silver, and in costly garments; ... the one half Queen Doña Elvira took, and Doña Sol the other. And when they had thus divided it, Doña Sol said that all which she had in the world should be for her nephew the Infante Don Garcia Ramirez, and with the good will of Queen Elvira his mother, she adopted him then to be her son, and she took him with her to Aragon, to the lands which had been given her in dower, and bred him up till he became a young man; and after the death of his father he was made King of Navarre, as may be seen in the book of the Chronicles of the Kings of Spain. And when all these things were done they departed each to his own home, and Gil Diaz remained, serving and doing honour to the bodies of his master the Cid and Doña Ximena his mistress.

XVII.

Now Don Garcia Tellez the Abbot, and the trusty Gil Diaz, were wont every year to make a great festival on the day of the Cid's departure, and on that anniversary they gave food and cloathing to the poor, who came from all parts round about. And it came to pass when they made the seventh anniversary, that a great multitude assembled as they were wont to do, and many Moors and Jews came to see the strange manner of the Cid's body. And it was the custom of the Abbot Don Garcia Tellez, when they made that anniversary, to make a right noble sermon to the people: and because the multitude which had assembled was so great that the Church could not hold them, they went out into the open place before the Monastery, and he preached unto them there. And while he was preaching there remained a Jew in the Church, who stopt before the body of the Cid, looking at him to see how nobly he was there seated, having his countenance so fair and comely, and his long beard in such goodly order, and his sword Tizona in its scabbard in his left hand, and the strings of his mantle in his right, even in such manner as King Don Alfonso had left him, save only that the garments had been changed, it being now seven years since the body had remained there in that ivory chair. Now there was not a man in the Church save this Jew, for all the others were hearing the preachment which the Abbot made. And when this Jew perceived that he was alone, he began to think within himself and say. This is the body of that Ruydiez the Cid, whom they say no man in the world ever took by the beard while he lived ... I will take him by the beard now, and see what he can do to me. And with that he put forth his hand to pull the beard of the Cid; ... but before his hand could reach it, God, who would not suffer this thing to be done, sent his spirit into the body, and the Cid let the strings of his mantle go from his right hand, and laid hand on his sword Tizona, and drew it a full palm's length out of the scabbard. And when the Jew saw this, he fell upon his back for great fear, and began to cry out so loudly, that all they who were without the Church heard him, and the Abbot broke off his preachment and went into the Church to see what it might be. And when they came they found this Jew lying upon his back before the ivory chair, like one dead, for he had ceased to cry out, and had swooned away. And then the Abbot Don Garcia Tellez looked at the body of the Cid, and saw that his right hand was upon the hilt of the sword, and that he had drawn it out a full palm's length; and he was greatly amazed. And he called for holy water, and threw it in the face of the Jew, and with that the Jew came to himself. Then the Abbot asked him what all this had been, and he told him the whole truth; and he knelt down upon his knees before the Abbot, and besought him of his mercy that he would make a Christian of him, because of this great miracle which he had seen, and baptize him in the name of Jesus Christ, for he would live and die in his faith, holding all other to be but error. And the Abbot baptized him in the name of the Holy Trinity, and gave him to name Diego Gil. And all who were there present were greatly amazed, and they made a great outcry and great rejoicings to God for this miracle, and for the power which he had shown through the body of the Cid in this manner; for it was plain that what the Jew said was verily and indeed true, because the posture of the Cid was changed. And from that day forward Diego Gil remained in the Monastery as longed as he lived, doing service to the body of the Cid.

XVIII.

After that day the body of the Cid remained in the same posture, for they never took his hand off the sword, nor changed his garments more, and thus it remained three years longer, till it had been there ten years in all. And then the nose began to change colour. And when the Abbot Don Garcia Tellez and Gil Diaz saw this, they weened that it was no longer fitting for the body to remain in that manner. And three Bishops from the neighbouring provinces met there, and with many masses and vigils, and great honour, they interred the body after this manner. They dug a vault before the altar, beside the grave of Doña Ximena, and vaulted it over with a high arch, and there they placed the body of the Cid seated as it was in the ivory chair, and in his garments, and with the sword in his hand, and they hung up his shield and his banner upon the walls.

XIX.

After the body of the noble Cid Campeador had been thus honourably interred, Gil Diaz his trusty servant abode still in the Monastery of St. Pedro de Cardeña, doing service to the graves of the Cid and Doña Ximena, and making their anniversaries, and celebrating masses, and giving great alms to the poor both in food and clothing, for the good of their souls; and in this manner he lived while Don Garcia Tellez was Abbot, and two others after him, and then he died. And his deportment had alway been such in that Monastery, that all there were his friends, and lamented greatly at his death, because he had led so devout and good a life, and served so trustily at the graves of his master and mistress. And at the time of his death he gave order that they should lay his body beside the good horse Bavieca whom he had loved so well, in the grave which he had made there for himself while he was living. And Diego Gil remained in his place, doing the same service which he had done, till he departed also. And the history saith that though Gil Díaz was good, Diego Gil was even better.

XX.

Eighty and six years after the death of the Cid Campeador, that is to say, in the year of the Era 1223, which is the year of the Incarnation 1185, it came to pass, that there was war between the Kings of Leon and Navarre on the one part, and the King of Castille on the other, notwithstanding this King Don Sancho of Navarre was uncle to the King of Castille, being his mother's brother. And this King Don Sancho entered into the lands of his nephew King Don Alfonso of Castille, and advanced as far as Burgos, and with his sword he struck a great stroke into the elm tree which is before the Church of St. John at Burgos, in token that he had taken possession of all that land; and he carried away with him a great booty in flocks and herds and beasts of the plough, and whatever else he could find, and with all this booty went his way toward Navarre. Now he had to pass nigh the Monastery of St. Pedro de Cardeña, where the body of the Cid Campeador lay. And at that time the Abbot of the Monastery, whose name was Don Juan, was a good man, and a hidalgo, and stricken in years; and he had been a doughty man in arms in his day. And when he saw this great booty being driven out of Castille, he was sorely grieved at the sight, and though he was now an old man, and it was long since he had got on horseback, he went to horse now, and took ten monks with him, and bade the strongest among them take down the banner of the Cid from the place where it was hung up, and he went after King Don Sancho who was carrying away the spoil. And the King when he saw him coming marvelled what banner this might be, for in those days there was no banner like unto that borne by any man in all the kingdoms of Spain; and perceiving how few they were who came with it, he halted to see what it might be. And the Abbot humbled himself before him when he came up, and said, King Don Sancho of Navarre, I am the Abbot of this Monastery of St. Pedro de Cardeña, wherein lies the body of Cid Campeador, your great grandfather; and for that reason presuming on your bounty and favour, I am come hither with this banner, which was borne before him in his battles, to beseech you that you would leave this booty for the honour of this banner and of the body of the Cid. And when King Don Sancho heard this, he marvelled at the great courage of the man, that he should thus without fear ask of him to restore his booty. And he said unto him after awhile, Good man, I know you not: but for what you have said I will give back the booty, for which there are many reasons. For I am of the lineage of the Cid, as you say, and my father King Don Garcia being the son of Doña Elvira his daughter, this is the first reason; and the second is for the honour of his body which lies in your Monastery; and the third is in reverence to this his banner, which never was defeated. And if none of these were of any avail, yet ought I to restore it were it only for this, that if he were living there is none who could drive away the spoils of Castille, he being so near. For the love of God therefore, and of my forefather the Cid, I give it to him, and to you, who have known so well how to ask it at my hands. When the Abbot heard this he was as joyful as he could be, and would have kissed the hand of King Don Sancho, but the King would not suffer this because he was a priest of the mass. Then the King ordered the spoil to be driven to the Monastery, and went himself with it, and saw the banner hung up again in its place, and abode there three weeks, till all that booty had been restored to the persons from whom it was taken. And when this was done he offered to the Monastery two hundred pieces of gold for the soul of his forefather the Cid, and returned into his kingdom of Navarre, and did no more evil at that time in the realm of Castille. This good service the Cid Ruydiez did to Castille after his death.

XXI.

Moreover when the Miramamolin brought over from Africa against King Don Alfonso, the eighth of that name, the mightiest power of the misbelievers that had ever been brought against Spain since the destruction of the Kings of the Goths, the Cid Campeador remembered his country in that great danger. For the night before the battle was fought at the Navas de Tolosa, in the dead of the night, a mighty sound was heard in the whole city of Leon, as if it were the tramp of a great army passing through. And it passed on to the Royal Monastery of St. Isidro, and there was a great knocking at the gate thereof, and they called to a priest who was keeping vigils in the Church, and told him, that the Captains of the army whom he heard were the Cid Ruydiez, and Count Ferran Gonzalez, and that they came there to call up King Don Ferrando the Great, who lay buried in that Church, that he might go with them to deliver Spain. And on the morrow that great battle of the Navas de Tolosa was fought, wherein sixty thousand of the misbelievers were slain, which was one of the greatest and noblest battles ever won over the Moors.

XXII.

The body of the Cid remained in the vault wherein it had been placed as ye have heard, till the year of the Incarnation 1272, when King Don Alfonso the Wise, for the great reverence which he bore the memory of the Cid his forefather, ordered a coffin to be made for him, which was hewn out of two great stones; and in this the body of the Cid was laid, and they placed it on that side where the Epistle is read; and before it, in, a wooden coffin, they laid the body of Doña Ximena. And round about the stone coffin these verses were graven, in the Latin tongue, being, according as it is said, composed by King Don Alfonso himself.

BELLIGER, INVICTOS, FAMOSUS MARTE TRIUMPHIS,
CLAUDITUR HOC TUMULO MAGNUS DIDACI RODERICUS.

And upon his tomb he ordered these verses to be graven also:

QUANTUM ROMA POTENS BELLICIS EXTOLLITUR ACTIS,
VIVAX ARTHURUS FIT GLORIA QUANTUM BRITANNIS,
NOBILIS E CAROLO QUANTUM GAUDET FRANCIA MAGNO,
TANTUM IBERIA DURIS CID INVICTOS CLARET.

And upon the walls it was thus written. I who lie here interred am the Cid Ruydiez, who conquered King Bucar with six and thirty Kings of the Moors; and of those six and thirty, twenty and two died in the field. Before Valencia I conquered them, on horseback, after I was dead, being the seventy and second battle which I won. I am he who won the swords Colada and Tizona. God be praised, Amen.

XXIII.

The body of the Cid remained here till the year of the Incarnation 1447, when the Abbot Don Pedro del Burgo ordered the old Church to be pulled down that a new one might be built in its place. And then as all the sepulchres were removed, that of the Cid was removed also, and they placed it in front of the Sacristy, upon four stone lions. And in the year 1540 God put it in the heart of the Abbot and Prior, Monks and Convent of the Monastery of St. Pedro de Cardeña, for the glory of God, and the honour of St. Peter and St. Paul, and of the Cid and other good knights who lay buried there, and for the devotion of the people, to beautify the great Chapel of the said Monastery with a rich choir and stalls, and new altars, and goodly steps to lead up to them. And as they were doing this they found that the tomb of the blessed Cid, if they left it where it was, which was in front of the door of the Sacristy, before the steps of the altar, it would neither be seemly for the service of the altar, because it was in the way thereof, nor for his dignity, by reason that they might stumble against it; ... moreover it was fallen somewhat to decay, and set badly upon the stone lions which supported it; and there were other knights placed above him. Whereupon the Abbot, Prior, Monks, and Convent, resolved that they would translate his body, and remove the other tombs to places convenient for them, holding that it was not meet that those who neither in their exploits nor in holiness had equalled him in life, should have precedency of him after death. And they were of accord that the day of this translation should not be made public, knowing how great the number would be of knights and other persons who would be desirous of being at this festival, for which cause they doubted least some misadventure would betide of tumults and deaths, or scandals, such as are wont to happen on such occasions; they were therefore minded to do this thing without giving knowledge thereof to any but those who were in the Monastery, who were of many nations and conditions, and who were enow to bear testimony when it was done; for there was no lack there, besides the religious, of knights, squires, hidalgos, labourers, and folk of the city and the district round about, and Biscayans and mountaineers, and men of Burgundy and of France.

XXIV.

So on Thursday, the eighth day of Epiphany, being the thirteenth day of January in the year of our Lord 1541, and at the hour of complines, the Abbot and Convent being assembled, together with serving-men and artificers who were called for this purpose, they made that night wooden biers that the tomb might be moved more easily and reverently, and with less danger. And on the morrow, which was Friday, the fourteenth day of the said month and year, the Convent having said primes, and the mass of Our Lady, according to custom, and the Abbot, Fray Lope de Frias, who was a native of Velorado, having confessed and said mass, the doors of the Church being open, and the altar richly drest, and the bells ringing as they are wont to do upon great festivals, at eight in the morning there assembled in the Church all the brethren of the Monastery, nineteen in number, the other fifteen being absent each in his avocation; and there were present with them Sancho de Ocaña, Merino and Chief Justice of the Monastery; Juan de Rosales, Pedro de Ruseras, and Juan Ruyz, squires of the house; master Ochoa de Artiaga, a mason, with his men; Andres de Carnica, and Domingo de Artiago, master Pablo and master Borgoñon, stone-cutters, with their men; and master Juan, a smith, with his; and all the other workmen and serving-men and traders who were in the house. And the Abbot being clad in rich vestments, and the ministers and acolites with him, with cross, candles, and torches burning, went all in procession to Our Lady's altar, where the sacrament was at that time kept, because of the repairs which were going on in the great Chapel; and all kneeling on their knees, and having recited the Pater-noster and the Ave-maria, the Abbot gave a sign, and the Precentor of the Convent began in plain descant the antiphony Salvator Mundi. And when the whole Convent had sung this, the Abbot said the verse Ostende nobis, and the verse Post partum virgo, and the prayer Omnipotens sempiterne Deus, qui es omnium dubitantium certitudo, and the prayer Deus qui salutis oeternoe, demanding the grace and favour of the Lord. When this was done they returned in procession to the great Chapel, before the tomb of the blessed Cid, and then the choir began the anthem Mirabilis Deus, saying it to the organ. And while this was singing in great accord, the workmen stood ready with their instruments in hand, to lift off the upper stone of the coffin, because it was well nigh impossible to remove the whole together, and also because the Abbot, Prior, and Convent, had resolved to see that holy body and relicks, by reason of the devotion which they bore to the blessed Cid, and that they might bear testimony in what manner he lay in that tomb, wherein he had been deposited to many years ago, as behoved them for the honour of the Cid and the authority of the Monastery.

XXV.

When the anthem was finished, the Abbot said the verse Exuliabunt saneti in gloria, and the prayer Deus qui es tuorum gloria servorum. And when all had said Amen, the Abbot himself, with a little bar of iron, began first to move the lid of the stone coffin; and then the workmen and others easily lifted it off upon the bier, and thus the tomb was laid open; and there appeared within it a coffin of wood fastened-down with gilt nails, the hair of the coffin being entirely gone, and great part of the wood decayed also. Within this coffin was the holy body, now well nigh consumed, nothing but the bones remaining entire. On some of the bones the flesh was still remaining, not discoloured, but with a rosy colour, and the bones, were of the same rosy colour, and the flesh also which had fallen from them. The body was wrapt in a sendal wrought after the Moorish fashion, with sword and spear by its side, as tokens of knighthood. As soon as the coffin was opened there issued forth a good odour, and comforting fragrance. It appeared that no part of the body was wanting: but this was not narrowly examined, by reason of the reverence which they bore it. After all this had been seen well and leisurely by all those who were present, the Abbot and his ministers passed a clean sheet under the coffin, and collecting into it all the bones and holy dust, covered it with another sheet, and took it out, and laid it upon the high altar, with candles and torches on each side; and in this manner it remained there all day, till it was time to deposit it in the tomb. And all this while the choristers sung to the organ, and the organ responded. And when the body was laid upon the altar, the Abbot said the verse Mirabilis Deus, and the prayer Magnifuet te Domine sanctorum tuorum beaia solemnitas. And when this was done he went and disrobed himself of his sacred vestments. And the workmen went and removed the stone lions, and placed them in the place where they were to be, and the tomb upon them. And the Convent went to perform divine service, which was celebrated that day at all the hours with a full choir. And at the hour accustomed, after this was done, the Abbot and the Convent invited all who were there present to be their guests, giving a right solemn feast to all; and the chief persons dined with the Convent in the Refectory. And that same day in the evening, after vespers, when it was about four o'clock, the workmen had removed the stone lions, and placed the tomb upon them, and laid the lid of the tomb hard by, and made all ready to fasten it down, so soon as the holy body should be laid in it. And at that time, the bells ringing again, and all being again assembled, the Abbot having put on again his vestments, which were of white brocade, and his ministers with him, went to the altar whereon they had laid the holy body, which had been right nobly guarded and accompanied. And the singers singing the while, he and his ministers took it and laid it with great reverence in the tomb, all seeing it when it was laid there, wrapt up and covered with the sheets. And in the presence of all, the workmen put on the lid and fastened it down. Then the Abbot began the Te Deum laudamus, and the singers continuing it, they went in procession to Our Lady's Chapel, where the most holy sacrament then was, as ye have heard. And the Abbot said the verse Benedicamus Patrem et Filium cum Sancto Spiritu, and the prayer Deus ad quem digne laudandum, and they all returned thanksgiving to the Lord. And the Abbot and the ministers went into the Sacristy, and took off their sacred vestments; and then he returned and again invited all who were there to a collation in the Refectory, which had been prepared by the servants of the Monastery. And when this was over they separated, each going with great content to his several occupation, praising God.

XXVI.

It was a thing of great consolation that there was not a person in that Monastery, who did not all that day feel great joy and delight in his soul. And there befell a thing of which many took notice, and which ought not to be passed over in silence, and it was this. There was a great want of rain in the land of Rioja and Bureva, and the district of Cardeña also was in want of water, though not in such great need, for it was long since any rain had fallen; and it pleased God that on the aforesaid

Thursday, the eve of the translation, at the very hour when the Abbot and his people began to prepare the bier, and make all things ready for opening and removing the tomb, a soft and gentle rain began, such a rain that to those who were out of doors it was nothing troublesome, and to the country greatly profitable, and pleasant unto all; and it lasted all that night, and all the day following, till the holy business of the translation was accomplished, and then it ceased. Now it was found that this rain had fallen at the same time and in the same manner, both in the country below Burgos, and also in Bureva, albeit that it rarely hath happened for rain to fall at one time in both provinces, because they are wont to have rain with different winds. It seemeth therefore that this blessed knight, who while he lived protected and defended that country with his person and his arms, beholding the service which was done him, and how he was remembered, favoured it at that time in heaven with his holy intercession, by sending that thing whereof it had then most need, which was water from heaven, in order that it might be made manifest that he never ceased to show favour to those who trusted in him, and to that Monastery of St. Pedro de Cardeña. And an account of this translation, and of all this which befell, was drawn up by the Abbot Fray Lope de Frías, and signed by all the brethren of the Monastery, and all the chief persons there present.

XXVII.

Now albeit this translation of the body of the blessed Cid had been made with such honour and reverence, there were many who murmured against it; and Don Pedro Fernandez de Velasco, Duke of Frias, who was then Constable of Castille, and the Municipality of Burgos, sent advice thereof to the Emperor Charles V. who was at that time in Flanders, beseeching him to give order that the tomb of the Cid might be translated back to its former place, and that of Doña Ximena also, which had been removed into the Cloisters of the Monastery. Hereupon the Emperor dispatched letters to his Governor, Cardinal Juan, bidding him see that the petition of the Constable and of the City of Burgos was fulfilled, and the Cardinal in obedience thereunto dispatched the provision here following.

The King.

Venerable Abbot, Monks and Convent of St. Pedro de Cardeña, know ye that we have ordered to be given, and do hereby give our edict unto you, to the following tenor. The Council, Justice, and Regidores, Knights, Esquires, Artificers and Good Men of the City of Burgos, have made a memorial to us the King, showing, that we well know the fame, nobleness, and exploits of the Cid, which are notorious to all, from whose valour there redoundeth honour to all Spain, and especially to that city whereof he was a native, and where he had his origin and birth place; and that one of the principal things which they who pass through that city, both natives of these kingdoms, and strangers also, desire to see, is his tomb and the place wherein he and his ancestors are interred, for his greatness and the antiquity thereof; and that it is now some thirty or forty days since ye, not having respect to this, neither bearing in mind that the Cid is our progenitor, nor the possessions which he left to your house, nor the authority that it is to the said Monastery that he should there have been interred, have removed and taken away his tomb from the middle of the great Chapel, where it had stood for more than four hundred years, and placed it near a staircase, in a place unseemly, and unlike that where it was placed heretofore, both in authority and honour. Moreover ye have removed with him the tomb of Doña Ximena his wife, and placed it in the Cloisters of the said Monastery, full differently from where it was. The which that city, as well because it toucheth us as for her honour, doth greatly resent; and albeit that as soon as it was known the Corregidor and three of the Regidores thereof went there to prevail with ye that ye should restore the said bodies to the place where they were wont to be, ye would not be persuaded; whereof the said city holdeth itself greatly aggrieved: and moreover it is a thing of bad example for Monasteries and Religioners, who, seeing how lightly the tomb of so famous a person hath been removed, may venture to remove and change any monuments and memorials, whereby great evil would accrue to our kingdoms. And the said City supplicateth and beseeching us of our grace, that we would be pleased to give command that ye should restore the bodies of the Cid and of his wife to the same place and form as heretofore. And the Cid having been so signal a person, and one from whom the Royal Crown of Castille hath received such great and notable services, we marvel that ye should have made this alteration in their tombs, and we command you if it be so that their bodies or their tombs have been indeed removed, as soon as ye receive this, to restore them to the same place, and in the same form and manner as they were before; and in case they have not yet been removed, that ye do not move nor touch them, neither now nor at anytime to come. And having first complied with this order, if ye have any cause or reason for making this removal, ye are to send us an account thereof, and also how ye have restored the said bodies and tombs to their former place within forty days, to the end that we may give order to have this matter inspected, and provide as shall be most convenient. Done in Madrid, the 8th day of the Month of July, in the year 1541. Johannes Cardinalis, by command of his Majesty. Governor in his name.

XXVIII.

This provision having been notified unto them, the Abbot and Monks made answer that they were ready to obey it, and that he would go and give account to the Lord Governor of what had been done. And the Abbot went accordingly to Court, and informed the Cardinal Governor of the translation which had been made; and that the tomb of the Cid had been removed to a place more decorous, and nearer the High Altar, and answering the site where King Don Alfonso VI. had commanded him to be placed in his ivory chair before he was first interred; and where the vault had been made wherein he had lain many years. And that the reason why the tomb had been moved was, that the passage from the Sacristy to the choir and the High Altar might be cleared; and that the reason why it had not been placed in the middle of the Great Chapel, was, that if that place were occupied, it seemed due to Queen Doña Sancha, the foundress of that House, or to King Don Ramira, who had held that place in the old Church. But notwithstanding all these reasons which the Abbot alleged, the Cardinal ordered him to obey the King's command. Hereupon the Abbot returned to the Monastery and determined to place the tombs of the Cid and of Doña Ximena in the middle of the Great Chapel, before it should be known in Burgos that the translation was to take place; and accordingly when those persons who would fain have been present made enquiry, they were told that the thing was done.

XXIX.

Now there have not been wanting over-curious persons who, because the Monastery of Cardeña is the first under the royal patronage, by reason that it is a foundation of Queen Doña Sancha, who is the first royal personage that ever founded a Monastery in Spain, and because King Don Alfonso the Great re-edified it, and Garcia Ferrandez the Count of Castile restored it, have said, that the Cid hath taken the place of these patrons. And when King Carlos II. was in this Monastery in the year 1679, he asked whose the tomb was which occupied the middle of the Great Chapel; and Fray Joseph del Hoyo, who was at that time Abbot, made answer, Sir, it is the tomb of Rodrigo Diaz, the Cid Campeador. Why then, said one of the Grandees, doth the Cid occupy the best place, seeing that this Monastery is a royal foundation? Upon this the Abbot made answer, that the Emperor Charles V. had ordered the Abbot and Monks to place him in that place; and King Carlos II. said, The Cid was not a King, but he was one who made Kings. And from that time till the present day the tomb of the Cid hath remained in the same place, and that of Doña Ximena beside it; and with such veneration and respect are they preserved, that they are alway covered and adorned with two cloths, whereof the upper one is of silk, and on great festivals they are adorned with one still more precious.

Many are the things which belonged to Ruydiez the Cid Campeador, which are still preserved with that reverence which is due to the memory of such a man. First, there are those good swords Colada and Tizona, which the Cid won with his own hand. Colado is a sword of full ancient make: it hath only a cross for its hilt, and on one side are graven the words Si, Si ... that is to say, Yea, Yea: and on the other, No, No. And this sword is in the Royal Armoury at Madrid. That good sword Tizona is in length three quarters and a half, some little more, and three full fingers wide by the hilt, lessening down to the point; and in the hollow of the sword, by the hilt, is this writing in Roman letters, Ave Maria gratia plena, Dominus, and on the other side, in the same letters, I am Tizona, which was made in the era 1040, that is to say, in the year 1002. This good sword is an heir-loom in the family of the Marquisses of Falces. The Infante Don Ramiro, who was the Cid's son-in-law, inherited it, and from him it descended to them. Moreover the two coffers which were given in pledge to the Jews Rachel and Vidas are kept, the one in the Church of St. Agueda at Burgos, where it is placed over the principal door, in the inside, and the other is in the Monastery of St. Pedro de Cardeña, where it is hung up by two chains on the left of the dome; on the right, and opposite to this coffer, is the banner of the Cid, but the colour thereof cannot now be known, for length of time and the dampness of the Church have clean consumed it. In the middle is his shield hanging against the wall, covered with skin, but now so changed that no blazonry or device is to be seen. In the Sacristy there are the keys of the coffer, a great round chest of sattín wood, the setting of the amethyst cup which he used at table, and one of the caskets which the Soldan of Persia sent with the myrrh and balsam; this is of silver, and gilt in the inside, and it is in two parts, the lid closing over the other part; its fashion is like that of the vessels in which the three Kings of the East are represented, bringing their offerings to Christ when he was newly born. On the upper part is graven the image of our Redeemer holding the world in his hand, and on the other the figure of a serpent marvellously contorted, per-adventure in token of the victory which Jesus atchieved over the enemy of the human race. That noble chess-board, the men whereof were of gold and silver, was also in the Monastery in the days of King Don Alfonso the Wise, but it hath long since been lost, no man knoweth how. Moreover there is in this Sacristy a precious stone of great size, black and sparkling; no lapidary hath yet known its name. The Convent have had an infant Jesus graven thereon, with the emblem of the Passion, that it might be worthily employed. It is thought also that the great cross of crystal which is set so well and wrought with such great cunning, is made of different pieces of crystal which belonged to the Cid. But the most precious relick of the Cid Ruydiez which is preserved and venerated in this Monastery, is the cross which he wore upon his breast when he went to battle; it is of plain silver, in four equal parts, and each part covered with three plates of gold, and in the flat part of each five sockets set with precious stones of some size; and with other white ones which are smaller; of these little ones, some are still left, fastened in with filigrane. In the middle of the cross is a raised part, after the manner of an artichoke, ending in white and green enamel; and it is said that in the hollow thereof are certain relicks, with a piece of the holy wood of the true cross. Verily, that part of the writing which can still be read implieth this, for thus much may at this day be discerned.... CRUCIS SALVATOR * * SANCTI PETRI * * PORTO. Of the four limbs of this cross the upper one is wanting. King Don Alfonso, the last of that name, asked for it, and had it made into a cross to wear himself when he went to battle, because of the faith which he had, that through it he should obtain the victory; of the lower limb little more is left than that to which the plates of silver and gold were fastened on. From point to point this cross is little more than a quarter.

XXXI.

There is no doubt that the soul of the blessed Cid resteth and reigneth with the blessed in Heaven. And men of all nations and at all times have come from all parts to see and reverence his holy body and tomb, being led by the odour of his fame, especially knights and soldiers, who when they have fallen upon their knees to kiss his tomb, and scraped a little of the stone thereof to bear away with them as a relick, and commended themselves to him, have felt their hearts strengthened, and gone away in full trust that they should speed the better in all battles into which they should enter from that time with a good cause. By reason of this great devotion, and the great virtues of my Cid, and the miracles which were wrought by him, King Philip the Second gave order to his ambassador Don Diego Hurtado de Mendoza, to deal with the Court of Borne concerning the canonization of this venerable knight Rodrigo Diaz. Now Don Diego was a person of great learning, and moreover, one of the descendants of the Cid; and being greatly desirous that this thing should be effected, he sent to the Monastery of St. Pedro de Cardeña, and had papers and depositions sent from thence, and made a memorial of the virtues and miracles of the Campeador, showing cause why this blessed knight should be canonized. But before the matter could be proceeded in, the loss of Sienna took place, whereupon he was fain to leave Rome and thus this pious design could not be brought about. Nevertheless the Cid hath alway been regarded with great reverence as an especial servant of God: and he is called the Blessed Cid, and the Venerable Rodrigo Diaz. Certes, his soul resteth and reigneth with the blessed in Heaven. Amen.

Robert Southey – A Concise Bibliography

The Fall of Robespierre (1794)
Joan of Arc (1796)
Icelandic Poetry, or The Edda of Sæmund (1797)
Poems (1797–1799)
Letters Written During a Short Residence in Spain and Portugal (1797)
St. Patrick's Purgatory (1798)
After Blenheim (1798)
The Devil's Thoughts (1799). Revised edition published in 1827 as "The Devil's Walk".
English Eclogues (1799)
The Old Man's Comforts and How He Gained Them (1799)
Thalaba the Destroyer (1801)
The Inchcape Rock (1802)
Madoc (1805)
Letters from England: By Don Manuel Alvarez Espriella (1807), the observations of a fictitious Spaniard.
Chronicle of the Cid. Translated from the Spanish (1808)
The Curse of Kehama (1810)
History of Brazil (3 volumes) (1810–1819)
The Life of Horatio, Lord Viscount Nelson (1813)
Roderick the Last of the Goths (1814)
Sir Thomas Malory's Le Morte D'Arthur (1817)
Wat Tyler: A Dramatic Poem (1817)
Cataract of Lodore (1820)
The Life of Wesley; and Rise and Progress of Methodism (2 volumes) (1820)
What Are Little Boys Made Of? (1820)
The Vision of Judgement (1821)

History of the Peninsular War, 1807-1814 (3 volumes) (1823-1832)

Sir Thomas More; or, Colloquies on the Progress and Prospects of Society (1829)

The Works of William Cowper (15 vols.) (Editor) (1833-1837)

Lives of the British Admirals, with an Introductory View of the Naval History of England (5 volumes) (1833-40); republished as "English Seamen" in 1895.

The Doctor (7 volumes) (1834-1847). Includes The Story of the Three Bears (1837).

The Poetical Works of Robert Southey, Collected by Himself (1837)